SLY FOX HOLLOW

A Novel

By

Brett Allen

HOGWASH PUBLISHING LLC

ISBN: 979-8-9881152-0-5

For the Dogman, wherever you are.

"Fear has a way of souring the serenity of life's finer moments. A sunset, for example, tainted by fear, is no longer something to be enjoyed, but a countdown to darker things. Fading light becomes fading hope. Monsters, living and imagined, thrive in the darkness of our minds."

"Professor" Clyde Clawson Cryptozoologist/Monster Hunter;
1968

TO: Office Of Records; Mishiimin County, Michigan
FROM: The Desk Of The Mishiimin County Clerk
DATE: January 16, 2022
SUBJECT: MEMORANDUM FOR RECORD

The following pages contain a detailed account of the events at Fox Hollow in the Fall of 2017, as recorded by the County Clerk of Mishiimin County. This narrative is a compilation of eyewitness accounts, records provided graciously by the Fox Hollow Police Department and Environmental Protection Agency, FBI character-witness interviews, personal recollections, hearsay, and garden-variety gossip. Provided items deemed too cumbersome to integrate into a coherent narrative have been added throughout, unaltered. Any gaps in provided accounts have been filled by the County Clerk himself. Some creative liberties were taken.

This report is intended to be a cautionary tale and it is the hope of this Clerk's Office that the records herein will shed light on the key players and events of October 31, 2017, the series of bizarre happenings leading up to the incident in question, and to generally describe how things got all mucked up in the first place.

Best Regards,
A.J. Hillberry
Mishiimin County Clerk

Note: A special thank you to the Local Apple Pickers Union #43 for providing numerous eyewitness accounts, to the Environmental Protection Agency for their cooperative information sharing, and, to a lesser extent, to the Federal Bureau Of Investigation, who arrived late to "The Incident" and were ultimately unnecessary, but which everyone agreed was a sweet gesture.

October 19, 2017

11:37 a.m.

William "Bomber" Merridan sat alone in the manager's office of Marty's Market with his feet propped on his desk. Taking a break from his purchase orders, he stretched his arms and gazed out through the half-shut blinds of the office window, surveying the Customer Service desk and checkout lanes of Fox Hollow's one and only grocery store. Bomber often found himself here, looking out upon the culmination of his thirty-three years of existence and wondering, if not a bit rhetorically, where the hell he'd gone wrong. Ordinarily, this dejection would trigger a defense in Bomber's brain, sending his mind jaunting off through the blinded window, over the service desk, and out the automatic sliding doors. Leaving the store behind, his thoughts would sail up and over Main Street, floating out above the endless orchard rows enveloping Fox Hollow, searching for the perfect place to hide and wait.

Today, though, his thoughts were not allowed to wander far.

Left of the Customer Service Desk, a man in a gray sweatshirt loitered near the drink coolers, his hood pulled low. Picking up a bottle of Fox Apple Juice, the man pretended to read the label before returning it to the shelf. Aviator sunglasses concealed his eyes which scanned the faces of patrons and employees moving about the checkout lanes. His nostrils flared and he smoothed his thick mustache, which appeared several shades lighter than his half-hidden eyebrows. His peculiar dress and suspicious behavior may have gone unnoticed in larger cities, where the per capita quota of weirdos, degenerates, and creepers is much higher, but in a map-dot like Fox Hollow he stuck out like a sore thumb.

Bomber was quickly gripped by the strange man's behavior, encouraged by the potential of criminal activity. A break from the daily monotony was welcome in any form.

Suddenly, as if triggered by Bomber's suspicion, the man sank both hands deep into his sweatshirt pocket and moved toward the cash registers.

"Here we go," Bomber whispered, dropping his feet from the desk. "Do it, I dare you."

The man in the hoodie paused near the service counter and scanned the room again. Bruce, the Customer Service cashier, addressed the man, which appeared to startle him. Bomber put one hand on his phone, prepared to make his heroic call to emergency dispatch.

The man gave Bruce a wary smile, shook his head, and moved toward the exit. Bomber sighed. He grabbed his pricing gun and, with one eye closed, took careful aim at the would-be criminal.

"Pew, pew, pew," Bomber sang before holstering the price pistol like an Old West gunslinger.

"Is this what I pay you for?"

Bomber swiveled his chair and discreetly elbowed the computer's mouse. His wolfman screensaver blinked away, leaving a blank purchase order glowing back at him.

Marty swayed in the doorway. A gray horseshoe of hair circled his head, ruffled like the down of a baby bird. His nose and cheeks were purple in a wash of broken capillaries.

"Sorry, Marty," Bomber said and feigned a renewed diligence toward the order. "Suspicious fella out there. Thought we had a robbery in progress. Shoplifter at the least."

"Arsonist would be preferred," Marty grunted. He shuffled

into the room, knocking his shoulder against a file cabinet before slumping into his desk chair. The smell of bourbon wafted in with him.

Martin VanGovern the Fifth came from a long line of grocers. Five to be exact. His great-great-grandfather, Martin VanGovern, Sr., had opened Marty's Market in 1878, making it the second-oldest establishment in the second-oldest town in Mishiimin County. In fact, the store had been a store long before the town had been a town at all. Marty's Market had originally been opened to service the clientele and employees of the town's oldest establishment, a brothel by the name of The Foxy Howl Inn, which, itself, serviced the hypocrisies of the puritanical residents of Mishiimin County's first oldest town, Cedar Mills, located ten miles west.

Known for being rather uncouth, Marty Sr. had carved the market's original slogan, *"WHORES GOTTA EAT,"* on a sign above the store's entryway. Eventually, an influx in population and the formal establishment of Fox Hollow proper brought with it the laws and moral rigidity that signaled the end of The Foxy Howl Inn. The brothel, along with the market's crass sign, slipped into local legend. While Fox Hollow grew, Marty's Market grew with it, exchanging prostitutes for fruit pickers as their primary patrons, and passing from one Martin to another, until finally settling in the resentful hands of Martin the Fifth, who often joked—mostly while drunk—about cleansing the family history through the catharsis of fire.

Marty pulled a bottle from his desk.

"The display for that new Fox Applesauce toxic waste is empty again," Marty sighed, pouring whiskey into a foam coffee cup.

"The Electric Bloo Goo?" Bomber asked. "I just filled the display this morning. That stuff is flying off the shelf."

"Why do they need to dye the applesauce blue?" Marty scoffed. "It's unnatural. They're peddling poison to children."

"What's good for Fox Applesauce is good for Fox Hollow, right?"

Marty made a gurgling noise in his throat.

"It ain't even a national product yet," he said. "It's another damn 'test item.' That's all we are to them: Fox Applesauce guinea pigs."

Bomber sighed. "You act like they're doing weird medical experiments on us."

Fox Applesauce *had*, in fact, briefly conducted medical experiments on Fox Hollow residents in the late 1920's trying to uncover physiological evidence supporting the famous axiom: "An apple a day keeps the doctor away." No number of apples per day was ever found to keep medical practitioners at bay, though thirty-six per day seemed the average amount leading to their immediate need. The research had been conducted on willing participants, however, all of whom were generously compensated.

Marty took a pull from his cup.

"The Fox family has been a blight on this town for over a hundred years," he said.

"Well, they're not even in control anymore," Bomber said.

After closing The Foxy Howl Inn, its proprietor, Silas Fox, had acquired the acreage around the former brothel, sowing the land with rows of apple trees, which he named the Sly Fox Orchards. Over the years, Sly Fox Orchards expanded, and in 1924, Silas's grandson Samuel Fox opened an applesauce production facility and Fox Applesauce was born. By the mid-1960's, the company had become a semi-national brand, a staple of Midwest children's lunchboxes, and the lifeblood of Fox Hollow. Nearly everyone in town worked for Fox Applesauce in some capacity. The town thrived for eighty-four years under a wave of pureed fruit—it's every open field converted to apple orchards, every able body employed as pickers, drivers, pencil-pushers, factory line-workers, botanists, chemists, chefs, taste-testers, logisticians, technicians, lawyers, and middle managers. Nearly every skill set was needed. And then, in 2008, after a series of family tragedies, the Fox family patriarch had sold his controlling interest in the company to the town's next richest man, Carl Longstreet, who quickly incorporated Fox Applesauce and moved all middle-class jobs to a facility in Dover, Delaware, in an effort to capitalize on state income tax breaks and other generous regulatory loopholes. With the middle class gone or unemployed, Fox Hollow limped along, barely kept afloat by the meager incomes of Local Apple Pickers Union #43, whose unskilled laborers maintained the orchards, facilitated the annual harvest, and operated the Fox Applesauce production plant.

"You shouldn't talk like that anyway," Bomber added in a hushed voice. He looked around the office suspiciously. "They have ears everywhere."

Marty rolled his eyes.

"You joke," Marty said, "but I wouldn't doubt it. Your uncle lets them get away with everything."

"Great-uncle," Bomber corrected.

Marty was pouring again and his divided attention sent whiskey sloshing over the cup's rim.

"He's not that great," Marty said, slurping the rogue puddle off a stack of invoices.

Bomber held his tongue and swiveled back to his computer. His great-uncle Cecil Merridan was the mayor of Fox Hollow and had been for the last seventy years, earning him the distinction of having been the town's youngest and oldest serving mayor. He'd run entirely unopposed for the last fifty of those years and his continuous presence at Town Hall had become part of the community's personality, another quirky characteristic of a charming Midwestern town. His position had become largely ceremonial in recent years anyway, with the Board of Aldermen unofficially consolidating most of the real power when Cecil's mental state began swerving over the centerline.

"I need you to close tonight," Marty slurred.

Bomber groaned.

"Can't do it," he said. "I've got plans tonight. Somebody else will have to cover."

Marty squinted at him.

"What plans do *you* have?"

Bomber pretended to be concentrating on his purchase order, which was still blank.

"Going on one of your little monster hunts again, aren't you?" Marty cocked an eyebrow.

"No, I have a date," Bomber lied. "And they're not 'monster hunts' anyway. It's cryptozoology. It's science."

"Oh, that's right," Marty laughed. "You're after your wolfman, or fox-boy, or whatever the hell you call it."

"Dogman," Bomber corrected. "The Michigan Dogman. There have been hundreds of documented sightings. Hundreds. It's a real thing—"

"Documented by who?"

"What?"

"You said 'documented sightings,'" Marty said. "Documented by who?"

"By the people who saw it."

"Like you?" Marty asked.

Bomber clenched his teeth.

"I'll have you know—" he started.

"Alright, alright," Marty said, raising his hands in surrender. "Don't get all wound up. Your Dogman's probably more real than this date of yours."

Bomber ignored him.

"Who's the girl?" Marty pried.

"Your mom," Bomber said.

"Ha!" Marty laughed. "Well, then you're monster hunting after all." He peered into the bottom of his cup before emptying it.

The store's intercom crackled to life: "Bomber, line one."

Bomber picked up the receiver.

"Bruce, can you please stop saying 'Bomber' over the intercom? It makes some customers nervous." Bomber told everyone his nickname was derived from the powerful way he used to throw a football in high school, but most believed it came from him "bombing" the biggest game in town history.

"Sure, whatever," Bruce said. "I have Mrs. Grayson here at the service desk and she needs help in Aisle Two again. She's asking for you specifically—again."

"Of course she is," Bomber said. "Can you tell her I'm busy and send someone else?"

"I really can't," Bruce said. Bomber could hear him smile. "We're swamped out here."

Bomber confirmed this through the window. He looked back at Marty, who was eyes shut, chin-to-chest, and still clutching his coffee cup of whiskey.

"Alright, I'll be right there."

Bomber hung up. He watched Marty for a moment longer and felt genuine sympathy for the man, who, as far as he could tell, had no life beyond the walls of the store and the bottom of a bottle. A man who'd remained the same unwaveringly miserable grump since the day Bomber had started working there fifteen years earlier. He stood to leave and caught his reflection in Marty's blackened computer monitor. Dressed in the same Marty's Market red polo, name badge, and khaki pants, he could've passed as a younger version of the whiskey-soaked grocer in front of him.

"Where the hell are you going?" Marty asked, his eyes still shut.

"I've got to go—"

"The correct answer is, 'To restock the toxic apple goo,'" Marty interrupted with a drowsy smile.

"Right," Bomber said. "But first I've got to assist the forever-helpless Mrs. Grayson in finding her canned salmon before she resorts to cat food again."

"Whores gotta eat," Marty mumbled as Bomber left the office.

"Good morning, Cecil," Doris said sweetly. Doris Grayson was seventy-eight years young and suffered from extended bouts of dementia where she relived the life of her early twenties. She frequently confused Bomber for a younger version of his great-uncle Cecil, which was understandable if you compared their high school yearbook pictures. Both had close-cropped black hair and a lean, bordering on wiry, athletic build, though Bomber had softened around the middle in recent years. They'd both been handsome, in an unassuming way, and were considered to be a "good catch" among the moms and grandmas of their respective generations. Doris had held a flame for the charismatic mayor in her youth, an adoration reciprocated frequently, but not steadily by Cecil. Her wholesome beauty had earned her the title of Miss Apple Blossom for five years running (1951-1955) at Fox Hollow's annual Harvest Festival, assuring her no shortage of male suitors whenever Cecil's attentions waned. Unfortunately, her social ease with the town's young men earned her a certain reputation still whispered and giggled about by the other blue-haired Bettys about town. Doris simply dismissed the talk as jealousy. Even as Bomber's fifth-grade teacher, she'd been striking to look at, though the flowy demeanor of her youth had been replaced by a staunch—some might say draconian—conservatism. Somewhere over the last twenty years, the old-age bus had hit Doris Grayson head-on.

"Good Morning, Doris," Bomber smiled. He'd found correcting her only led to drama.

Doris wrapped her shriveled fingers in Bomber's and they shuffled off toward Aisle Two.

"When are you going to ask me out, Cecil?" Doris cooed. She pouted a wrinkled lip. "There're plenty of other fellas dying for my attention."

"I don't doubt they're dying," Bomber mumbled. Doris's fingers were ice cold.

Soon they were standing in front of the canned fish in Aisle Two.

Bomber tried to think of what Cecil might have said: "I'm sorry, Doris, but I've got a town to run. Perhaps someday, when things settle down, I can take you on a proper date. That is if I don't run for President."

He winked.

Mrs. Grayson's eyes went wide and she snatched her hand away.

"What in god's name are you talking about, William?" Mrs. Grayson was back.

"I—uh—"

"I'm sorry, young man, but I'm much too old for you."

Bomber's face was as red as his Marty's Market polo.

"And don't you think *you're* a bit old to be fantasizing about becoming President? You barely passed fifth grade. No offense to you, son, but not many washed-up high school football stars or Bigfoot-nuts become President."

"Dogman," Bomber sighed.

"What?"

"I'm a Dogman—" Bomber stopped. "Never mind."

"Dogman, huh?" Mrs. Grayson said. "Your uncle said he saw a dog*boy* down by the ol' Kissing Pond. Maybe they're related."

"Uh-huh," Bomber rolled his eyes.

"They say the storm drain down by the Kissing Pond leads all the way back to the Fox Family Mansion."

Bomber pretended to listen. Everyone in town knew the old stories of the Fox Family Mansion's history as the Foxy Howl Inn brothel, but no one ever talked about it. It wasn't a history to be proud of to be sure and like all past sins, it was a subject actively avoided.

"They say it's how they used to sneak in the booze and the hookers during Prohibition," Doris said.

"Who is 'they'?"

"Course, the booze is legal now, so it's strictly an entrance for working girls these days."

"Uh-huh."

"Kind of demeaning if you ask me, but then again, I don't make a living on my back."

Bomber dropped two cans of salmon into Doris's basket.

"This isn't the brand I like," Doris complained, holding up a can. "Where's the kind with the kitty on the front?"

"We can't sell you those anymore," Bomber explained. "Those are for cats and you don't own a cat."

"Fine," Doris said, waving him off. "I'll find it myself."

She tottered off, her orthopedic shoes scuffing on the tile floor. Bomber thought to pursue her and explain the earlier confusion.

"Goodbye, Cecil," she called over her shoulder, giving a wave with her free hand.

Bomber shook his head and the intercom crackled: "Bomber to the service counter, please."

6:48 p.m.

Shadows crept like gnarled fingers through rows of apple trees. From a grove of Red Delicious, Cecil Merridan stumbled forward, pushing through a flap he'd cut earlier in the chain-link fence. A "No Trespassing" sign rattled behind him. Gasping, he scrambled up the ditch embankment to Old Dickerson Road as fast as his ninety-two-year-old legs would allow and promptly threw up on his leather shoes. Off to his left, among the fruit trees, came the sound of snapping branches.

"Back, you devil!" Cecil warned. His throat was dry and weak. He shook vomit from his wingtips and picked up his shuffle again. Glasses flecked with sweat, he squinted down the deserted gravel road, barely making out his old town car in the failing light. Laughter seeped from the trees, which would've been terrifying had the old man's hearing aids been at full volume.

"You won't make it," came a savage voice.

"What?" Cecil huffed.

"I said, you won't make it," repeated the voice, louder now.

"You're not real," Cecil shouted. From his pocket he produced a small prescription bottle and fumbled with the lid.

"You can't get rid of me with your pills," the voice roared and laughed. It seemed to come from both sides of the road.

Cecil stumbled as the lid came free and he sprawled into the dirt. A hip shattered. His chin split. His glasses disappeared into the shapeless void and he groped for them among a sea of white pills and loose gravel. There was more laughter from the trees.

"You'll answer to the authorities," Cecil yelled. "You're just some little punk."

The laughter stopped.

"Don't call me 'little,'" the voice hissed.

"What?"

A fuzzy shadow emerged from the apple trees and climbed onto the road. Cecil heard the unmistakable crunch of his glasses underfoot.

"I said. Don't. Call. Me. Little," the blur said again, stepping closer.

"What—what are you?" Cecil asked.

There was a long silence. "I'm Fox Hollow's original sin," the blur finally said.

Cecil squinted, his eyes filling with fuzzy hues of orange and black and white.

"What the hell does that even mean?" he snapped with the curmudgeonly confidence of an elderly man who is aware he's about to die and just wants to move the damn thing along. "I mean, actually. What the hell *are* you?"

He was answered by a flash of fangs as the last sliver of sun disappeared behind the trees.

NOTE: No known witnesses. Narrative liberties drawn from crime scene photographs shared with this Clerk's Office by an anonymous member of the Fox Hollow Police Department.

7:54 p.m.

Sheriff Connie Hayes sat at her computer reading yet another email from Ms. Carol Meyers on the subject of her awful cat. Connie rubbed her temples and wondered why the hell she'd ever come back to Fox Hollow. She could've been a cop anywhere.

She looked around her office. The walls were sparse, save for a few vintage photographs of Fox Hollow left by her predecessor, Sheriff Peter T. Barnstorm, who'd been ousted from the position a year prior. In the far corner, a metal shelving unit held a library of well-worn police manuals and legal books. In an effort to negate the sterility of the metal rack, a fake fern had been wedged in beside the books, its dull green leaves drooping under a fuzzy coat of dust.

Sheriff Connie, as everyone called her, hadn't had time to settle into her office, as her appointment to the position had been as rapid as her predecessor's exit. Ex-Sheriff Barnstorm, as corrupt as he was tall, had left the department in tatters. His lengthy career as the insufferable, yet uncontested, town sheriff had come to an abrupt end as a result of an in-depth, investigative report conducted by the local newspaper, *The Fox Howler*. The report dug deep into the inflated budget of the Fox Hollow Police Department and detailed an egregious misuse of annual funds for military-grade weapons and tactical gear, such as body armor, Kevlar helmets, assault rifles, crew-serve machine guns, night-vision optics, anti-tank weapons, heated toilet seats, anti-tank mines, various models of grenades, and a light-armored vehicle with a mounted fifty caliber machine gun that Barnstorm had named "Mollie's Revenge" after his ex-wife. Unable to justify the fraud, waste, and abuse, Barnstorm was forced to step down. Though an elected position, the title of Sheriff was bestowed upon then Patrol-woman Connie Hayes who was one of the only Fox Hollow officers under Barnstorm to come out of the report clean. This was due largely to Connie's well known moral rigidity, but also because Barnstorm was a sexist bastard and left her out of "the know" on pretty much everything anyway.

Adding insult to injury, Barnstorm had left with nearly half the department's personnel, misogynistic loyalists who couldn't stomach working under the direct command of a woman—one of Native American descent no less. So the year had been a building year, hiring new officers and putting out all the small fires Barnstorm had left in his wake. Despite her efforts, Connie knew the town's residents still lacked faith in her. All except Ms. Carol Meyers, that is. And her damn cat. There was nothing particularly distasteful about the cat itself. No mangy fur or leaky eye or anything of the sort. The damn thing just liked to run free, no doubt feeling oppressed by the depths of Ms. Carol Meyers' overbearing love. So, every week, the nasty little beast would go missing and every week Carol would lose her mind. And every weekend the little beast would return and Carol would laugh at whatever eviscerated vermin it presented on her doorstep. Connie typed a quick response:

Ms. Meyers,

Though I understand your worry regarding the comings and goings of Mr. Fuzzbottom, it is not the job of the Fox Hollow Police Department to track down wayward pets. Especially those who have historically returned of their own volition. The officers of this department are far too busy responding to emergencies, investigating crimes, and upholding the peace to be bothered with these requests. It is my suggestion that, if you find cats too difficult to manage, perhaps you should look into less ambulant animals. Perhaps a goldfish. Or a rock. Whatever you choose, please stop emailing me about it.

Sincerely,

Sheriff Hayes

P.S. If I were your cat, I'd run, too.

Connie looked out her window into the open office area. It was a slow night, even for Fox Hollow. Two of her officers shuffled papers on their desks, fighting heavy eyelids. A third had his head down completely. She sighed and held the backspace key, watching her honest email disappear.

* * *

Dear Ms. Meyers,

I will send Officer Householder to your home first thing tomorrow morning to assist in locating Mr. Fuzzbottom. We're all praying for his safe return.

Warm Regards,

Connie

Send

Connie sighed.

This scenario had played out too many times. A needy request. A harsh and hasty email. A moment of pause. Select all. Delete. Sometimes Connie would catch herself grimacing a fake smile while typing her politically correct responses. It was good practice for face-to-face interactions. Ever since Fox Applesauce's massive reorganization, forced pleasantries were the status quo around town. Happy masks hiding worried minds.

There was a knock on her office door.

"Enter."

Sergeant Householder leaned into the room. Connie was always surprised by his height and his height made him exceptional at retrieving runaway cats from apple tree branches.

"Hey-ya, boss," he said, scratching nervously at his temple. "You mind if I duck out a few minutes early today?"

Connie looked at her watch. 7:56 p.m.

"We're kind of swamped here," she said. "But I think we can handle the last four minutes without you."

"Thanks, boss," Householder grinned.

"But don't be late tomorrow morning," Connie said. "I've got a super important assignment for you. First thing. Real gritty police work."

Sergeant Householder eyed her. Her stone face rarely gave up any clues.

"It's not Ms. Meyers's cat again, is it?"

Connie grimaced a smile. Good practice.

"Sorry," she said. "Mr. Fuzzbottom's a rascal."

Householder knocked his head gently against the doorframe.

"Come on, boss," he said. "That's not police work. That's not even fireman work. Hell, last time the cat wasn't even missing. Carol had locked it in the upstairs bathroom by accident."

Connie suppressed a smile.

"I know it's dumb, but we don't have a lot else going on and people like Ms. Carol Meyers can make a lot of noise in a small town if they want to. You'll be done in ten min—"

"Egg salad," Householder interrupted.

"What?"

"Egg salad," he repeated. "Every time I go over there, she rewards me with an egg salad sandwich."

"That doesn't seem—"

"I hate egg salad sandwiches."

"You find the cat," Connie said. "I'll eat the sandwich."

Sergeant Householder left her office muttering about egg salad and Connie went back to her emails. Most were boilerplate, but there was an interesting one about a suspicious man in a gray hoodie loitering outside of Marty's Market. She loved those kinds of emails. It always ended up being someone well known in town who didn't want to be seen buying condoms or leaving the back room of the video rental store.

Emails complete, she grabbed her keys and checked her watch: 8:01 pm. Maybe tonight she could finally spend some time with her son.

Her phone buzzed.

"This is Sheriff Hayes," she answered.

The office was quiet except for a few keyboard clicks from the night officer and static coming from the dispatch radio. Connie knocked over three chairs as she sprinted out the door.

10:15 p.m.

It was an unseasonably warm evening for mid-October and Bomber wished he hadn't worn so many layers. He sat with Bruce on the backside of a rock pile that separated an orchard from a small, swamp-filled gully. The tree frogs were deafening and the hardiest of the summer's mosquitoes still droned lazily past their ears.

"Why did you paint your face black?" Bruce whispered.

"Because we're supposed to be hiding," Bomber whispered back. They were both dressed, at Bomber's insistence, in home-sewn camouflage. Garments Bomber had crafted from a set of old drapes, a gaudy pattern of foliage mixed with green and red apples.

"I don't think it's helping," Bruce said, looking up at the full harvest moon above.

"It would've worked better if *both* of us had done it," Bomber whispered.

"It's bad enough you made me wear these ridiculous clothes," Bruce grumbled, sweeping long black hair out of his eyes and over his ears. "They're too tight and feel like sandpaper."

He shifted and pulled at the fabric, which was stretched over a developing gut. Bruce had always been out of place in the woods, which was odd considering his heritage. Like many kids his age, Bruce's comfort zone was located directly in front of his gaming console. *His* camouflage was a Che Guevara t-shirt and gray sweatpants. A recent high school graduate, he'd decided to take a year to "find himself," but had instead been recruited to find a Dogman.

"That's probably because they're made of old curtains," Bomber whispered. "But they're highly effective."

"How do you know?"

"What?"

"How do you know they're effective?"

"Have we been spotted by any Dogmen yet?"

"No."

"Bingo," Bomber said. "Now keep it down."

"Sorry," Bruce said. He was silent for a few moments. "So

why are we here again? I don't mean, like, existentially. I mean, like, why did you choose this location?"

"Natural lines of drift," Bomber whispered.

"Natural lines of *what*?"

"Drift," Bomber stated. "Animals, especially elusive animals, like to stay out of sight of people and predators, correct?"

"Correct."

"Well, we're the predators tonight," Bomber smiled.

"Mom wouldn't approve of me hanging out with a predator," Bruce interjected.

"Shut up," Bomber said. "If you'll notice, we're at the end of a long gulley. To our left, the land rises to meet County Line Road. To our right, the land rises to meet another orchard. Animals will stick to low ground areas, to avoid being silhouetted and seen."

"But there are plenty of low ground areas around here. Why this spot?"

"On the other side of the swamp is Bill Hardy's farm. You may've heard that last week, two of Bill's calves were found dead. Mutilated, to be more precise."

"My mom said it was probably coyotes," Bruce said.

"That's because your mom doesn't see the signs," Bomber said. "I talked to Bill in the store yesterday. Poor guy was all amped up. He said the calves were ripped to shreds, but it didn't look like anything was eaten. I don't know of any kind of natural animal that'd do that."

"I've heard polar bears do," Bruce said.

"I'm fairly certain they don't make it this far south," Bomber said.

"That's not what I'm suggesting."

"I've gathered tons of intel on the Michigan Dogman. I've read all the sighting accounts, old and new. I've researched all the old lore. One consistency I've found is the Dogman retreats to swampy areas after encounters. So whatever tore up those calves, would've headed right into the swamp in front of us."

"Impressive deduction," Bruce said.

"Well, Mr. Hardy did mention there was a blood trail leading to the swamp," Bomber said. "So that helped."

The radio in Bomber's hand crackled.

"We've been out here for two hours," came a voice over the radio. "How long are we sitting tonight?"

"As long as it takes," Bomber whispered into the radio. "Now keep it down. Dogmen have keen ears."

"I'm bored," came the voice over the radio. "And I don't see why I have to be out by myself on the edge of old man Hardy's field. If he spots me, he's gonna shoot my ass for sure."

"You're the only one of us with para-military experience," Bomber said.

"The police academy is not 'para-military experience.'"

"He won't spot you," Bomber said. "He's out of town."

"Seriously? Then why the hell am I way back in the swamp. I'm going to sneak up through the field and get a closer position."

"Don't—"

"It'll be fine. I have para-military experience."

"Sergeant Householder," Bomber hissed. "I said don't."

"Too late. Moving."

"Dammit," Bomber threw down his radio. "He's going to blow the whole op."

Bruce sat quietly as Bomber brooded.

The radio crackled again.

"Oh my god," came Householder's voice.

Bomber and Bruce both scrambled to pick up the radio, but Bomber won out. "What?"

"I've found tracks," Householder said.

"What kind of tracks? Never mind, we're coming up. Good work, Sergeant."

Bomber put down the radio and turned to Bruce. "You're up, kid."

"What do you mean 'I'm up'?"

"Tracks," Bomber said. "You're our track guy."

"How am I the track guy?"

"Because you're part Ottawa Indian," Bomber explained.

Bruce paused. "Wait," he said. "Do you think, because I'm a quarter Indian, I know all about animal tracks?"

Bomber stared back at him.

"Don't you?" he asked slowly.

"No," Bruce said. "And I feel like that's racist or something. Of course, I shouldn't be surprised, coming from a guy in blackface. Also, we prefer 'Native American.'"

"It's camouflage," Bomber said, pointing to his face.

"It's idiotic," came a voice from behind them.

Bomber and Bruce both jumped. On top of the pile of boulders, Sheriff Connie stood silhouetted by the moon, her jacket pushed back behind the handle of her sidearm.

"Mom!" Bruce yelped. "What are you doing here?"

"I was going to ask you two geniuses the same thing," Connie said. "Besides trespassing, obviously. I've been trying to get a hold of you for hours."

"Welp, this whole night's a bust," Bomber complained, climbing to his feet.

"You don't know the half of it," Connie said to Bomber. "I was looking for Bruce to find you. I'm afraid I have bad news," she said. "Terrible news, actually."

"If Marty finally burned the store down, I won't be as disappointed as you'd think."

Bomber laughed. Connie didn't.

"There's no easy way to say this," Connie said. She concentrated hard on sounding sympathetic. "Your uncle was found in a ditch off Old Dickerson Road earlier tonight. It appears to have been a pretty savage animal attack. The mayor is dead."

October 20, 2017

3:45 p.m.

Rumors flowed fast in the applesauce capital of the Midwest. Bomber believed it had something to do with the Fox Hollow's encompassing patchwork of orchards, interconnected rows and columns of fruit trees carrying hearsay and gossip from point to point like electrons through a circuit board. Bomber's life had been the data source for the town's rumor-computer several times before. First in high school and then again after his "encounter."

By the next morning, the entire town had heard of Cecil Merridan's death. Sheriff Connie and the Fox Hollow PD had kept the gruesome details closely guarded, so naturally, everyone was already an expert. Rumors buzzed about wild beasts, eviscerations, police cover-ups, and even a botched alien abduction. Bomber had tried to make it through his shift at the store, but the assault of sympathetic small talk was too much. Marty had been surprisingly sensitive, allowing Bomber to clock out early.

"I won't even dock yer pay," he'd slurred sadly, sloshing an arm against Bomber's back.

If he was being honest, Bomber's distraction had little to do with sorrow for his great uncle. He did feel bad, but he'd never been close with Cecil—no one had besides Doris—and everyone around town seemed to agree that, though Cecil's death was "untimely," at ninety-two years old, he'd had a good run. Even Bomber's parents, who had recently become permanent Florida snowbirds, accepted the news with a "that's a shame," before explaining their impending absence from the funeral.

In truth, Bomber was more perturbed about being left out. "A savage animal attack," as Sheriff Connie had phrased it, was the bread and butter of any self-respecting cryptozoologist, but he'd not been allowed anywhere near the investigation. This was disheartening, but not entirely surprising given his lack of credentials and rocky history with Sheriff Connie. But still, after ten years as the town's unofficial Dogman expert, it would've been nice to be consulted.

Bomber grappled with this as he stared out the truck window watching rows of trees zip by. Bruce was giving him a ride home from the market in his rusted-out Ford Ranger, which threatened to rattle apart over every pothole. Bomber didn't own a vehicle and hadn't driven in nearly a decade. Not since the night of his encounter.

After high school, Bomber had developed a bit of a drinking problem—a rather public drinking problem that held its roots in the very same blown football game that some say earned his nickname. On the fateful night of his encounter, Bomber had spent the evening in his typical manner, belly-up to the bar at the town's only watering-hole, The Tree Of Knowledge Bar & Grill, getting thoroughly blitzed on Budweiser tall-boys and shots of Jim Beam. The bartender, a slender, tattooed man called Snake for the way he stuttered his S's, had traded a free beer for Bomber's keys just seconds before last call and then booted him out of the bar.

Fueled by drunken rage at Snake's treachery and fresh out of favors from friends, Bomber had no choice but to walk the four miles home. His trek quickly took on an adventurous feel, his mood buoyed, and before long he was cutting through large swaths of Fox Applesauce orchards and boisterously singing 90's pop songs planted in his brain by the bar's karaoke machine, hours earlier. It was only after scaling an unexpected chain-link fence and singing Chumbwamba's "Tubthumping" for the third time that Bomber had begun to get the sense he was being followed. His exuberance soon gave way to paranoia, which soon gave way to panic, and he'd hurtled himself down rutted orchard rows at top speed as snapping branches and panting breath closed in behind him.

When asked, Bomber would insist his self-induced driving hiatus was a direct result of his encounter, citing that if he'd been driving he'd never have been pursued by the nightmare-beast and that his mountain bike, now his only mode of transportation, forced him to slow down and become more in tune with his surroundings. He would often add his lofty line: "You have to break from the ordinary to see the extraordinary." This was usually met with eyerolls, of course, but Bomber didn't care because he figured it to be the most profound thing he'd ever thought up, though he wasn't entirely sure it hadn't come from a sports drink commercial or something similar. The truth of the matter was far less glamorous, as Bomber's car had broken down shortly after his encounter and he hadn't the money or desire to fix it.

"Thanks again for the ride," Bomber said, as Bruce slowed the truck.

"Just wanted to make sure you were doing alright," Bruce said. "Marty said you were a real shit-show today."

"He's one to recognize a shit-show."

Bruce nodded and the truck crunched to a halt with Bomber's window inches from his mailbox. The box was overflowing with envelopes, none of which were stamped.

"Geez," Bruce said. "You always get that much mail?"

Bomber shook his head.

Bruce turned into the driveway and they sat in front of the house while Bomber opened and scanned the letters. There were a few sympathy cards, but most were hastily-scrawled accounts of Dogman sightings around town. One even included a crude sketch that looked more like a house cat on steroids than any Dogman rendering Bomber had ever seen.

"Guess I'm not so crazy after all."

"Everyone else being crazy doesn't make you *not* crazy," Bruce said.

Bomber frowned.

"I visited Mom at the station this morning," Bruce said. "She was too busy to talk—per usual. Householder said the dispatch lines have been clogged with calls reporting sightings of strange creatures. No consistency, though. To be fair, he said a large number of calls were from Ms. Carol Meyers anyway, about her missing cat. I guess the call volume got so burdensome, that Mom declared an emergency town meeting for tonight."

"They all laughed at me," Bomber said.

Bruce took the page and examined the mutant cat sketch.

"Householder said they don't have a lot of details they can share yet, but he said Mom is hoping to put people's minds at ease or at least steer the rumors in a more believable direction."

Bomber stuffed the stack of envelopes into his jacket pocket and opened his door.

"No offense," he said, as he climbed out. "But your mom lacks vision. She's going to explain it away as some type of 'normy-animal,' like a coyote or cougar or something else lame."

There was an awkward moment.

"Are you coming or what?" Bomber asked.

Bruce stumbled from the truck. He'd never been invited inside Bomber's house, but he and Householder had long suspected the existence of a secret Dogman Command Center.

Bomber lifted his bike from the bed of the truck and they started up the walkway.

"Make sure you stay on the cement path," Bomber warned.

"When was the last time you mowed?" Bruce asked. The yard was knee-high grass that rippled in the breeze. The house itself was in a sad state of decay. Bomber's busy schedule of work and Dogman-related activities left little time for maintenance.

"Can't mow," Bomber said. "Tall grass hides the tripwires."

"Tripwires?"

"Tripwires trigger the floodlights," Bomber said, unlocking the front door. "And the floodlights kick on surveillance cameras."

"Makes sense."

"Try not to touch anything until we get downstairs," Bomber instructed.

Bomber's home had the feel of a decades-old crime scene. A

once happy home, left untouched in the wake of some horrific act, still hiding secrets of a long-abandoned cold case. Every surface was tinged with gray and furry with dust. The drapes were of the same design as Bomber's homemade camouflage and Bruce suspected there was a naked window elsewhere in the home.

In the living room, old family photos were still on display over an outdated television. A bookshelf-turned-trophy-display dominated the opposite wall and a portrait-sized school photo of Bomber was prominently displayed, his cocky smile sandwiched between frosted tips and a puka shell necklace. Bruce couldn't recall ever seeing Bomber with a similar smile. Medals, ribbons, and rows of football trophies cluttered the remaining shelves.

Bomber led them to a flight of stairs and they descended into the basement. As they rounded the landing Bruce came face-to-face with a monstrous statue, causing him to stumble backward. The body, originally a department store mannequin, was draped with strips and bits of animal fur, piecemealed like a jigsaw puzzle and then glued or stapled into place. The mannequin's limbs had been swapped for the appendages of taxidermied canids, human legs replaced with those of a timber wolf, forearms now the forelegs of a coyote. The head was that of a red fox and was comically disproportionate to the rest of the body.

"Don't mind Rex," Bomber said, patting the fox head. "He guards the place. I'm trying to recreate the Dogman I saw, but pieces are hard to come by."

"Where do you get the parts?" Bruce asked.

"Taxidermy black market," said Bomber, as if this were a completely normal thing to say. "And yard sales. The tail is 'Lycaon Pictus' or 'African Wild Dog.' A rare find. Got it from Ernie Smith, whose uncle used to go on all those safaris."

The Frankenstein-Dogman unsettled Bruce, so he diverted his attention to the rest of the basement, which was clearly Bomber's entire living space. Along the right-side wall was a small kitchenette, piled high with dirty dishes. On the far side of the room, a twisted mass of sheets spilled over the side of an old futon. Hanging behind the couch-bed was a framed poster of Bomber's personal idol, Buck Wildes, a YouTube-famous cryptozoologist and self-acclaimed monster expert. In the poster,

Buck stood confidently in attire best described as "redneck-chic," while a silhouette of a Bigfoot loomed in the background. Buck's name was emblazoned across the bottom in an audacious, tiger-stripe font.

Along the wall, opposite the kitchenette, was Bomber's meager command center and Bruce did little to hide his disappointment. Six old televisions were stacked in a two-by-three rectangle on a plastic folding table. Each had a grainy, live feed streaming from the yard outside. Above the TV array was a large corkboard filled with newspaper clippings, torn notebook pages, and doodles of canines with human features. Seven sketches in total, each labeled by its type and variation. Alongside the corkboard was a map of Fox Hollow and the surrounding areas. Dozens of brightly-colored push-pins peppered the map.

"Watch out for the gear," Bomber warned, pointing to an assortment of old snares and fur trapping equipment piled precariously in the corner. Bomber was particularly proud of a large bear trap lying menacingly out front (though, in actuality, he'd purchased it second-hand over five years before and had yet to pry open its rusty mandibles).

"The red pins are the confirmed incident sites," Bomber said, pointing to the map. There were two red pins and he pointed to each. "One is *my* encounter and one is from yesterday's attack." Each pin held a tiny tag, dated accordingly.

"Are those really *confirmed*?" Bruce asked.

Bomber ignored the question. "Notice the red pins are close together," he said. "Dogmen are notoriously territorial. It's likely our specimen lives close by and stays within a certain radius. The blue pins are areas I've determined to be 'high probability areas' or 'HPAs.' These hold optimal Dogman terrain, as well as suitable cover and concealment for observation. The yellow pins are sites which have already been staked out, with, uh…limited success. The blue pins usually become yellow pins, unfortunately, but that's the nature of cryptozoology."

"And the green pin?" Bruce asked, pointing to a lone green pin on the edge of town.

"That's a 'you-ee,'" said Bomber.

"You-ee?"

"U. E.—Unconfirmed Encounter," Bomber explained. "It predates my incident by five years, but it's all secondhand info. The *victim*, for lack of a better term, was no longer available for questioning by the time I learned of the incident."

"Who was it?"

"Your mom knew him," Bomber said. "Young guy named Wagner. He used to run the karate school in town. Sensei Wagner. Kind of a dorky dude, but nice enough. He helped a lot of troubled teens gain self-confidence and learn to love themselves and junk like that."

"What happened to him?"

"He blew his own brains out with a 12-gauge shotgun in the middle of his dojo."

Bomber shook his head. Bruce cringed.

"Anyway, he told some students about his sighting right before he died. There are correlating details in the story, so I thought it worth noting."

Bruce seemed distracted. Even frustrated.

"What's wrong?"

"I don't know," he said. "It's just the way you talk about this stuff all the time—"

"What?"

"—I just thought there'd be more to your command center."

"How so?"

"I don't know. I guess I had a different picture in my head. I pictured one of those see-through, glass-map-wall-deals you see in military movies. And some flashy computer screens with satellite imagery and live chat feeds with other Dogman hunters. Maybe some sonar/radar deals. I don't know. I definitely thought there'd be more blinking lights and blip sounds."

"Blip sounds?"

"And I thought it'd be more dimly lit. The fluorescent lights down here are a buzzkill."

"You Millennials whine a lot," Bomber said.

"You're a Millennial, too."

"Barely," Bomber said. "And perhaps you forget I'm operating on a grocery store manager's salary from my parent's basement."

"That's the most Millennial excuse I've ever heard," Bruce

said.

Bomber bit his lip.

"I can see I've already upset you," Bruce added, "so I might as well ask. Why do you live in the basement when you've got the whole house to yourself?"

Bomber looked as if he'd never considered it.

"Gotta stay agile," he said.

"What?"

"Listen. You want to be part of Team Dogman, right?" Bomber asked.

"Can we come up with a better name?"

"Your first official assignment—" Bomber said, retrieving the stack of letters from inside his jacket pocket, "—since you apparently don't know anything about tracking, is to go over these letters, find any good leads, and mark the locations on the map. Use the gold pins."

Bruce reluctantly took the stack of letters. "What do the gold pins represent?" he asked.

Bomber stared at him as though he'd been asked a trick question.

"They represent the letters we just received," he said. "Please try to keep up."

7:45 p.m.

Normally, a town meeting would have been Bomber's worst nightmare, but he held onto hope that Sheriff Connie might let slip some useful details of her investigation. The meeting was to be held in the Fox Hollow High School gymnasium to accommodate the expected large turnout. Bomber arrived early and killed time perusing the trophy cases in the main foyer. He tapped the glass window as he read the years on the regional football trophies.

"1997, 1998, 1999, 2000—."

A small dusty space had been left where the 2001 season trophy should have been, a space where a ten-year winning streak had ended.

"An empty space, like the one in my soul," Bomber whispered. He felt very dramatic saying this out loud.

Bomber had been Fox Hollow's starting quarterback since the latter half of his sophomore season and held the school record for career passing yards by the end of his junior year. He'd led the team to two regional championships, one state championship, and was being actively scouted by several collegiate programs. Off the field, he'd dated Gloria Fishman, undeniably the most popular girl in school, and was head over heels for her, though she was high maintenance and frequently cruel in a stereotypical "mean girl" fashion. His best friend had been Sylvester Fox, better known as Sly, who was the heir to the Fox Applesauce fortune and, at the time, the suit performer of the school's mascot, a cartoonish plush fox uncreatively named Foxy. Sly was the perfect friend for an idol teen boy and his family's exorbitant wealth provided endless funding for their teenage mischief, which, whether large or small, was waved off with a "boys-will-be-boys" attitude by members of the community who were either passionate about football or passionate about staying employed. The infallible king of Fox Hollow High, Bomber's life had been a teen movie cliche, right down to the high-stakes championship game of his senior year.

In the final minutes of that vicious last game, Cedar Mills had eked out a three-point lead. Seconds remained on the clock, but the fans of Fox Hollow weren't worried.

The end zone was in striking distance.

Cold November mist clung to the air.

The ball snapped and Bomber faded quickly into the pocket, scanning for his favorite receiver.

There, in the far-left corner, he found him. Right where he should be.

Bomber's arm cocked and the crowd fell silent. But there was something else in that far corner, beyond the receiver. Beyond the game. Outside the field fence, Foxy had his back to the action. Sly had removed his big, stupid, fox-head and there were arms wrapped around his scrawny, stupid, human-neck. As Sly swayed around, Bomber could see Gloria locked passionately on his lips. He launched the ball at his new target.

Bomber shook off the memory. The whole thing was rather "Casey At Bat" as you can imagine and he rarely allowed himself to think of it, let alone dwell on it or let it affect his mood. A crowd had formed in the foyer and he set off toward the gymnasium, pushing through the throngs and avoiding eye contact with anyone who might share his embarrassing memory. A hand reached out and momentarily grasped his shoulder.

"I'm sorry for your loss," a woman sniffled. A tear trickled down her cheek.

"That was sixteen years ago, Debbie," Bomber snapped without breaking stride.

Bomber picked a seat in the center of the bleachers and studied the high school hieroglyphics carved into the wood benches. Mostly crude penises and four-letter words. He was sure his own work was there somewhere. Occasionally people would stop to offer their condolences, confirm rumors, or ask for Bomber's take on the Dogman's role in the whole tragic ordeal. The latter was usually done with obvious tongue-in-cheek, but Bomber was used to the backhanded comments by now.

In the center of the basketball court stood a lonely microphone stand. Far behind it, the town's Board of Aldermen sat in a neat row of folding chairs. Five in total, the Board of

Aldermen's unofficial chairman, Patrick McConnell, sat closest to the mic. A short, stocky man of Irish descent, McConnell was also the VP of Operations for Fox Applesauce and a heroic figure about town. After the corporate relocation, it had been McConnell's impressive quarterly stats that kept the production facilities from suffering the same fate, saving the town from a full-on implosion. His favorable financial reports came at a price, however, and there were substantive reports of mistreatment directed at the company's migrant fruit pickers, who'd recently unionized as a result. McConnell was rumored to carry brass knuckles in his breast pocket and was often referred to as "The Leprechaun" behind his back. Love him or hate him, he produced results. He would often say that the people of Fox Hollow didn't owe him anything, in the way people who feel they're owed something often do.

To the left of McConnell, in the next three chairs, were Abe Carver, Trevor Wright, and Thad Archer. All of whom were employed by Fox Applesauce in some capacity and were quite uninteresting in every other regard.

In the final chair, at a noticeable distance from the rest, was Gloria Glass, formerly Gloria Fishman and Bomber's high-school sweetheart. It should be noted here that the term "sweetheart" is used only in the nostalgic sense and shouldn't persuade anyone to think of her in any other light than the cold-hearted succubus she truly was.

After graduation, Gloria had a brief stint as a Fox Applesauce spokesperson, modeling in several ads and cementing herself as a local celebrity until a risqué photo shoot of her own creation cost her the gig. Most of the town's women agreed that the resulting sauce promotions went overboard in objectifying women and over-sexualizing apples. The men in town were mostly fine with it. Attempting to leave judgmental eyes behind, Gloria left Fox Hollow and suffered two long years of hard partying at Michigan State University before finally sinking her claws into E. S. Glass, a pretentious aspiring writer with a hearty trust fund. They'd married quickly at her behest and moved back to Fox Hollow at his. He'd found the town "quaint" and hoped it would serve as an inspirational place to write about the struggles of the blue-collar man. He'd gone so far as to acquire the town's sole newspaper, promising to revitalize *The Fox Howler* to its former glory.

Which is why his suicide came as such a surprise two years later.

Gloria, who only seemed upset about the unfavorable light in which she was cast through the whole ordeal, was often heard making disparaging comments about her late husband. It was rumored she'd even told her grieving mother-in-law that "the only decent thing your son ever wrote was his suicide note and even there the main character was flat." The town just accepted this as Gloria's unique brand of grieving.

When the spotlight faded, Gloria's life became an unsatisfying spiral of hot yoga, empty merlot bottles, and daytime TV talk shows. Even the sale of her late husband's classic car collection couldn't bolster her spirits. She finally hit rock bottom when she was briefly detained by law enforcement after aggressively accosting an Animal Control Specialist, who'd been patrolling the neighborhood in response to several sightings of a large fox. Her purported mistreatment by the Fox Hollow Police Department led to a very public meltdown and a series of rather odd domestic disturbance calls, despite her living alone. Then, just when things seemed darkest, social media entered her life like a white knight. She found herself transformed. In her mind, she was no longer the old, selfish Gloria, but an informed champion of the people. Her hard-line opinions, sculpted by specialized algorithms, unqualified bloggers, and coercive posts limited to a hundred and twenty characters or less. She didn't just have a cause now, she had *all* the causes and she weighed in on social issues of menial interest with ever-increasing tenacity, gradually making her the champion of a formidable following of tiger-moms, angry gay men (lesbians still found her abhorrent), animal rights activists, militant environmentalists, amateur socialists, anti-gun lobbyists, communist sympathizers, and a handful of low-level Hollywood celebrities. Her cyber-victories revitalized an old dopamine addiction and her need for power became insatiable, until, one day, at a town hall meeting, she simply took a seat alongside the other Aldermen and never left.

Bomber hadn't spoken to Gloria since Sly's funeral and the

two had actively avoided each other for the better part of sixteen years. That is, until now.

The clomp of McConnell's work boots echoed around the gymnasium as he made the long march to the microphone. Reaching up, he lowered the mic to its lowest level.

"If I could have everyone's attention, please."

He cleared his throat in a theatrical manner and the gymnasium fell silent. Despite his height, his freckles, and his short-sleeve button-up, Patrick Seamus McConnell was an intimidating presence.

"As all of you are aware, Cecil Merridan is dead." He paused to let this sink in, despite his acknowledgment that everyone already knew it. "Our condolences to the Merridan family."

Everyone looked at Bomber, who, not knowing how to react, waved awkwardly as though acknowledging an achievement.

"In light of Cecil's passing," McConnell continued, "and because we are now entering election season, it has been decided amongst the Board of Aldermen that a mayoral election shall occur on an expedited schedule. Anyone who wishes to run for the position of Town Mayor may come by Town Hall tomorrow to officially register."

He paused again, expecting this news to make a larger splash. The town had stopped observing the election ritual altogether in the mid 80's.

"Are there any questions at this point?" McConnell asked. "Yes, you there, in the back."

Everyone turned to see a large woman in a majestic horse shirt standing in the back row.

"We was told this meeting would be about how Mayor Merridan died," she said. "How did Mayor Merridan die?"

"You were misinformed, my dear," McConnell said. "This meeting was called to determine the succession plan for the mayoral office."

There was a collective groan from the audience.

"I don't see how it's relevant," McConnell said with an air of concession, "but perhaps Sheriff Connie could shed light on the circumstances of the deceased." He motioned to Connie, who stood near the exit. "Sheriff Connie, could you oblige us?"

Connie shook her head.

"Well, there you have it," McConnell said. "The man was ninety years old and feeble as a foal. A light breeze could've taken him out."

"I ain't ever heard of a light breeze tearing a man's throat out," the woman yelled.

There were murmurs of affirmation from the audience, indicating no one else had heard of a light-breeze-massacre either.

"Maybe we ought to ask Bomber instead," someone shouted. "Seems more likely it was one of his werewolves anyhow."

A laugh rippled through the bleachers and Bomber's face flushed. The sound of heels clicking was heard once again. Sheriff Connie grabbed the microphone, edging out McConnell who was obviously displeased with having his announcements derailed.

"Fine," she snapped. "I suppose you all deserve some peace of mind, but I don't have much to give. I'm sure the rumor mills are working overtime, so here are the details I can share at this time. Mayor Merridan is dead. He was found along Old Dickerson Road. His wounds were consistent with an animal attack."

"What type of animal?" yelled the horse shirt woman.

"Jesus, Debbie," Sheriff Connie said. "If I knew that, I'd have said. The investigation is being handed over tomorrow to the Cedar Mills branch of the Department of Natural Resources. The DNR will be better equipped to identify the animal, track it, and capture it."

Bomber raised his hand. Sheriff Connie ignored him.

"It's likely this is just an isolated incident," she continued. "But please keep a close watch on your small children, pets, and, of course, the elderly. Most importantly, please refrain from spreading unverified information regarding the attack." She gave another sharp look at Bomber. "Rumors and monster stories are toxic. We're all adults here. There are no such things as werewolves, Bigfoots, or Dogmen."

Bomber frowned. He looked at Gloria, who was smiling and staring straight at him. Sheriff Connie returned to her post by the exit and Bomber could hear his name in the whispers all around. McConnell commanded the mic again.

"As I was saying," he said. "A proper election will be held at the beginning of November. Per the town charter, at least two debates will be held prior to the election. Times and locations will be forthcoming. That is if anyone decides they want the silly job."

McConnell straightened himself and adjusted his tie.

"In the interim, as Senior Alderman of the town council, I will be assuming the full duties of interim mayor for the next two weeks. Not that there are a lot of duties to assume."

"Not so fast," shouted Gloria.

Before McConnell could protest she was ticking across the gymnasium on thin stilettos, waves of blonde hair bouncing on her shoulders. Her slick red pantsuit was an inferno racing to consume Patrick McConnell. She snatched the microphone and leaned in. "Sorry to interrupt your little coup d'etat, Pat."

"What in God's name are you talking about, Gloria?" McConnell groaned.

"I'm talking about this not-so-subtle takeover you're aiming for here." Gloria poked sharply at his shoulder.

"I don't like being poked," McConnell said. His face was as red as his hair. "Or being called 'Pat.'"

"I'll bet you don't, buster," she said, poking once more for good measure before addressing the bleachers. "This man is a fox in sheep's clothing. He intends to use and abuse his self-appointed position to further Fox Applesauce's vile anti-environmental agenda."

"What?" he shouted. "What 'anti-environmental agenda'?" His voice was distant as Gloria had taken full control of the microphone.

"Not today, Mr. Senior Alderman," Gloria hissed.

She clapped her hands twice. A door at the back of the gymnasium clattered open and three women filed in. Two held a retractable movie screen between them and trotted in tandem. The third woman pushed a media cart, equipped with an ancient overhead projector, which had been commandeered from the school's library. The movie screen was quickly erected in the center of the basketball court, while the projector was placed a few feet from the mic stand. The efficiency of the drill suggested numerous test runs had been made. The gymnasium lights clicked off as the overhead projector flickered on, revealing a blurry image of a weathered document. A particular paragraph had been circled in red.

"The official town charter of Fox Hollow states as follows," Gloria said. "'Section 12C, paragraph three. In the event the serving mayor becomes incapacitated or deadened and is no longer able to perform *his*'—gender bias, by the way—'mayorly duties, he can and should be succeeded, posthaste, by his next of smartly kin, therein, until a rightly successor may be determined in due process of the electoral procession.'"

Bomber didn't like how that sounded.

"The town charter was written in 1892, Gloria," McConnell argued. "There were about twenty people living here at the time. And clearly of limited intellect."

"You hear that, Fox Hollow?" Gloria shouted. "He undermines the document that is the very cornerstone of our great town. *And* he calls your forefathers 'simpletons.'"

"I didn't call anyone a simpleton," McConnell growled.

"The fact of the matter, Pat, is that law is law. And since Cecil Merridan has no other 'smartly kin' in Fox Hollow, there is only one obvious choice." Gloria turned back to the crowd. "Ladies and gentlemen, your new interim mayor, Mr. William 'Bomber' Merridan!"

Gloria's team of tiger moms simultaneously lit three large flashlights, converging their beams on Bomber's face. He squinted and held his hands over his eyes. Exactly two people in the audience began to clap but quickly stopped. Bomber waved awkwardly again.

"This is ludicrous," McConnell grumbled.

"Lights!" Gloria shouted. The gymnasium lights clicked on. Everyone squinted. "I'm sorry, Pat. What part of this is ludicrous? Perhaps you think our precious town charter is ludicrous. Perhaps you think the rule of law is ludicrous."

Gloria turned back to the audience.

"Perhaps Mr. McConnell here would like to see this town descend into anarchy!"

One person in the back began to clap.

"Christ, Gloria," McConnell said, pinching the bridge of his nose. "What makes you think Bomber even wants the job? The guy spends his days stocking shelves and his nights chasing imaginary monsters. He doesn't have a damn clue how to run a town."

"It doesn't matter what he wants," Gloria yelled, waving her copy of the town charter above her head. "It matters what—"

Her eye caught Bomber who sat with his hand raised high in the air, yet again.

"Oh, hon," Gloria said. "You're the mayor now. You don't need to raise your hand."

Bomber stood on the bench where he'd been seated. He felt an energy welling up in him.

"Mr. McConnell is right," he said. "I don't have a clue how to run a town. And I know a lot of you out there don't have a real high opinion of me. In fact, I'd wager most of you think I'm a bit of a crackpot." There were nods of affirmation through the bleachers.

"And an alcoholic," someone shouted.

"Yes, thank you. *Recovering* alcoholic, actually," Bomber corrected. "What I'm trying to say is, despite it all, this town has always been my home. I love Fox Hollow and I'll try my hardest to be the best damn mayor this town has ever seen. For the next two weeks. You know, besides my dead uncle."

"Great uncle," someone corrected.

"For Fox Hollow," Bomber shouted, thrusting a fist into the air.

No one clapped.

Bomber remained in the bleachers as people filtered out. Gloria still prowled the lacquered floor, glad-handing folks who'd stuck around to gossip. She kept shooting him meaningful glances, as if she'd like to talk. He wanted no part of it.

A few people had slapped Bomber on the back and offered their support. Several more had stopped to speculate on what Sheriff Connie might be hiding and ask for his theory on the so-called "animal attack." He had just launched into an explanation to poor Mrs. Johnson about the differing bite radii of indigenous canis species and how they conflicted with reported Dogman attacks when a voice came from below.

"I hope you know what you're doing," Sheriff Connie said. She stood a few steps down with her hand on her service pistol.

Mrs. Johnson, too polite to interrupt before, took her opportunity to escape.

"I'll manage," Bomber said. "And since I'm mayor now, you can share details of the investigation, right? You probably *have* to."

Sheriff Connie studied him for a moment. She had a strong jaw that set firm when she was irritated, which was pretty much every time she spoke to Bomber. From a young age, her grandfather, leader of the local Ottawa tribe, Chief Herman Hayes, had taught her strength, patience, and grace. Conversely, her own father had taught her nothing but an unhealthy distrust of people by vanishing when she was only four years old. Raised on a nearby reservation, she never quite fit in with her peers at school. Being in this gymnasium brought back hard feelings.

In high school, she and a small band of eccentric friends would practice Goju-ryu karate on the high school's lawn during the lunch hour. This small reprieve from the day was often tainted by ridicule from Bomber, Sly, and their Neanderthal football cohorts. Even her devotion to her dojo couldn't stave off her low self-esteem and, with baby Bruce in her belly most of her junior year, Connie had the odds stacked against her. It all reached a climax the summer after graduation when Connie discovered the body of her karate instructor, Sensei Wagner, sprawled across his dojo mats on an idle Tuesday morning, his big toe still caught in the trigger assembly of the shotgun he'd used to sully the sanctum with chunks of skull and brain and flesh. After giving the police her statement, Connie had driven straight to the local Army Recruitment Center. She would not be beaten by this town like Sensei Wagner. Her grandfather and her extended family on the reservation helped to raise Bruce and after five years in the Military Police, two decorated tours in Iraq, and a graduation from the Mid-Michigan Police Academy, Connie returned to Fox Hollow where she became the town's first female officer.

"No, I don't have to share anything," she answered Bomber flatly. "And I meant, 'I hope you know what you're doing' because the police department's payroll is processed at City Hall. If my guys don't get their bread, they won't work. All you have to do is keep the wheels from falling off for two weeks. Don't dick it up."

She turned abruptly and headed back across the gym, a slight smile gracing her thin lips. Bomber watched her go. Every interaction with Sheriff Connie left him feeling an inner shame for the way he treated her school. When he looked back, Gloria had appeared, her plastic face stretched by a man-eating smile.

"Gloria," Bomber sighed.

"Bomber," Gloria said, nodding with mock seriousness.

"What do you want, Gloria?"

"So hostile," she said. "I just wanted to make sure you were alright with these—new developments." She faked a smile. "I know I kind of put you on the spot and, Lord knows, you can be a bit shaky under pressure. Plus you've got a lot going on with all this Dog-boy stuff."

"I'm fine," Bomber snorted.

"Good," she said. "You're not entertaining ideas of trying to *stay* mayor, are you? I don't think it would suit you. Plus, rumor has it, 'yours truly' might be throwing her hat into the election ring tomorrow."

She winked, but Bomber was only half listening. He'd caught sight of a man near the emergency exit. Dressed in the same hoodie and sunglasses as the Unabomber wannabe from Marty's the day before. Bomber looked for Sheriff Connie but she was long gone.

"Bomber, did you hear me?" Gloria asked, shifting into his line of sight.

"Yeah, yeah," Bomber said. "Good luck and all."

He quickly moved down the stairs, determined to make his first act as interim mayor a citizen's arrest of an obvious criminal, or at the very least a potential criminal.

The man in the hoodie noticed Bomber noticing him. As Bomber pushed through a cluster of gossipers, the man backed toward the emergency exit.

"Hey! You! Stop right there!" Bomber called, jogging with his hand in the air, like he was hailing a taxi.

The man was out the door before anyone in the gym saw him,

leaving Bomber waving to nothing and no one.

"Stop!" Bomber yelled. "Your mayor commands you."

Bomber pushed through the emergency door and stumbled onto the sidewalk. Across the street was an empty parking lot and beyond it, an arborvitae hedge separated school grounds from city homes.

"You better run!" Bomber called but wasn't sure why.

Somewhere down the block, a dog began to bark.

October 21, 2017

8:17 a.m.

On the east end of Main Street, a district of Fox Hollow known as "Old Town" had once welcomed citizens and visitors with its quaint 1950's Americana, but now the classic charm of Cecil Merridan's "living time-capsule" was quickly losing ground to the poisons of the digital age and a lackluster, plastic world. Mom-and-pop shops, whose broad front windows once offered enticing peaks at their wares under hand-painted glass murals, were all but replaced with cell phone stores, mega-chain pharmacies, and a never ending rotation of quick-service food franchises, their windows wallpapered with flashy corporate advertising and impossible-to-beat deals on products people didn't know they needed. Everywhere, trappings of the uninspired modern world crept in like an invasive species.

Earl's Barber Shop had remained true to the old order. The barber pole still twisted slowly out front, but old Earl wasn't cutting much hair anymore. Bomber had gone to Earl's for as long as he could remember and was still fond of the old man's colorful stories: his jump into Normandy, his brief stay in a Nazi P.O.W. camp, and his endless battles with "the goddamn Krauts." But now, at 93 years old, Earl had an unnerving shake in his scissor-hand and most of his regulars had quietly found new barbers. The shop still opened daily, at 8 a.m. sharp and Bomber was one of the few who still braved Earl's chair. Loyalty was worth a sketchy cut. But mostly, the barbershop now served as a meeting place for a handful of elderly men who'd sit around sipping weak coffee and griping about lost time, liberal sons-in-law, and the newest generation of soft young punks destroying the America for which they'd so passionately fought.

Across from Earl's was Robinson's Family Pet Store, which had opened when Bomber was only a child. He had fond memories of family visits, where he'd marvel at all the furry animals his mother would never allow. Shortly after opening, as part of a promotional stunt, Robinson's Family Pet Store acquired two "exotic" creatures to add to their inventory of otherwise ordinary house pets. The first was a one-month-old American Alligator named Alice, whose ugly disposition made her hiss and snap at anyone who dared cross in front of her Plexiglass enclosure. The second was a two-year-old scarlet macaw named Ms. Chitters. If Alice couldn't hurt you physically, Ms. Chitters would hurt you emotionally. Bought cheap from a failed local comedian, Ms. Chitters was trained to respond to heckling audience members with a laundry list of scathing insults. As intelligent as she was mean, Ms. Chitters used her stage talents to relentlessly badger the pet store patrons, with brazen affronts such as:

"Nice face, melon head."

Or:

"Fatty-fatty, numb-nuts."

Or the go-to:

"Your mother's a tramp."

While trying to remove Ms. Chitters from high traffic areas, the Robinsons quickly discovered an odd curiosity, in that the two tropical creatures seemed to pacify one another in close proximity. Their cages were placed side-by-side and the customer harassment lessened.

In his teenage years, Sly had taken particular offense to Ms. Chitters's "yo momma" jokes (his own mother had disappeared on him and his father) and would frequently drag Bomber along to the Robinson's Family Pet Store for the sheer purpose of retribution. Screaming "Polly want a cracker" at the top of his lungs, Sly would shake the birdcage violently until Mr. Robinson inevitably threw both boys out. The parrot, deserving or not, became so distraught from the abuse that, after time, she would attack the brass bars in a frenzy of red, green, and blue feathers at the mere sight of Sly. Ironically, both Ms. Chitters and Alice had outlived him and were still residents of the pet store. Alice, now over six feet long, was far too dangerous to sell, while Ms. Chitters had been sold several times, but would become doleful and silent without her reptilian friend and would eventually be returned when her feathers began to fall out. The pair had become unlikely celebrities in town and the pet shop's store-front mural featured a smiling alligator with a brilliant macaw perched atop its lumpy head.

Town Hall stood on the west end of Old Town like a capstone on the end of nostalgia. The building was modestly sized and built of burnt-orange brick, a decorative white cornice wrapping the upper level. A small veranda stretched from the main entrance, ending at two thick, Roman columns before descending to a cobblestone walkway leading back to Main Street. The building, and its landscaping, had gone largely unchanged since its original construction in the summer of 1914.

Central in the walkway was a great stone pedestal, upon which stood an enormous bronze statue, gleaming under the morning sun. Bomber, clad in a tie for the first time in ages, stood before it, battered briefcase in hand. He watched curiously as a large—some might say "freakishly large"—robin dipped and dived, pecking fiercely around the statue's face. For a split second, Bomber thought the bird's eyes appeared orange.

It had been years since Bomber had stopped to admire the bronze warrior, frozen in eternal combat. The soldier's legs were bent, driving forward into some unknown fray, his mouth agape in an eternal battle-cry, though Bomber had always felt he appeared to be yawning. Years ago, the soldier had gripped a rifle in one hand and a grenade in the other, his arm cocked and ready to throw. It had been a fierce display of patriotic bravery and, therefore, was an intolerable affront to decency, according to Gloria Glass. In an effort to remove images of violence from public spaces, Gloria had lobbied to have the statue altered. Ultimately, the rifle was hack-sawed off, replaced with an picker's basket, and the grenade was painted a shiny red to resemble an apple. Gloria had not received permission to make these changes, but no one dared object, fearing accusations of blood lust, warmongering, toxic masculinity, or general brutishness.

Bomber waved his briefcase, attempting to shoo the bird from the sleepy soldier-turned-apple-picker, before using a crumpled tissue to wipe filth from the black plaque on the pedestal:

PFC Sylvester "Sly" Fox III
March 5, 1984 - August 8, 2003
KIA - Najaf, Iraq - Operation Iraqi Freedom
"The Hometown Hero Of Fox Hollow"

The statue seemed ironic to Bomber, considering the depth to which Sly had despised Fox Hollow. He'd often confided in Bomber his desire to escape his birthright, viewing it more as a pending prison sentence than a winning lottery ticket. The summer after graduation was a tumultuous time in the town's history, a period still lightly referred to as "Sly's Rebellion." Over a three-month stretch, the town was terrorized with toilet-papered trees, cellophaned cars, graffiti tags, and exploding mailboxes, destroyed by pop-bottle-bombs made from concoctions of various volatile cleaners. Ex-Sheriff Barnstorm, Connie's predecessor, was deep in the Fox family's pocket and did little to impede the destruction, but when a delayed bottle-bomb ruptured and permanently blinded Frank the Postman, Sly had to face the music. Judge Trotter, who was very much *not* in the Fox family's pocket, presided over the case and despite Mr. Fox's considerable political influence, gave Sly the choice of three years in prison or a stint in the U.S. Army. Sly happily chose the Army. When asked why, he'd feigned a patriotic calling, but Bomber knew he was simply drawn to the promise of sanctioned acts of violence.

"Scram," Bomber yelled, swinging his case overhead. The enraged bird took a swoop at him before sailing off across Main

Street and over the police station. From behind the police station, he thought he heard an engine backfire or a firearm discharge. Bomber wondered if the bird was some distant, vengeful relative of the many Sly had slain with his Daisy BB gun.

Sly's mother had disappeared when he was nine, under circumstances never made clear to the general public. Rumors, of course, abounded. The predominant theory was she'd run off with one of her several lovers, but this supposition was weakened when all of her known side-pieces were found to be accounted for around town. The next theory was that Mr. Fox had killed her. This seemed most likely to Bomber, though no one could provide evidence. Mr. Fox, like his father and his father before him and his father before him, had a terrible temper. A mean streak a mile wide, as they say. Some said it was hereditary, others theorized a perpetuated system of childhood neglect, and a handful still rumored an old Ottawa Indian curse. Whatever it was, it was likely the reason for Sly's own dark side. A child psychologist might have diagnosed Sly with a complete lack of empathy—as well as several other sociopathic trait markers. Sly would occasionally come to school with mysterious bruises on his arms or face, but Bomber never had the courage to ask, nor Sly the courage to tell.

The summer of Sly's tenth birthday, he and Bomber had taken to building and launching model rockets in the clearing around Scum Pond—all that remained of Doris Grayson's "Kissing Pond"—at the center of the original Fox Orchard. Sly had quickly grown tired of standard launches, insisting "manned missions" were the wave of the future. Bomber had protested meagerly, not wanting to seem lame or soft, but Sly proceeded without him, sending dozens of Scum Pond frogs into low orbit. Every creature returned to earth the same, a crispy shell of black and green. Bomber voiced his discomfort with the whole operation, but Sly only laughed.

There'd been other instances of Sly's developing cruelty over the years. There'd been the drive-by "ketchup-packet-assaults" on local homeless—namely Carl Longstreet—and the systematic debasing of the high school's unofficial karate club to name a few. Bomber had, regretfully, been a willing participant in both.

There'd also been a parking lot brawl or two, where Sly had pummeled his opponent in a trance-like rage, long after the other boys went limp. Even his stint as the high school's mascot was done with ill intent. His rude, confrontational behavior accepted as part of Foxy's boisterous personality. Each instance had spurred a brief awareness in Bomber, a partial epiphany that bled into a nagging doubt about his friend, but his immaturity and desire for acceptance had suppressed his will to speak up. And so he never did.

Bomber hadn't spoken another word to Sly after the big-game-betrayal where Bomber's heat seeking spiral had knocked out Sly's top right canine. He didn't so much as say goodbye before Sly left for Basic Training. The town had made a big to-do about his leaving, holding a parade in his honor, which didn't sit well with the family of Blind Frank the Postman. News of Sly and his exploits slowly faded, until a year later when the U.S. invaded Iraq and two men in Army greens arrived at the Fox Family Mansion with a folded American flag. Details of Sly's death were disseminated to the town via *The Fox Howler*, not yet in the hands of E. S. Glass. The final account of Private Fox's death had read like an award citation, romantic and full of guts and glory. His last act on earth: an effort to save an injured comrade from the murky waters of the Euphrates River while under withering enemy fire. Neither soldier would see shore again. It seemed, despite Bomber's assessment, Sly had died selflessly. Bomber had misgivings about the report's accuracy, but even he eventually swallowed the story, finding it difficult to hold a grudge against a hero, though he still felt bad about the space frogs.

"He sure was something else, wasn't he?"

Bomber nearly dropped his briefcase. He turned to find Gloria, high heels in her hands. She was substantially shorter without her shoes and she tiptoed across the uneven cobblestones.

"He was an animal," Bomber said.

Gloria sighed in agreement and they stared up at the soldier's shining face for an awkward moment. Bomber hoped she'd leave. Or be struck down by the vengeful hand of God. One of the two.

"They're going to kill it, you know?"

"What?"

"Whatever killed Cecil," she said. "A bear, a cougar, your Dogman, whatever it was, the DNR is going to find it and put it down."

"Why would you care?" Bomber asked.

Gloria gasped in fake astonishment.

"I care about all living things," she boasted.

Bomber rolled his eyes.

"The real question is, why don't *you* care?" Gloria added. "I'm not saying I believe your stories, but if I were you, I'd want to find the creature and salvage my reputation."

Bomber was silent. He hadn't considered what the authorities would do if they captured the Dogman. Or if they'd even attempt capture at all.

"Perhaps it's something to bring up in the Council Meeting," Gloria chirped before daintily padding off toward the town hall entrance.

The mayor's office had been flooded with condolence flowers and Edith, the mayoral secretary, shuffled about the lobby making sure every gardenia, carnation, and lily was appropriately positioned. At 81 years old, Edith had been the mayoral secretary for nearly as long as Cecil Merridan had been in office. Bomber could only imagine the despair she must be feeling and thus wished to avoid an interaction at all costs. He wasn't proud of this, but he wasn't great at comforting people either, especially the elderly. Social encounters, in general, had been difficult lately. His job at the store required him to interact with his fellow townspeople on a rapid and repetitive basis. The speed and volume of which made anything more than the superficial exchange of pleasantries next to impossible. Everyone spoke to him, but no one really *said* anything. He knew everyone but knew no one. His ability to make deeper, personal connections had slowly waned, a skill seeping out of him unnoticed until, in a moment like this, it was unsuccessfully summoned from an empty tank. Fortunately, Edith's botanical distraction was complete enough to allow him to tiptoe past her to his late great uncle's office.

Bomber clicked the heavy wood door behind him. The air in the office was thick with the smell of stale pipe tobacco and the combined mustiness of seventy-year-old furniture and ninety-year-old men. Bomber's first step drew a tremendous creak from a warped floorboard. He froze and listened. From beneath the door, a pleasant tune wafted in, as Edith went on humming a familiar, but not quite recognizable, church hymn.

The office was old, but charming. An ancient oak desk commanded the room and two faded olive chairs faced it for the more intimate encounters of Cecil's previous open-door policy. Behind the desk, two flag poles displayed the American flag and Fox Hollow flag (See Historical Addendum #1) respectively, giving the scene an air of officiality and seriousness. Between the flags, a large window offering an up-close view of a white picket fence had been left propped open and a cool draft filtered in. The east wall of the room held a built-in bookshelf from floor to ceiling, though there were only ten books in the whole structure, mostly autobiographies of 19th-century politicians. The rest of the space was occupied by various trophies and plaques Cecil had been awarded—or he'd awarded to himself—and a variety of potted plants that, judging from their brown leaves, had synthesized their last photons. The west wall could hardly be seen. Its face was covered with a patchwork of black plastic, wood, chrome, and brushed nickel frames, containing photographs of Cecil at every major town event over the last seventy years. The pictures were hung in careful order, from oldest to newest, starting with a black and white photo of his inauguration in 1946. The final photo was of Cecil and several leaders of the local pickers union as they bobbed for apples at last year's Harvest Festival. Everything in between was a hall-of-fame gallery of the town's best memories, a visual history of the unity his great-uncle had fostered for almost three quarters of a century.

Bomber slid the window shut and sat down at the desk. The old chair belched ancient air. The desktop was mostly clear, save for a small lamp, a magnifying glass, a "World's Best Mayor" coffee-mug-turned-pen-holder, and a sprawling desk calendar, completely devoid of entries except the recurring council meeting at 9 a.m. on Tuesdays. The meeting for which Bomber had come but was woefully unprepared.

He placed his briefcase on the desk and popped it open. It was empty, aside from a sandwich he'd packed for lunch. He would need a notepad and pen—and perhaps a clipboard to really drive home his commitment and professionalism. Checking the desk, he found the upper-right drawer contained an assortment of pens procured from local businesses, which had not been deemed worthy of the desktop mug. The middle drawer was filled with hard candy, mostly of the butterscotch variety. No doubt pilfered from annual parades or bought on-the-cheap in post-Halloween sales. In the middle of the candy was a lone packet of Fox Applesauce's Bloo Goo.

"Poor guy was suicidal," Bomber muttered.

The bottom-right drawer contained a nearly full fifth of Whistle Pig rye whiskey and two lowball glasses. Bomber made a note to clear these out, lest temptation take hold. In addition to not driving since his encounter, he'd also given up alcohol completely.

The drawers on the left side were locked, with no key to be found. The lock required an old-fashioned skeleton key and Bomber was certain he'd have remembered seeing it in a previous drawer. The keyhole was surrounded by knicks and scratches and sizable divots had been gouged in the top of each drawer, suggesting the key had been lost for some time and Cecil had tried to pry the drawers open, probably under the influence of the Whistle Pig.

"I nearly blew your brains out."

Bomber's head snapped up. Edith stood in the doorway, a small watering can in one hand, a tiny Derringer pistol in the other. The weapon was still leveled at Bomber.

"I'm sorry?" Bomber sputtered, holding his hands out, as if they could stop a bullet.

"I nearly blew your brains out," Edith repeated in her raspy voice. She lowered the small pistol. "I heard drawers clank'n about and I figured we were being burglarized again. Didn't realize you'd snuck in, on account of it being odd behavior for your first day."

Bomber's face flushed.

"I'm sorry," he said. "You seemed busy and I didn't want to be a bother. I can't imagine how hard this must be, after so many years."

Edith's laugh was abrupt as she shuffled into the room and began watering the dead plants. Her arm shook as she lifted the can.

"Young man, I was happy for him."

"Sorry?"

"Boy, you're about as hard of hearing as he was," Edith nearly shouted. "I was happy for him, I said. The man was ninety-two years old. When you get to be our age, you start to wonder if the good Lord forgot about—WA-CHOO!"

Edith's sneeze nearly knocked her over and Bomber winced, expecting the pistol to discharge. Water sloshed from the can as she braced herself against the bookshelf.

"Bless you," Bomber said, coming around the desk.

Edith waved him off.

"God'll bless me when he finally takes me," she said, with a pleasant smile. "I just hope when I go, it's as exciting as it was for ol' Cecil. I'd like to go out in a blaze of glory." She yanked her pistol up again, pointing it at nothing in particular. "Guns blazing."

"Well, I hope you don't go too soon," Bomber smiled.

"What an awful thing to say to me," Edith complained. "I just told you I'd like to die."

Bomber shifted uncomfortably.

"I only meant that it'll be nice to have an experienced mayoral secretary around to keep me in line."

"Mayoral Administrative Assistant, Mr. Merridan," Edith corrected, shuffling toward the door. "It's the twenty-first century. We don't use the word 'secretary' anymore. Ms. Gloria insisted upon it. She said it's demeaning. And that's a selfish reason for you to want me alive."

"I'm sorry," said Bomber. "I'd only like you alive for two more weeks, please. Just until the new mayor takes over."

"As you wish, Mr. Merridan, but so you know, Cecil wouldn't have wanted you here. He didn't want you to pursue politics. He always said political families were gross, incestuous affairs. So if it gets you out of here, I'll give you two weeks—for Cecil—but not a second longer." She reiterated this last bit by absently poking the pistol in his direction

"Thank you," Bomber said. "And please, call me Bomber."

"I won't," she replied. "WA-CHOO!"

Another sneeze nearly blew her out the door and Bomber cowered from the gun. She turned and eyed Bomber suspiciously.

"Do you own a dog, Mr. Merridan?" she asked.

"No, ma'am."

"I'm allergic to dogs, Mr. Merridan."

"I assure you, if I owned a dog, I'd be the first to know."

"Must be those close calls with the 'Dogman' then," she said mischievously as she shuffled out the door. "Don't be late for your council meeting, Mr. Merridan."

9:06 a.m.

Ms. Carol Meyer sashayed around her kitchen, cleaver in hand, humming her favorite hymn. She had just received word from the Fox Hollow P.D. that, after days of polite reminders, the strapping Sergeant Householder was finally en route to her home. She felt bad, at first, for taking the morning off from her volunteer duties at The Golden Years Assisted Living Facility, a dreary home for the elderly where she played endless games of cribbage, euchre, and backgammon with the town's forgotten loved ones, but she was optimistic that Mr. Fuzzbottom would soon be safe and she would be enjoying a nice lunch with her knight in shining armor.

On a low note in her hymn, she brought the cleaver down, slicing an egg salad sandwich in half. She herself wasn't fond of egg salad, but she knew it was Sergeant Householder's favorite and she wanted to show her gratitude. Once the sandwich was neatly plated, she placed it in the refrigerator and removed the sandwich from the day prior, placing the halves into a plastic baggy.

"Lunch and a to-go bag," she smiled to herself. "I spoil you, Sergeant."

She stopped and listened. Something was scratching at the back door.

"Mr. Fuzzbottom?"

She crossed the kitchen and opened the door, expecting to find her wayward orange tabby with some freshly murdered rodent, but the concrete steps were bare save for the dark blood stains of past kills.

She stood in the doorway, taking in the sun and wondering if she should change into a shirt with a lower neckline before the good Sergeant arrived. The sound of an approaching tractor could be heard down the orchard rows that stretched out behind her home. The air tasted of pesticides. The noise and taste were reminders of the dismay she'd felt when the vast fields that once flanked her home had been purchased and converted to orchard. For a brief moment, she wondered why they were spraying in late October, but then something caught her attention.

At the back of the yard, in the border hedge of skip laurel that held the orchard at bay, leaves rustled vigorously.

"Mr. Fuzzbottom?" Carol called. She crouched down but couldn't get a good look. Knowing if she pursued him, he'd run, Carol turned and entered the house, leaving the door hanging open. She picked up her humming once more, occasionally glancing at the door. She even poured new food into Mr. Fuzzbottom's dish, purposefully letting the pieces fall from an exaggerated height to maximize the din created in the tin dish.

She had just returned to the stove, where more eggs were boiling—this time for a funeral luncheon at the church—when she heard the back door creak.

Play it cool, Carol, she thought.

She turned her head only slightly, letting her peripherals do the rest. A giant shadow stretched across the green-white-checkered tile. She whipped her head around and gasped, nearly falling back onto the hot burner.

"Shoo!" she pleaded. "Get out of here!"

A ragged beast blocked the doorway. Nearly the size of a cougar, it was almost unrecognizable as a cat. Patches of orange fur dotted an otherwise hairless, but muscular, body and a small red collar constricted its veiny neck so that it wheezed as it slinked into the kitchen. A small bell on the collar jingled merrily.

"Mr.—Mr. Fuzzbottom?" Carol whimpered.

The beast lifted its head with just a glimmer of recognition. Orange lightning cracked its blackened eyes. Its jowls lifted and quivered. Carol reached for the cleaver.

ADDENDUM #1

SUBJECT: A Brief History Of The Fox Hollow Flag

DESCRIPTION: The Fox Hollow Flag features an orange and white fox head in profile, set upon a solid, black background. Inside the fox's mouth, pinned carefully between two triangular teeth, sits a pristine, green apple.

HISTORY: In the early days of America, taverns and brothels were often the first signs of "civilization" on the otherwise rugged frontier. In order to draw customers, early businesses needed to advertise across large swaths of land. Unfortunately, though cunning and resourceful woodsmen, most fur trappers and huntsmen were illiterate bastards. To circumvent the communication gap, tavern- and brothel-owners carved pictures, or pictograms, into wood placards and placed them along established roadways and prominent trails. In our specific case, The Foxy Howl Inn used a fox head for obvious reasons. The green apple, though innocent as it seemed, was a subtle reference to "sins of the flesh," original sin, or the Temptation of Eve. Fur trappers, huntsmen, and other passersby would know of The Foxy Howl Inn by word of mouth and would be on the lookout for their particular carvings, trail markers promising the fulfillment of their carnal cravings.

CURRENT USE: The Fox Hollow Flag, despite its impure past, is still displayed at all major town functions. Most notably, the fox head and apple are still used as the school's logo, which is displayed on athletic uniforms, buildings, and official documents.

****

Bomber tried, but the council meeting couldn't keep him there. He drifted in and out of consciousness, while pieces of McConnell's agenda wormed into his brain creating disjointed dreams that skipped across his mind's eye. Environmental concerns of Fox Applesauce. A bit about missing migrant workers. Something about a group of militant vegans. And then, finally, the meeting was gone.

In his dream, he was running down an orchard row under the misty glow of a full moon. The trees were gnarled, ancient things, their branches thick with water sprouts which lashed at his cheeks and grabbed his shirt with their sharp fingers. He was taking heavy, panicked breaths.

He stopped in a clearing of trampled grass. At its center was a mangled mass of fur and flesh and bone. Moonlight shined off a heap of wet entrails, a gray island in a pool of ink-black blood. Bomber bent down to inspect the animal. Steam rose from the carcass.

A branch snapped.

"Who's there?" He whispered. He didn't wait for a response. He was running, occasionally stumbling in deep tractor-tire ruts. He ran until his lungs and legs begged for mercy. It was close now. He could hear footsteps and breaking branches.

He glanced over his shoulder as he ran.

Nothing.

He glanced again.

There. A few yards back. A black mass pulsed in and out of moonbeams. An apparition with glowing, orange eyes. A fuzzy specter.

"Get back," Bomber shouted, a shameful crack in his voice.

Bomber felt a resurgence of energy, of hope, as he spotted a chain-link fence and a dirt road beyond. He had to make it over.

From behind him, a mournful howl curdled his soul. He couldn't help it. He looked again and that's all it took. His foot caught the edge of a tire rut, sending him sprawling.

In his dream, Bomber's head hit the fence post. At that same moment, in the real world of the town council meeting, his chin slipped from his hand, cracking hard onto the desk. The conversation around him stopped.

"Are you okay?" McConnell asked, out of obligation.

"I'm fine," Bomber said, rubbing the jaw. His face reddened, as he studied the wood grains of the table.

"Listen, Bomber," McConnell said. "No one could think any less of you if you didn't attend these meetings. I'm sure you'd prefer to be doing just about anything other than discussing the streamlining of small businesses licensing."

"You said 'could,'" Bomber said.

"What?"

"You said 'no one *could* think any less of me,'" Bomber repeated.

"I'm sure I said '*would*,'" McConnell said. He checked his watch. "Besides, shouldn't you be at Marty's right now?"

"I traded shifts."

"How fortunate for us all."

"I've actually come with a purpose," Bomber said. He straightened his back and folded a page of his legal pad, to create the illusion he'd been taking notes.

"Please, don't keep us in suspense," McConnell said.

Bomber cleared his throat.

"It seems to me, you've all got a problem. A Dogman problem."

The room was a mixture of groans and sighs. Gloria, who'd been uncharacteristically amenable throughout the meeting, gave him an encouraging smile.

"Fine, fine," Bomber continued. "I understand you're not ready to accept the Dogman theory yet. That's on me. In this day and age, belief requires hard evidence, which I've failed to provide. A problem I plan to remedy soon. But even so, Dogman aside, you've got a wild beast on the loose. There's no denying that. And there's no denying that after ten years' experience, I'm the town's foremost expert on the tracking and trapping of wild game."

"What have you successfully caught?" McConnell asked.

Bomber ignored him.

"I understand Sheriff Connie has requested the help of the

Department of Natural Resources. I don't fault her for following procedure. But I fear they may simply kill the creature—if they can even find it. As a scientist, this doesn't seem prudent. We could be dealing with an undocumented species, here. Killing the creature could be a major blow to the scientific community."

Bomber was proud of himself for using the word "prudent," but he could see the council wasn't sold.

"Also, the majority of the tracking will be done on Fox Applesauce lands, correct?"

Nods from those council members who were still paying attention.

"And there are several orchards still being harvested, correct?"

More nods.

"It's no secret that Fox Applesauce's late-season harvest is done primarily by migrant workers, many of whom have work statuses that are questionable at best. Don't try to deny it. Everyone knows and nobody cares. But it might be safe to say that uniformed DNR officers lurking about could make your workforce…uh, skittish—that is if they don't jump-ship entirely. Therefore, I'd like the council's permission to form a task force, with members of my choosing, to capture the beast. Alive."

"Granted," McConnell said.

"Really?" Bomber asked, surprised.

"I don't know what you think this is," McConnell said, leaning in. "But none of us give a rat's ass what you do, where you do it, or who you do it with. You don't need our permission. You can form whatever you'd like. A task force, an exploratory commission, a torch-and-pitchfork mob, we don't care."

Bomber beamed. "And you'll have Sheriff Connie rescind the invitation to the DNR?"

"No," McConnell said flatly.

Bomber frowned.

"Sounds like I'll have to get out in front of them," Bomber said, mostly to himself.

"I can't believe this dip-shit is the interim Mayor," Thad Archer interjected. Gloria continued to smile.

"That's a nice segue into our final topic for today: the

mayoral election," McConnell said. "If one becomes necessary, we'll do it by the books. The voting will be held in line with State and Federal elections on November 7. Per the town charter, there will be a minimum of two public debates. Abe is currently working to secure venues for each."

This was apparently news to Abe, who scribbled furiously on his legal pad.

"'*If* one becomes necessary'?" Bomber interrupted.

"Yes, Bomber," McConnell said. "'*If*.' There are currently zero people interested in being the mayor of Fox Hollow. I'll be shocked if anyone volunteers to run at all."

"What happens to me if no one runs?" Bomber asked. "I remain interim mayor?"

"Minus the 'interim,'" McConnell sighed. "Things would continue on as normal. You would remain the public face of City Hall. Your duties would include parade grandmaster, groundbreakings, rousing pre-football game speeches, public Dogman rants—things like that. You could even designate a citywide Dogman Day if you'd like."

"I don't want to be mayor," Bomber said.

Gloria was on the edge of her seat, looking ready to pounce.

"Bottom-line," McConnell said, "the council will continue to run the show behind the scenes and everything will be hunky-dory."

"And that, my dear, is where you're mistaken," Gloria said. She popped from her seat like a coiled spring. "I am hereby resigning from my seat on the Board of Aldermen."

Abe, Thad, and Trevor gaped at her. Everyone knew what was coming next.

"Fine," McConnell said, unamused by her theatrics. "The council, minus Gloria, will continue to run the show."

"You're wrong there too, buster," Gloria said, poking McConnell in the shoulder.

"Don't poke me, Gloria."

"I'm taking this opportunity to announce to you clowns that I'm running for mayor. And when I win, and I *will* win, the mayor won't be some spineless, empty shell you can push around." She thumbed toward Bomber. "Your reign of terror will be over,

McConnell."

"Reign of terror?" McConnell laughed.

"Reign. Of. Terror." Gloria repeated. She checked her watch. "I'm off. The campaign trail awaits. I have an exclusive interview with *The Fox Howler* in thirty minutes."

"You mean the newspaper *you* own?" McConnell rolled his eyes.

Gloria turned to Bomber and gave him a wink. With that, she strutted out the door, her high heels clattering across the ancient floorboards.

McConnell closed his eyes and put his forehead on the table.

"Well, well, well," Bomber sang. "Look who's napping now."

FOX HOLLOW POLICE DEPARTMENT

Dispatch Call Transcript
10/21/2017 - 17:31

VH: Vince Hodges, FHPD Dispatcher
JH: Jason Householder, FHPD Sergeant
CH: Connie Hayes, FHPD Sheriff

VH: Patrol Car Four-Five, this is dispatch, over.
JH: Go ahead dispatch.
VH: Just checking in. Expected you back a while ago. Everything okay?
JH: Roger, dispatch. Got waved down by Mrs. Callahan in the Eden Hills neighborhood.*BREAK* She thought some kids were lighting fireworks behind her house. *BREAK* Went to check it out.
VH: Good copy. Was it?
JH: Was it what?
VH: Kids lighting fireworks?
JH: Hell if I know. Didn't find a thing. On my way back now.

STATIC

VH: Patrol Car Four-Five, this is dispatch, over.
JH: Go ahead, dispatch.
VH: Sheriff Hayes wants to know if you stopped to help Ms. Carol Meyers this morning, over.

STATIC

VH: Patrol Car Four-Five, this is dispatch, over.
JH: Yeah, yeah, I'm here, dispatch.
VH: Did you copy last?
JH: Roger. Good copy. Negative. I was unable to meet Ms. Carol Meyer this morning.

STATIC

VH: Sheriff Connie wants to know why. *BREAK* She

seems angry.

JH: Lost track of time. Will go over first thing in the morning. Promise this time.

STATIC

CH: Patrol Car Four-Five, this is your damn boss. *BREAK* You're damn right you'll go over there first thing in the morning. You're lucky I haven't heard from her today. If I get one more snarky message from her before morning, I'll have you stopping at her house as part of your daily routine for the next month. Copy?

STATIC

JH: Roger. Good copy, boss.

6:45 p.m.

The sun was low and a stiff autumn breeze cut through the orchard. A few apples remained in the branches. Pockmarked with scabs and wormholes, they'd been deemed undesirable by the picking teams. They swayed like pendulums, marking time, as Bomber, Bruce, and Householder walked between the rows. Bomber could see Bruce shivering. He shuddered too, as sweat slipped down his back and cooled along his beltline. Bruce was no doubt wishing he was home in front of his Xbox, but Bomber had insisted they hunt tonight. "The first official operation of Task Force Dogman," he'd said, before rattling on about being sanctioned by the Board of Aldermen. Neither Bruce nor Householder had the heart to tell him no.

"I just don't understand," Bruce said, "why we aren't setting up a hide site like we usually do? I didn't sign on for an all-night death march. I don't even walk this far in World of Warcraft." He shifted an aluminum baseball bat from one shoulder to the other.

"We're not hiding tonight. We're changing our tactics," Bomber said, folding his map and tucking it into a newly sewed pocket on his homemade apple camo. He didn't really need the map, but felt it gave his team confidence in his leadership when he was seen consulting it. "You probably would've heard me explain this earlier if you weren't on your cell phone all the time."

Bruce put his phone back in his pocket.

"I'm not," he said. "And you sound like my mom." He paused. "By the way, in case you want to know, Facebook is blowing up about Gloria running for Mayor."

"I'd be more interested if Gloria blew up," Bomber said.

Householder laughed.

"I guess we're not worrying about being quiet tonight either?" Bruce asked. "And don't we usually do this after dark?"

"Didn't you hear *anything* I said earlier?" Bomber asked. "Forensics placed Uncle Cecil's death right about sundown. And he wasn't a real stealthy guy." He stopped to examine a broken branch. "Hiding hasn't been working. And with the DNR hot on our heels, we don't have time to be sitting around. We've gotta make the Dogman come to us."

"So we're bait?" Bruce asked.

"We're bait," Householder confirmed.

"We're not bait," Bomber said. "Bait doesn't carry weapons."

Bomber also carried a baseball bat, a dinged-up Louisville Slugger he'd received for his twelfth birthday. He'd never actually played an official game of baseball, but Sly had used it more than once to demolish mailboxes. Sergeant Householder carried a special shotgun he'd "borrowed" from work. It was loaded with less-than-lethal bean bag rounds.

"Shouldn't we have real ammunition?" Bruce asked.

"We're not trying to kill it," Bomber said.

"But it's definitely going to try to kill *us*," Bruce said. "And even though we have it outnumbered, I'm going to put my money on the Dogman."

"Who said there was only one of them?" Householder asked.

Bruce tightened his grip on the bat.

"Householder is right," Bomber said. "We shouldn't make assumptions. We don't know how many Dogmen or Dogwomen —Dogpeople?— we're dealing with. We also don't know what drove it—or them—to kill. There aren't any previous accounts of Dogman-related deaths. Of course, we shouldn't make assumptions there either. There have probably been plenty of gruesome Dogman deaths, wrongfully attributed to other predators. Either way, if we come across it, don't bash it too hard."

"You know what I think?" Bruce asked. "I think you white people are finally getting what you deserve for stealing my people's land."

"You're only a quarter Native American, so it's only a quarter your land," Bomber said.

"We prefer 'Indian.'"

"Cecil was old," Householder said, "but he wasn't old enough to have stolen your ancestor's land."

"No, but he certainly had no problem reaping the benefits," Bruce said. "Maybe the curse is real after all."

"I don't believe in curses," Bomber said.

"He believes in Dogmen, but not curses," Householder laughed.

Bomber held up his hand, signaling them to stop. He crouched down. Bruce and Householder did the same.

"What is it?" Bruce asked.

"Shhhhhh," Bomber hissed.

"Sorry, I thought we were trying to get killed," Bruce whispered.

"There," Bomber said, pointing downhill to where the orchard row ended. There was a small clearing separating the orchard from a thicket of buckthorn bushes. The sun had dropped below the horizon and visibility was dwindling. Someone or something stood in the clearing.

"What is it?" Householder asked.

"I don't know," Bomber said. "But I'm going to try to startle it."

"That seems like the most logical thing to do," Bruce said.

Bomber picked up a drop-apple and, staying as low as he could, launched it toward the figure. He was pleased he still had aim, but his distance was lacking. He'd intended for the apple to land in the woods beyond the figure, but it fell short, striking the figure with a loud *thwack*. Bits of apple exploded everywhere. The members of Task Force Dogman held their breath.

Nothing. The figure didn't move.

"Alright," Bomber said. "Let's go. Householder, you lead with the shotgun."

They moved in a tight group with Sergeant Householder out front, his shotgun at the ready. All three strained to see against the dying evening light. They were nearly on top of it before they could tell the figure was actually a life-size 3D archery target. A black bear, standing erect on its hind legs. An iron chain had been looped around its neck and a large chunk of raw meat dangled on a hook against the bear's chest.

"What do you suppose this is all about," Bomber asked. He approached the bear, intending to poke it with the baseball bat.

Before anyone could answer, Bomber's foot snagged something in the tall grass and he stumbled. There were several loud clicks from the treeline and the nearly dark orchard was flooded with blinding white light. Task Force Dogman shielded their eyes and cursed.

"Who's out there?" Bomber shouted.

No answer.

They stood in a circle around the faux bear, each facing out with their weapons raised. Bruce whimpered slightly.

"Come out and show yourselves," Bomber shouted.

No answer.

"DNR?" Householder whispered.

"Unlikely," Bomber said. "Kind of a slip-shod way of baiting an alpha predator. This is the work of amateurs, for sure."

"Seems like a better plan than walking the woods with a stick and a prayer," Bruce said.

Bomber ignored him.

"Look," he pointed.

Chest height on the trees where the lights were mounted were little camouflaged boxes. Bomber walked over for a better look.

"Trail cameras," he declared. "Clear Vision Cams. These babies are top of the line. Three hundred bucks a pop. I can see four of 'em from right here. They might be amateurs, but they're well-funded amateurs."

"Who do you suppose 'they' are?" Householder asked.

"No clue. But these cameras use cell signals to transmit pictures directly to the owner's phone. Whoever put 'em here, already knows we're here."

Bomber took a step back and flipped the bird to the closest camera.

"Whoever it is, I can assure you, they're not a sanctioned Task Force like us."

"So what do we do?" Bruce asked.

"We steal all their stuff," Bomber said. He started to unstrap the nearest camera.

"Oh no," Householder said, pointing a finger at himself. "Cop, remember. Maybe if they hadn't caught me on camera already, but you said it's far too late for that."

"Fine," Bomber said. "We're not stealing. We're gathering their equipment so no one *else* steals it. We're being good Samaritans. They've got our picture. They know who we are. They can come get their junk back anytime. Then we can have a little chat about territory encroachment."

Householder looked uneasy, but Bruce was already removing the next camera.

"They're not even supposed to be out here," Bomber said.

"Neither are we," Householder offered.

"We're a Task Force," Bomber nearly shouted. "And I'm the mayor. And you're a cop. And a quarter of this land belongs to Bruce. We're the best hope this town has. Our mission trumps everything, including property boundaries and petty theft laws. Now give me a boost, so I can steal these lights."

October 22, 2017

1:00 p.m.

Coughlin Funeral Home was the third-oldest establishment in Fox Hollow. The family patriarch, Rory Coughlin, had set up shop shortly after Marty's Market in 1887, officially making the fledgling town an acceptable place to die. Despite the sensitive nature of their work, the Coughlin clan held the reputation of being callous toward their clientele and unscrupulous in their means of acquiring new business. It was rumored that Rory Coughlin himself, on a few unprovable occasions, had been responsible for creating new funeral business during slow months. He'd even tried to piggyback off Marty's Market's slogan, but "Whores Gotta Die" did not catch on and probably did the funeral home more harm than good. The current owner, Tommy Coughlin, though less prone to such strong-arm tactics, was still known to pay off local retirement homes for access to their patients' medical records, allowing for more targeted marketing and projections on future income. His brutish, fire-haired twin sons were known to take bets amongst their unsavory friends as to who the next Coughlin customer would be. All in all, the Coughlins were tolerated simply out of a lack of options. Their business sign welcomed citizens and visitors alike as they entered

Fox Hollow from the east:

Coughlin's Funeral Home
Est. 1887
"Nothing is certain, but Coughlin's and taxes."

In the soft-lit funeral parlor, Bomber stood staring down at the lifeless face of his late, great uncle. He was bleary-eyed from the all-night hunt, which gave the appearance he'd been crying over the deceased, but he expected to be tapped on the shoulder at any moment by some would-be monster hunter demanding the return of their high-end surveillance equipment. Around the room, townspeople milled about looking for friends and relatives in vintage photos collaged over no less than twenty large, cork-board easels. A project Edith had undoubtedly been working long before Cecil's death. Bomber was fortunate she'd taken on the task, as he was Cecil's only relative in attendance and hadn't had the forethought to decorate for the dead. Bomber's parents had never been on bad terms with his great uncle, so it was no surprise they'd sent their deepest sympathies manifested into a large wreath of roses, which hung behind the casket.

There was a tug on Bomber's sleeve and he turned to find the wrinkled face of Mrs. Doris Grayson staring up at him. Bomber swallowed hard. This would be difficult for her to process.

"Hello, Doris."

"Hello, Cecil," Doris replied. Her eyes became watery. "I'm so sorry you died."

"Thank you, Doris," Bomber replied, shooting a sideways glance at the corpse next to him. "It's not all bad. It's quite relaxing actually."

Doris mustered her strength and lifted onto her tiptoes to peer over the edge of the coffin. Bomber stared at her wrinkled face, waiting for any sign of recognition.

"They did a wonderful job on you, Cecil," Doris said. "Though they could have given you more color in your cheeks. You always had the rosiest cheeks after making love."

Bomber winced as a tear slipped from her eye.

"Are you going to be okay, Doris?" he asked.

The old woman regained herself and placed her shriveled hand on his arm, in the way old folks do before delivering important news or juicy gossip.

"I heard there was going to be a luncheon after the service. Is that true?" She asked.

Bomber smiled.

"I believe so, Doris, but the luncheon won't be here. It's going to be over at the Third Reformed Church at noon."

"Oh, good!" Doris exclaimed. "Ms. Carol Meyers over at the 3RC makes the best egg salad sandwiches in town."

She licked her lips hungrily.

"I hear she uses smoked paprika instead of regular. Doesn't seem too Christianly. But it *is* sinfully good. You know what I mean, Cecil?"

"I'm afraid I *don't* know what you mean, Doris, no."

Doris didn't hear him or didn't care.

"Say, do you think Mr. Longstreet will be attending the service? He's an interesting fellow, that one. I'd really enjoy it if I got a seat next to him."

She licked her lips hungrily again.

"You'd really enjoy *my* funeral if you could sit by Mr. Longstreet?" he asked accusingly.

"Don't be conceited, Bomber," Mrs. Grayson accused. "This isn't *your* funeral, it's Cecil's. And excuse an old woman for trying to make new friends. It seems that funerals are the only social events I get invited to these days."

Bomber flushed.

"I'm not sure if Mr. Longstreet will be here," he said. "I don't know that he and my uncle were especially close. Or even on speaking terms."

As if on cue, the front door of the funeral parlor burst open and the crowd parted like a living curtain. In the doorway, backlit by the late-morning sun, was Carl Longstreet, arguably the most interesting, or at least the most confusing, man in Fox Hollow. He was, per usual, dressed to the nines in an ensemble reminiscent of a caricature of a late nineteenth-century robber-baron. On his head, he wore a comically tall top hat which was too skinny to properly circumference his head. Its perch, atop his slicked-back gray hair, was slightly off-kilter and his neck jostled with constant adjustments, like a street performer in a balancing act. Over his right eye, or sometimes his left, he wore a monocle, which fell out constantly, often getting caught in the waxed curvature of his mustache. He wore a cream-colored tuxedo jacket with two soiled tales which flapped against the back of his pant legs, causing him to walk with an occasional startled skip. In his hands he carried a glossy, black cane, its handle a custom-fitted golden apple. He wore tattered fingerless gloves, no doubt an homage to his past. For you see, the most interesting thing about Mr. Carl Longstreet was not his strange attire or his magnificent wealth, but the extraordinary way in which he came about them.

Carl Longstreet hadn't always been rich. Quite the opposite, in fact. For all of Bomber's youth, Carl had been Fox Hollow's resident panhandler. A drifter. A bum. A town constant, he'd spend his days drifting between intersections, accosting people for spare change, or dumpster diving behind Harold's Hamburger Shack. For most of the year, he was all but ignored unless being harassed by delinquent teens—namely Sly. But every Christmas, the town would adopt him and the twelve local churches would squabble over whose turn it was to show him Christ-like charity. He would be fed, bathed, and clothed, but never elevated above his current station.

Then, shortly before Christmas of 2008, Carl simply vanished. The town feared the worst, going so far as to take out "Have-You-Seen-Me" ads in local newspapers and sending search parties traipsing through knee-deep snow, over acres of orchards. It would be a year later when Carl's picture resurfaced on the front page of *The Fox Howler* under the headline, "Local Homeless Wins Big In State Lottery." As it turns out, Carl had done what drifters do best, drift. According to the article, he'd spent the better part of the previous year hitchhiking south before a discarded lottery ticket, found in a fast food dumpster, altered his life forever and transformed Carl from a dirty, stinking vagabond, into one of the richest men in West Michigan. With his winnings, Carl returned to Fox Hollow like a conquering emperor and in a shocking turn of events, purchased the Fox Family Mansion and the controlling interest in the Fox Applesauce Company. No public statement was ever made by Mr. Fox or his representatives.

Carl kept mostly to himself, though there were rumors he threw exclusive parties at the old mansion. Extravagant affairs attended by the country's wealthy elite, evidenced only by the lights and music emanating from behind the high estate walls and the occasional trickle of limos, sports cars, and blacked-out SUVs through the town's gravel back roads. To Bomber's knowledge, no one from Fox Hollow had ever been invited.

Of late, Carl had been spotted around town with a new chauffeur, a clean-cut young man of sturdy build. No doubt a measure of personal security. Together, they'd cruise the streets of Fox Hollow in Carl's stretch limousine with no real purpose, occasionally stopping so Carl could rummage through the trashcans of his old haunts. When asked about this curious behavior, Mr. Longstreet would simply reply, "old habit" with a wink of an eye and a doff of his awkward hat.

Skipping the guest registry at the parlor entrance, Carl made his way across the room like a celebrity on the red carpet, occasionally stopping to shake hands and give stiff hugs. Even now, with their eyes downcast, people Carl greeted would wipe their hands post-shake or check a patted shoulder for transferred grime. Old habits, indeed.

Carl's chauffeur, clad in mirrored sunglasses and a white-walled, high-and-tight haircut, moved steadily behind him. The young man was well-dressed, but not over-dressed like his employer and he seemed to be scanning the room behind his glasses. Bomber assessed the man must be ex-military.

"Fine morning for a funeral," Carl said, approaching the casket. He peeked quickly at the corpse, then looked away in disgust. "What an awful tie. Who would put a man in such a thing before putting him in the ground for all eternity?"

He stared at Bomber accusingly. Bomber looked around for Doris, but she had apparently wandered off.

"Mr. Coughlin took care of all the arrangements," Bomber said.

"Leave it to that tasteless Mick to desecrate the body of this good man," Carl grumbled. "You should have called me. I have hundreds of ties better than that one. The best ties. I could have loaned you ten."

Carl watched with detachment while people filed into the chapel where the funeral service would be held.

"You must be the grand-nephew and the new, illustrious interim mayor. I don't believe we've met," Carl said, extending his hand. "Carl Longstreet, Sr."

"We've met before," Bomber said, shaking his hand. "Several times. I'm a manager at Marty's Market. You come in every now and then for malt liquor."

"Old habits," Carl laughed. He looked sideways at his chauffeur, who shook his head disapprovingly. "Ah, yes. I *do* remember you. Bomber, is it not? You're the chap who dillied up the big football match a number of years back, correct?"

Bomber's face reddened.

"And now you go about looking for ghosts?"

"Dogmen," Bomber said, embarrassed. "They're like werewolves. But different."

"Fascinating," Carl whispered. His face held a look of genuine interest.

His chauffeur shook his head again.

"Pardon me," Carl said. "I'm being rude. This young man to my left is my personal bodyguard, campaign manager, and chauffeur, Carl Longstreet Jr. Oh, and he's also my son."

"I didn't realize you had a son," Bomber said.

"Neither did I," Carl snort-laughed. "Turns out, winning the lottery is a wonderful way to reconnect with long-lost family."

"He couldn't have been so long-lost, to have the same name," Bomber observed.

Carl turned to Junior. "What was your name before?"

Junior opened his mouth to speak, but Carl cut him off.

"He doesn't remember," Carl said. "But it was a terrible name. He had it legally changed."

Bomber could tell Junior was rolling his eyes behind his sunglasses.

"That's dedication," Bomber said.

"Six hundred and thirty-five million dollars' worth of dedication," Carl replied.

"And, I'm sorry, did you say he is your campaign manager?"

"Ah, yes. You caught me. As it turns out, I've decided to make a run at the mayor's seat, now that old Cecil has kicked the bucket. I guess you could say that I'm gunning for your chair."

"Well, you'll be welcome to it," Bomber said. "The whole thing has been quite a surprise to me. I'm sure I'll be more than happy to give it up after the election."

By now the parlor had all but emptied and people were taking their seats in the chapel.

"You won't have an easy win," Bomber cautioned. "You'll have some stiff competition now that Gloria Glass is running."

"Ah, yes. Ms. Glass. She's quite the looker. The competition won't be the only thing that's stiff." Carl winked, causing his monocle to fall out. He tried to give Bomber a playful jab with his elbow but missed.

"Good God," Bomber recoiled.

"I'm kidding. At my age, I need pills for that anyway," he said, looking away ruefully.

"Well, I don't think she should be taken lightly," Bomber said. "She can be very tenacious. Vicious even. Seriously. Watch your back."

Organ music drifted in from the chapel and the Coughlin twins began to wheel the casket out of the parlor. Carl watched them vacantly.

"Yes, yes. She has quite the reputation. And I've also heard about the raccoon incident, which is why I'm not all that concerned."

"That was unfortunate," Bomber recalled.

Early on in her rise to social justice warrior-hood, Gloria, at the helm of *The Fox Howler*, had taken on a cause which was now simply dubbed "The Raccoon Incident."

According to Gloria's research—none of which was ever made public—thousands of scavenging animals were killed, maimed, or displaced annually, after being inadvertently dumped from roadside waste bins into the backs of garbage trucks, their meals ending at the business end of the truck's trash compactor. It was Gloria's contention that garbage-men should provide early warning to these unsuspecting animals, with a minimum of three solid knocks on each waste bin before disposal. A secondary battle soon erupted over the term "garbage-men" being sexist and demeaning. The town now recognized such employees as gender-neutral "Mobile Waste Disposal Specialists."

After state wildlife agencies rejected her petition for financial support, citing the premise as "ludicrous," Gloria took matters into her own hands and what started as a front yard protest culminated with a restraining order from the Mobile Waste Disposal Specialist's Union and two counts of disturbing the peace. In a last-ditch effort, Gloria, greased up with baby oil and a bottle of merlot, slipped into a pleather Catwoman suit, donned a raccoon mask, and folded up into her own garbage can. The wine and the wait proved to be too much and Gloria awoke moments before the compactor came down. Her screams could not be heard over the truck's engine and did nothing more than attract the unwanted attention of several similarly-fated raccoons who, in their confusion, savagely attacked her. Fortunately, the pleather had stopped the majority of the lacerations and the compactor flattened the angry mob of vermin moments before breaking Gloria's femur. No one in town was happy to see her hurt—save for the beleaguered garbage-men—but most were simply relieved to see her latest crusade literally crushed out of existence.

"Gentlemen, the service is about to begin. If you could take your seats."

Tommy Coughlin had snuck up behind them.

"Yes, yes," said Carl. "I suppose we should get inside, Mr. Interim Mayor." He turned to Tommy. "You've done a wonderful job with the body, Mr. Coughlin."

"Well, thank you," Mr. Coughlin beamed.

"Yes, it's nice when the funeral home director doesn't make a big to-do about making the corpse look alive or even presentable. It really helps those in mourning to solidify that the dead are in fact dead."

Mr. Coughlin held his smile over grinding teeth.

"I look forward to providing you the same service, Mr. Longstreet," he said.

Junior chuckled as Bomber slipped through the tension and entered the chapel.

"He makes me lie down in green pastures, he leads me beside quiet waters—"

Pastor Mast had just begun the service as Bomber made his way to the seats nearest the pulpit, which were reserved for family and close friends. As the pastor of the Third Reformed Church of Fox Hollow, Pastor William Mast was a staple of the Fox Hollow community. Despite being one of twelve pastors in the immediate area, he was largely seen as the town's premier conduit to God. He was pastor to the other pastors and was even rumored to provide counsel to Father O'Shay, the town's only Catholic priest. When he spoke, he did so slowly and conscientiously, and people listened.

It wasn't until Bomber had taken his seat next to Edith that he noticed Carl and Carl Jr. had followed him down the aisle. Carl gave a wave of acknowledgment as they took two empty seats directly across the aisle. To Bomber's surprise, the seats had been reserved for them with labeled place-cards.

Bomber leaned over to Edith, who was fanning herself with the funeral service program.

"Are you giving a speech?" Bomber whispered.

"Shush, boy," she hissed. "The Pastor's readin' the Bible. Show some respect. This is my favorite part."

"Yea, though I walk through the valley of the shadow of death—" Pastor Mast recited. Edith mouthed the words as he read.

"You do know when it says 'yea', it doesn't mean 'yay,'" right? It's not saying, 'Yay! I'm walking through the valley of the shadow of death.'"

"Hush your mouth," Edith hissed again. "You read it your way, I'll read it mine."

Bomber shook his head and smiled.

"Do you know why Carl Longstreet and his new son got reserved seats up front?"

Edith sighed, realizing she was fighting a losing battle.

"Mr. Longstreet said he would like to say a few words. He said he had some kind things to say about Cecil," she said.

"That's odd. I didn't realize they were friends."

"They weren't, that I know of," said Edith. "But he paid me one hundred dollars, so he can talk us all to death, for all I care."

"Edith," Bomber scolded.

"Edith," Pastor Mast called, beckoning for her to come up on stage.

Bomber stood to help her up, but she swatted at him with the program fan.

"I ain't a cripple," she snapped and began hobbling toward the stage. Pastor Mast received a similar rebuke as he tried to help her up the side stairs.

Edith's eulogy started sweetly enough, with fond recollections of the former mayor and the decades they'd worked together. She was nearly five minutes in when uncomfortable and intimate aspects of their close-quarters relationship began to drop into the speech. Nothing overtly sexual was mentioned, but there were strong enough undertones, euphemisms, and exaggerated winks to make Pastor Mast shifty at his post near the casket. Eventually, Edith's speech descended into a jealous rant and after her third reference to some type of age-triggered suicide pact, Pastor Mast intervened and a watery-eyed Edith returned to her seat.

"And now, for some reason unbeknownst to me," Pastor Mast said, his brow wrinkled, "Mr. Carl Longstreet would like to say a few words."

Carl stood and handed his cane to Junior. With a clean jerk, he straightened his waistcoat and tuxedo jacket and made his way up the stage stairs to the pulpit. He'd removed his top hat, but a ring still dented his greasy hair. From his pocket he removed a pair of small glasses and several wrinkled index cards.

"Ladies and gentlemen," he said with a throat-clearing cough. "I thank you for the opportunity to speak today about this great man. I want to share with you a fond memory of Mayor Cecil Merridan."

Bomber was relieved that the speech was not a campaign announcement.

"As many of you know, I came to Fox Hollow in the Summer of '87. I was a lonely drifter. Not a penny to my name. Without a pot to piss in, as they say."

Pastor Mast frowned, as Carl continued.

"I remember the day as though it were yesterday. It was a particularly hot July afternoon and I had hitched a Fox Applesauce freight car returning from a Chicago delivery. With no belongings, I toured the town at my leisure, eventually finding myself out front of our beautiful City Hall. I was of the mind to pick my first panhandling position—location is everything, you know—when an older gentleman in a black bowler hat called for me to stop. He must've been able to tell by the state of my dress and the depth of my cheeks that I hadn't had a square meal in quite some time. Instead of shooing me along, the kind man invited me to his home. I remember the dinner was sub-par. Typical bachelor fare. Some shoddy TV dinner if I recall correctly," Carl chuckled and looked off, lost in memory, "but it filled an empty belly. We whiled away the evening, Cecil and I, chatting at his kitchen table about nothing in particular. He even shared with me a finger of his cheapest whiskey. A generous man."

Carl wiped the corner of his eye.

"And before I left that evening, Ol' Cecil said to me something I'll never forget. He looked me dead in the eyes and said, 'Hank'—I'd told him my name was Hank, out of distrust—he said, 'Hank, I like you, but there'll be no filthy beggars in my town. So get a job or get the fuck out.'"

Carl laughed abruptly. Pastor Mast turned crimson.

"You see," Carl continued, "despite his flaws, Mayor Merridan, or Mayor-Merr, as I liked to call him behind his back, understood the finer nuances of ruling a town."

Junior shook his head.

"Sorry, I mean 'running a town,'" Carl corrected. "To have order and peace, you must have control. Control over the riff-raff who wander across borders. But over the years, our town's borders, in conjunction with Mayor-Merr's mental stamina, became lax. Wild animals now ravage our fine citizens." He motioned to the casket. "But that's not all. Roving bands of high school heretics raid our town from their dens in Cedar Mills. They ravage our yards with toilet paper, forks, and plastic wrap, they destroy our mailboxes with pipe bombs."

The teens from Cedar Mills *had* been a scourge on the citizens of Fox Hollow for decades, with only a brief respite during Sly's Rebellion. It'd become a passage of rights for the adolescents of Cedar Mills to take up unprovoked arms against the small town they perceived to be inferior to their own.

"And it's not just the Cedar Mills youth," Carl went on. He was getting quite excited now. "The panhandlers! The panhandlers are out of control. You can't go anywhere without being accosted for money. Now, I know what you are thinking: 'Pot calling the kettle black,' right? Well, I'm rich now and it's unbelievably annoying. Besides, the panhandlers today don't have the charisma we did in *my* day. Not a single one of them is willing to dance for their dinner. And their signs—don't get me started on their signs. So damn depressing all the time." He wiped imaginary tears from his eyes with both hands. "*Boo hoo, I can't feed my eight children, boo hoo.* Maybe stop having kids if you don't have any money!"

He was shouting now and Junior motioned for him to wrap it up. Pastor Mast shot daggers at them both.

"Right, right. I digress. The point is, with Mayor-Merr gone, God rest his ruthless, cold-hearted soul, this town is vulnerable. Vulnerable to the threats from outside our apple-rich borders. The Cedar Mills hooligans, the panhandlers, the Dogmen—I'm looking at you Bomber."

Bomber blushed as a muffled chuckle rippled through the rows behind him.

"But this town is also vulnerable from the threats within," Carl continued. "The Gloria Glasses, who'd like nothing more than hippy-dippy, free-loving, socialist anarchy."

Murmurs of agreement could be heard, accompanied by a single, "Amen."

"That's why, I, Carl Longstreet Senior, am announcing my run for mayor of Fox Hollow."

He paused for the gasp that didn't come. Three people began to clap.

"Thank you," Carl said, attempting to doff his top hat, but finding nothing. "I'll now open up the floor for questions."

"You most certainly will not," Pastor Mast shouted. He was standing now and his face was fire. "This is a funeral, not some muckraking campaign rally. You come off that stage immediately."

"Whoa, calm down there, Pastor," Carl said. "I'm a God-fearing Christian, just like you."

Carl looked to Junior who nodded in confirmation.

"I'm not trying to pay any disrespect here," Carl continued. "In fact, quite the opposite. This man who lays before us, dead as a doornail, was probably the single greatest proponent of the American political system in this whole damn town. Pardon my language, Pastor, but I think he'd have considered it an homage for me to announce my candidacy here today."

"Not. Another. Word." Pastor Mast hissed. He circled toward the stairs, stage right, while Carl quickly descended the stairs, stage left.

"I'll be answering questions at the luncheon following the service," Carl shouted, as he returned to his seat next to Junior. "Vote Longstreet!"

"That would've been worth it without the hundred dollars," Edith whispered with a delighted smile. Bomber decided he'd not be attending his dead, great-uncle's luncheon no matter how good the egg salad was supposed to be.

The chapel had cleared within fifteen minutes of the service's end and Bomber stood alone, staring down at a dead mayor. The Coughlins had boosted the collar of Cecil's shirt, trying to hide the extensive work done to repair the jagged wounds on his throat. Small fingers of lacerations crept above his collar like dirty secrets seeping out from beneath his pristine, white dress shirt. Two rows of tight stitches ended under his chin on either side of his mouth, giving him the look of a ventriloquist's dummy. Bomber felt shame. The man in the casket was a blood relative, but he knew nothing real about him. He was, to Bomber, what he'd been to the rest of the town; simply, "the mayor," whose legacy would be that of "the good ol' days," whether his actions had influenced them or not.

Bomber wondered what his own legacy would be if he were to drop dead right there in the funeral home. Nothing good, he thought. Nothing compared to Cecil—or Sly. Nothing but a blown football game, a history of public drunkenness, and a vacant manager's slot at Marty's Market that would, no doubt, be filled within a week. And let's not forget "monster hunter," which would draw much snickering at his funeral. He supposed he'd be happy if people showed up to his funeral at all. He knew his days as a cocky jock and then as the town drunkard had set a lot of people against him and he feared his sobriety and general affability of recent years would not be enough to atone for past sins. He feared facing his infractions individually and directly.

Pastor Mast had concluded the service by talking briefly about fear.

"We must not let our lives be ruled by fear," he'd said. "Whatever creature is to blame for poor Cecil's death will be found, caught, and dealt with. Until then, we must lean on one another. Watch out for one another. Our unity in God's love will overcome fear. You *are* your brother's keeper and neighborly love and good charity will carry us through these uncertain times."

Pastor Mast's legacy would never be in question. Even the staunchest of atheists in town could look to him for inspiration and reassurance. After the funeral, he'd floated through the room shaking hands and administering hugs where needed. Everyone who spoke with him walked away with a smile. Everyone except Carl Longstreet, who'd spent several minutes posing with Bibles and kneeling in phony prayer while Junior snapped pictures on his phone, undoubtedly to be used as campaign propaganda for the evangelical crowd. Bomber had watched as Pastor Mast pulled him and Junior aside. A hushed but heated exchange occurred behind the chapel's piano before the two Longstreets exited to the backstreet by way of an emergency exit. Pastor Mast took a concentrated moment to gather himself and caught Bomber's eye before returning to his flock. His smile had been strained and eyebrows raised in a "can-you-believe-those-guys" manner.

Bomber was startled, as a large hand settled on his shoulder. He turned to find Mr. Coughlin standing behind him, flanked by his two Neanderthal sons. Between the three of them, the entire chapel aisle was blocked. Mr. Coughlin's sons were brutish fellows with matching shocks of red hair kept much too long, so that it dangled over their dull eyes. No one could ever remember their names. They were just "The Coughlin Twins."

Mr. Coughlin looked as though he wished to say something comforting but couldn't find the words.

"Thank you for your services today," Bomber said, trying to take the pressure off him. "Everything was very smooth. Is there anything else you need from me?"

Mr. Coughlin nodded and his sons moved to either side of the casket.

"We need you to leave," he said. "We're closed."

The Coughlin Twin at the head of the casket slapped the lid with his massive hand and it slammed shut over the old, dead mayor.

4:37 p.m.

Much to Doris Grayson's dismay, the egg salad sandwiches never arrived at the Third Reformed Church's post-funeral luncheon. And though the volunteer staff at the 3RC was fully prepared to serve standard ham sandwiches, they were met with stiff resistance from several elderly attendees who'd been bused over from The Golden Years Assisted Living Facility and had been looking forward to the funeral egg salad with great anticipation ever since the news of Cecil's death. They demanded to speak with Ms. Carol Meyers immediately. When it was discovered Ms. Carol Meyers was not even on the premises, a red flag was raised. This was very unlike her in all respects, as she never missed a town social event, no matter how macabre. Even with a wayward cat, it was unusual and Sergeant Householder, who'd conveniently forgotten his mission yet again, was quickly dispatched to check on her.

Obviously, no members of the community or press were being allowed beyond the police tape closing off the Meyers' residence and Sheriff Connie had no intention of wavering. It was far too grim. But she knew, even now, rumors were beginning to circulate about Ms. Carol Meyers' death. Rumors of a nearly-decapitated corpse found on the kitchen floor, still clutching a cleaver. Rumors of Carol's ripped, not sliced, neck and most of her vital organs spread across her checker-tiled floor. They'd probably be talking about poor Mr. Fuzzbottom too, who hadn't escaped the carnage. Several large chunks of his orange and black fur had been found splattered across the ceiling and the once-pristine, white cupboards.

Sheriff Connie's forensic team concluded Carol had been dead for over a day by the time Sergeant Householder arrived, by which point the egg salad sandwiches had spoiled, though no one seemed concerned with those any longer.

Connie stood in the back doorway, forcing herself to take in the full scene. Her officers stepped carefully around the kitchen in plastic shoe covers, photographing and documenting every inch. Their faces were pale and they made *urp*ing noises with their throats that intermixed with the clicking of the cameras. She finally couldn't take it any longer and turned away.

Sergeant Householder stood at the property edge, facing the orchard. Connie made her way across the lawn, trying not to breathe too deeply. The air was bitter with the taste of pesticides and the lawn, completely enclosed by apple orchards, made her feel claustrophobic. The trees stood like soldiers, ready to overrun this last patch of unconquered turf.

"I think it's safe to say whatever got Mayor Merridan, got Ms. Carol Meyers, too," she said, raising her voice to speak over the drone of an approaching sprayer.

Sergeant Householder nodded but didn't speak.

Sheriff Connie hated this touchy-feely junk. It was her least favorite part of the job, but she accepted it as a necessary facet of leadership.

"It's not your fault," Connie said.

Householder hung his head.

"If she'd have hung herself or shot herself or opened some veins in the bathtub, then yes, you could probably blame yourself," Connie said. "But this—" she pointed back to the house, "—this wasn't going to be stopped by a police courtesy call two days ago."

Householder nodded and they stood for a moment listening to the unseen sprayer moving away into the orchard.

"Why do you suppose they're spraying right now?" Householder asked. "They've already harvested this section."

Connie shrugged.

"Preventive spray, I guess," she said. "Or they're trying to poison us all, so they can turn this whole map-dot into one big orchard when we die."

Householder nodded.

"Alright, enough of this sad-sack junk," Connie said. "Carol ain't getting any less dead and we've got work to do if we want to prevent more people from getting their necks ripped out. Are you with me?"

This seemed to rally Householder a bit.

"Yes, ma'am," he said, wiping the back of his hand across his nose.

"Good," she said. "I want a town-wide curfew put in place.

Nobody's out after sundown, without prior approval. And even when people are out during the daytime, they should be encouraged not to travel alone and to stick to populated areas. Got it?"

"Got it," Householder said.

"And as a personal caveat, that means no more traipsing all over hell-and-gone with Bomber's goddamn Task Force. Same goes for Bruce. I'm not going to lose my only son and my best officer because that dill-hole wants to catch a science project."

Connie was getting worked up and she liked the feel of it.

"That curfew is going to upset a lot of folks," Householder said. "People aren't going to appreciate being told what to do."

"It's for their own good," Sheriff Connie said.

"Some won't see it that way. There's gonna be push-back."

"Bring on the wolves," Sheriff Connie said. They both looked around cautiously. "Metaphorically, of course."

October 23, 2017

8:11 a.m.

Bomber had traded his morning shift at Marty's in preparation for the emergency town council meeting he was sure would be called at City Hall. The rumors about what happened to Ms. Carol Meyers were grim, to say the least. Bomber had been among a crowd of rubberneckers the night before, but despite his newfound political clout and several minutes of rather unabashed begging, he'd been denied access to the crime scene and was forced to wait for the same meager morsels being fed to the on-scene reporter from *The Fox Howler*. Neither Connie nor her officers would confirm the details of the scene, but their sickly expressions spoke volumes. Sergeant Householder, looking especially green, had issued an emergency warning imploring citizens to avoid traveling alone and unnecessarily. He also instated, per Sheriff Connie's directive, a night-time curfew, even though both the Meyers and the Merridan attacks had happened during daylight hours. The most conservative members of the town were already beginning to rabble-rouse about restricted rights and authoritarian control. Some were even calling for the immediate removal of "Comrade Connie."

Not wanting to miss the meeting, Bomber arrived at City Hall well before sun-up. After an hour in the empty conference room, Edith had shuffled in with her watering can and explained the emergency meeting had been held the night prior, while simultaneously flashing her new string of faux pearls bought with Carl Longstreet's dirty, funeral-speech money. Bomber was furious about being snubbed from the meeting, but knew he couldn't take his anger out on Edith, who'd probably have just clubbed him with her watering can anyhow. To top it off, Sheriff Connie had left a firmly-worded note on the mayoral desk calling for the immediate disbanding of Task Force Dogman, citing a lack of professional training and the rising risk levels of their "nocturnal buffoonery." She'd even had the Board of Aldermen sign the note, driving home its officiality. Bomber kicked himself for comprising his entire team of people emotionally and professionally tied to the one woman in town who hated him most. He didn't like the idea of hunting alone, especially after the events of the last few days. He needed a new team and, more urgently, he needed breakfast.

Traffic on Main Street was sparse due to the new travel restrictions and Jeanie's Appleseed Diner, which was usually slow anyway, was completely empty. A bell above the door chimed Bomber's arrival and a "Please Wait To Be Seated" sign greeted him at the empty hostess podium.

"Be right there," came a voice from the kitchen.

The day's edition of *The Fox Howler* was already on the newspaper rack by the front door. Bomber grabbed a copy and, throwing caution to the wind, blew past the hostess station, choosing the booth by the front window. His favorite spot. He spread the newspaper on the dirty tabletop, hoping for some new information on "The Meyers Incident."

"You gotta be kidding me," he whispered.

The front page was dominated by an expose featuring the two mayoral candidates. More than half the page was eaten by photos of the dueling, amateur politicians. Gloria's photo was a professional— yet provocative—portrait showcasing a healthy dose of cleavage beneath a plunging, cashmere neckline. No expense had been spared in airbrushing. Carl's photo was far less flattering and appeared to be a grainy security camera still-frame from his dumpster-diving days. In it, he appeared to be eating a sandwich he'd salvaged moments earlier. The contrast of the photos was not surprising considering Gloria's ownership of *The Fox Howler*. Originally known as *The Fox Hollow Times*, Gloria's late husband had attempted to reinvigorate the failing publication by rebranding it "The Fox Howler," despite the fairly common knowledge that foxes don't howl. This was the first of many journalistic failures for the small paper but given its lack of competition and tendency to perpetuate and validate the rumor mill, it limped on. After her husband's suicide, Gloria had retained ownership of the press, but farmed out all aspects of its operations to the most competent individuals she could find who were willing to captain a sinking ship.

At the bottom of the page, below the candidate profiles and in much smaller font was an article chronicling the few known details of the Ms. Carol Meyers mystery, its few correlations with Mayor Merridan's death, and a whole plethora of speculations delivered by some of the town's least educated and most vocal. For Bomber, the article only confirmed the more believable rumors he'd already heard and he couldn't help feel slighted once more that he hadn't been asked to weigh in on any Dogman-type connections.

"What can I get ya?" Jeanie sighed. "Besides a pair of glasses, so you can read the goddamn sign."

She forced a smile.

"A dishrag would be nice," Bomber smiled. "This table is filthy." He folded up the paper and pushed at some crumbs with his fingers. "And can I get a menu?"

Jeanie, by Bomber's count, was the eighth owner of the Appleseed Diner. Only a year ago, it had been Johnny's Appleseed Diner and before that, Faye's (or Billy Jo's or something rednecky). Needless to say, the diner had never fared well, but Bomber hoped Jeanie would have a better go of it. She'd been a year behind Bomber in high school and, like many of his schoolmates, he'd not treated her kindly. A regret for which he actively tried to remedy with light flirting in the hopes it made him seem endearing—which it did not. That's not to say that Jeanie did herself any favors. With six kids at home, ranging from two years old to fifteen and all by different fathers, she was perpetually teetering on a catastrophic mental and emotional breakdown. What manifested was a steady flow of sass and snark, with sporadic bursts of white-hot rage. These traits rarely fared well in the customer service industry.

Jeanie spoke through a clenched jaw.

"I imagine if you'd have waited to be seated, I'd have put you at a clean table and given you a menu to boot."

"Sorry," Bomber said, using a napkin to corral more toast crumbs. "I just really like the window seat. I like to be able to gaze out on my domain."

Jeanie rolled her eyes.

"The menu hasn't changed, Your Excellency. What do you want? The usual?"

"I've changed, Jeanie," Bomber announced. "I'm the mayor now. I need a breakfast befitting my position. Menu, please."

Jeanie produced a paper tri-fold from her apron and sailed it across the table.

"Can I start your Royal Highness off with something to drink?"

"Yes," Bomber said, sitting up straight. "I'll have a mocha latte."

"One black coffee, coming up," Jeanie grumbled, heading back to the kitchen.

On the edge of the booth, another newspaper was wedged between the window and the condiment carrier. It was different from the one spread out in front of him. Bomber unfolded it and laid it out over the other paper. *The Fox Hollow Post* was a publication he'd not seen before. Like *The Fox Howler*, the entire front page was occupied with side-by-side shots of the opposing mayoral candidates—Carl Longstreet looking slick in his top hat and tux and Gloria, battered and bandaged, in what remained of a pleather cat costume so many years ago. It was clear who was buttering the bread of *The Fox Hollow Post*.

There was a knock on the window. Bomber retracted instinctively, causing the cracked plastic booth to wheeze. There, in the window, was the mustachioed man in the gray hoodie and sunglasses. Bomber could see his own horrified reflection in the lenses. There was a long moment of tension before the sandy bristles of the man's mustache curled, revealing a toothy, white smile. He motioned to the empty seat opposite Bomber. Bomber glanced at the seat, then back at the sunglasses. This was interpreted as approval and the man gave a double thumbs-up before entering the restaurant. The bell on the door announced him.

"Sit wherever you'd like," hollered Jeanie from the back. "Everyone else does."

The man removed his sunglasses as he slid into the booth. His eyes were alarmingly green and Bomber felt an uncertain familiarity with him, as though he'd known him in a past life or they'd been foes in a mostly forgotten dream. Bomber's heart was pounding. He discreetly reached for his butter knife, but, realizing the utensils were still rolled in his napkin, grasped the whole bundle instead.

"You've got some nerve," Bomber said.

"More than you know," said the man. He smiled and Bomber was again struck with the feeling he'd met the man before. Even his voice was familiar.

"What makes you think I won't call the cops on you right now?"

"I fear we're getting off on the wrong foot," the man said.

The man brushed back his hood revealing close-cropped, black hair, white-walled on the sides, and tapered high. From his upper lip, he peeled away the bushy, sand-colored mustache revealing a more modest black mustache, curled slightly at the ends, with tiny bits of glue still speckled throughout.

Bomber's jaw dropped.

"Like I said, I think we're getting off on the wrong foot," the man said, extending his hand to shake. "I'm Buck. Buck Wildes."

"You—you're Buck Wildes," Bomber stammered.

"Yes. That's what I just said. Nice to meet you too, Mr. Mayor."

Buck mimed a handshake with the air.

"*Interim* Mayor," Bomber said absently before snapping out of his shock. He snatched up Buck's hand. "I'm sorry. Nice to meet you, too, Mr. Wildes. Huge fan."

Buck Wildes was a household name in the cryptozoology

community and something of a monster-hunting legend. His persona was that of the consummate woodsman, as quick with an axe as he was with a joke. Buck's natural charisma and rural charm, along with the high production value of his films, had landed him in the top-rated spots among cryptozoological-themed channels on all major online video sharing platforms. With a career spanning over a decade, Buck had been everywhere, including three years in the Pacific Northwest tracking Sasquatch, two in Florida slopping through swamps for Skunk Apes, two years in New Mexico ranging the desert for Chupacabra, and a year in Vermont diving for "Champ" the Lake Champlain sea monster. He'd even endured a six-month stretch in New Jersey, trying to shed light on the whole 'Jersey Devil' myth. Along with his videos, Buck was hugely popular across multiple social media platforms, where he promoted wildlife conservation, responsible hunting, and clean eating. He was a gun shooting, flag-waving advocate of freedom and personal accountability in all things. In videos, he always wore a sleeveless flannel shirt, showcasing chiseled, tattoo-riddled arms, and a camo hat with an American flag patch, of the style popular with military veterans. He was loud and boisterous and passionate about the monsters he sought. A true believer. To Bomber, he was a rockstar. Like Ted Nugent with a high-and-tight.

"Great. Two customers and they both choose the only dirty booth." Jeanie was back at the table. She poured Bomber's coffee and ran a dingy rag over the table before flopping another menu down.

"What can I get you to drink?" she asked Buck.

He ordered a black coffee and unleashed another trophy smile. Jeanie was clearly struck by his green eyes. She smiled the smile Bomber had been trying to coax out of her for years.

"You got it, hon."

"Are the cinnamon buns messy?" Buck asked, browsing the menu. As he spoke, he removed his hooded sweatshirt, revealing his signature cutoff flannel and bronze, muscular arms.

"They can be a bit sticky," Jeanie confessed. She had one hip cocked unnaturally high.

"I do love a good messy bun," Buck winked.

Jeanie giggled and patted the frazzled hive of hair pulled loosely behind her head.

"And a bowl of plain oatmeal, if you please," Buck added.

She scribbled on her notepad and turned to Bomber.

"And you?" she asked flatly, as her high hip deflated. "You know what you want?"

"I'll have the usual," Bomber said, not taking his eyes off Buck. He hadn't so much as touched his menu.

Jeanie snatched the menu and, noticing Bomber's dumbfounded stare, turned back to Buck, eyeing him suspiciously. She opened her mouth to speak, but then thought better of it and retreated to the kitchen.

"Sorry about her," Bomber said. "Folks around town aren't exactly open-minded to the paranormal stuff like you and me. She's probably never seen your videos. People are pretty set in their ways here and nothing exciting ever happens—at least it never used to. So, one might be excused if an—overactive imagination—got the best of them. I guess, what I'm trying to say is, I'm sorry about chasing you out of the gym the other night."

"Forgiven," Buck said.

"It's understandable though," Bomber said, taking a sip of his coffee. "The disguise I mean. Given the nature of your work. I bet you get recognized wherever you go. I mean, other than here, obviously."

"Yes, I—," Buck started.

"One thing I don't understand though," Bomber interrupted. "How did you get here so fast? I saw you before I even knew Cecil was dead." Bomber's eyes went wide. "Unless—unless you're behind the killings?"

Buck raised an eyebrow.

"Sorry," Bomber said. "Doing it again. But it *is* a legit motive. Giving yourself a juicy story to draw in viewers."

"I thought it might look bad," Buck said. "Which is another reason for the disguise. I should've told you already, I'm sorry about your uncle."

"Great uncle," Bomber corrected.

"I'm sure he was," Buck consoled. "He must've been. He's the one who contacted me about coming to Fox Hollow to hunt the Michigan Dogman."

Bomber was speechless. His uncle had been a secret believer.

"Cecil wrote to me about some strange occurrences around town," Buck said. "He even said his grand-nephew—I'm assuming he meant you—had a first-hand encounter. Said you were something of an expert on the beast."

Bomber straightened in his seat. The vinyl booth wheezed with pride. Buck stopped speaking abruptly.

Jeanie returned to the table with the cinnamon bun in one hand, the bowl of oatmeal in the crook of her elbow, and a double-grip on a mug and a full pot of coffee in the other. She placed the food in front of Buck. The cinnamon bun was the size of his head and smothered in warm, gooey frosting. The oatmeal looked like gray gruel in comparison. Buck smiled at Jeanie graciously, as she filled his mug with coffee. The two men sat silently, waiting for her to finish. She eyed Buck with suspicion again, as she topped off Bomber's cup.

"I might be crazy," she said to Buck. "But I saw you when you walked in here. Didn't your mustache change color?"

"Don't tell anyone," Buck smiled. He dangled the fake mustache like a cat dangling a dead mouse.

"Okay," she laughed a confused laugh. "Tell anyone what?"

"Are you serious?" Bomber nearly exploded. "You're really going to stand there and tell me you don't know who this is?"

Jeanie looked uncomfortable now. She searched Buck's face, wondering if it was an old classmate or a local fatty who'd dropped some pounds.

"This is *the* Buck Wildes," Bomber scoffed. "He's only the greatest cryptozoological documentarian of our generation."

Jeanie still looked confused and Bucked waved it off to show there were no hard feelings.

"I make monster-hunting videos for YouTube," Buck simplified.

Jeanie nodded politely.

"Got it," she said in a tone that suggested Buck's attractiveness had just nose-dived.

"Buck, this is Jeanie Jinks," Bomber said. "She's the owner of this fine restaurant. For the time being anyway."

"Hush your mouth, Bomber Merridan," Jeanie snipped, then turned to Buck. "It's nice to meet you, Mr. Wildes. I'm sure your movies are—very entertaining." She turned back to Bomber. "Your stupid omelet will be up in a minute."

They watched her march back to the kitchen.

Buck took his phone from his pocket and arranged his coffee, silverware, and oatmeal-gruel in an aesthetically pleasing way.

"Hold on one sec," he said. He took several pictures of his food, leaving the decadent cinnamon bun well outside the frame, and then fiddled with his phone some more. "And—#healthyliving."

He clicked the screen one last time and then returned the phone to his pocket.

"Gotta keep the Instagram algorithms happy," he said, sliding the bowl of oatmeal toward the window and the pastry toward his stomach.

"I didn't know Cecil even believed me," Bomber said. "I didn't think anyone did."

Buck shrugged. He picked up his silverware and began dissecting the cinnamon bun.

"I guess he believed you enough to call in the big guns," he grinned, pointing his fork back at himself.

Bomber was a little hurt by this revelation. Even in the limited world of cryptozoology, his own flesh-and-blood hadn't counted him competent enough to confide in or publicly support.

"Why now?" Bomber asked. "What were the 'strange occurrences' he mentioned?"

Buck shrugged again, his mouth full of dough.

"That's the kicker," he said between chewing. "He contacted me last week via snail-mail. Didn't give me any detail. Said he was worried the letter might get intercepted. Said he had evidence and it was time-sensitive. What do you suppose he meant by that?"

Bomber pretended to think but was concentrating on not seeming overeager. Not that Buck would've noticed anyway, his head was low as he forked in big bites of bun.

"Local legends state the Dogman only appears once every ten years," Bomber said. "And most often in years ending in seven. Like now."

"That's an odd set of parameters," Buck said.

"I think it has something to do with lunar cycles," Bomber said. "And maybe barometric pressure. Seven is generally a pretty unlucky number anyway, I guess. But it's been this way since the first recorded sighting back in 1887."

"And how long ago was your encounter?" Buck asked.

"Ten years ago," Bomber whispered ominously.

"Well, at least Cecil pointed me to the right person," Buck smiled. His plate was empty and the extra frosting had been scraped clean. "We have to find this thing, before the DNR or some other hillbilly kills it. The whole scientific community depends on it. I feel like this could be 'the big one.'"

"That's what I've been saying," Bomber whispered. Validation was a warm hug.

"How about you fill me in on everything you know tonight?"

"Are—are you asking me on a stakeout?"

"Come by the Fox Den Motel tonight around 7:00 pm. Room 12. Come armed with your top three High Probability Areas," Buck said, as he put his sweatshirt back on. "We can talk more on the way out. I wanna hear the details of your encounter and more on the local legends."

Bomber was speechless again. He'd dreamed about monster hunting with Buck Wildes for nearly a decade.

"And," Buck continued, "you can return all of my gear you stole the other night."

Bomber's face flushed, as Buck produced his phone again and displayed the trail cam photo of Bomber and his rigid middle finger.

"Of course," Bomber said. "Of course."

"Don't worry about it," Buck said. "I've had far worse. Like the time I got jumped by a bunch of meth-heads while on a Bigfoot stakeout near Snoqualmie Pass in Washington. They took everything. My equipment. My money. Even my clothes. You ain't been embarrassed until you've stumbled bare-ass onto the I-90 during the evening rush."

"I don't remember that episode," Bomber said.

"I do," Buck said with a haunted look.

"What about the curfew?" Bomber asked. "Nobody's

supposed to be out after dark. Sheriff's orders."

Buck smiled his winning smile. Icicles of frosting still clung to his mustache.

"Celebrities can usually finagle special treatment."

Buck scooted out of the booth and stood next to the table. He gave a tentative look toward the kitchen door where Jeanie had disappeared and pulled his hood back over his head.

"Listen," he said. "I need to keep a low profile for now. Can't have rival crypto's finding out what I'm up to and creeping in on our territory. If we're going to be working together, no more public introductions. No one else needs to know I'm here. Got it?"

"Right," Bomber said. "Of course."

Buck nodded.

Halfway to the door, he turned around.

"I forgot to ask," he said. "Why does everyone call you 'Bomber'?"

"I'm a bit of a local legend myself," Bomber said, nearly scalding himself on a sip of coffee. This seemed to satisfy Buck and the bell above the door announced his departure. Bomber leaned back and the vinyl booth wheezed with excitement. Task Force Dogman was born again.

9:46 a.m.

Bomber blew on his hands as the market's automatic doors slid open. Two cashiers stood at their registers chatting idly. Bruce was at the customer service counter, helping Clarence Peterson with pop-can returns. Bomber had decided that Clarence was a robot, fueled exclusively by cheap beer. Once the Director of Strategic Marketing for Fox Applesauce, Clarence now arrived every morning, like clockwork, cashing in a case of empty Bort's Beer cans for the ten cent per can deposit. The deposit money was then used to supplement the purchase of a new case of Bort's Beer, after which he'd head home to begin the process of draining them for the next day's return.

Bomber stopped as he passed the newspaper display. Normally reserved exclusively for *The Fox Howler*, the rack was now divided, and the new *Fox Hollow Post* was in the choice position. Bomber snagged a copy of each paper and spread them out on the corner of the customer service counter.

"What a crock," Bomber said to himself.

"What's a crock?" Bruce asked, as Clarence Peterson shuffled off to the beer aisle.

"What're you doing here already?" Bomber asked.

Bruce typically worked the ten-to-six shift and was never even a second early. In fact, he was regularly several minutes late.

"Mr. VanGovern asked me to open for a while, since you're a bigshot now."

"Just call him 'Marty,'" Bomber said. "It's weird when you call him 'Mr. VanGovern.'"

"So, what's a crock?" Bruce asked again.

"The headlines in these papers," Bomber said, drilling down with his finger. "There have been two people slaughtered in less than a week by the Dogman. Hell, Ms. Carol Meyer's blood is still drying and she barely gets a footnote at the bottom of the page."

"Mom said it's all gonna get explained in a reasonable way," Bruce said, pulling *The Fox Howler* toward him.

"Mom said *meh, meh, meh*," Bomber mocked.

"Mom also said you'd be irritable this morning," Bruce said. "Is that why you're late? Were you up late setting Dogman traps around your house last night?"

"No," Bomber lied. "I already have plenty of traps rigged. And not that it's any of your business, but I was trying to fulfill my mayoral obligations. Something I could've done, had I not been subverted by your totalitarian mother and that sniveling Board of Aldermen."

He took a deep breath.

"Please don't tell your mom I said that," he added. "On a positive note, I got to meet someone famous this morning."

Bruce was fixated on the newspaper.

"Don't you wanna know who I met?" Bomber asked.

"You said it wasn't my business," Bruce said. He flicked his eyes up. Bomber was about to burst. "Fine. Who'd you meet?"

"I really can't tell you," Bomber smiled. "He wants to keep a low profile. He asked me to keep our relationship a secret."

"My eighth-grade girlfriend asked me to do the same thing," Bruce said, losing himself for a moment to some distant pain. He shook off the memory and tapped the picture of Gloria.

"She's gonna make an awesome mayor."

"You're going to vote for *her*?" Bomber asked. "She's a monster."

"She can't be worse than Captain Top-Hat there," Bruce said, pointing to Carl's grungy photo. "Gloria is looking out for us little guys. She wants to raise the taxes on the rich folks and increase the minimum wage."

"But the only 'rich folk' in this town *is* Carl," Bomber said.

"Bingo," Bruce said.

"You get minimum wage because you're a part-time cashier at a podunk grocery store," Bomber said. "You took a week off last month to go to the Cedar Mills' Comic Con."

"So?"

"So, the Comic Con was only three days long," Bomber said.

Bruce shrugged.

"Costume prep takes time," he said. "Anyway, this job's still not enough pay to live on."

"I'm sure if you wanted to earn more, I could convince Marty to make you a night manager or something. Get you some additional responsibilities and a pay raise."

Bruce looked horrified. "Forget it," he said. "I want to get *paid* more. I don't want to *work* more. Besides, I don't want to get stuck here forever. No offense."

"I didn't take offense until you said 'no offense,'" Bomber said.

"Honestly, this whole election thing has gotten me thinking about going into politics," Bruce said. "I could really make some changes. Really help the little guy—people like me, being crushed by the oppression of late-stage capitalism."

"The only thing you're being crushed by is late-stage laziness," Marty snapped as he emerged from the back hallway. "And you can help the little guy by restocking the Bloo Goo like you were told."

"I'm being oppressed," Bruce whispered to Bomber.

"It's called 'being employed,'" Bomber whispered back.

"Bomber, you're late," Marty said, studying the bottles of liquor on the back wall.

"I'm sorry," Bomber said. "Mayoral duties this morning."

"Save it," Marty said. "Bruce already ratted you out. Said he saw you at Jeanie's."

Bomber shot Bruce a look. Bruce shrugged.

"It was a working breakfast," Bomber said, still glaring at Bruce.

Marty ignored him.

"I want you to gather up all *The Fox Howler*s and pitch them in the trash," Marty said.

"Sir, I can't," Bomber said. "We've already paid for them. We need to sell them."

"Well, at the very least, I want you to deface your ex-girlfriend's picture on every copy," Marty said, slurring a little. "Maybe give her a mustache. Or some devil horns or snot or something."

"Can do, Sir," Bomber laughed.

"I wasn't joking."

"Yes, Sir," Bomber said. "So you're a Longstreet supporter?"

Marty found the bottle he was looking for on the bottom shelf.

"I'm a Longstreet supporter for the sole reason that he's *not*

Gloria Glass," Marty said. He was already twisting the top off his prize as he disappeared back down the hall.

Bruce shook his head. "Marty has no clue," he said, pulling his phone from his pocket. "Longstreet is a fascist. Check out this campaign video he posted last night."

Bruce pushed "play" and handed the phone to Bomber. A green apple materialized, superimposed over a waving American flag. "America The Beautiful" played and a voice-over began, which Bomber recognized as Tim Gunderson, the high school football announcer.

"*Fox Hollow. A town of hard working, honest folks. A town built from the ground up by ingenuity and the relentless spirit of its citizens. Once the embodiment of free-market enterprise and the cradle of the American Dream.*"

The music turned ominous.

"*But that dream was sharted—*"

"I think he meant 'shattered,'" Bruce said, over a sound-effect of breaking glass.

"*—by Junior Alderman and confirmed vegan, Gloria Glass,*" the announcer continued.

Multiple unflattering pictures of Gloria flashed across the screen, including one of her pushing away a hamburger in disgust.

"*Gloria Glass wants to strip you of your freedoms and security. Gloria Glass wants to give your rights to the rodents who plague our trash cans, endangering our children and small pets. Gloria Glass believes in open borders with Cedar Mills. A policy which has likely taken the lives of two Fox Hollow citizens in under a week.*"

"Are they suggesting someone from Cedar Mills is killing people?" Bomber asked.

Bruce shushed him.

"*Gloria Glass wants to increase taxes to fund unwanted entitlement programs—programs meant to breed dependency and flood our streets with dirty, disgusting vagrants.*"

A photo of a homeless man with his face blurred out flashed on the screen. Bomber was sure it was an old photo of Carl.

"*In 2008, a business tax pushed by Gloria Glass became a key factor in the sale of Fox Applesauce and the destruction of our once great town. Gloria Glass killed Fox Hollow.*"

A large, red circle-slash slammed down over the infamous image of Gloria in her tattered raccoon costume.

"*Now Fox Hollow can return the favor!*" the announcer stated triumphantly.

"Is he suggesting we kill Gloria?" Bomber asked.

The screen changed to a shot of Carl Longstreet standing on Main Street, just down from Jeanie's Appleseed Diner. He poked his finger absent-mindedly at the flap-cover of a public trash bin and peered inside. Someone off-camera cleared their throat.

"*Oh! Hello there,*" he said, doffing his top hat to the camera. "*Good day to all the fine citizens of Fox Hollow. As we mourn the passing of our long-time, beloved mayor, let us not tarnish his legacy by electing a successor unfit to fill his void. You deserve a leader who will work hard for your best interest. As a community leader, I, Carl Longstreet have funded numerous community youth programs—*"

He was, of course, referring to a brief foray into philanthropy a few years back when he established an outreach program for at-risk teens. The program quickly dissolved when it became apparent that Carl was sending local youths out to beg for change on high traffic street corners, while he pocketed the lion's share of their earnings. Each kid was expected to recruit friends for an increased share in what amounted to a "panhandler pyramid scheme."

"*—and in my early days I was solely responsible for alleviating the homeless epidemic within our town.*"

In his day, he'd been the only homeless person in Fox Hollow. His rise in social status made his statement true. As the video continued, Carl strolled down Main Street, habitually glancing into public trash cans as he passed.

"*If you elect me as your mayor, I promise to rebuild this city to its former glory. I promise to create more jobs for those who are hungry— hungry to make an honest living. And finally, to increase border security, preventing acts of terrorism from those murderous Cedar Mills teens. Together, we can fight for Fox Hollow. Together we can take the Longstreet to victory.*"

Carl ended his speech at Town Hall in front of the great bronze statue of Sly Fox. A flag waved in the background and he forced an awkward smile. The voice-over returned.

"Paid for by The Committee To Elect Carl Longstreet."

Bomber handed the phone back to Bruce.

"Production value was good," Bomber said. "But he seems out of touch. And demented."

"A relic of the old world," Bruce said loftily, putting his phone away.

"I don't know what that means."

"It means things are changing, Bomber. I'm sorry about Cecil's death, but it's created an opportunity for positive change."

"Literally nothing has changed here in the last ten years," Bomber said. "People here are incapable of accepting even the slightest deviation from normal. Why do you think my uncle was mayor for seventy years? Why do you think the town imploded when Fox Applesauce headquarters relocated?"

"Why do you think no one believes a Dogman is terrorizing the populace?" Bruce offered.

"That's exactly my point. The amount of change this town can handle is limited to the variety of the neon food coloring in their applesauce. So, if you'll excuse me, I need to go restock the Bloo Goo *again.*"

Bomber put the final swoop on a handlebar mustache he'd added to Gloria's picture before walking off toward the back room.

"The revolution is at hand," Bruce called.

10:05 a.m.

Sheriff Connie stood beside Householder's desk with her arms folded across her chest, a perplexed look on her face.

"Can I help you, Sheriff?" Sergeant Householder asked.

Connie said nothing. She was staring at the holding cell in the back of the office.

"Ma'am?" Householder tried again. He straightened some papers, suddenly conscious of the disorder on his desk.

"Where the hell did *they* come from?"

She pointed to a man and woman sitting opposite each other in the holding cell. They were both in their mid-20s—maybe early 30s, but well-maintained or artificially augmented. The man was sullen in a navy suit, the jacket folded next to him on the bench. One pant leg was torn off at the knee, exposing a black sock coated in dried, brown burrs. There was a tear in the other pant leg and filth on his shirt. A loosened tie hung from his neck like an untethered noose. He was handsome, you could tell that even through the grime on his face. The woman was beautiful, but equally disheveled in an emerald-green cocktail dress which barely stretched over her large, counterfeit breasts. Her raven hair, it seemed, had at one point been styled with elegant waves, but was now a mess of wild tangles. A small twig was still adrift just above her shoulder. The couple was whispering back and forth. Angrily. Connie wondered if they'd been caught copulating in the orchard.

"Oh. Those two. Yeah, they were brought in early this morning," Householder said. "Officer Parks said he got a call around 2 a.m. from Pastor Mast. These two were apparently drunk as skunks, trying to break into the church. He said they were hysterical. Ranting about a demon chasing them." Householder said. "I guess the fella kept yelling 'sanctuary,' at the top of his lungs, like in that hunchback film."

"Who are they?" Connie asked.

"The man is Nigel Peters."

"That sounds familiar," Connie said.

"Not surprising," Householder said. "He just directed the movie, *When In Ancient Rome*, which was a box-office smash."

"I don't know it," Connie said.

"Also not surprising," Householder said. "It was a romantic comedy—about Roman gladiators."

"And the woman?"

"The woman is a—" Householder checked a notepad, "— Becca Bones. She's an actress." He paused. "An *adult film* actress."

"I like how you pretended not to remember her name." Connie smirked.

Householder blushed.

"What the hell are they doing in Fox Hollow?" Connie asked. She knew the answer before she'd finished the question.

"Spillover from another Longstreet party, I assume," Householder sighed.

"They say anything about what chased them?"

"Nah. They just woke up a few minutes ago," Householder said. "Neither of them will say a word to us without a lawyer, which is dumb, 'cuz Pastor Mast isn't pressing charges and nothing was damaged. Their hangovers are punishment enough."

Sheriff Connie nodded and headed back toward her office.

"Keep on them," she said. "If they were chased by something, it could be the same 'something' we're looking for."

"Yes, Ma'am," Householder said.

"Say what you want about ol' Carl," Connie said, "but he knows how to party."

12:07 p.m.

An abandoned electric scooter created a bottleneck in the cookie/cracker aisle. Bomber pulled the handle-trigger and the starter clicked. A green light in the center display blinked sadly and then faded out completely.

"Damn you, Ron-Boy," Bomber said.

Ron "Ron-Boy" Carson and his mother, Big Mama Carson, were two of the market's regulars. Ron-Boy, whose nickname originated from his overprotective yet somehow neglectful mother, had been two years ahead of Bomber in school and their years on the football team had briefly overlapped. Ron-Boy had been a great football player because what he lacked in formal education and interpersonal skills, he made up for in anger, aggression, and sheer physical mass. He was the type of guy who'd mop up mayo with a handful of French fries, then put you in the hospital for watching. He'd made one hell of a lineman.

After high school, Ron-Boy made his living in the same way Big Mama did: shuffling to and from the mailbox to collect Social Security checks, state food-assistance checks, disability benefit checks, insurance payout checks, and other amounts awarded through an array of frivolous lawsuits. Together, they were making more than Bomber could imagine and even had an in-ground pool installed behind their mobile home the previous summer.

Every Monday and Thursday afternoon, like clockwork, Ron-Boy and Big Mama would arrive at Marty's in their rusty van, its handicap placard ticking like a pendulum off the rear-view mirror. Big Mama was always dressed the same, sporting a skintight tank top which popped the folds of her back like a broken can of biscuits. Her enormous belly was always tucked into a dirty pair of electric pink spandex, held together by nothing more than the sheer grace of God. Ron-Boy's dress was less risqué and more varied, as he rotated through an assortment of colored sweatpants, carefully coordinated with a collection of XXL T-shirts he'd acquired from local garage sales and thrift stores. Each shirt was a souvenir of a vacation Ron-Boy never took: Disney World, the Grand Canyon, Key West, the Daytona 500, the Indy

500, Rocky Mountain National Park, SeaWorld San Diego, and The Alamo, to name a few. To Bomber, Ron-Boy was a walking reminder of when folks in town had the disposable income to travel and as the shirts faded, how far removed from those times they'd become. Today Ron-Boy was sporting an epic eagle, soaring majestically over Mount Rushmore. *South Dakota* was scrawled across the bottom in swooping font.

The two Carsons had zoomed off on the store's two Cruiser-2000 electric mobility scooters, per their normal ritual, but twenty minutes later Bomber spied the pair again in the frozen section, sans one scooter. Big Mama was still in hers, but Ron-Boy was waddling behind, dramatically dragging the tips of his shoes, a scowl bunching his chins. The task of locating and retrieving the heavy scooter was now on Bomber.

The scooter was surprisingly hard to push. With one hand on the seat-back and the other steering, Bomber felt like he was slogging it through thick mud.

"I think they work better if you sit on them," said a voice behind him.

Bomber turned, ready to spit venom, only to find Pastor Mast smiling back at him.

"Hello Pastor," he said, straightening up. "I've been bested by the infamous Carson Gang once again. Members of your flock, aren't they?"

Pastor Mast grimaced playfully.

"Probationary sheep still, I'm afraid," he said. It was no secret that the Carson duo had been caught skimming money off the collection plates mid-service. Their defense had been that part of the money was coming back to them anyway, in the form of the church's charitable giving and it shouldn't be looked at as stealing, but more of a "cash advance." Sheriff Connie had offered to take them down to the station, but Pastor Mast, opting for compassion, settled for a stern lecture, to which the Carsons had half-heartedly listened while they scrolled through their phones.

"Perhaps we'll get through to them one day," Pastor Mast said.

"Stranger things have happened," said Bomber, steadying himself for another push.

"Speaking of strange happenings," Pastor Mast went on. "I wanted to apologize. I never had the opportunity to speak with you at your great uncle's funeral. I wanted to offer my condolences."

"No apology needed," Bomber said. "You had your hands full with the funeral crashers."

Pastor Mast scoffed.

"Can you believe the nerve of that fellow?" he asked, shaking his head. He turned and perused the wall of cracker options. "Using a funeral as a political rally. Cecil actually sought my counsel a few weeks back regarding Mr. Longstreet's—"

Pastor Mast stopped.

"Mr. Longstreet's what?" Bomber pressed.

"Mr. Longstreet's—decadent—parties," Pastor Mast continued. "Hedonistic things from what I can tell. Don't get me wrong, what Mr. Longstreet does behind the walls of his estate is his business. But when it spills out into Fox Hollow, it's an issue. There's enough competition for people's souls these days."

"I can't say I know of anyone who's been invited to a Longstreet party," Bomber said. "I always just assumed they were for his hoity-toity friends."

"That may be true," Pastor Mast said, "but just this morning, two of his guests tried to break into my church. They were out of their senses. Drunk or maybe even on drugs and raving about a demon chasing them."

Pastor Mast noticed Bomber's spine straighten and shook his head.

"Don't start, Bomber," he chastised. "It was not your werewolf. The sinners in question were so out of sorts a rogue squirrel would've brought them to their knees. They were belligerent, so I was forced to call the authorities."

Bomber didn't press further but was pleased to have fresh intel for Buck.

"So you won't be voting Carl Longstreet for mayor?" Bomber asked with a wry smile. "You'll be a Gloria Glass man?"

"I'll vote for neither," Pastor Mast said.

"Neither?" Bomber asked. "But it's your civic du—"

"Call me old-fashioned," the Pastor said, putting a box of

wafers into his basket, "but the lesser of two evils is still evil."

Bomber decided moving the scooter could wait and he sat in the cracked plastic seat.

"I don't think anyone worthy is going to step up," he said.

"That's the problem nowadays," Pastor Mast said, putting another box of wafers into his basket. "We've become a nation of finger pointers. The emotional abuse of public service, though often well-earned, makes the very thought of it terrifying to most reasonable people. All that's left are the narcissists and charlatans and crooks who've sold their souls long ago."

"Wow," Bomber said. "Tell me how you really feel."

"I wish my son Billy were back," Pastor Mast sighed. "He'd have the spine for it, but he's still off playing Army. He's probably too hot-headed for it anyhow."

He added another box of wafers to the basket.

"Anyway," he said. "I don't want either of those yahoos going around telling people they've got 'the God vote.'"

He looked pleased with his wafers and turned back to Bomber.

"And what about you, Mr. Interim Mayor?" He asked. "You're well-known around town. Ever consider joining the family business?"

"I've got too many skeletons," Bomber laughed.

"But yours aren't in the closet," Pastor Mast smiled. "Memories are short, Bomber. And politics seems to be nothing more than a succession of distractions. Perhaps it's time to put childish things aside and give this town something new to look at."

Childish things? Bomber thought.

"You could be the lesser of *three* evils," Pastor Mast winked and continued down the aisle, leaving Bomber, once again, stranded and surrounded by crackers.

12:49 p.m.

Connie emerged from her office a pale shade of green. She typically had an iron gut, but there was nothing typical about the brutality of Ms. Carol Meyers's death or the gruesome crime scene photos she'd been analyzing for the last hour.

"Householder," she said, still staring down at an open file. "Do you have any Tums?"

She was met with silence. Householder was not at his desk. She checked her watch and was surprised to find it had been several hours since they'd last spoke. She cursed, realizing she'd missed a lunch date with Bruce, who hadn't so much as called to remind her. He was used to it now, she supposed.

Officer Hodges sat behind the dispatch radio doing his best to look busy.

"Where'd he go?" Connie asked.

"Patrol duty, Ma'am," Hodges said. "A while ago."

Connie nodded.

"And them?" she asked, pointing to the empty holding cell.

Hodges fidgeted, unsure if the answer was going to get him reamed.

"Longstreet came and picked them up," he said. "Not Carl. The younger one. The son. I guess he's Carl, too, though."

"Did we get anything useful out of them?" Connie asked.

Hodges shook his head. "They weren't talking, Ma'am. Just rich folks doing rich folks things."

5:45 p.m.

Bomber arrived early to Room 12 of the Fox Den Motel. He worried about appearing overeager but knocked anyway.

"'Bout time," Buck shouted through the door. He was in typical Buck Wildes wardrobe— his flannel cut-off tucked into olive army-fatigue pants, which were tucked into black combat boots.

"You're gonna freeze," Bomber told him. "Throw this on."

He removed two hoodies from his backpack, made of apple-patterned drapes, and tossed one to Buck, who looked skeptical.

"When in Rome," Buck said and slid the scratchy material over his head.

He eyed Bomber's backpack, which looked to be loaded with rocks.

"What else ya got in there?"

Bomber opened the flap, proudly displaying his giant, rusty bear trap.

Buck raised an eyebrow and, without a word, moved to the back doors of a white utility van parked outside his room. The Virginia vanity plate read "MONSTER1."

"Voila!" he said, throwing open the rear doors.

The interior of the van was a cryptozoologist's dream. The cargo hold, which had been separated from the main cab by a steel plate bulkhead, had been outfitted with racks, cages, and bins containing gizmos and do-hickies of every sort. There were motion sensors, spotlights, trip wires, and trail cams lining the walls. A large black bin, marked with a variety of "CAUTION," "HAZARD," and "FLAMMABLE" stickers, sat against the sidewall. The word "PYROTECHNICS" was stenciled on the front. A large black case labeled "Thermal Imaging Devices / Night Vision Goggles" was padlocked to the neighboring rack. All the lids had been propped open for Bomber's viewing pleasure. Along the opposite wall was a gun rack with several funky-looking rifles.

"Tranq-guns," Buck said, following Bomber's gaze. "For taking down big game."

Sprinkled in were leftover gadgets from other cryptid hunts. A scuba tank lay beneath a shelf next to a bucket containing several thick lengths of unfinished wood. Bomber recognized them as Sasquatch calls from Buck's episodes in the Pacific Northwest.

"How did you afford all this gear?" Bomber asked. There had to be several hundred thousand dollars' worth of equipment.

"Sponsors," was all Buck said.

"Are those Claymore mines?" Bomber asked, pointing at a stack of curved metal cases inside the pyro-box. His bear trap suddenly felt inadequate.

"Yes," Buck said. "I take perimeter security very seriously."

With his shock and awe campaign complete, he started lowering and locking lids.

"You have a location in mind?" he asked.

"I did, but there's been a change of plans," Bomber said. "I may not have slick equipment, but I have the freshest intel."

6:08 p.m.

Pastor Mast slid the last letter into the Third Reformed Church's marquee road-sign and dusted off his hands. He stepped back to inspect his work for spelling errors, still cautious after his "DOG IS GOOD" mistake a few weeks back. He'd been proud of his quip while speaking with Bomber earlier in the afternoon and the sign now read:

"THE LESSER OF TWO EVILS IS STILL EVIL"

His upcoming Sunday service would be one of caution. A reminder to his flock that their faith should lie with God and not the empty campaign promises of women or men of questionable motivation. Especially those whose moral ambiguity had long been public knowledge.

A jacked-up truck sped by and laid on its horn, causing the Pastor to jump. The driver shouted something from the passenger window that sounded like: *Longstreet.* Pastor Mast watched him drive off but refrained from shaking his fist. Coming from the other direction was a white utility van. As it passed, he clearly saw Bomber Merridan, clad in his ridiculous apple-drape-camo, duck down in the passenger seat.

So much for putting childish things aside, he thought.

Before picking up the box of extra letters, he briefly considered turning on the marquee's lights, big glowing bulbs which lined its edges. The sign had been a gift from the church's Tuesday night bingo club, but while the gesture was appreciated, the reverend had balked at the glitzy feature, stating that this was Fox Hollow and not the Las Vegas Strip. He was now reconsidering his admonishment. Attendance had been uncharacteristically low of late. Perhaps a little "flash" was what he needed.

"I'll bring them in the old-fashioned way," he said to himself, shaking off the temptation.

He was nearly back to the church doors, when something across the parking lot caught his eye— something long and dark just inside the wall of apple trees, on a small strip of grass that sloped into the parking lot. He looked at the church and then at the object. His back ached from bending over the sign and the box of letters was heavy.

If you leave it there, you're just as bad as the litter-bugs, he thought. Putting the letters down, he trudged across the long asphalt lot. Before he reached the object, he knew what it was: the missing pant leg of the drunkard from the night before.

He bent down and pinched the navy-blue material between his thumb and forefinger. Though ripped across the top, the pant leg was still mostly intact. All except the area which would've covered the man's heel. There the cloth was shredded as though by tooth or nail and upon closer inspection, the strands of tattered fabric were crusty and hard. Chewed and left to dry. Across the back of the leg were several short, orange hairs.

"Curious," Pastor Mast said out loud.

6:47 p.m.

After quickly consulting the map, Bomber and Buck plotted the most likely path of two drunks stumbling between Fox Mansion and the Third Reformed Church. They'd left Buck's van, lovingly referred to as "The White Whale," parked on the dusty shoulder of Old Dickerson Road, not far from where Mayor Cecil had been disemboweled and de-throated. The sliding side door of the van was permanently welded shut to accommodate the equipment racks and Buck had secured the rear doors with a series of steel bar locks that would've put Fort Knox to shame.

Loaded down with two hunting bags full of gear and a sleek tranquilizer gun, they set off down an orchard row, being careful not to turn their ankles on the dropped apples hidden in the tall grass. On their heads, they wore mounted GoPros to ensure Buck caught "all relevant footage" for his next viral video. He insisted Bomber look directly at him whenever he spoke and they stopped occasionally to set up snares and tripwires wherever they found trampled grass or other telltale signs of life. Buck rigged the trip wires to high-definition cameras, which he diligently hid in the gnarled crooks of nearby trees. All of his devices were then synced to a tablet kept in the satchel strapped across his chest.

"Nowhere to hide now, ya bastard," he said after every successful sync.

It was dusk when they settled into their hide site, a jumbled construct of downed branches, piled near a natural chokepoint that separated the orchard from dense, swampy woods. Bomber recalled similar forts he'd built with Sly when they were kids.

"Whiskey?" Buck whispered. He offered up a silver flask.

Bomber shook his head and wriggled around a thick branch jabbing at his side.

"I don't partake," Bomber said. "Nothing torpedoes a story's credibility faster than bourbon on the breath. Learned that the hard way."

"Good on you," Buck said. He took a healthy pull. "So what'd yours look like?"

"My what?"

"Your Dogman, man," Buck said. His smile glowed in the

fading light.

"Oh, right," Bomber said, feeling a little foolish. "Canine Type, Variant One."

"Come again?"

"Canine Type, Variant One," Bomber repeated.

"No, I heard you," Buck said. "I'm just not sure what that means."

He could see Bomber's look of skepticism.

"Listen," Buck said. "I learn by doing. I wasn't a Bigfoot expert on Day One. I made myself learn, by hitting the woods hard, by talking to the locals, and by learning the legends of the indigenous people. Now, no offense, but this Michigan Dogman of yours isn't nearly as sexy as Bigfoot."

Bomber was surprised to find himself offended.

"There aren't any *Dogmen For Dummies* handbooks out there and there aren't a lot of folks clamoring for answers on the Dogman," Buck continued. "Or there didn't used to be. Not to mention, every region has their own nuances when it comes to monster legends. A sasquatch in northeast Washington state just ain't the same as a sasquatch in the Florida panhandle. That's why I link up with local experts like you. Fair?"

"Fair," Bomber agreed. He liked being called "expert" instead of "crackpot."

"So school me, Teach," Buck said, leaning back against the stick wall.

"Well," Bomber said, "experts acknowledge two types of Dogmen: the 'Type Three' and the 'Canine Type' and both have multiple variants or subcategories. The Type Three Dogmen are characterized by humanoid bodies—a sasquatch body, to put it into relatable terms. Though both types ambulate bipedally, the Type Threes have legs and arms like ours."

"Ambulate bipedally?"

"It means they walk upright," Bomber said.

"I know what it means," Buck said. "I'm trying to figure out why you wouldn't just say 'walks upright.'"

"Sorry," Bomber said. "Didn't want to sound unprofessional. The first recorded Dogman sighting in Michigan was a Type Three, believe it or not. Just northeast of here in Wexford County in 1887. Two lumberjacks were terrorized by a creature with a dog's head and man's body."

"Couldn't have been a man in a big fur hat?" Buck asked.

"It was said to be seven feet tall, with cold blue eyes—"

"So, a Swedish man in a big fur hat?"

"—and had a fierce howl like a human scream," Bomber said dramatically.

"Humans also have 'human screams,'" Buck said, which earned him an annoyed look from Bomber. "Sorry, it's my job to be skeptical. Please go on."

"The variants of the Type Three are really just due to head shapes and sizes. One has a wolf head. Another has a sasquatch-like head with a dog's muzzle. The third has a more squashed face, like a pug mated with an ape. Some people think those might be distant relatives of the common baboon, but those people are idiots. Obviously, baboons are not common here."

"Obviously," Buck said. He took another pull from his flask before adding: "Idiots."

"The Canine Type is the most common, by far. Both types are considered members of the Canidaes Family, but it's the Canine Type that resembles dogs and wolves most. Hence the name. Their body structures are similar to the average wolf, but they ambulate bi— they *walk* upright. There are four variants of the Canine Type. Variant One is basically a timber wolf walking upright. Variant Two is more of a hyena on hind legs—maybe a little taller. Variant Threes, the most common, are much taller and jacked like bodybuilders, with wolf heads. Hollywood bases their werewolves on Canine Type, Variant Threes."

"Or maybe people base their sightings on what they've seen in the movies," Buck suggested. Bomber ignored him.

"The most famous Canine Type, Variant Three sighting was back in 1937, in Paris, Michigan. A guy named Robert Fortney was attacked by a pack of wild dogs. He said the alpha dog was enormous and walked on two legs."

"Ambulated bipedally," Buck said matter-of-factly.

Bomber sighed.

"Variant Fours are even larger, with huge heads. They're the most aggressive of all seven variants and have been reported to eat other Dogmen.”

“Hold the phone,” Buck said, sitting up. “You’re telling me, people have not only reported seeing Dogmen, but they claim they’ve seen Dogmen eating other Dogmen?”

The sun was well below the horizon and the branches were turning black above them.

“Listen,” Bomber whispered, “you wanted to know what I know.”

They sat in silence, watching fireflies ignite and then flicker out. In the swamp, the tree frogs started their cadence.

“Oh,” Bomber said, “and some folks say Dogmen can use telepathy to communicate with people, but you’d have to be a real loon to buy into that.”

“Clearly,” Buck said. “So, if I’m recalling accurately—and I think I am—you saw a walking timber wolf?”

“Well,” Bomber said. “The thing is—”

Buck’s ever-present smile drooped, tugging the tips of his mustache.

“You gotta be joking,” he said. “You didn’t even see it, did you?”

“I did,” Bomber said, shifting uncomfortably. “I was just slightly—severely—inebriated. But I did see—*something*.”

He straightened. “I did see it,” he said with confidence, as though confirming it to himself for the first time. “Canine Type, Variant One.” He paused. “Only—”

“Only what?”

“Only, it was miniature,” Bomber said.

“Miniature?”

“Smaller than anything I’ve read about,” Bomber confessed.

Buck rubbed the bridge of his nose.

“You’re sure you didn’t just see a regular ol’ coyote?” He asked.

“It was smaller than a coyote,” Bomber said.

“Smaller than a coyote? Christ. No offense, but all this seems a bit insane now.” Buck pulled at his sleeve, indicating the apple camo shirt. “You’ve spent ten years chasing a drunken glimpse? And one that doesn’t even fit the accepted descriptions? Not to mention using such a flimsy encounter as a basis for enduring relentless ridicule from the town. Who does that?" He shook his head. "And worst of all, using it as an excuse to pass up good whiskey."

Bomber felt sick.

"I get it," Buck said. "I really do. In a town like this, there ain't a lot to hang your name on and just like Hollywood, any publicity is probably good publicity. I just wish I hadn't been lured in on a hoax."

He took an aggressive pull from his flask.

"It is not a hoax!" Bomber's jaw had been locked so tight it hurt. "It was no drunken hallucination. No trick of the eyes. Canine Type. Variant One. Miniature." His fists were clenched at his side. "And if you don't believe me, I'm not sure what the hell I'm doing here," he snapped.

Buck considered him a moment and once again his grin broke through the gloom, reflecting the moonlight. "Spoken like a true believer," he said. He leaned forward and slapped Bomber on the knee. "It's good to see someone with a little passion left. A little fire in the belly. I've worked with folks who're quick to bail on their convictions with the slightest friction. Good on you for sticking to your guns." Buck leaned back and tucked the flask back into the satchel. "Sorry for hounding you. Had to be sure you're a serious hunter and not one of those 'Weekend Werewolfers.'"

10:27 p.m.

The latch of Connie's front door clicked behind her. She leaned back, letting the darkness of the apartment wash over her. From the front door, she could see down the hall to the bedrooms. Light seeped from a crack in Bruce's door, but that didn't mean he was awake. It was common for Connie to find him asleep with an Xbox controller balanced on his chest.

She slipped off her shoes and went to the kitchen where she removed her pistol from its holster. As she'd done each night for over a decade, Connie mounted a stepping stool and deposited her weapon in a small safe kept in the cupboard above the refrigerator. Sure, Bruce was an adult now and the gun-safe was probably overkill, but on the other hand he'd been a particularly angsty teen, prone to fits of depression, and showed little signs of changing. It couldn't have been easy growing up the fatherless, quarter-Indian son of a cop. Kids can be so cruel anyway. Connie knew that first-hand.

Better safe than sorry, she thought. She closed the safe and spun the dial. She remembered all too well where the combination of depression and firearms could lead.

Her eyes fell on the stack of papers, folders, and small boxes next to the safe. Awards she'd accumulated from four years of Army service, one tour in Iraq, the Police Academy, and the community she served. Awards she'd never had the time or ambition to frame and hang around the small apartment or bring to the office to give it some character. She wasn't one for self-aggrandizement anyway.

"Mom?" Bruce called from down the hall.

"Yeah," Connie replied. "I'm home."

"Do we have any clear tape?" Bruce yelled.

"My day was fine," Connie yelled. "Thanks for asking."

Silence.

"How was your day?" Bruce yelled.

Connie sighed.

"I think we have some packing tape," she yelled. "Give me a sec."

"And markers too?"

"What are you doing in there?" Connie yelled.

There was a thumping on the floor from the apartment below. Connie cringed. They'd woken Edith again.

Connie opened the refrigerator. The shelves were mostly empty except for a half-gallon of expired milk, a brown iceberg lettuce wedge slowly liquefying in its bag, and a door full of off-brand condiments.

She shook her head and shut the door. Searching the kitchen drawers, she found a roll of clear packing tape.

"How is it you work at a grocery store, but we never have any damn groceries?" Connie asked, coming down the hall. She pushed Bruce's door open and tossed him the tape, which he bumbled and dropped. He was sitting on his bed with a giant piece of poster board in front of him. A fifty-two-inch flat-screen TV glowed on the wall—Bruce's latest purchase with the money he claimed he never had. It was paused on a Gloria Glass campaign video.

"You didn't give me any money to buy groceries," he said as he bent to retrieve the tape.

"You have a credit card," Connie said. "That I pay for. Get some food tomorrow."

"Okay," Bruce grumbled. He went back to coloring big block letters on the poster board.

"What're you making?"

"A sign," Bruce said. He discreetly moved a pillow, trying to block it from view. "Did you find any other markers? I might need some glue, too. And maybe glitter."

Connie moved around the bed. The sign read, "*GLORIA BE TO GOD*" in block letters.

"Don't tell me you're campaigning for that spiteful hag?"

"Mom!"

"I'm sorry," she said, "but Gloria is the worst person I've ever met. And I meet criminals. All day. It's my job."

"She's worse than Carl Longstreet?" Bruce asked.

"Carl's an idiot," Connie said, "and he doesn't understand social norms. And yes, all indicators point to him being an awful person too. But Gloria is much worse."

Bruce went back to coloring his sign.

"Gloria is going to help the 'little guy,'" he said. "She's going to elevate those of us who are being oppressed."

Connie reached down and grabbed the remote from the bed and clicked off the huge TV.

"Your life is an endless struggle," she said. "If you're not too busy being oppressed tomorrow, buy some food after work."

She started out the door.

"What about the investigation?" Bruce asked. "Anything new you can tell me?"

"Yeah. Turns out Gloria Glass is the murderer," Connie smiled.

"Har, har," Bruce said.

"No, we handed off the investigation to the DNR today," Connie said. "Their initial assessment pointed to a black bear—"

"Or some other *normy animal*,'" Bruce muttered.

"You know I don't like you hanging around Bomber Merridan outside of work," Connie said as she left the room.

That night, Connie dreamt she was a shepherd in a lush, green field which rolled infinitely in all directions. Her flock was all about her. There were scores of identical white sheep, too many to count, grazing on the endless hills. The herd's movements were fluid and hypnotic, like ocean waves. Connie took comfort in them and the sheep were neither happy nor sad, but content in being fed and watched over.

Suddenly, there was a hair-raising bleat. Connie turned to find a circle had opened in the flock. In the center was a dead ram. Its throat was a shredded mess of wet red wool and pink pulpy tissue. The stomach was ripped open, leaving entrails in a shiny, coiled pile beside it. Before she could reach the ram, there was another scream. She turned again to find a dead ewe lying only a few feet away. Another scream. And another. She turned and turned, but could never identify the assailant, until all but one of her sheep were dead, a small lamb far off in the field. She began running toward it, through a pasture rife with death. At her feet, blood seeped through the green grass, spraying with each footfall. But her feet were not her own. They were the hooves of a sheep. She looked at her hands, which had also become hooves.

I guess I'm a sheep now, she thought.

There was an ease in this thought. A surrender. Or maybe a realization that she'd been a sheep the whole time. She could not tell.

She looked up toward the lamb. Behind it, a black mass formed. A living thing that billowed up like thick smoke. From within the darkness, a mouth took shape. A mouth filled with razor teeth of silver and gold, hovering under sharp orange eyes. The mouth smiled a wicked smile. Connie felt no fear of the creature, only fear for the lamb. Her lamb, which continued to graze, unaware of the danger enveloping it.

Connie tried to shout but could only bleat like the other dying sheep. The black smog curled and bent low. The large jaws loomed close to the lamb's head. Connie galloped on all fours now, her hooves spraying blood in her wake. Her movement caught the little lamb's attention. It looked up, green blades of grass dripping with blood poked from its lips. It opened its little lamb mouth to speak.

"Gloria be to god," the little lamb croaked in Bruce's voice.

The creature snapped its ruthless maw, removing the lamb's head with a spurt of crimson. Connie woke in her bed still thrashing and bleating.

11:55 p.m.

"Anubis."

Bomber snapped awake. For a split second he forgot where he was. He rubbed his eyes and squinted into the dark.

"What?"

"Anubis," Buck whispered again. "The ancient Egyptian god of the underworld, the one who ushered the dead into the afterlife. Before that he was known as Wepwawet. He had the head of a jackal."

"So?"

"In ancient Greece," Buck continued, "they had the Legend of Lycaon. King Lycaon of Arcadia and all his sons, to be precise. They were cursed by Zeus for serving him a bad meal. The main course was the roasted flesh of one of Lycaon's own sons."

"Gross," Bomber said.

"Zeus thought so, too. He turned the whole family into wolves. Werewolves. In Japan, they have the Kitsune. They are magic, shape-shiftin' little fox-buggers. Tricky little bastards, according to legend. The Aztecs had Xolotl and I'm one hundred percent sure I'm pronouncing that wrong. He was their god of fire and lightning. Had the head of a dog. The list goes on."

Bomber's mind was still foggy.

"Why are you telling me all of this?" he asked.

"Perspective," Buck said. "You spoke earlier about the first Dogman sighting being in the late 1800s. I'd argue that people have been seeing Dogmen since the very beginning. And since they couldn't explain what they saw, they deified them. Turned them into gods. Or found other ways to explain them. You're not chasing some crazy vision, man. You're connecting with the past. Humans never change. Sure, we adapt to the times, but we never truly change. We're all just cavemen with fancier toys."

Bomber wasn't in the mindset for any existential ponderings. He shivered and ran a hand over his jacket sleeve. The thick drape material was wet with dew. High overhead, the moon was dim behind thin wisps of clouds, dousing the orchard in a flavorless gray.

"Doesn't sound like you're lacking in Dogman knowledge

after all," Bomber said.

"On the contrary," Buck said. "I had no idea about the types and variants. That's what's great. Every region adds its own spice. The Dogman here in Michigan is much different than, say, the Chupacabra of the southwest or the Beast of Bray Road next door in Wisconsin. They're all dog-creatures, sure enough, but everything I learn gets turned on its head the second I move."

"You were Googling all that stuff on your tablet while I was sleeping, weren't you?" Bomber asked.

"I get surprisingly good service out here," Buck said, patting his satchel.

"What time is it?"

A pale glow illuminated Buck's eyes.

"11:58 p.m.," he said. "Your turn to take watch."

Bomber shifted to a better position among the rocks and ruts, while Buck leaned back and rested his head on his backpack.

"So you and the Fox kid used to be best buds, huh?" he asked.

"I suppose so," Bomber said. "How did you know about that?"

"One learns a lot when digging into a small town's history," Buck said. "What happened there? Between you and the Fox kid, I mean."

Bomber wasn't particularly interested in talking about the subject.

"Stole my girl," he said.

"There's always a girl."

"It was for the best," Bomber said. "Sly never brought out my best self. I'm still trying to repair the damage I did around him."

Buck was silent.

"We used to throw some crazy-big parties not far from here though," Bomber said. "Down by the old Kissing Pond."

"Kissing Pond?"

"Yeah, it's a man-made drainage pond south of the Fox Mansion," Bomber said. "It's where the old folks used to go to make out."

"Gross," Buck said.

"I mean when they were young," Bomber said. "Like in the

1940s and 50s. I didn't mean there are a bunch of senior citizens sneaking down there to get freaky. They couldn't anyway. Fox Applesauce fenced off the whole area and turned it into an 'R and D' orchard—that's Research and Development."

"I know what R and D means," Buck said, sitting up. "What are they R and D'ing?"

"No clue. They just threw up a chain link fence one day and a bunch of 'No Trespassing' signs. They're always cooking up crazy new products and testing them on the town. I imagine they're just growing new breeds of apple for test batches. Stuff like that."

Buck was silent again.

"You must've been in the Fox Mansion a few times, right?"

"Not once," Bomber said. "Never made it past the front door."

"How come?"

"Sly's dad was a monster," Bomber said. "And his mom ran off when he was only nine years old. Some say Mr. Fox used to beat her and that's why she ran. Others say she was having an affair. A lot say it was both. Whatever it was, Mr. Fox didn't handle it well."

"What happened to him?"

Bomber shrugged.

"Sold the company after Sly died," he said. "Took the money and ran. He probably bought a Tuscan villa or an island somewhere—where he hunts people for sport. Or he's building a bio-fueled rocket to Mars. Or funding a private war in a Third World country. Whatever rich jerks do in retirement."

"Nobody knows where he went?"

"Just rumors," Bomber said. "The Fox Hollow Special."

"Sounds like there's no love lost from you," Buck said.

"He ruined the town I lo—"

Bomber stopped. A glowing light flickered on over the horizon off the northeast corner of the orchard. It reminded him of the glow of a stadium and there was a warm feeling of nostalgia.

"Football game tonight?" Buck asked, following Bomber's stare.

"Wrong direction for the school stadium," Bomber said. "And

way too late."

"What's off that way?"

"Fox Mansion," Bomber said. "Longstreet Mansion now, I guess. Probably another one of Carl's fancy parties."

The distant sound of bass drums trickled into the hide sight, mixed with the occasional muffled cheer from a crowd. Buck got to his feet.

"I need to stretch my legs," he said. "I'm going to go check it out."

Bomber started to rise too, but Buck put his hand on his shoulder.

"This whole area is covered in sensors, cameras and trip wires," Buck said. "You hang back and monitor everything. It's your turn to watch." He handed Bomber the tablet and left the tranquilizer gun leaning on the branches where he'd been seated.

Bomber wasn't thrilled with the idea of being left alone.

"The mansion is a long way," he said, "and surrounded by high walls."

"Plenty of trees to climb," Buck said. He reached down and picked something from the ground.

"You probably better take this, too," he said, holding out a small device.

"What is it?" Bomber asked. He took the object, finding it attached to a wire.

"That's the clacker for the Claymore mines," Buck said, a little too casually. "I placed a circle of 'em around our position while you were sleeping."

"Jesus, Buck," Bomber gasped. He thrust the detonator back at Buck. "I don't want this."

Buck recoiled. "Please be careful with that," he gasped. "It never hurts to be over prepared. There's ten out there, with interlocking blast areas. Three hundred and sixty degrees of security, all daisy-chained together."

"This is Fox Hollow, not Nam," Bomber hissed.

"A couple clacks will do it, but don't use it unless you have to," Buck said.

"Obviously."

"Seriously. It'll mess some shit up."

"No, I get it," Bomber said, holding the cord and letting the detonator dangle.

"I shouldn't be long," Buck whispered, checking his watch. "I have our location on my GPS. If you see or hear anything, hit me on the walkie-talkie. I'll radio when I'm on my way back, so you don't accidentally blow me away."

He lobbed the walkie to Bomber, which hit his stomach with a dull thud. Bomber winced. By the time he'd safely put down the clacker and picked up the handset, Buck had disappeared.

An hour passed. Then another. Bomber moved from one heightened state of alertness to another. The temperature had dropped again and the tree frogs were silent. All around him, the night was interrupted by the scurrying of nocturnal animals, sometimes barely audible over the distant sounds of drums and thumping music. A nearly full moon cut silver streaks between branches. Time moved in odd intervals.

The strange glow on the horizon finally died, like the sun had stalled and then decided against starting a new day. The music faded with it. Another half hour passed.

He must've lost his way, Bomber thought. *Or fell down a ravine. Or broke his ankle on a drop-apple. Or the Dogman fucking ate him.*

The walkie-talkie offered nothing but static. He tried again. Ten channels. Nothing but hisses and crackles.

He looked at his watch. If Buck was not back in five minutes, he'd go after him.

The minutes ticked away. Five. Ten. Fifteen. Each time, Bomber told himself he'd give Buck five minutes more, convinced that's what the monster hunter would want. Less movement. Higher probability of success. He strained his eyes into the darkness, hoping each shadow, each swaying branch, was Buck returning.

Crack.

He froze. The sound of snapping branches came from his far left.

He was about to call to Buck but stopped.

The branch-snaps stopped, replaced by a heavy, raspy

breathing, like a dog panting. The sound drew nearer.

Bomber searched the ground next to him. Finding the detonator for the claymore mines, he was suddenly grateful for Buck's extreme preparedness. He lifted his head cautiously for a glimpse of the savage thing coming his way.

Breathe, he thought. He could hardly hear anything over the drumming of his heart.

Bomber estimated the animal to be five to six feet in length and roughly two hundred pounds. It was not visible yet, so he figured it must be walking on all fours, which ruled out his Dogman. He figured it to be a small bear, but a cougar wasn't impossible in lower Michigan either. Rare, but not impossible. His imagination set in. Perhaps a timber wolf had snuck across the Mackinac Bridge. Or maybe some other apex predator had escaped from one of those unlicensed zoos run by unqualified hicks. He tightened his grip on the clacker as he imagined a Bengal tiger sinking its fangs into his tender neck.

A mound of field stones separated Bomber from the approaching noise. The grass behind the rocks swayed and separated. Bomber held his breath.

A small creature emerged, scrambling on four legs to the top of the rock pile. As it reached the crest, the silver moonlight washed over its fur, dark with a hint of burnt red. Bomber sighed. A common red fox sat at the peak of the pile, looking this way and that. It sniffed the air and panted dramatically.

Had it been chasing something? Or was it being chased? Perhaps Buck had kicked it up in the underbrush.

Bomber was about to stand, once again concerned for Buck. The fox beat him to it. As though morphing into an entirely different creature, the small fox stood skillfully on its hind legs. Its shoulders were set back and its head high, but only for a moment. It quickly doubled over, with its front paws—or were they hands? — on its knees. It panted heavily, as though it'd just crossed the finish line of a marathon. It burst into a fit of chest rattling coughs and then spit a wad of mucus onto the rocks before standing again. Around its waist was a black band and Bomber wondered if maybe it'd been tagged by the DNR. This theory was immediately torpedoed when the fox used its front paws—hands, they were definitely *hands*—to slide the band around, revealing a pouch on the other side. A fanny pack.

The hell? Bomber thought.

From inside the waistband, the fox produced a pack of cigarettes and silver lighter. It casually took a seat on the highest rock and pulled a cigarette from the pack with its front teeth. The lighter flickered, lit the cigarette, and the fox took a long, stiff drag. He then produced another object from his fanny pack and after several seconds of fiddling, held it to his ear.

"Hey," the fox spoke.

The fox SPOKE.

Bomber pinched his own leg. It hurt. There was silence in the orchard. Every living creature was listening in disbelief.

"It's me," the fox said into the phone. "Trail went cold. Lost the scent." There was a brief silence."No, I'm not smoking again." The fox crushed his cigarette out on the rock. "If there was anybody there, they didn't see anything anyway."

Silence.

"Yes, I'm sure."

There was another long silence and the fox's long snout twisted into a frown.

"Listen, dammit," he snapped. "Don't you forget who's in charge here. If I say it's not a problem, it's not a problem."

Silence.

"I'm sorry," he said, his tone relaxing. "I love you, too."

He leaned back on one arm, his feet swinging lazily over the edge of the rock. Bomber had removed his GoPro and it was lying out of reach on Buck's bag. His phone was deep in his pocket and he didn't dare illuminate the screen anyway.

"I was thinking," the fox said. "Since I'm out here, I'd like to take care of our problem-child—take him out of the equation before he has an audience tomorrow."

Silence.

"No. Alive."

Silence.

"Yes, I'm sure. Have the van brought around. I have other plans for him."

Silence.

"Yeah, yeah," he said. "Love you, too."

The fox hung up the call and tucked the phone back in his fanny pack. He stood up, stretched his lower back, and then did a deep toe-touch. His red and white tail pointed skyward.

Despite the ominous phone call, the fox's casual limbering put Bomber momentarily at ease. He knew any photo or GoPro video would be grainy and blurry at best, so he reached for Buck's tranquilizer gun instead. A branch behind his head shifted, which dislodged two others, creating an obscene noise. Bomber was a stone.

The fox froze, too. His triangle ears erect and quivering, he slowly turned his long face toward the tangle of branches.

Bomber held his breath as the fox hopped from the rocks, cocking his head from side to side. The Claymore clacker was closer than the tranquilizer gun and seemed the smarter choice. Bomber picked it up, but by the time he looked back the fox was inside the perimeter of the mines, its eyes now locked on his. The white fur around its mouth peeled back with a faint quiver, revealing sharp, glistening teeth. There was a guttural rumbling as it snarled—or was it smiling? And the smell—was that Axe Body-Spray?

His senses utterly confused, Bomber remembered the clacker in his hands. It was possible the noise would frighten the fox or at least cause an adequate diversion, giving him an opportunity to run. It was his only shot. He closed his eyes and squeezed the clacker in rapid succession, like Buck had directed.

Clack *Clack* *Clack*

Nothing.

Bomber looked up. If it had been a smile on the fox's face before, it was definitely a snarl now. In one hand it gripped the frayed end of the detonator wire. The other end poked from between its razor teeth. It dropped the cord, moving in through the small entrance of the stick-fort. The fox was short, but menacing—stocky and muscular. It stood over Bomber, who sat quaking in his nest of branches. The fox leaned in and bared its teeth, saliva dripped in slow strands from the thick whiskers of its chin. The moonlight hit just right, sending a gold flash off the fox's right canine. The sharp tip of its nose was inches from

Bomber's face.

Bomber closed his eyes tight. "Please don't kill me," he moaned.

The fox's hot breath hit him before its words even registered. "You can't kill what doesn't live."

There was a long, tense silence. Bomber opened his eyes, finding himself alone once again.

October 24, 2017

8:11 a.m.

Buck held the frayed det cord and scratched his head. He'd returned from his recon of the Fox Mansion just before sunup, having been bested by the estate's towering exterior walls. He explained that his GPS had gone on the fritz when he approached the mansion, leaving him clueless for his return. He'd eventually stumbled onto a blacktop road and walked several miles, taking several wrong turns, before ending up back at The White Whale.

"A fanny pack, you say?"

Bomber prepared for a barrage of ridicule.

"Yes," he confirmed. "A black fanny pack."

Buck nodded.

"And how tall?"

Bomber held his hand so that it hovered around his belly button. In his head, he was already assessing the changes he'd need to make to Rex, his basement Dogman statue.

Buck scratched his head.

"Confirms your 'miniature' sighting, I guess. And you say he stole my tranquilizer gun?"

Bomber nodded. The tranquilizer gun had been the only thing missing after the fox had vanished. Buck was hot about this at first, but conceded it was partly his fault for leaving it out of reach.

"I really wish it hadn't chewed through the cord," he said. "Daisy-chaining these together took some time."

"You don't seem as shocked as I thought you'd be," Bomber said.

"Oh, I am," Buck said. "I just didn't think we'd find him this quick."

"Him?"

"Yes, the Dogman," Buck said quickly. "That's why we're out here, right?" He walked over to the rock where the creature had made a phone call of all things. Bomber was still trying to wrap his mind around the sight.

Using a small forceps he'd produced from his pocket, Buck plucked a crumpled cigarette butt from the top of the rock. He inspected it closely, smelled it, and dropped it into a small plastic baggy.

"Fascinating."

Bomber watched as Buck continued to work, silently interrogating the entire area. He worked with an efficiency born of repetition and no small amount of professional training, which, based on the quality of his equipment, he most certainly could afford. Buck made rough sketches of a set of paw prints he found near the rock pile, then scoured the area for bits of fur or, as he put it, "a jackpot of excrement." He explained that he could identify most animals by the size, shape, and contents of their feces. He found none, but Bomber was still envious of the skill set all the same and made a mental note to get better at identifying shit.

"I wish Bruce were here," Bomber said. "He could track it. He's part Indian."

"Native American," Buck corrected. "Unless you mean he's from India, in which case I don't see how that's relevant."

"Well, what do we do now?" Bomber asked. "Nobody's going to believe this."

"You're right," Buck said. "'Cause nobody's going to hear about it."

Bomber had figured this would be Buck's position.

"We have to say something to the police," Bomber said. "People are being killed. We'd be withholding evidence or something. If we stay silent and it kills again, that's on us."

Buck got up from the ground where he'd been sniffing a rather prominent paw print. He put a dirty hand on Bomber's shoulder.

"To be blunt," he said with a sympathetic smile, "people already think you're a bit off your nut. Sheriff Connie would chuck you in the looney-bin if you start spoutin' what you just told me."

Bomber knew Buck was right. There was no way Sheriff Connie would take him seriously, nor would anyone else in town.

"So what do we do?"

Buck bent down and pulled a hand-held video camera from one of the backpacks.

"The bread and butter of all Cryptozoologist Documentarians," he said, his smile beaming. "Close encounter dramatic re-enactments."

8:48 a.m.

"Next question."

Connie backed up and the two reporters pursued, thrusting their recorders at her.

"Was the reverend involved in anything—sordid?" Tina Chen asked, one eyebrow cocked expectantly. Tina Chen was *The Fox Howler*'s lead investigative reporter and had arrived at the Third Reformed Church ahead of her rival from the new *Fox Hollow Post* by about thirty seconds, which was only about thirty seconds behind the arrival of Sheriff Connie and her officers. She was still perplexed at how the reporters had found out so quickly.

We must have a mole in the department, she thought, absently nodding her head in agreement with her own assessment.

"Oh," Tina squealed excitedly. "What was it? Was it really bad? Pornography? Pedophilia? Dendrophilia? Sex dungeon?" She raised that eyebrow again.

"What? No," Sheriff Connie said. "No. It's nothing like that at all." She looked back at the church's parsonage, where officers were coming in and out like bees from a hive. The storm door on the front entrance hung open on one hinge, the way they'd found it.

Two hours before, Connie had been sitting at her desk with a steaming cup of coffee, mentally preparing for another dive into two case files full of grisly photos, when her phone rang with a call from Patrick McConnell.

"Connie," McConnell had said. "I need you to come down to the Third Reformed. There's been an incident—I think. Please be discreet. No sirens or lights."

His voice had been stiff and matter of fact, but then again, so was McConnell.

"What happened?" Sheriff Connie had asked.

"I just told you," McConnell said. "There's been an incident. Probably. I think. Please hurry." The phone went dead before Connie could question further.

McConnell, a long-time deacon of the Third Reformed Church, wasn't one for drama, or police for that matter, so Connie had rushed out the door, recruiting Sergeant Householder along the way. When they'd arrived they found McConnell standing alone in the front yard, pale freckled arms crossed over his barrel chest and trademark short-sleeve dress shirt.

McConnell explained that Pastor Mast had failed to show for the church's 8:30 a.m. service. Since this was uncharacteristic of him, McConnell had went next door to check on the aging reverend, only to find the parsonage storm door hanging off-kilter and the inside door ajar. Furniture had been flipped, dishes smashed, papers crumpled and shredded. There was even a butcher's cleaver lodged in the drywall near the television in the family room. A quick search failed to turn up Pastor Mast but did uncover a spatter of blood on the edge of a crucifix, which appeared to have been ripped from the wall.

By that time, Tina Chen and her rival reporter had arrived with their respective photographers and Connie had to intercept them before they could take photos through the parsonage windows.

"Can you confirm this was another brutal attack by the Wolfman?"

Sheriff Connie didn't recognize the reporter from *The Fox Hollow Post*, but he was a muscular thing with a jawline as strict as the high fade in his hair. Ex-military, she figured.

"Dogman," Connie corrected, immediately hating herself and then hating Bomber.

"So you confirm?" the reporter asked, though it was more a statement and he scribbled furiously in his notebook.

"No, I don't confirm," Connie said. "There's nothing I can share with you at this time, other than that we're still unsure of the whereabouts of Pastor Mast. We have no reason to suspect he's in any danger, but we are taking all necessary precautions."

She didn't feel bad lying to the reporters, given their respective papers' recent articles. To her, lying to liars was a net-zero. Two wrongs making a right. And besides, they knew she was lying anyway. The entire Fox Hollow P.D. wouldn't have been called in for "necessary precautions," but she wasn't going to give them an inch. Connie turned to head back to the church, while the reporters shouted more questions.

Tina Chen: "Is the Fox Hollow PD covering up a religious sex ring?"

Muscley Reporter: "Was the reverend eaten or just disemboweled by the Dogboy?"

Chen: "How many humans have been sex trafficked by the Third Reformed Church?"

Muscles: "How many more Fox Hollow citizens do you think will be slaughtered by the Wolf-Thing before your department comes up with any real answers?"

Sheriff Connie stopped and took a deep breath. Her attempt at soothing herself only oxygenated her rage. She turned slowly, ready to unleash a torrent, but something caught her eye. Creeping slowly down the road, as though trying to sneak past, was a white utility van. From the passenger seat, Bomber Merridan stared at her, slackjawed.

8:54 a.m.

"We're not stopping," Buck said.

"We have to stop," Bomber said. "There are police everywhere. Something happened to Pastor Mast."

"That's exactly why we can't stop."

"Pull the van over," Bomber demanded.

Buck complied and rolled the van to a halt on the dirt shoulder.

"We'll only be a minute," Bomber said. "I want to make sure the pastor is okay."

"There's no 'we,'" Buck said. "You can go, but I'm out of here. Us Cryptos Guys are outlaws and cops don't like people in our line of work. We tend to fan the flames of fear. Make folks paranoid, ya know? Cops tend to aim for the opposite effect. Most of 'em anyhow."

Bomber was aware of Buck's numerous run-ins with local law enforcement over his tenure as a monster hunter. The line of work went hand-in-hand with flagrant and repetitive trespassing and, as Bomber now realized, the utilization of military-grade munitions, which he was all too sure Sheriff Connie would also frown upon. Bomber had always thought trading barbs with local law enforcement was just part of the drama built into Buck's videos. Another juicy angle to draw in viewers. It hadn't occurred to him that a star like Buck might face real consequences after too many infractions.

"Can you just wait here a minute?"

Buck shook his head. "Sorry, bud. No can do. I saw a couple reporters down there. One of those cameras gets a shot of me and my cover is blown. You'll have to find your own way home."

Bomber sighed. Pastor Mast had always been kind to him, even after Sly had convinced him to toilet-paper the parsonage in the fall of their Junior year. Maybe "kind" was the wrong word. Paternally stern. But fair. In the wake of their recent conversation, Bomber felt compelled to check in on him.

Bomber shut his door and Buck peeled away, kicking up a trail of dust and gravel. With the taste of road dust in his mouth, Bomber walked back to the Third Reformed Church and slipped behind a crowd of rubberneckers, held back by a loose barricade of Fox Hollow police cruisers. Most of the crowd was dressed in their Sunday best, members of the pastor's congregation wondering what was going on. At the far end of the crowd, the two Coughlin twins hovered like fat buzzards, craning their necks to sniff out any future business for their father.

"Mr. Interim Mayor," someone called.

Bomber looked over to see a muscular man in a dark suit coming toward him with a hand-held recorder. The man looked like a professional assassin.

"John Trojan. *The Fox Hollow Post.* Can you comment on this morning's Wolfman attack?"

Bomber winced at the words, partially at the misnomer and partially because it confirmed his fear. He opened his mouth to speak, but was cut off, literally and figuratively, by Sheriff Connie who'd run between squad cars to insert herself between Bomber and the reporter.

"You most certainly cannot."

She took Bomber by the shoulder and guided him through the crowd. Not gently either. Like a football player, she stiff-armed him toward the end zone. On the other end of the squad cars, she let him go, but not before adding a small shove.

"What gives?" Bomber asked.

"What are *you* doing here?" Sheriff Connie asked. She continued walking up the concrete path toward the parsonage door. Bomber followed but then she stopped and spun on him.

"I was passing by," Bomber said. "I saw the police cars and Pastor Mast is a friend. I was worried."

"I saw you. In the van. Whose van was that?" Connie pressed.

"Just a friend from out of town," Bomber said. No lie there.

"A friend you broke curfew with? To go monster hunting?" Connie pointed to Bomber's apple-drape camo hoodie.

Bomber blushed. Busted. "I guess so."

"You guess so?" Sheriff Connie got right up in his face and stuck a firm finger in his chest. "I could arrest you for that. You just don't get it, do you? This isn't high school, you cocky prick. This isn't the goddamn Bomber Show and we aren't your supporting cast. I'm the Sheriff of this town." She removed the finger from his chest and pounded at the badge on hers. "The damn Sheriff. I put the curfew in place and you can be damn sure I expect it to be followed."

"It's not that big of a deal—"

"It *is* a big deal, you arrogant twit!" Connie spat. "For three reasons. One. By some stroke of voodoo, black-magic bullshit, you're the *de facto* Mayor right now. So if people see you disregarding the rules, they think they can do it, too. Especially when it's you, cause you're not important enough to get away with it. So then I have to be the bad guy and clean up your mess. Which leads me to Number Two. I don't want to clean up any more messes. I don't want my officers to have to clean up any more dead bodies, either. Don't mistake this for caring about you. I couldn't give two shits if you get slaughtered, but it makes my guys squeamish to clean up guts and it gives poor Officer Hodges bad dreams, which then I have to hear about and pretend to care about and I'm not a damn psychologist." She drew a breath. "Now, Number Three. And this is a big one. You're now a suspect. Yeah. Congratulations. Because you couldn't stay home, you now have no alibi for where you were when Pastor Mast disappeared. So maybe I should take you in after all."

Connie was winded and put her hand on her pistol for dramatic effect.

"Disappeared?" Bomber asked.

"Yes," Connie conceded. "Disappeared. Missing. Gone. The parsonage is a disaster. Our mystery animal dragged him away, apparently."

"I don't think this was just some animal," Bomber said. He quickly continued before Connie could get her eyes all the way to the back of their sockets. "And I don't mean Dogman stuff either. I think there's more going on here."

He thought back to the fox on the phone.

"What do you mean?" Connie asked. She folded her arms across her chest.

"We drove by here last night and Pastor Mast was putting up a new message on the road sign," he said. "It read, 'The lesser of two evils, is still evil.' He'd come up with it during a talk we had yesterday afternoon. He was pretty proud of himself."

"So?"

Bomber pointed to the road sign. Discarded letters littered the lawn around the sign, gleaming under the midmorning sun. Only two words from the original message remained on the sign:

"*STILL EVIL*"

Sheriff Connie looked unimpressed.

"We've been here for almost an hour now," she said, pointing to the crowd of churchgoers beyond the police cars. "Any one of these folks could've walked over and done that. I saw those two Coughlin goons lurking around. That seems like something those Neanderthals would do."

Bomber couldn't deny it and probably would have agreed if he hadn't come armed with the knowledge of a miniature Dogman. He wished he had some way of presenting this knowledge in a believable way. Why couldn't the Dogman have been some ravenous beast? Why'd it have to talk, use cell phones, smoke cigarettes, and make horrible, though practical, fashion choices?

"We know it was an animal," Connie continued. "We found a pile of scat on the kitchen counter."

Bomber was thrown by this news.

"'A jackpot of excrement,'" Bomber whispered to himself.

"What?"

"Nothing," he said. "You say you found animal poop on the kitchen counter?"

"Yes," Connie said. "And it's doubtful it belongs to either of the Coughlin twins." She smiled slightly at her own joke.

"Well, that's good, isn't it?" Bomber asked. "You can test it to determine its origin, right?"

"Not me personally, but it's already on the way to the Cedar Mills DNR lab. We don't have the equipment here because a certain member of the Board of Aldermen blocked funding for it last year."

"Gloria?"

"Gloria," Connie said. She shook her head. "I might resign if that wench ends up mayor. She was worse than you in high school."

"People can change," Bomber said.

"You think Gloria has changed?"

"No, definitely not. I was talking about me."

"Sheriff?" Householder said. He'd just stepped out from the front door. "I thought you might want to see this—Oh, hey, Bomber."

Bomber waved.

Householder held up a clear plastic bag with a wad of blue fabric inside.

"What is it?" Sheriff Connie asked.

Householder dipped a pair of forensic tongs into the bag and lifted out the soiled cloth. It unfolded into the bottom half of a trouser leg.

"Found them in the Pastor's trash," Householder said.

"The mystery of the pornographer's pants is solved," Connie said. "You've done it, Sergeant. Except we knew the pant leg was missing and more than likely lost around here. The Pastor probably found it in the church lawn and threw it away."

Householder's smile faded. Connie felt bad for being callous.

"However," she said. "I hadn't considered the two drunks as suspects, but they certainly do have a motive. They're famous, I guess, and their story would be an embarrassment if it ever got out. Powerful folks don't like loose ends and they certainly don't like sitting in jail cells for hours. Good work, Sergeant."

Householder's smile came roaring back.

"Are you talking about the drunks from Longstreet's party?" Bomber asked.

Connie and Householder looked surprised.

"Pastor Mast told me about that, too," Bomber said, "when he was sharing his disdain for Carl Longstreet. They got into it pretty good after Cecil's funeral."

For the first time Bomber could remember, Connie didn't respond with an eyeroll.

"That's two motives linked to Mr. Longstreet," she said. "I'd say that warrants a social call." She pulled her car keys from her pocket and pointed one at Householder. "You're in charge until I'm back." She looked at Bomber, then at the church's sign. "And get someone to dust for prints on that marquee board. I want to know who the wise guy is."

"Yes, ma'am," Householder said and then jogged off to find a lower-ranking officer to boss around.

There was an awkward silence between Sheriff Connie and Bomber.

"I have one more question," Bomber said.

"What?" Connie asked, irritated.

"Can I get a lift home? My ride left me."

Connie looked at him. Then at the reporters waiting eagerly to harass them again. She couldn't have Bomber running his mouth unsupervised. She sighed, as though processing some great defeat.

"Come on."

9:25 a.m.

Pebbles pinged off the undercarriage of Sheriff Connie's Dodge Charger as it cruised over the loose gravel and potholes of 36th Street. Like everywhere in Fox Hollow, fruit trees lined the roadside, their uniform rows running off to the horizon. It was late in the picking season, but branches still hung low under the weight of Ida Reds, Goldrushes, and Northern Spies. Even on Sunday morning, Bomber occasionally spotted groups of migrant workers picking diligently as the rows zipped by.

Sheriff Connie hadn't said a word since they'd left the church. Bomber suspected she was still mad about his disregard for her curfew and unwillingness to share Buck's identity.

"What do you suppose he sees in her?" she asked suddenly.

"Sorry?"

"Bruce," Connie said. "What do you suppose he sees in Gloria? He's campaigning for her. I thought I raised him better. I thought he had more sense."

Bomber shifted in his seat and wondered if she truly wanted an answer. This woman who hated him was now asking his opinion on personal, family matters. He feared saying anything that could be misconstrued as an attack on her parenting. He wanted to make amends with Connie, but this was a precarious spot. Anything he said or did, could and would be used against him in a court of Connie.

"Well, I—" Bomber started.

"I can't figure out if he actually believes her rhetoric," Connie interrupted. "It doesn't take a rocket scientist to realize Gloria's literally Hitler. Gloria Hitler. That should be her name."

She looked at Bomber expectantly.

"I—um—" Bomber stammered.

"I mean, you above anyone else should know she's a monster. She doesn't care about anyone. She's just jonesing for more power. And Bruce is buying it, hook, line, and sinker."

Bomber took the opportunity to redirect the blame.

"Maybe he feels like the rest of us," he said. "Betrayed. Mr. Fox pulled the rug out from underneath the whole town when he sold the company, all to put more coin in his pocket. Makes you realize how much we're all at the mercy of a few select people. That kind of realization can make anyone's footing feel shaky. Evil as she may be, Gloria's saying the things a lot of people want to hear right now."

Connie gave him a look.

"That was surprisingly astute," she said.

"You get a pretty good pulse on people when you work at a small-town grocery store for seventeen years."

The tension in the car seemed to soften and Connie focused back on the road.

Bomber hadn't said what he'd been thinking. Having worked with Bruce for two years, he'd heard more than a few saucy comments about Connie's work obsession and had seen Bruce's dejected face every time Connie canceled or forgot a lunch date. Bruce would claim his frustration stemmed only from the fact that Connie's dedication to duty never elevated their standard of living—as if money were an acceptable conciliatory award for a mother's attention. Bomber was sure Bruce's political leanings, whether he knew it or not, were a bid for attention.

Bomber, too, wondered why Connie did it. The Sheriff of Fox Hollow was a thankless job, tainted further by the corrupt legacy of Ex-Sheriff Barnstorm. The town had not yet regained trust in the precinct, which is probably why Connie put in so many long hours.

He stared out the window and tried not to think about how he'd contributed to crippling Connie's self-esteem in school, and how that might have led to her obsessive need to succeed and impress. For a moment, Bomber allowed himself a fantasy where Connie thanked him begrudgingly for his role in shaping the strong woman she'd become. The fantasy made him feel ill the moment he thought it.

"Well, what kind of shit-show is this?" Connie grumbled, slowing the car to a roll.

Six women marched in a tight circle just outside the wrought-iron gates of Fox Mansion. They were dressed identically in black yoga pants and tight pink track jackets, half-zipped to showcase low-cut white tank tops and maximum cleavage. Their hairstyles, though varying in artificial color, were all the same. Long, meandering curls cascaded down their backs, barely covering the message, *Gloria Be To God*, screen-printed on their jackets. Their makeup, thick like warpaint and painstakingly applied, bore the toll of their endless marching. Perspiration caused primers, powders, glosses, concealers, and liners to sag and streak, exposing secret pimples, crow's feet, frown lines, bags, and the occasional cold sore. But they marched on in their knee-high designer boots, oblivious to their failing faces and hoisting picket signs high above their melting heads.

"End Illegal Pesticide Testing"

"No Blood For Applesauce"

"Hands Off My Junk, You Bum"

"Go Back To Your Dumpster, Oscar" (This one had a delightful rendering of Oscar The Grouch wearing a top hat and monocle.)

"Gotta hand it to Gloria," Connie said. "She's ruthless."

Gloria hadn't wasted time in her smear campaign against Carl. Within an hour of his funeral home speech, ads began running on the local country music station, casting the one-time homeless man as a disconnected elitist pig. Then, in direct contrast to the radio messages, she began circulating fliers featuring an image of the old millionaire picking through a local trash bin. The fliers made accusations of everything from trespassing and loitering to identity theft and indecent exposure.

Sheriff Connie crept the patrol car slowly toward the circling tiger-moms, who only relented after she was nearly on top of them. Connie lowered her window a few inches.

"Out of the way," she yelled, shooing them the way one might shoo a muddy dog. The women conceded, but not without icy stares and mouthed curses. One woman flipped them the bird.

"Real classy, Tammy," Connie shouted, pulling past them and up to the gate.

"You're not going to make them leave?" Bomber asked.

"As long as they stay on the road and don't go onto Carl's driveway, there really isn't anything I can do," Connie said.

"How do we get in?"

Connie pointed to a small squawk box, embedded in the stone where the gate met the high compound wall.

"Give it a buzz," she said.

Bomber hesitated. He had concerns about being mauled by tiger-moms. He was about to exit the car when the gates swung open unprompted, relieving him of his duty.

"Smile," Connie said, seeing Bomber's confusion. She pointed to a security camera mounted on the wall. "We're on closed-circuit TV."

"Carl has definitely tightened security since he bought the place," Bomber said.

The driveway was at least a quarter-mile long and cut through an enormous expanse of perfectly manicured lawn, which was possibly the largest chunk of land in Fox Hollow unoccupied by apple trees. The mansion resembled a classic southern plantation, plucked from a Dixie estate and dropped into the heart of the Midwest. In the tradition of antebellum architecture, a stately colonnade ran the full length of the building, its pillars supporting an ornate portico that shielded the front porch from sun and rain. Two rows of identically spaced windows lined both floors, most drawn tight with crimson curtains. In the center of the lawn was a bronze statue of an apple tree. Beneath it, a nude woman—also bronze—stretched erotically to pluck an apple from its branches. Coiled around the trunk, a serpent lured the woman into eternal damnation.

On the roof, Bomber could see several men in gray and green uniforms watching them through dark sunglasses. They were athletically built, with military-style patrol caps, and intimidating guns strapped across their chests. One appeared to be speaking into a radio.

"Carl's a paranoid fellow, I guess," Bomber said, pointing up at the security team.

Connie parked near the front door and left the car idling. She drew in several deep breaths with her eyes closed, the one useful stress-relieving trick she'd taken from a complimentary yoga class a few weeks back at the town's only studio, Wild Goose Yoga, owned and operated by the very same Tammy Schmidt who'd just flipped her the bird outside the mansion's front gate. The ninety-minute yoga session had revealed three things to Connie: she wasn't as flexible as she used to be, she was unrelatable to other women her age, and she was not above snickering at the accidental flatulence of otherwise prim and proper housewives. The post-stretch meditation had, however, proved useful and the deep-breathing technique became a favored coping method when faced with the unavoidable task of dealing with exceedingly stupid people.

"I'm going to let you come along," she finally said. "For two reasons. Number one: I don't trust you not to touch anything in my car."

Bomber nodded in agreement.

"And number two: Carl Longstreet is a famously chauvinistic ass-wipe. Unfortunately, he's also a rich, chauvinistic ass-wipe who donates a lot of money to the force. My force. I'm hoping he'll view you as something akin to a man and therefore open up about his parties, his guests, and his beef with Pastor Mast."

"Something *akin to* a man?"

"Just do me a favor and keep your mouth shut," Connie said. "No talk about Dogmen, no details about the disappearance, no mention of your 'jackpot of excrement' or whatever you called it."

Bomber reddened and Connie exited the car before he could respond.

The front door was flanked on each side by two regal stone foxes. Affixed to the door was a giant knocker, which to neither of their surprise was shaped like an apple, secured by a thick, brass ring.

"For Christ's sake, don't these people ever get sick of all the damn apples?" Connie asked. She lifted the giant knocker and rapped it against the door. While they waited, Bomber watched a group of Hispanic men work diligently on the mansion's landscaping. They were mostly middle-aged men and were all dressed in matching forest green polo shirts. Each shirt bore the same fox-head emblem, sewn over the right breast. The men stole nervous glances at Bomber and Connie. Bomber wondered if they were concerned about the legality of their work status and if they came from the same pool of migrant workers hired by Fox Applesauce Co. He raised his hand in a half wave and they immediately turned their backs.

Odd.

The door rattled. Someone on the other side was struggling with a series of locks and latches. The handle shook violently, followed by the sound of cussing and more latches being manipulated. This repeated several times before the door swung open, revealing an irritated Carl Junior.

"Apologies," he said, flattening wrinkles from his dark suit jacket. "The locks are from the original construction and can be tricky. Come in. Quickly."

"Why all the locks anyway?" Bomber asked. "We live in Fox Hollow, not Detroit."

Junior forced a smile, as they stepped inside. He scanned the lawn outside before closing the door and resetting the top-most lock.

"Security is paramount to Mr. Longstreet," he said. "Especially after the recent attacks."

"You call your dad 'Mr. Longstreet'?" Sheriff Connie asked.

"Mr. Longstreet insists upon it," Junior said. "At least until we know each other better."

The entrance opened into a large foyer, with a cathedral ceiling pierced by a spectacular crystal chandelier. At the center of the foyer, a larger bronze fox sat on a marble pedestal, howling lustfully at the chandelier above. The floors were also marble and polished to a high sheen. This was the room Bomber had only caught glimpses of as a child, waiting for his friend at the front door.

Two long hallways extended off each side of the foyer, each lined with closed doors of equal spacing. The symmetry of the setup reminded Bomber of a hotel and he wondered if each door hid identical rooms, with identical fixtures, furniture, and linens. Some doors were numbered. Perhaps relics from the brothel days.

On each side of the fox statue, rounded staircases hugged the foyer's exterior walls as they ascended to meet at a landing on the floor above. The stairs were covered in a stream of maroon carpet, patterned with green and yellow apples. It was an interior design atrocity and Bomber appreciated that Connie made no attempt to disguise her disgust.

"To what do we owe the pleasure of this visit?" Junior asked with half-hearted congeniality.

Bomber started to speak, but Connie shot him a look.

"We need to speak with your fath—with Mr. Longstreet about a few town matters," she said. "I assume he's here?"

"Mr. Longstreet is in the middle of a bath," Junior said. "I'd be happy to relay a message to him if you'd care to leave one."

"We'll wait," Connie said.

Junior smiled.

"It could be quite some time," Junior said. "He enjoys bathing very much—after so many years without."

"Tugs at the heartstrings," Connie said. "How about you go tell him we're here and he can decide how long he'd like to have a Sheriff's patrol car parked outside his front door. Ms. Glass and her pit vipers out front will have a field day with whatever story they concoct."

Junior's smile faded. "Stay right here," he ordered, then turned, clicking his heels together in a sharp, militaristic way, before starting up the stairs. Bomber and Connie watched until he disappeared over the landing of the floor above.

"Tool," Connie muttered.

A painting on the opposite wall caught Bomber's attention and he moved around the fox statue for a better look. The framed canvas stretched from floor to ceiling in the space between the stairs, the top shrouded in darkness from the shadow of the landing overhead. Several dim floor lights gave the figures on the canvas an eerie illumination.

The painting depicted a frontiersman, dressed head to toe in buckskins, towering over an indigenous woman on her back among several felled trees. The woman was backing away from the settler who had his axe raised high above his head, his manic eyes eliminating any confusion about his intent. The woman, however, showed no fear. Instead, her eyes were dagger-sharp, her mouth wide in a defiant yell. The crown of her head was covered in a strange headdress, woven with feathers and beads. She wore a colorfully patterned blanket like a poncho, secured with a leather sash adorned with bear claws and animal bones. The blanket spread like a wing over one raised arm and her knobbed finger pointed accusingly at her attacker. In the background, several other natives could be seen scattering into the trees, pursued by more settlers with muskets and axes and clubs.

Bomber read the tarnished placard at the bottom of the frame:

"The Curse Of Progress"
October 23, 1877
Silas Morgan Fox teaches European customs to local savages.

Connie stepped up beside Bomber.

"Pretty messed up," he said, his voice barely above a whisper, as though trying not to disturb the patrons of some fancy art gallery.

Connie made a noise in her throat that was equal parts annoyance and agreement.

"Have you ever seen this before?" Bomber asked.

Connie shook her head.

"No, but I'd heard about it," she said. "The Fox family and my tribe have a—complicated past." She spit on the painting.

Bomber looked at her, his jaw slack.

"You know what I like about this painting?" Connie asked. "Not a single apple in the whole damn thing."

Bomber laughed.

Connie smiled. Slightly.

"This is nice," Bomber said, meaning their brief connection.

"Shut up."

There were footsteps on the landing above and they moved back out near the statue. Bomber had to side step to avoid catching his temple on the sharp point of the fox's tail. Junior descended the stairs, looking more irritated than ever.

"Mr. Longstreet will be right down," he said. "I see you've been appreciating the artwork and not staying put, as I'd requested."

Bomber wasn't sure if he was referring to the painting in general or if he'd spotted Connie's loogey slinking down the canvas.

"I wouldn't call *that* art," Connie said.

"Mr. Longstreet sure loves his foxes and apples," Bomber said, trying to ease the tension.

"Obviously they were left here by the Fox family," Junior said. "Mr. Longstreet never took an interest in redecorating, so most of the artwork has remained in its original place."

"Mr. Fox didn't take anything with him?" Connie asked. "Why?"

Junior shrugged. "I've been told his departure was—hasty."

Carl appeared at the top of the landing. He was missing his trademark top hat, and his dangling monocle had been replaced by a pair of binoculars hanging around his neck.

"Junior, I've finally managed to get these aimed on-target," Carl shouted without looking down. "Those trollops are still out there. At least they had the courtesy to wear tight yoga pants. Hubba-hubba. Am I right?"

Junior coughed the way you do when you want someone to shut the hell up. Carl looked down to see his guests but didn't seem embarrassed in the slightest.

"Sheriff Connie, how nice of you to finally grace us with your presence. I only called thirty-one minutes ago," he said, pulling a gold pocket-watch from his tuxedo coat.

"You called?" Connie asked.

"Of course," Carl said. "Those women out there are a nuisance and I want them removed from my property immediately or else."

Connie's eyebrows raised.

"Or else what?" she asked, placing a hand on her pistol grip.

"Er—or else—" Carl stammered. "It was just a figure of speech. I want them off my grounds."

"Well, good news for you," Connie said. "Those women are not on your grounds. The road is a county road. They have every right to be there, as long as they're not destroying anything, publicly intoxicated, throwing feces, or being generally disturbing."

"I'm generally disturbed," Carl announced.

"I don't doubt that at all," Connie replied.

Junior checked his watch.

"Well, Sheriff," Carl said, "if there is nothing to be done about the harlots in the road and you didn't get my call, why exactly are you here?" He looked over at Bomber, as if noticing him for the first time. "And Mr. Interim Mayor, how good to see you again. I was unaware that police ride-alongs would be a perk of my new job." He sneered. "Or perhaps you were in Sheriff Connie's custody for other reasons?"

"We're here—" Bomber started, but Connie cut him off.

"We're here to ask you about a couple guests from your party the other night," she said. "The drunks who tried to break into The Third Reformed Church."

Carl chuckled. "You think those two might be somehow responsible for Pastor Mast's disappearance?"

"How did you know about it?" Bomber asked before Connie could.

Carl shook his head and ran fingers through his gray, slicked-back hair. "This is Fox Hollow," he said. "I probably knew about it before you did. And I can assure you, my former guests had nothing to do with it. In fact, they were beyond grateful to the good reverend for not pressing charges. Getting caught in a church could be quite an embarrassment in their line of work. Besides, they departed as soon as they left the police station. Junior here brought them to the airport himself."

Junior nodded and Connie jotted something down in a notepad.

"So you believe Pastor Mast's disappearance was the responsibility of *someone* and not *something* this time?" Carl asked, raising an eyebrow.

Bomber opened his mouth but was stopped cold with a glare from Connie.

"We're exploring multiple leads," she said.

"No, no," Carl scolded. "I'd like to hear what Mr. Merridan has to say on the subject. It occurs to me now why he's along for the ride. No doubt he has some interesting theories, anchored on his belief in fantastical fauna?"

Carl and Junior looked at Bomber expectantly.

"Well—" he started. Connie shook her head. "Well—would I be able to use the bathroom? I've gotta 'go' pretty fiercely." He really didn't but could think of no better way to take himself out of the spotlight.

Junior looked to Carl, who nodded. "Follow me," Junior

sighed.

Junior was uneasy leaving Connie alone with Carl. He walked fast, guiding Bomber down the western hall, past the identical doors—their only difference being the hotel-like numbers.

"Are these numbers from when this place was a whorehouse?" Bomber asked.

Junior said nothing.

At the end of the hall, they turned left into an identical corridor. The doors down this hall were mostly unmarked until they reached one that read "WATER CLOSET." Junior pulled out a large ring of keys, unlocked the door, and ushered Bomber inside.

"Be quick," he grunted.

Bomber closed the door and stood over the toilet in the tiny restroom. On the other side of the toilet was a small window blocked by—surprise, surprise—apple-themed curtains.

Clack, clack.

The muffled sound of wood striking wood came through the window and Bomber, ever so slightly, pulled the curtains apart and peered out. The view was of nothing in particular, only the side yard of the mansion, some decorative bushes, and the enormous stone wall beyond.

Clack, clack, clack.

The sound came again, but this time it was off to the side. Outside of the field of vision allowed by the small bathroom window. Bomber pressed his face close but could see nothing.

Clack, clack.

Suddenly, two men came into view. They were dressed like the landscapers he'd seen earlier, in dirty jeans and worn work boots. Both men carried rakes, but held them low, where the metal meets the wood pole. One man was backpedaling, holding his rake high above his head and parallel to the ground. The second man pursued him, hammering blow after blow with his own rake against the first. Finally, the defending man's arm slipped and the next swing caught him crisply on the crown of the head. The man yelped. Bomber winced. The attacking man's lips were moving, but Bomber could hear nothing. Instead, the victorious man struck a few poses with his rake, as though instructing the other on what he could've done better. The defeated man rubbed his head and nodded dolefully.

There was a knock at the door and Bomber jumped.

"Hurry up in there."

Bomber flushed the toilet and exited the small bathroom.

"I didn't hear any peeing," Junior said.

"I sat down to pee," Bomber said. "I don't like when weirdos are listening in."

Junior locked the door behind him and they made the trek back to the front door in silence. In the foyer, Connie was sitting on the staircase with her chin in her hands, while Carl drifted wistfully around the room ranting about his marvelous mansion.

"You'd be surprised at the number of secret rooms and passages in this place," he was saying. "A real labyrinth."

Junior coughed to announce their return, derailing Carl's train of thought.

"Ah, yes. I guess the point I was trying to make, fanciful fairy-tale creatures aside," he looked at Bomber as he said this, "is I'm certain the real culprits are those conniving Cedar Mills teenagers. Spawns of Satan. The whole lot of them."

"We'll look into it," Connie said. She stood and motioned Bomber toward the door.

"When I'm mayor, I'm going to build a wall to keep those little bastards out," Carl yelled, suddenly all worked up.

Junior deflated him with an angry look and Bomber noted a hint of fear in the old millionaire.

Junior stepped to the front door and opened it a crack. He poked his head out and looked around, then opened it further.

"I hope you got the answers you were looking for," he said in a way that suggested he didn't hope for that at all.

"We didn't really—" Connie started.

"Oh, shit! Get out, fast," Junior shouted, shooing them both out the door.

Confused, Connie and Bomber stumbled through the door, which slammed behind them. They could hear locks being fastened and Junior's steady cursing.

"What was that about?" Bomber asked.

Connie pointed to the front lawn. On the other side of the

"Original Sin" statue, Tina Chen was snapping pictures with a comically large telephoto lens.

"This is private property," Connie yelled, "and you don't have permission to be here."

Tina Chen was already on a dead run across the lawn, back toward the gate, which had inadvertently been left open.

They were descending the stone stairs back to the patrol car when there was a shout from the side yard. They turned to find one of the Hispanic landscapers running toward them, with another man in hot pursuit.

"*Cuidado con el perro del infierno,*" the man shouted hysterically.

The second man was quickly on him and wrapped his arms around his panicked friend's chest. The hysterical man struggled and then relented, allowing himself to be pulled back.

"*El solo esta loco,*" the second man called, spinning a finger near his own temple.

"This town '*esta loco,*'" Connie said, as they climbed back into her patrol car.

12:30 p.m.

Bruce felt anxious. And when Bruce felt anxious, he liked to eat. He sat alone at his usual table in Harold's Hamburger Shack, listening to the chants coming from outside. The view from his seat allowed him to see a good stretch of Main Street, almost to the parking lot at Marty's Market, where he'd need to return within the half hour.

The city blocks between were littered with political endorsement signs, placed by residents and store owners declaring their allegiances. People wore T-shirts, hats, pins, jackets, and novelty socks promoting their candidate of choice wherever they went or slapped divisive bumper stickers on their modest sedans and minivans. Public altercations between the rival factions were becoming the norm. Tensions were high.

The curfew had done little to deter the Longstreet supporters, who quickly took a "you can't take our freedoms" stance, leading to an actual increase in the evening and nighttime activity around town. Many on Team Longstreet also began exercising their Second Amendment rights, making a point to open-carry whatever they deemed appropriate from their home arsenals. They claimed the guns were for protection, but it was no secret they enjoyed the nervous looks from their free-loving rivals on Team Gloria.

Team Gloria—or "The Glass-Jaws," as Team Longstreet called them, for their perceived fragility—were not as adept at direct confrontation. Instead, they'd begun an insurgency of sorts, perpetrating acts of yard-sign destruction, thievery, pro-Gloria graffiti, and other stunts of petty vandalism. Their major conflict with the Longstreeters had little to do with the candidates' actual policies and more to do with the curfew defiance. They feared if the beast kept claiming victims, it'd keep coming back for easy meals. They argued that if people stayed home and cut off the creature's food source, perhaps it would move on to massacre a different town instead. The Longstreeters were quick to point out that Cecil Merridan had been attacked before sundown, Pastor Mast at his home, and poor Ms. Carol Meyers had been attacked both at home *and* during the day. Neither side actually listened to the other, so argument of logic went unheard.

Bruce's anxiety stemmed from the rising tensions. He'd told himself it was all necessary. No meaningful change could come without conflict. Old archaic ideologies, like cornered animals, would not die easily. He looked down at his unopened burger. Then to the empty seat across from him.

He checked his phone.

"*Still coming?*" He texted his mom. He waited for the three dots indicating a pending response, but they never came.

The chants from outside were louder now. Through the windows, Bruce could see a group of protesters marching circles on the sidewalk in front of the restaurant. News of the attacks had spread across the county, prompting unwanted attention. A day ago, a group of professional animal rights agitators had arrived from Cedar Mills to ensure the ethical treatment of whatever species the murderous beast turned out to be. Known as The Coalition for Animal Safety, Security and Environmental Sustainment, or The Coalition of A.S.S.E.S. for short, their members were easily recognized by their dirty dreadlocks, tight man buns, loose woman buns, gauged ear piercings, wobbly braless breasts, and the pungent scents of essential oils. They'd established a regular protest outside of Harold's Hamburger Shack, attempting to kill two birds with one stone—though they'd never use that phrase—until more information on the beast came to light. They marched endlessly with large poster boards depicting sad, baby cows being hacked to bits or the image of an adorable werewolf pup, with big sad eyes. Their presence had already incited several altercations with regular townsfolk. In every instance, cameras from *The Fox Howler* had been there to capture the "barbarity" inflicted upon the Coalition of A.S.S.E.S. by gun-wielding Longstreeters who were just trying to get a quick lunch. Harold stood at the window and shook his head.

"Quite a sight, isn't it?"

Bruce turned to find Gloria Glass standing behind him. His chest tightened. She was dressed in a form-fitting, bright green pencil skirt with a matching blazer. The white blouse underneath was unbuttoned just a little too low. Her hour-glass figure struck a pose under her long blonde hair which had been piled high on her head in a powerful up-do, every strand perfectly placed. Two wisps hung down from each temple, framing her face seductively. She was flanked on each side by two beautiful women in black pantsuits and dark shades. Bruce felt the immediate desire to gain her approval or impress her by saying something smart and witty.

"What?" he croaked.

"There's change in the air," Gloria said, looking proudly out the window. "You can smell it." She sniffed the air and turned up her nose. "Unfortunately 'it' smells like dead animal meat."

Bruce discreetly slid his tray to the side, trying to hide his uneaten burger.

"May I?" Gloria asked, motioning to the seat across from him. "Or are you expecting someone?"

"By all means," he said. "I wasn't expecting anyone." He wished it didn't feel so true.

Gloria took a seat and her bodyguards took up positions at the end of the table facing out into the restaurant, their firm butts calling for Bruce's attention. He fought the urge to look, focusing instead on the table in front of him.

Gloria smiled.

"In school," she said, "I wouldn't have been caught dead sitting with a guy like you."

Bruce chuckled nervously.

"Don't laugh," Gloria chided like a patient mother. "It's not okay. I was a different person then. A bad person. But people can change, Bruce. Do you believe people can change?"

"Yes," Bruce said. He was amazed that Gloria Glass even knew his name. "But why are you telling me all of this?"

"Two reasons," Gloria said. "Number one: I wasn't particularly kind to your mother in school, which I deeply regret. And if I'm going to be mayor, we're going to cross paths a lot more. I'd like very much for you to help me convince her that I *am* sorry. Can you do that for me?"

"Yes," Bruce said again. This was not at all the heartless succubus his mom and Bomber had warned him about.

"Two: A little bird has told me you've become quite the advocate for my campaign. Is that correct?"

Bruce blushed. "Yes, ma'am." He looked over and noticed Harold was no longer watching the protesters. Instead, he was watching their secret meeting, but still shaking his head.

"Wonderful," Gloria smiled. She leaned forward over the table, pushing her cleavage to new heights. Bruce tried desperately to maintain eye contact. "I'd like to offer you a secret position on my campaign."

"A secret position?"

"Yes," she smiled. "Mr. Longstreet may have the money, but we have the cunning. I need you to be my Guerilla Marketing Manager. As the former mascot of Fox Hollow High School, you have a unique talent for rallying a crowd. Plus your job at Marty's puts you smack-dab in the main hub of the town. You'd be perfect at it."

"I—I guess I can try," Bruce said. He smiled. "I've kinda already started actually."

Gloria reached forward and patted his hand. "I know you have, hon," she said.

Bruce melted.

"I do need to ask you one favor," Gloria said.

"Anything."

"You still have your Foxy costume, right?" Gloria asked.

Bruce nodded. The school had permitted Bruce to keep the costume after he graduated, as they had intentions of upgrading the aging Foxy.

"Excellent," she said. "As you know, the first debate between myself and Mr. Longstreet will be happening in just a few days. I'd like you to attend and I think it would be wonderful fun if you attended as Foxy. You know, rally up my side of the crowd."

"Won't that make it look like the school is endorsing your campaign?" Bruce asked. "I'm not sure if I'd be allowed—"

"Oh, who cares what the school thinks?" Gloria said. "It's easier to ask for forgiveness than permission. A good Guerilla Marketing Manager is a man of action. Am I right?"

"I make all kinds of costumes for ComicCon. I could make you a different—"

"A good Guerilla Marketing Manager is a man of action," Gloria repeated.

Bruce nodded. "I'll be there," he said. "Foxy will be there."

Gloria smiled a big white smile. She tapped the table and her bodyguards took a step out. She got up from her seat, smoothed her skirt, and turned to face Bruce again.

"One last thing," she said. "Anyone working on my campaign, secret or not, shouldn't be seen eating in a blood-thirsty, trash-hole establishment like this."

With that, she exited the Hamburger Shack with her two bodyguards in tow. Bruce stared hungrily at his still-wrapped burger for a full minute, digesting what had just happened and nothing else. He gave Harold a helpless shrug as he discarded the burger into the waste bin, stacked his tray, and pushed through the exit.

12:36 p.m.

An urgent town council meeting had been called and, despite the dire circumstances, the Board of Aldermen had all been rather sour about having their Sunday interrupted. All except Patrick McConnell, who was business as usual. Upon arrival, he'd callously handed Bomber a stack of legal documents, which he informed was a stipulation to Cecil Merridan's last will and testament, as well as a quitclaim deed transferring ownership of Cecil's home and land to the Fox Applesauce Corporation. The stipulation had been inexplicably added the month prior. Bomber was to have the estate cleared of personal belongings within two weeks when it was scheduled to be razed, cleared, and absorbed into Orchard #37. A process that was already underway with Ms. Carol Meyer's property.

Sheriff Connie had kept the meeting agenda focused on what information could and could not be released to the public through a press conference to be held within the hour. The debate between her and McConnell had become heated, to say the least, with Sheriff Connie wishing to share pertinent info only, while omitting anything that might cause widespread panic. McConnell's stance was to omit everything entirely and pretend the situation was normal, going so far as to suggest they push the narrative that Pastor Mast had answered an urgent call from the Lord and was off building orphanages in the Congo or "some crap like that" for the foreseeable future. Much to everyone's surprise, Bomber finally stepped in and laid out the course of action to be taken. Sheriff Connie was to provide a bare minimum of information to satisfy curiosity and ease the fear of the town. McConnell would then address the crowd about increased travel restrictions and a tightening of the curfew, so as not to appear that Sheriff Connie was instituting martial law. Much to Bomber's surprise, the plan was accepted, giving his confidence a much-needed shot in the arm. It was then unanimously decided that Bomber should be nowhere near the press conference due to the likelihood of him spouting off something ridiculous about Dogmen and blowing the whole thing entirely. With his afternoon now clear, Bomber called Buck at the hotel and arranged for them to meet at the Appleseed

Diner. They had much to discuss about the night prior and the morning's events.

When he arrived at the diner, Bomber was surprised to find Jeanie's name painted over on the front window. The restaurant had been renamed "Terry's Appleseed Diner." Terry Smedleck was the diner's former dishwasher and Jeanie's apprentice chef. He was a wiry little thing, barely out of high school, but already balding. While seating Bomber at his window booth, Terry gleefully reported that Jeanie was pregnant again and had immediately thrown in the towel, both literally and figuratively, when she'd received the news. As it turns out, seven children in a single-parent home is the sweet spot in regard to state-sponsored income assistance programs and she needed only to quit her job to fall beneath the necessary income requirements. Her confidence in the financial leap-of-faith was further bolstered by her fervent belief in an inevitable Gloria Glass victory, which would mean the rollout of a new municipal welfare program to pad her income further.

"A nine-month lottery ticket," she'd told Terry, as she fastened a Gloria campaign button that read "Voting For Two," just above her tiny baby bump, which was more French fries than fetus.

Bomber decided to wait for Buck with a slice of Jeanie's warm apple pie, which was now Terry's warm apple pie and, though the same pie, decidedly less appealing. The events of the day ran through his head, dominated by the image of a fox on a phone.

The mere fact that he was thinking about a talking fox made him feel utterly insane and he was almost grateful when his concentration was broken by the sound of shattering porcelain.

"Jesus, Ron-Boy, calm down," Bomber heard Terry plead. Bomber peeked around the booth to find Ron-Boy Carson's enormous frame looming over a table of four teenagers, apparently on a double date. His fists were mallets, clenched at his side, and his face was a deep crimson, which clashed with the burnt orange Fox Hollow First trucker cap on his head, a flashy piece of campaign flare worn by the most ardent Longstreet supporters. Ron-Boy's family had been dirt-floor-poor for as long as Bomber could remember, so why they'd support a candidate with no sympathy for the lower class was beyond him.

"You Cedar Mills sons-a-bitches ain't welcome in here," Ron-Boy spat.

"It ain't your place, Ron-Boy," Terry begged, while staying well out of range of Ron-Boy's massive mitts. "They're paying customers, so they sure-as-shit *are* welcome here."

"Goddammit, Terry, these Cedar Mills punks are stealing all our jobs," Ron-Boy growled, which was ironic because he'd literally never held a job. His jowls shook and he squinted hard like an actor trying to remember his lines. "And you saw what they did to ol' Pastor Mast last night."

"You were at the Third Reformed Church this morning?" Terry asked.

"Well—no. We ain't allowed back yet. But I heard about it," Ron-Boy said. "Heard it was Cedar Mills punks. Buncha little terrorists if you ask me."

"Why don't you just sit down and eat your meal, Ron-Boy?" Terry pleaded.

"I ain't eatin' next to these dirtbags, they make me sick. Makes me sick you'd even serve 'em here."

One of the teens murmured something and Ron-Boy lost it.

"What'd you say to me, you little shit?" he snapped. He leaned over their table, his enormous belly hanging out the bottom of a "What Happens In Vegas, Stays In Vegas" t-shirt. It settled in a blob on the tabletop, threatening to overtake the plates on either side. The two girls recoiled in horror. With a swing of his great paw, Ron-Boy grabbed one of the boys by the back of the head and forced it down hard into his meatloaf special. The boy sputtered profanity and mashed potatoes as he came up for air.

"Y'all punks need to learn yer place," Ron-Boy snarled.

Half the other patrons of the diner were ignoring the outrageous scene, while the other half watched through their phone screens as they recorded the whole ordeal. Only one person spoke up, but it wasn't a voice of reason.

"Get 'em, Ron-Boy," came a questionably female voice from the booth in back.

"Oh, I'll get 'em, Ma," Ron-Boy called back.

Terry spotted Bomber peeking around the booth and his eyes pleaded for help. Bomber looked sadly at what remained of his mediocre slice of apple pie.

"Nobody's getting anybody," Bomber called, sliding from the booth.

"This doesn't concern you, grocery boy," Ron-Boy said.

He swung his belly toward Bomber and it squeaked across the glossy tabletop.

"Unless one of you is a Dog-Boy," he said, pointing at the teens and then laughing, delighted by his joke.

"Clever," Bomber said. "But it actually does concern me. As acting mayor, all matters of Fox Hollow concern me. Especially acts of harassment and assault by the town's resident cretin."

Terry shook his head. Two customers, who'd sat down only moments before the row, put down their menus and made for the door. Terry shouted an apology. There was a terrific grunting from the back booth, followed by the shrill screech of bare skin against cheap vinyl. Finally, two pale legs the size of tree trunks emerged from the booth, followed shortly by Big Mama Carson. At the edge of the booth, she rocked herself to her feet and steadied her belly, which was tucked into a pair of dirty, teal-colored short-shorts, serving double duty as spandex. Her shirt was a yellow tent and read "Don't Tread On Me" above a coiled snake. The snake was divided and misshapen, with portions lost in the folds of fat and its head drowning in a large ketchup stain.

"What'd you say to my boy?" she growled.

"Don't get all riled up, Mama," Ron-Boy said, suddenly very docile. "Your dia-bee-tees, remember?"

"Hush up, Ronald, I had my sodas, I'll be fine."

She waddled down the row of booths.

"Now, I'll ask you again," she said, out of breath from her ten-foot trek. "What'd you jus' say to my boy?"

Bomber gulped.

"I said, he has no right to be harassing these kids. They're just trying to have a quiet dinner," Bomber said.

"We're not kids, you moron," one of the Cedar Mills girls snapped.

Mama Carson laughed.

"See," she said. "See all that sass. Even to you. And you tryin' to help 'em. They come around here talkin' down to everyone and scarin' folks right outta their minds and our very own mayor wants to take their side. Not only that, but he's going to go around insulting my boy, even though he knows right-well that my boy's simple."

"I ain't simple, Mama," Ron-Boy said, his cheeks reddening.

"Sure you're not, boy," she said, with the flick of her wrist. "But you, Mr. Fake-Ass-Mayor, *must* be simple if you think yer gonna call my boy a 'crouton' and get away with it."

"That's not what I—"

"Come on, Ronald, defend your honor, boy," she said to her son, who was now standing deflated behind her.

Ron-Boy straightened as best he could.

"Right, Mama," he said, his fists balled into meat clubs once again. He squeezed, with some difficulty, around his mother and squared up in front of Bomber. The bells above the entrance chimed and Bomber imagined more customers hurrying out to avoid being witnesses to his impending murder.

"I'm not looking for a fight," Bomber said, raising both hands.

Ron-Boy cocked back one of his mighty mallets, reeling back for a lumbering swing. Bomber instinctively raised both arms to his face, closed his eyes, and braced for impact. There was a sickening thwack of flesh impacting flesh, followed by a tremendous bellow and a thud that shook the floor and rattled dishes.

Big Mama Carson shrieked.

"I've been accosted," Ron-Boy screamed. He was a pile on the floor pinching his nose, which spurted blood between gasps.

Buck stood next to Bomber, still holding his post-impact pose, as though surprised by his own act.

"You struck my boy," Mama Carson screamed. She grabbed a plate from the Cedar Mills teens and smashed the top half against the table, splattering them with meatloaf, mashed potatoes, and shards of porcelain. She gripped the remaining jagged, half-moon in her hand like a great claw.

"I'm warning you, lady," Buck said. "I know Krav Maga."

He tensed his hands into an odd bird-claw posture.

"Figures you two commies would be mixed up with the Russians," Mama Carson shouted and started slashing at the air in front of her.

Bomber and Buck backpedaled around the tables in full retreat.

"You cut it out now, Miss Carson," Terry shouted. He was standing near the service window in the back. A telephone was pressed to his ear, its cord disappearing through the window. "I'm calling the cops right this minute."

"Yer bluffin'," Mama Carson yelled, her bloodshot eyes still locked on Buck.

"I ain't. I just bought this place. Can't have you tearing it down on Day One," he said. "I know you don't want any trouble for Ron-Boy either. You guys pack up and leave and I'll hang up this phone right now."

Mama Carson seethed. Her belly heaved violently, threatening to pull loose from the cocoon of her unflattering shorts.

"Your meal is on the house if you go right now," Terry added.

A switch flipped. Mama Carson straightened up, tossing her dinnerware weaponry onto a nearby table.

"Get up," she said to Ron-Boy, who was still whimpering on the blood-stained carpet. "Turns out you jus' gotta rough some folks up around here to get a little justice."

She helped Ron-Boy to his feet, nearly losing her balance as well. The two of them shuffled toward the door, with Big Mama's flip flops sounding their departure.

"This ain't over, Mr. Phony Mayor," Big Mama said. "We gonna have words next time I need groceries."

The bells announced their exit and Bomber sighed, knowing she was right. Buck tried to apologize for the violence, but Terry was too busy bouncing between the remaining customers, comping meals and making apologies of his own.

"Do you really know Krav Maga?" Bomber asked, as they returned to his booth. The air hissed from the seats in a long sigh of relief.

"Not in the slightest," Buck said, shaking out the hand he'd used to strike Ron-Boy. "Haven't been in a fight in years. Hurts something awful, to tell you the truth. May I?" He pointed to Bomber's glass of ice water. Without waiting for a response, he slid it over and placed his fingers deep into the glass.

Bomber proceeded to fill Buck in on the developments of the day. He told him about Pastor Mast's disappearance—which Bomber was referring to as an "abduction"—about Sheriff Connie's minimal, but monumental, concession that something strange was afoot, about the "jackpot of excrement," and finally about the odd trip to the Fox Family Mansion. Buck was particularly interested in the mansion and asked questions about its layout and security.

"To be honest, it felt like a tacky apple-themed hotel," Bomber said. "And the grounds maintenance crew was extremely strange and undisciplined."

Bomber picked up his fork and pushed the remaining pie around his plate.

"What's eating you?" Buck asked.

Bomber sighed. "This election is getting ugly. I'm disappointed in a lot of folks I thought I knew."

"Your town is completely bat-shit," Buck said, swirling his fingers around the ice cubes.

"It wasn't always like this," Bomber said. "Fox Hollow used to be a nice place to live. As American as apple pie, as they say."

Buck considered this as he pulled a wad of napkins from the table's dispenser.

"Are you sure it was great for everyone?" he asked. "From what I've seen, this town has some deep-seated anger issues. Like some real next-level tribal stuff. In my experience, that type of resentment doesn't come out of nowhere."

The word *tribal* hung with Bomber a moment, but he couldn't place why.

"In your experience as a Bigfoot hunter?" Bomber asked.

"I know that's sarcasm," Buck said, "but yes, as a Bigfoot hunter. But also in my experience as a human. This job has taken me into parts of this country you don't ever hear about. Poor towns and villages, tucked into the back corners. The fringes of society. I've seen whole towns without electricity. Honest to God.

Most of those people don't live there because they want to. They live there because they have to. Or they don't know where else to go, what else to do. Sure, America is great and all, but it was never great for them. It's a fallacy to cast a rosy net of nostalgia over everyone."

Bomber thought again about the awful way he'd treated Connie and her friends in school. About the "practical jokes" he and Sly had played and the high likelihood they'd been the only ones laughing. And then he had the hard realization that, perhaps, what he'd always mistaken as good-natured ribbing about his Dogman quest, was not so good-natured at all. Perhaps he wasn't as well-liked in town as he thought.

"I think it's pretty safe to say, whatever it was you saw in the orchard last night took Pastor Mast," Buck said.

Bomber felt a lump in his throat. There was nothing he could have done at the time or any way he could have known where his inaction would lead, but maybe if he hadn't shut his eyes to it, the evil wouldn't have been allowed to persist.

"We need to come clean to Sheriff Connie," Bomber said. He was matter of fact about it and clinked his fork resolutely on his dirty plate. "And if she doesn't believe us, we make it public right away."

Buck pumped his hands in front of him. "Let's not be hasty. People around here already think you're nuts. What makes you think they'll believe you now?"

"I don't care if they believe me or not," Bomber said. "Carl and Gloria are using these attacks as a wedge to divide the town. It's my duty to provide the people of Fox Hollow with the truth, wherever I can. Even if they won't believe it."

"Give me three days," Buck said. "Give me three days—with your help, of course—to find this *thing*. If we're no closer to finding it after three days, we can tell Sheriff Connie and she can go ahead with having you committed to a psych ward."

Bomber nodded.

"Three days," Bomber said. "But no more splitting up out there. No more going off on your own to *investigate something*. When we're out there, we stick together."

"Fair," Buck said.

The Cedar Mills teens were heading for the door and, despite their incident with Ron-Boy, seemed quite upbeat. Bomber could only assume Terry had comped their meals, too. One of the girls veered off and approached their table. She wasn't more than sixteen and wore her makeup thick like a mask, dulling small ranges of acne across her over-blushed cheeks. She had all the self-confidence of a filtered photo and smiled insincerely as she looked them both over.

She zeroed in on Bomber.

"Your big mouth got my jeans ruined," she spat, pointing to a small red stain on her pant leg. "My dad'll be sending you a dry-cleaning bill, loser."

To drive her point home, she reached over and flipped Bomber's plate into his lap.

"Oops," she said, with the sarcasm of a thousand blazing tweens.

Satisfied, she turned and marched out, her friends cackling behind her.

"I might vote for Longstreet, just to get that fence," Bomber grumbled.

Buck slapped the table dramatically.

"No distractions," he commanded. "We need to focus on the task at hand. The one true threat to Fox Hollow. The Dogman. Or Foxboy. Or whatever the hell. We start tonight."

11:07 p.m.

It was late when Sheriff Connie finally made it home, an occurrence that wasn't unusual before, but had now evolved into routine. She was tired, but most of all she was irritated. Her drive home had proved just how many people were ignoring the curfew she'd put in place. One home had been hosting a fraternity-style party on their front lawn, complete with strobe lights, thumping music, tiki torches, red Solo cups, and an iced-up keg in a kiddy-pool. The party was dotted with the orange hats of Longstreeters.

Screw 'em, she thought. *Let 'em get eaten.*

Then she thought of all the paperwork a "Person-Gets-Eaten Incident" requires and was filled with momentary dread. She shook it off, along with her shoes inside the front door. The lights were off—all except the sliver of light coming from under Bruce's door.

"Okay," she whispered to herself. "Do what you need to do."

Her first order of business was to apologize to Bruce for missing lunch—again. He surely was aware by now of the incident surrounding Pastor Mast, so Connie hoped he'd understand.

She gave his door a soft knock, having learned her lesson about entering a teenage boy's bedroom unannounced.

"Bruce?" she called.

No answer.

She pushed the door open and gasped.

The smell was like a punch in the face. Had she not been used to it, she'd have assumed the room had been ransacked much like the church parsonage. Bruce was gone, but the floor was piled high with dirty clothes, comic books, old gaming systems, and heaps of art supplies and fabric rolls from his Comic-Con costume creations. There was a clear space in the corner, where his Foxy costume had been sitting since last Spring. Several severed spiderwebs twisted in a draft of air. The absence of the mascot costume was concerning. There was nothing productive Bruce could be doing after dark, dressed like a giant cartoon fox.

Connie pulled out her phone to text him, stopped, and slid it back into her pocket. He was an adult now—legally at least. He deserved his space and her absentee parenting hadn't earned her the right to pry.

She stepped carefully across the room to pick up a plate of pizza crusts from the floor. As she bent down her elbow cracked the corner of Bruce's desk.

The computer monitor on the desk blinked. She rubbed her elbow and stared at the screen. At first, she couldn't place the man staring back at her from the paused YouTube video, but then it hit her. It was the driver from the white van.

"Bomber, you son-of-a-bitch," she whispered.

ADDENDUM #2

SUBJECT: Competing Headlines

DESCRIPTION: The following are the competing headlines of both *The Fox Howler* and *The Fox Hollow Post* in the days following the disappearance of Pastor William Mast Sr. The intention of this addendum is to highlight the misinformation and misdirection used egregiously by both media outlets to further the causes of their aligned candidates.

FOX HOWLER HEADLINES:

October 24: Fox Hollow Police Confirms Holy Pervert
October 25: Gloria Glass Rebukes Beast Bungling Bomber
October 26: Fox Applesauce Co. Endorses Elitist Scum For Mayor
October 27: Gun Nuts Turn Mostly Peaceful Town Into Shooting Gallery
October 28: Fox Hollow Faces The Longstreet To Doom

FOX HOLLOW POST HEADLINES:

October 24: Police Consult Local Dogman "Expert" At Holy Crime Scene
October 25: The Messenger Of God's Wrath
October 26: Communist Camp Spreads Ideological Filth In Fox Park
October 27: 'Glass-Jaws' Shatter Over Hell-Hound Hunts
October 28: Unfit To Lead: Why Gloria Glass Can Kiss Our A**

October 29, 2017

11:15 a.m.

The morning following Pastor Mast's disappearance, the headlines of the town's dueling newspapers were not surprising. Neither publication mentioned any details of the disappearance, the crime scene, or any statements provided by Sheriff Connie and Town Hall. This was likely due to the incident being a disappearance and not a gory massacre, and therefore not fitting nicely into a pre-established narrative. Instead, the papers ran their typical divisive articles, with *The Fox Howler* victimizing the "misunderstood creature" and the *The Fox Hollow Post*, appealing to the evangelical crowd, dubbing the beast a "messenger of God's wrath," sent to cleanse the town of Gloria Glass's cult of hedonistic followers. *The Fox Hollow Post's* article featured an impressive artist rendering of Cerberus, the three-headed hellhound, snarling his way through a grove of apple trees.

Bomber was disturbed by the tensions building in town but had little time to address them in the capacity of Interim Mayor. Since their last meeting in Terry's Appleseed Diner, he and Buck had spent every possible moment hunkered down in hide sites, abandoned deer blinds, and hilltop lookouts, trying to catch another glimpse of the Dogman. They decided it was best to be prepared and Buck now totted a double-barrel shotgun Bomber had discovered while clearing out the belongings from his Great Uncle Cecil's home. Bomber wasn't entirely comfortable with guns, but he also wasn't entirely comfortable with the Vietnam-era claymore mines Buck continued to place around their position each night. Buck did eventually confess the mines weren't entirely legal and that he'd purchased them from a black-market Army surplus store outside of Albuquerque, New Mexico, when an extended Chupacabra hunt had landed him in a territory contested by multiple Mexican drug cartels.

Despite the illegal arms, Bomber became further enamored with the epic persona that was Buck Wildes. Before and after stakeouts, Buck would regale Bomber with tales of his adventures. While none of his stories ever involved actual monsters, they were, more often than not, colorful anecdotes of how not to handle encounters with wild animals, spontaneous weather anomalies, and confrontations with backwoods meth makers, moonshiners, and other jumpy hillbillies. As an avid fan, Bomber was mostly familiar with the stories and while Buck presented them as failures and shortcomings, Bomber saw them as pure gold—the chronicles of a life rich with experience and far from his own mundane existence. Bomber began to see himself as an apprentice to the Master, Buck Wildes. A squire to a cryptozoological knight.

While his relationship with Buck was flourishing, other aspects of his life were in decline. Marty's Market, like the town, was also subject to rising tensions and Bomber would often hear muted whispers of dissension among the cashiers, baggers, stockboys, bakers, deli workers, and butchers. He knew Bruce was at the core of it all, catching him in hushed conversations, tucked away in stock rooms, cooler cases, and low traffic aisles. Bruce would make pointed gestures toward the manager's office, followed by a surprisingly accurate impersonation of Marty taking pulls from an imaginary liquor bottle. The dissatisfaction among the workers was mounting and Bomber made a number of attempts to appeal to Bruce's sensibility, but was only met with bristling responses, most of which didn't make sense.

"Typical white male," Bruce would say. Or "you're just a tool of the patriarchy," or "my body, my choice," or "Boomers gonna boom."

On top of everything, the clearing of Cecil Merridan's home had been slow and Bomber had struggled to find anything worth keeping, aside from the shotgun and a teal-blue mint-condition 1967 Cadillac DeVille under a car cover in the garage. The keys were nowhere to be found and, due to his driving hiatus, Bomber would need someone else to drive the thing anyway. He considered asking Bruce, as a way of extending an olive branch, but when he arrived at the Customer Service counter, he found it vacant. What he did find was an overstuffed bag of garbage leaning against the liquor shelf. He shook his head, hefted the bag, and headed for the stockroom, where there was an emergency exit to the dumpsters outback.

Cutting through the store, he rounded the corner of the soda aisle and nearly collided with the backside of Ron-Boy Carson. Big Mama and Ron-Boy were earlier than usual and neither noticed Bomber as they stacked two-liters of cola into Big Mama's electric scooter. Ron-Boy was a sight to behold. On his head, he wore an ill-fitting skateboard helmet, retrofitted with a child's walkie-talkie duct-taped over his right ear. On his chest was an armor plate-carrier vest, similar to those used by S.W.A.T teams and Special Forces soldiers. The side straps of the coyote brown vest must have been too small, as they'd been cut away and replaced with a single ratchet-strap, fastened around his abdomen. The silver ratchet bounced on his back and the excess strap dangled into his asscrack, which was proudly on display above red cotton gym shorts. A crude skull had been cut from cardboard, painted white, and taped to the back of the vest. Instead of his regular Velcro shoes, he now wore a pair of black leather combat boots, which, to his credit, were spit-shined to a high gloss. None of this was nearly as shocking as the real-life assault rifle dangling from a carabiner attached to the shoulder of his vest.

Bomber cringed watching the rifle bounce off Ron-Boy's gut as he slung Cokes and Mountain Dews from shelf to basket. He knew the rifle would make a lot of customers uneasy, but "open carry" was legal in Michigan and Ron-Boy was within his rights. Bomber also rationalized that any confrontation on the matter would simply feed into Ron-Boy's desire to be provocative, not to mention Big Mama was still looking to settle the score after Buck's stiff right hook. He decided to hurry on to the next aisle and live to fight another day.

The air near the dumpsters was a thick stew of rotting meat and produce, brined in curdled milk. A sourness more tasted than smelled. Bomber buried his nose in the crook of his arm. Every few steps he raised his eyes to gauge his distance to the dumpster. The art of this unsavory task was to see from how great a distance one could launch the trash bags and score a direct hit, thereby minimizing smell saturation, trash-water splashback, or the less-frequent raccoon ambush.

The trash bag sailed smoothly into the dumpster and impacted on the bare floor, sending vibrations echoing up its metal walls. The fading vibrations gave way to a new noise. Several loud shrieks filled the dumpster. Thrashing claws scratched and scraped wildly against the bin's metal interior. Bomber backed up. The thrashing stopped. Everything stopped. Even the sounds of traffic on Main Street seemed to stop. All that could be heard was the distinct sound of heavy breathing, followed by wet snuffs and snorts.

Bang.

Something exploded. Bomber ducked low out of instinct. The burst echoed in the dumpster, then escaped like a specter into the rancid air.

Bomber looked behind him to see if anyone else had heard the commotion. Not a soul around. He edged closure to the dumpster and listened.

Silence.

He gave the dumpster a slight kick. The metal hummed and then went silent.

Cautiously, he peered over the edge. The inside of the bin had been painted crimson with blood. Chunks of fur and hide and bone and little bits of purple-gray intestine slithered slowly down the walls, leaving trails in the blood like gory snails meandering to the rusty floor. In the far corner, four large paws sat upright, each severed mid-shin with jagged tibias pointing skyward. A long rope-like tail was glued to the wall behind them. Bomber watched in horror as the disembodied parts melted into a purple sludge and dissipated into the pooling blood.

Bomber pulled his hand from the dumpster's edge. He checked them frantically for blood and then wiped them across his pant legs for good measure.

What the hell had happened? What was in that bag of trash?

"Cecil! The bastards moved the women's bathroom again."

Bomber looked back to find Doris standing outside the emergency exit, clutching her shopping cart. She looked around in a daze, confused by the natural light. He hurried toward her, trying to reconcile what he'd just witnessed.

"Ms. Grayson, please go back inside," he coaxed. "I'll take you up to the restrooms."

"So formal, Cecil," Doris said. "Nobody but Father McCallister calls me Ms. Grayson."

She giggled and continued prattling on about people who were long dead before Bomber was even born. They made their way back through the stockroom, where Bomber was careful to remove boxes and debris from Doris's path, while simultaneously checking over his shoulder, as though a monster were about to burst in behind them.

Maybe it was a giant sewer rat that'd found a pack of Alka-Seltzer? They say that can happen to seagulls. Seagulls that eat Alka-Seltzer explode—don't they?

He was sure he'd heard that somewhere.

If it can happen to seagulls, it can happen to rats, right? Seagulls are just flying rats after all.

Bomber held the stockroom door open for Mrs. Grayson, who pushed her cart slowly back into the store as she continued talking about God knows what.

"—my father was shuttling pickers from the Indian reservation again the other day," Doris was saying, "and he let me ride along. I dare say he won't be letting that happen again. What with the way those Indian boys were looking at me. Of course, I did wear my best sundress, just to make them ache a little."

She smiled mischievously and then frowned at the lack of

response from Bomber, who she still believed to be Cecil.

"I swear, Cecil," she pouted. "Somedays, it seems I can't catch your eye or ear no matter how hard I try."

Bomber stopped and turned to her. He didn't have the spare brainpower to play along with the pretending-to-be-Cecil game. He was irritated. Not because of her talking, but because she wanted him to be someone else and deep down he wanted to be someone else, too. Shame hit him. Shame for feeling irritated with this kind woman who couldn't help her confusion.

"I'm sorry, Doris," he said. "It's been a wild couple of days. Lot of Dogman activity and I'm trying to get to the bottom of it."

"Dogman?" Doris asked, her eyes wide. "Like the curse the Indian fellow told us about? I thought he was teasing. Trying to scare us."

Bomber perked up.

"Indian curse?"

Doris seemed pleased to have finally caught Cecil's ear.

"Oh Cecil," she cooed. "You remember. You were there. At the party by the Kissing Pond? You must remember. It was the first night we made love, right there in the orchard."

Doris batted her eyes, but at her age, it appeared to be an involuntary spasm or the onset of a brain aneurysm.

"Refresh my memory," Bomber said. "For old time's sake."

"Oh, Cecil, you bad boy," she pretended to scold. "Well, you were taking off my—"

"No!" Bomber stopped her. "Refresh my memory about the curse."

Doris frowned.

"Oh, I can't remember all of it," she said. Her voice turned choppy and less confident. "There was something about a crazy old medicine woman cursing the town's founder. Turned him into some kind of monster or something. Anyway, the Indian fellow was trying to convince us the beast lived right there in the old storm drain by the pond. You must remember. You told him, 'The only thing what comes out of there are the hookers from Fox Mansion.' I remember it, 'cause everybody gasped at that the same way they gasped about the monster."

"I don't understand," Bomber said.

Doris screwed up her face. She was trying to focus but couldn't pick a target.

"The old rumor," she said. "The old rumor is that the storm drain connects to the mansion. They say it's how they used to get the prostitutes and some of their higher-profile clients in and out."

Bomber had heard this rumor before.

"The Kissing Pond has to be at least a mile from the mansion," Bomber said, but Doris didn't respond. She was staring at the floor, trying to reconcile two realities into one. Bomber gripped her shoulders.

"Doris," he commanded, with a shake. "Who was it that told us about the curse?"

"Red—skins—" she croaked.

"Yes, yes, I know you said it was the redskins," he pleaded. "But which Indian? I need a name."

"No. I need some redskin potatoes, Bomber. And the bin was empty," Ms. Grayson snapped. "And I can't believe you'd use such a derogatory term for Native Americans. Truly despicable. I'm sure I don't need to tell you Mr. VanGovern will be receiving a complaint about your slur."

For just the slightest moment Bomber wondered if a solid bop to her old head would disconnect the wires again, but then he felt bad for having such a thought and hung his head. The bottom of Doris's cart was lined with boxes of Bloo Goo.

"You like that stuff?" Bomber asked, pointing at the boxes.

"No, I just carry it around for fun," Ms. Grayson said and then her face relaxed.

"I'm just saying, it can't be very good for you."

"It's sweet of you to be concerned for my health, Cecil," Doris cooed.

"Yes!" Bomber nearly shouted. He grabbed Doris by the shoulders again. "Who was the Indian boy who told us about the curse?"

Doris looked thoughtful.

"It was the chief's boy if I remember right," Doris said. "Herman Hayes. Herman being his Christian name, but all of us girls call him Swinging Timber for a very particular reason."

She wink-spasmed.

"Jesus, Doris," Bomber said.

"Oh, come off it, Cecil," Doris said. "You're no angel either. I should know."

Bomber continued walking with Doris to the produce department, while she unloaded all the reasons she knew Cecil was a dirty bird. By the time they'd arrived at the empty redskin potato bin, Bomber again felt nauseated, but for new reasons. He instructed Doris to wait there while he checked in with the produce manager about the potatoes, which Doris balked at, insisting she was still looking for the women's restroom, and headed off back toward the rear stockroom.

Bomber returned to the front of the store to find Bruce back at his post, passing out "Gloria Be To God" buttons to a few of the other cashiers.

"Marty's not going to approve of that," Bomber pointed out.

"I'll tell him to shove it," Bruce scoffed. "He's too drunk to remember it anyway."

Bruce launched into another litany of complaints, but Bomber barely registered them. His mind bounced between exploding dumpster vermin and old Indian curses and talking fox men and boisterous internet monster hunters. He didn't understand any of it. Or why, it seemed, he was at the center of it. He felt like his whole life had been leading to the convergence of these oddities. The thought left him feeling energized, almost happy, which in itself felt odd considering the tragedies necessary to get him there.

"I've been speaking with some of the other employees," Bruce said, "and nobody here is happy with how we're being treated. It's 2017 for god's sake and we're still being given derogatory titles like cashier and bagger and stockboy—which should be changed to a gender neutral stockperson at the very least—and expected to do thankless jobs for peanuts."

"How are those job titles derogatory?"

"They're demeaning in their simplicity," Bruce said. "Our jobs are difficult and hard and people are mean to us. A lot. We deserve complicated, important-sounding titles to command more respect."

"Such as?" Bomber asked.

Bruce looked down at a notebook he'd been writing in.

"Food Supply System Engineers," he announced proudly.

"That seems cumbersome, but I'm sure Marty won't care if you all change what you call each other."

"I'm talking to the others about unionizing—" Bruce said.

"He'll definitely have a problem with that," Bomber said.

"—and demanding higher wages."

"He'll probably just hire a whole new staff."

"And that's why we need Gloria," Bruce proclaimed, as though his half-baked idea had brought them full circle.

"Right," Bomber said. "Not to change gears here, but I need to talk to your great grandpa. You think he'd be at home?"

"Why do you need to talk to my Paw Paw?"

Bomber winced at the use of the childish nickname.

"It's nothing," he said. "I need to follow up on something Ms. Grayson said during one of her episodes. It's Dogman stuff."

Bruce eyed him suspiciously.

"You're not going to try to get *him* to track the Dogman, are you? He's like ninety-five years old."

"Do you know where he'd be or not?" Bomber asked.

Bruce looked at his watch.

"It's still early, so he's probably at Earl's with all the other fossils in town."

"Your great grandpa is an Earl's guy?"

"I know," Bruce said. "It's weird. Paw Paw says they're all friends, but he doesn't trust old white men. I think he goes there so he can keep an eye on them. It's a classic 'keep your enemies close' kinda thing."

"Smart," Bomber said. "You could take a lesson from him in dealing with Marty."

Bruce shrugged and walked toward the cash register where a customer was waiting.

"He's unreasonable," Bruce said. "And the only way to fight unreasonableness is with equal and opposite unreasonableness."

12:05 p.m.

While Bomber had spent the last few days trespassing through swaths of Fox Applesauce orchards and woodlands, Sheriff Connie had done the same but with a slightly different motive. While Bomber and Buck searched for Dogmen, Sheriff Connie searched for any signs of Pastor Mast, but a week of search parties, forensic teams, and cadaver dogs had produced no leads. It was as if the pastor had vanished into thin air. In her frustration, she considered that maybe The Rapture had happened discreetly and Pastor Mast had been the one and only soul worthy of being plucked from this hell-town.

As news of the strange happening leaked from Fox Hollow, so did the rumors of wild beasts lurking in the surrounding areas. Hunters from around the state arrived in droves, making the pilgrimage in hopes of bagging the "Fox Hollow Hell-Hound," as some were calling it. In one instance, Sheriff Connie and her search party had crashed through a thicket, only to find themselves staring down the business end of several twelve-gauge shotguns. The hunters feigned disappointment over their spoiled hunt, but the cracks and quacks in their voices suggested they were relieved at not being violently dismembered by an evolutionary anomaly. To make matters worse, the hunters-of-fortune were constantly getting mixed up in violent run-ins with the group of vegan-hippy-wannabes from Cedar Mills, who'd set up a filthy tent city in Fox Park and spent their days protesting against Harold's Hamburger Shack.

Connie sat at her desk and took a long slow breath. Normally, she'd be happy to get away from her desk, but she'd spent so much time in the field over the last several days that sitting still felt alien. A blue folder sat in front of her, a photograph of Buck Wildes paperclipped to the front. The photo had been stolen from Buck's Facebook page where he was listed as a "Celebrity/Influencer." In the picture, he stood with one bare foot inside a prodigious humanoid footprint. Connie drummed her fingers and stared at the picture until a new email dinged on her computer.

"Wonderful," she moaned. "What does my buddy, Pat

McConnell, want this time?"

McConnell had been seeking frequent updates on the investigation and had been growing agitated at the lack of progress.

Sheriff Hayes,

I'm emailing with a request for security support this afternoon. As you may know, Gloria has been making a large push for the working-class vote and has informed us she will be making an appearance, against my wishes, at Orchard 54 today. It's a bullshit move, if you ask me. Most of the workers there are on temporary work visas and shouldn't be voting anyway. Far be it from me though to stand in the way of a crazy lady. Anyway, her presence seems to breed confrontation and our workers are already scared shitless about being in the orchard with whatever beast is out there, so I'm hoping I can get a couple officers to provide security around 2pm today. Just to make sure things don't go off the rails and to put my people's minds at ease.

Any developments in the investigation? Keep me posted. Fingers crossed nobody else gets slaughtered.

Pat

Connie rolled her eyes, hit the intercom button, and called for Sergeant Householder. He appeared moments later with several folders under his arm.

"Please tell me those aren't for me," Connie said.

"These aren't for you," he said slowly. He placed them on her desk and cautiously slid them toward her. "Mostly just incident reports to review, really. Altercations between neighbors and some destruction of property stuff."

"I can't wait until this damn election is over. Doesn't even matter who wins," she said. "And speaking of the election, do we have anybody we can spare this afternoon to go out to Orchard 54 and make sure Gloria doesn't get her pretty little head bashed in?"

Householder grimaced.

"This afternoon is going to be hard," he said. "We've got four guys over at the Fox Applesauce production plant for a Longstreet event. Plus, set up for the Harvest Festival started today, so we've got two guys at Fox Park to make sure nobody kills each other and to clear out the dirty, vegan hippies. Then I've got three officers at the middle school getting prepped for the debate tonight. Other than dispatch, that's all we have."

Connie thought for a moment.

"Pull the guys from the middle school," she said. "We have hours until the debate. They shouldn't need them for any technical setup anyway."

"Will do," Householder said. He looked down at her desk. "Are you a fan or something?"

"What?"

He pointed at the picture of Buck Wildes.

"Oh God, no. I should've figured you'd know about this guy, too."

"Know about him? It's hard not to. Bomber's constantly sending Bruce and I his videos."

"Well, if you're not careful, you'll end up *in* one of those videos."

Householder looked confused.

"Bomber didn't tell you?" Connie asked. "Some task force leader he is."

"Tell me what?"

"He's been tooling around with Mr. Buck Wildes for the last week. I saw him with this joker on Sunday outside Third Reformed. Didn't piece it together until last night. Seems our little town has drawn the attention of a bona fide second-rate pseudo-celebrity."

Householder frowned. "I can't believe he didn't tell me," he said, more to himself than Connie. "Did he tell Bruce?"

Connie shrugged. "I'd ask him if he'd ever return my texts."

"Everything all right there?"

"It's fine."

"You think he has something to do with all this?" Householder asked, raising his eyebrows. "Buck, I mean. Not Bruce."

"It crossed my mind," she said. "This nut-ball just happens to show up right when mysterious attacks start happening around town? What better way to boost ratings as a phony monster-hunter than to be your own phony monster?"

Saying it out loud helped steel Connie's suspicion.

"Not to mention, his mustache is creepy as all hell," she added.

"You think Bomber is in on it?" Household whispered, looking around as if the office were bugged.

"Bomber's an idiot," Connie sighed. "But he's no murderer. I can see him getting swept up in his hero-worship enough to not notice what's really going on. He's the perfect mark for a guy like Buck. A small-town simpleton with something to prove, who's already completely sold on the Dogman junk."

She thought for a moment.

"And then again, maybe Bomber *does* know. And maybe he *is* in on it. Maybe he's tired of being a decade-long joke. How well do you really know anyone?"

Householder thought back to all the late nights with Bomber, listening to his half-cocked theories and the way he spewed Dogman "facts," as if saying them over and over somehow made them less outlandish. He thought about the sometimes-desperate tone in Bomber's voice when he spoke about the Dogman and how he felt sorry for him, embarrassed for him. But also how he sometimes felt a similar excitement. That maybe, just maybe, there was something more to this boring old town.

"It's all just a theory," Connie said. "Hopefully it's wrong. We need to do some more digging. People will surprise you, House. And disappoint you."

1:21 p.m.

The sky was overcast and the smell of damp leaves intermingled with dying earthworms and a slight tinge of pesticide. A jacked-up 4x4 truck roared down an otherwise empty Main Street. Metal poles attached to the truck's tailgate bowed under the weight of two giant "Longstreet To Victory" flags, each the size of bed sheets, billowing behind. The driver laid on his horn as he passed Krystal's Crystals, a new-age gift shop on the edge of Old Town. The shop had a new—some might say audacious—mural painted on the front window depicting a voluptuous Gloria Glass riding atop a fierce dragon which itself was blowing waves of rainbow flames across a building that looked suspiciously like the Fox Applesauce headquarters. "Burn the patriarchy" was scrawled across the bottom. An arm extended from the truck's window and a middle finger extended from that arm.

Bomber shook his head, watching it all from a bench next to Earl's Barber Shop. He knew there were hillbillies and hippies alike in Fox Hollow, but the election had really drawn them into the open, giving them a safe space and a spotlight. It even seemed to amplify these traits in people he'd once considered normal, unleashing some weird animalistic pride in their own intolerance. Even those who'd once prided themselves on free love, inclusivity and community had become close-minded, compartmentalizing themselves into groups of varying degrees of radical progressiveness, each small cell exploding with a confused mixture of joy and anger at the very thought of their own moral self-righteousness and the bigotry of their foes.

Bomber had phoned Buck, who had shown considerable interest in the potential of an old Indian curse, referring to it as a "highly marketable new angle" and they agreed to meet at Earl's inside the hour. Marty had hit the bottle hard all morning, leaving Bomber no choice but to place Bruce temporarily in charge of the store under the agreement there'd be no further talk of unionization or violent coup d'état while he was away.

Buck appeared on the bench next to him, disguised again in his large sunglasses and fake mustache.

"The guys in Earl's are all old as dirt," Bomber said. "Nobody's gonna recognize you. Nobody in there even knows what YouTube is."

"Better safe than sorry. How is this the first time you're hearing about this curse?" Buck asked. "Isn't this geezer's great-grandson on your crew, for god's sake?"

Bomber shrugged.

"He's not that great," Bomber said. "Bruce has spent most of his life playing Xbox and trolling celebrities online. He doesn't strike me as being interested in family heritage. As for the curse, I knew there was *a* curse, but I never knew it had any tie-in with the Dogman stuff."

"Still, it's a small town," Buck said. "Seems like it would be common knowledge."

"Unless it's been actively covered up," Bomb suggested. "Slaughtering indigenous people and stealing their land isn't really an origin story to boast about."

"So it's a curse and a conspiracy now?"

"Look, it's probably nothing. Doris Grayson is bonkers," Bomber said. They stood and headed for the swirling barber poles. "Fair word of warning, these guys are suspicious of outsiders. You might want to let me do the talking."

Whatever conversation had been taking place inside the old barbershop died the moment they walked in. Silence hung with the stale smell of cigars, barbicide, and mentholated muscle balms. Old, weathered heads stared at them beneath white combovers and shiny domes. On the back wall was a giant American flag and beneath it, a flag of the 82nd Airborne, reading "All American" across the bottom. Scattered around the walls were grainy black-and-white pictures of serious men in serious uniforms. On a small table in front of the flags was a shadowbox containing several medals including two Purple Hearts and a Bronze Star. The room was lined with mismatched chairs, collected from garage sales around town, some at the homes of the very men sitting upon them now. Some of the chairs were empty—more than last time Bomber had visited.

He knew the men from their glory days as church leaders, town council members, assistant football coaches, chili cook-off champions, Harvest Festival coordinators, and Marty's Market regulars. Most had been the backbone of Fox Applesauce's doomed local management but retired before pensions died and the business's bottom-line became priority over employee satisfaction. They'd been the pillars of employee picnics, with handshakes that hurt and soothing smiles hiding silver tongues. They seemed gigantic in memory. But now, in their twilight they withered and stooped, their noses and ear lobes swelled as their faces sank inward. Their silver tongues loosened by minds no longer tethered to hopes of climbing social or political ladders. They spoke dreamily of the "good old days" and harshly of anything new. Their conversations would be blunt and shocking to outsiders and they spat words like "liberal" and "Democrat" and "hippies" with the same venom they'd used to speak of Nazis and Communists years before. Their jokes were often racist or misogynistic or not really jokes at all but were not told out of malice but ignorance. Bomber wondered if they'd always held such beliefs and said such things. He wondered if, in his youth, the gravity of their casual prejudices had simply been lost on him. These men were a searing reminder of his own finite existence and that people are rarely all they outwardly display.

Earl sat in his own barber chair with a steaming Styrofoam cup. Out of habit, he hopped from his seat and began dusting its surface with a straw hand-broom, leaving the chair dirtier than before. The men around the room stayed silent, staring at Bomber and Buck as if they'd kicked in the door. There was no shortage of "Fox First" ball caps and "Longstreet To Victory" buttons, though Earl and his shop displayed no signs of partisan favor.

"Who's first in the chair?" Earl asked, flapping out the wrinkles of a weathered apron.

Bomber looked at Buck, who shook his head.

"Sorry, Earl," he said. "No haircuts today—"

"What?" Earl interrupted. He leaned his "good ear" forward, displaying an industrial size hearing aid, which emitted a high-pitched whine.

"I said, we aren't here for haircuts today," Bomber shouted.

"Then why the hell are you here?" Earl asked, looking disappointed with scissors convulsing in his wrinkled hand.

"We're looking for Herman Hayes," Bomber said.

"Who?" asked one of the men along the wall.

"Chief Hayes," Bomber said. "Chief Herman Hayes."

"Hey Herman," one man shouted, prompting a man at the back of the room to lift his gray head. "These two youngsters are looking for you."

The man rose to his feet, revealing his surprising height. He was old, but he was sturdy, with eyes like black pools behind wrinkled copper skin. His hair was cropped close on the sides, tapering up into a dramatic gray flattop, a hairstyle he'd not changed since his long, black locks had been sheared by an Army barber in 1951 before he left for Korea. His stride was still long and powerful and the sleeves of his black, nylon bomber jacket zipped as he walked toward them. He clutched a fountain soda from Harold's Hamburger Shack; a white straw poked up between fingers that looked like gnarled tree roots. The men around the room chuckled.

"Whaddaya want with this old savage?" one of them called.

"Hey Herman, they probably want to smoke 'em peace pipe," another laughed.

Chief Hayes made no effort to acknowledge their jokes.

"I've been expecting you," he said. His voice rolled like thunder through a river canyon.

He took a gurgling drag from his straw and slipped between Bomber and Buck, out the door and onto the main street sidewalk. The door closed behind them, abruptly ending the heckling from within. Chief Hayes took a seat on the bench, motioning Bomber and Buck to sit.

"Sorry to interrupt your morning," Bomber started.

"It's okay," Chief Hayes smiled. "I was tired of those old white racists anyway."

"Bunch of jerks," Buck said.

Chief Hayes looked at Buck, as if for the first time. His eyes narrowed looking over his obvious disguise.

"They don't pretend to be something they're not," he said.

The small patches of cheeks between the bottom of Buck's glasses and the top of his mustache flushed red. He removed the sunglasses and pushed back his hood.

"And besides, they are my friends," Chief Hayes continued. "Your generation is too sensitive to understand. You should hear the things I say about *them*."

"You said you've been expecting me," Bomber said. "What did you mean?"

"I meant what I said. I've been expecting you," Chief Hayes said. "I've been expecting you for several months. Since your uncle visited me."

"Cecil visited you? About what?"

"The curse, of course. Isn't that why you're here?"

"Yes. So the curse—it's real?"

Chief Hayes took another long draw from his straw.

"It depends on what you mean by 'real.'"

"So she isn't all crazy," Bomber said to himself, before adding. "Cecil never told me. Doris Grayson did."

Chief Hayes smiled, his eyes alive with a distant memory.

"Darling Doris," he whispered. "It's been years. She is quite the woman."

"Sure," Bomber said, dismissively.

"Did she tell you what they used to call me?"

"Yes, yes," Bomber said. "We're all very impressed. Can we talk about the curse?"

"Wait," Buck said. "What did they call you? Who's '*they*'?"

"It's not important—"

"The girls," Chief Hayes said, "they used to call me Chief Swinging Timber."

"What girls?"

"All of them," Chief Hayes winked.

"Can we get back on track here?" Bomber asked. The idea of Chief Hayes and Doris Grayson in the throes of passion was too much. "Tell me about the curse, please."

Chief Hayes's smile faded and he began speaking in a slow, rhythmic narrative detailing the struggles of his people from the time the first European fur trappers trespassed in their territory in the late 1600s, to the 1820s and 30s when New Englanders began relocating to Western Michigan in earnest. He spoke of land grabs, treaties, double-crosses, betrayals, and blood. He spoke of government "acts," relocations, forced migrations, skirmishes, scalpings, and massacres. He spoke of the 1807 Treaty of Detroit, where his people, the Ottawa, along with the Ojibwe, Potawatomi, and Wyandot people, had been pressured to sign the accords, surrendering a large portion of the state to white settlers and how this was just the beginning. He spoke of The Indian Removal Act of 1830 which forced entire communities of natives to give up the small reservations they'd retained and how they were relocated to Iowa and then to Kansas and how over half the Ottawa population had been wiped out by starvation, malnutrition, and disease. Bomber could not recall being taught any of this in his American History classes.

"But not all Ottawa went peacefully," Chief Hayes said. "There were pockets of resistance for decades. Small tribes who would not go quietly. There is a legend of one such tribe in this land when it was not yet named Fox Hollow. The tribe was led by an old medicine woman who claimed to be endowed with great powers by the spirit Nanabozho, a trickster god and shapeshifter. Certain of her abilities, she convinced the young braves of the tribe to join her in her fight against a nearby settlement that had begun clearcutting the forest of her people. She believed, through a series of rituals and sacrifices, she could transform herself and her warriors into the strong and cunning creatures of the forest— bears, wolves, cougars, wolverines—to confront and destroy their white enemies. Her braves, having seen her perform great acts of healing and felt the sway of her influence in hunts and battles, rallied fanatically to her side. On the eve of a long winter, she sent the youngest of her braves, my great grandfather, to deliver a message to the leader of the trespassers, a Mr. Silas Fox, that their presence would no longer be tolerated and if they did not abandon their attempts to usurp the land, he and all of his companions would be destroyed."

Chief Hayes took another long drag of his soda.

"My great-grandfather was not allowed to return to his people. Mr. Fox held him captive, which infuriated the medicine woman. She ordered her braves to paint their bodies in accordance with the ritual she'd created—a way she felt would most please Nanabozho. She blew smoke over them from a carefully crafted mixture of herbs and had them drink an elixir of broth, boiled from the bones of the animals they would become. Then she gathered her braves and confronted Mr. Fox and his party where they labored in the forest. They stood on the edge of the clearing, their bodies a terrifying and confusing jumble of painted patterns, glistening in the sweat of the food poisoning brought on by the spoiled broth and acrid smoke. The medicine woman pointed to the settlers and shrieked her incantation: "May the beasts of this land be a curse upon your hearts."

Chief Hayes' straw sputtered. He gave the ice inside a shake.

"Whoa," Buck murmured. "Did they transform into animals?"

Chief Hayes raised an eyebrow.

"Of course not, fool," he said, "but the medicine woman charged anyway and her braves followed, confident the charge—the reckless thrust into violent battle—would unlock the animal within."

"So what happened to them?"

"Mr. Fox was no stranger to violence or theft. He had ordered his companions to carry their guns with them into the forest that day. When the braves charged, they simply dropped their axes and took aim. As the warriors began to realize their painted hands were not becoming savage claws, the settlers fired on them, dropping half among the felled trees and stumps. The medicine woman was among them. The remaining braves, feeling foolish and betrayed by their leader, scattered into the woods and were pursued by the white men. Mr. Fox, however, stayed back. He found the medicine woman, still clinging to life among the corpses of her followers. His rifle was no longer loaded, so he raised his ax to her. He demanded she beg for her life and the lives of her braves and for the life of my great-grandfather. She spat upon his face. And in the delirium of her blood loss, she screamed a new incantation: 'May the beast of your heart be a curse upon this land.'"

"Damn," Bomber whispered. "What happened then?"

"He split her head in two."

They were all silent for a long moment and Bomber recalled the painting from Fox Mansion.

"What happened to your great-grandfather?"

"He managed to escape in the confusion."

"And what about the bodies?" Buck said. "That would've been a lot of bodies to dispose of without drawing attention."

"They were not white bodies," Chief Hayes said. "So they would draw no attention."

"Okay, hold up," Buck said, pinching the bridge of his nose. "So the predominant theory is that this Silas Fox guy, from a hundred and fifty years ago, is the Dogman. And he's running around killing people in Fox Hollow."

"Yes," Bomber said.

"No," said Chief Hayes. "Silas Fox is dead and gone. He is buried in the oldest section of Winesap Cemetery. The curse is a bloodline curse."

"But Mr. Fox is the only remaining descendant," Bomber said.

"That we know of," said Chief Hayes.

"But he skipped town years ago," Bomber said.

Chief Hayes shrugged. "I've told you all I know."

Bomber wondered if Sly had known about the curse.

"Why now?" Bomber asked. "Why would the killings start happening now?"

Chief Hayes nodded.

"That is the question," he said, as he stood. He rattled the ice in his now empty foam cup. "I'd better get back inside. If I'm gone too long, the white men will steal my seat."

"But how do we break the curse?" Bomber asked.

Chief Hayes stopped by the door.

"It's a blood curse," he said. "The bloodline must end."

Bomber and Buck were left sitting on the bench as it began to rain.

Bomber stood on Gloria's front porch, full of apprehension. She was the one person who'd possibly known Sly better than he. Buck had dropped him off, but declined to go with, claiming it would be far less awkward if Bomber went on his own. He then clarified that he meant it would be far less awkward for himself but seemed entirely unapologetic about it. Buck was not quite sold on Chief Hayes's story anyway. Apparently, Mr. Wildes was a bit pragmatic when it came to monster hunting and was cautious to hitch his wagon to anything delving into the outlandish world of magic and spirits. Evolutionary anomalies and anthropomorphic wildlife, however, were fine.

Bomber took a deep breath, let it out slowly, and knocked on the door.

No response.

There were no lights on inside. The rain had stopped, but the overcast sky was still a gun-metal gray. Bomber peered inside a window into Gloria's family room. Even in the dim light, the room looked uninviting. The type of spotless showroom that's off-limits to children or pets and looks like the owner was waiting for *Better Homes and Gardens Magazine* to show up for a photoshoot. On the mantle above a gas fireplace was a black-and-white portrait of Gloria. It was a candid shot of her in an orchard—probably right behind her house—picking an apple and laughing flippantly over her shoulder at some unknown joke or reacting to news that pumpkin spice lattes were back at Starbucks.

Under the portrait was an array of religious symbols and statues mounted on wood stands. A golden Buddha. A circular Yin and Yang. The four outstretched arms of Vishnu. Beneath them was a wicker basket holding two rolled-up yoga mats. On the wall nearest the entryway was a large, intricate crucifix and beneath Bomber's nose, just inside from the windowsill was an end table whose surface was tiled with a mosaic of the Star of David. On the table was a copy of the Koran, its spine crisp and unbroken. All these things were dim and dull, as though coated in a fine layer of dust. Bomber shook his head and for a moment felt sympathy for Gloria. He knew what it was like to lack direction, back when his only deity had been a bottle of Jim Beam.

"You're wasting your time," came a voice from behind him.

Bomber turned to find Rick Reynolds, one of the town's three mailmen. Rick was a gaunt Vietnam veteran who wore his long hair pulled back into a gray ponytail. He was known around town as "Slick Rick."

"Gloria hasn't been around here for a few weeks now," Slick Rick said.

"Where has she been?"

Slick Rick shrugged as he stepped around Bomber and jammed a stack of envelopes into an already-packed mailbox mounted next to the front door. Half the stack fell to the ground and Rick made no attempt to recover the mail before bouncing back off the porch.

"I guess there are a few secrets left in this old town," he said.

2:43 p.m.

Sheriff Connie grumbled her way down an orchard row, trying to keep a quick pace while avoiding ankle-shattering tractor ruts and dried burdocks that grabbed at her ankles and pants legs. She'd received an agitated call from Patrick McConnell, claiming Gloria and her campaign team were causing "civil unrest" during their visit. Householder had already left for the Longstreet event and couldn't be raised on the radio, so Connie took the opportunity to get out from behind her desk.

"You're too late," called McConnell as she approached. He was leaning against the back of a flatbed truck, which held four crates, each half full of apples. Around the truck were several picker's baskets, overturned and spewing fruit. Wooden ladders poked intrusively into branches, but no one occupied them. McConnell was alone. He ran his hands down his face in frustration.

"What happened here?" Sheriff Connie asked. "Where is everyone?"

"She stole 'em all," McConnell growled. "Came in here for her little campaign event, which I was nice enough to allow, then started squawking about poor working conditions, shoddy equipment, and unfair wages. Next thing I know, her and her band of pit-viper hussies have my migrant workers all riled up and chanting 'apples for apples' or some goddamn thing and then they all threw down their gear and marched out of here with her."

Sheriff Connie suppressed a smile.

"She was spouting all kinds of stuff about unionizing, too. Can you believe that?"

"Yes."

"They already have a damn union," he spat. "At least the legal workers do."

"Were there *illegal* workers out here?"

"I want you to arrest her."

"Doesn't sound like she did anything illegal," Sheriff Connie said. "Jerk-move, for sure, but nothing illegal."

McConnell pulled a hand from his pocket. It was clenched red around a set of brass knuckles. He rapped the knuckles against the iron frame of the flatbed thoughtfully.

"I went to check on the crew a couple rows down and they were all gone, too," he said. "Just vanished. You must have seen them on your way in. Between the two crews, there had to be thirty people."

"Didn't see a soul," Connie said. She was looking for an exit in the conversation.

"Odd," McConnell said. "Most of 'em got here on the back of these flatbeds. If you didn't pass them walking back to town, where the hell did they go?"

"Beats me, Pat," Connie said. "And frankly, the mode of transportation for your mutinous crew of illegal workers is not really my primary concern right now. Did you have anything else for me or did I come out here for nothing?"

McConnell waved her off and Sheriff Connie turned to leave.

"Oh, there is one other thing," McConnell said. "Maybe best if I get ahead of it—" He paused and looked sheepish, like a kid who let a swear word loose in front of his parents. "I may have said some things to Gloria in the heat of the moment that I'm not proud of."

"This is supposed to be surprising?" Sheriff Connie said.

"Well," McConnell said, "I may have made some threats. Pretty vicious stuff in retrospect. Empty threats, obviously. I'd never actually hurt Gloria. I just wanted you to know. In case she files a complaint or something. She seems like the type who'd tattle. And embellish."

Connie looked McConnell up and down. For the first time Connie could remember, perhaps the first time in his life, McConnell's short stature was his most noticeable feature. He was, for lack of a better term, deflated.

"Noted," Connie said with just a touch of sympathy.

3:13 p.m.

The rain had cleared and bits of blue peaked through the clouds, but Bomber was lost in thought about the old curse as he tramped over soggy leaves plastered to the sidewalk leading back to Marty's Market. He'd received an angry call from Marty, who'd returned to the store—presumably for another bottle of whiskey —and found Bruce riling up the stockboys in the back room with what Marty referred to as "socialist propaganda." Marty had been so worked up over Bruce's rabble-rousing he hadn't addressed Bomber's absence at all. Instead, Marty made it very clear that Bomber had better get Bruce under control before he "gave him the ax," which, after hearing the legend of the medicine woman's murder, left Bomber with some unpleasant imagery to deal with.

Crossing Main Street into Marty's parking lot, Bomber's ears picked up an insensible, droning chant: "An apple a day keeps the doctor away. And so does unaffordable healthcare."

Several of the store's high-school-age employees, who looked confused and nervous by the whole situation, marched in a circle, pumping homemade protest signs into the air.

Leading the pathetic protest, from the tailgate of his pickup, Bruce strutted like a prize rooster in the full Foxy mascot costume, howling his social unrest through the mouthpiece of a megaphone.

Marty stood outside the store, right in front of the automatic sliding doors which slid open and closed sporadically, unable to determine his intention. His arms were folded and his characteristic foam cup rested against a flabby bicep.

"The bastards have unionized," he shouted, as Bomber approached.

"They've what?"

"Unionized," Marty vomited the word. "Formed a committee and everything. Your buddy Bruce appointed himself president. Business has come to a halt."

Bomber scanned the group of protesters. "Looks like it's just the baggers though."

Marty laughed. "Those are just the active protesters. The rest of the imbeciles are pulling some 'non-violent resistance' crap.

They had it all orchestrated. As soon as it struck two o'clock, all the cashiers sat down on the floor at their stations, the baggers walked out, stock-boys laid down in the aisles, bakery ladies just up and vanished. It was actually pretty impressive."

"You seem remarkably calm about all of this," Bomber remarked.

Marty tipped his foam cup and peered inside.

"Between you and me," he said, "I'm fairly drunk."

By now, Bruce had spotted Bomber and, assuming Marty was talking trash, came to defend his honor. He fumbled from the truck with his big, plush feet and hands. The costume's "Fox Hollow High School" jersey had been replaced with a white "Team Gloria" shirt.

"Don't believe anything he tells you," Bruce yelled through his megaphone. With one hand, he struggled to remove the huge fox head. His face was flushed and black hair was plastered across his sweaty forehead. He looked like he might pass out from the exertion required to move the bulky costume. "Whatever he's telling you is a lie."

"He was telling me you formed a union and staged a protest for better wages and health benefits."

"You better believe it," Bruce said. "We're calling ourselves the United Coalition Of Food Supply System Engineers."

"Engineers?" Marty scoffed. "What are you engineering?"

"Supply systems," Bruce said, defensively. "Our jobs are hard and we deserve more important titles than derogatory terms like 'bagger' and 'cashier' and 'stockboy'—which should be changed to a gender-neutral 'stock-person,' by the way."

"You oppose job titles which accurately describe the sole function of your employment?" Marty asked.

Bruce gathered himself. He clearly hadn't prepared to defend his position against reasonable arguments.

"I—we oppose your labels. We regularly have to perform duties outside the scope of a defined job and we deserve a title that captures our labor-fluidity."

"Labor-fluidity?" Marty rolled his eyes.

Bomber shifted uncomfortably between the two.

"Cute button," Marty said, pointing at a large button pinned to Foxy's shirt. It read "Gloria Be To God" in big letters above an adorable baby raccoon with a halo, which was lifting its furry arms reverently towards the heavens among a background of clouds.

"Is that supposed to be one of the dead trash-compactor raccoons?" Bomber asked.

Bruce started to respond, but Marty cut him off.

"My sign is bigger," he bragged, pointing to the store's roadside sign. The sign no longer featured the weekly special of ground beef at ninety-nine cents per pound—which Bomber knew was only on sale because it was about to expire—but instead bore the familiar campaign tagline, "Take The Longstreet To Victory."

"I can't believe you support that war criminal," Bruce muttered.

"War criminal?" Bomber asked.

"Everyone knows Fox Applesauce uses harmful pesticides," Bruce said. "We're all gonna get cancer. You said yourself that the Blue Goo is poison. And who's in charge of it all? Carl-frickin'-Longstreet: War Criminal."

"That 'war criminal,'" Marty said, "used his lottery winnings to single-handedly prop up Fox Applesauce, and subsequently this town's economy. So without that 'war criminal,' you wouldn't even have a job to be a petulant little prick about. Maybe you should be a little more grateful."

"He's the one who moved all the jobs out of Fox Hollow in the first place," Bruce yelled.

"Because it was good for the company," Marty yelled back. "What's good for the goose, is good for the gander."

"What does that even mean?" Bruce's face was purple.

"It means, do your damn job."

Bomber looked around. Customers and protesters alike had begun to gather around the escalating argument.

"Guys, maybe we could take this inside—"

Neither Bruce nor Marty were listening.

"I still have a job?" Bruce asked incredulously. "I assumed you'd have fired me by now."

"I can't fire you for going on strike. You're in a union now," Marty said. "If you're going to be a union president you should learn a little about how they work."

"You're not my dad," Bruce said.

"I could be," Marty taunted. "Do you even know?"

Bruce sputtered. A tantrum was imminent.

"Let's take this into the office and try to find some common ground," Bomber said soothingly.

"I have no common ground with this old white fossil," Bruce announced. "He's just a perpetuation of the good ol' boy system. You can't get anywhere in this town unless you're a white male."

"You *are* white," Marty said. "Still not sure if you're a male, though."

"I'm a quarter Native American," Bruce shouted, then he raised the megaphone. "Down with the patriarchy! Down with white America."

This caused hesitation on the picket line and whispers among the gathering crowd. The murmurs were quickly drowned out by the blaring sound of Bruce Springsteen's "Born In The USA," which was thumping from the Carson's rusty van as it screeched into the parking lot.

"What are they doing here again?" Bomber asked. They never visited the store twice in one day.

The van sped through the parking lot and looked as though it might slam through the store's side wall. This prompted an optimistic gasp from Marty, followed by a disappointed groan when the van skidded to a halt, a few feet shy of impact. Ron-Boy lunged from the car with all the grace and agility of a walrus. He was still dressed in his homemade tactical get-up with his AR-15 rifle slung across his chest, which he pretended to air-guitar while grossly misinterpreting Springsteen's lyrics. From the passenger seat, Big Mama Carson sat stone-faced with her eyes locked on Bomber. The van's side door rolled open and large, corn-fed country boys began to pile out, all decked out in mismatched camouflage, homemade body armor, and various echelons of weaponry. The clown-car of combat cosplayers produced an additional seven men and two women, the last of which stumbled out waving a yellow "Don't Tread On Me" flag. The motley militia stood around adjusting their gear, guns, and groins before plodding over and forming a line facing Bruce's protesters in an attempt to be intimidating.

"What's all this about?" Marty asked. "Who are all these people?"

Bomber recognized one or two in the group, but most must have come from out of town. Ron-Boy stepped up as the group's spokesman, which wasn't an encouraging sign.

"We're the local, unofficial branch of the Michigan Militia," he announced. "Perhaps you've heard of the Apple Knockers Brigade?"

"No."

"Well that's us," Ron-Boy said, sucking in as much of his gut as he could. He jerked his thumb over his shoulder. "We're here to provide you some security from these socialist bastards."

He pointed accusingly at Bruce and the protesters.

"I'm fine, thanks," Marty said.

"Nonsense," Ron-Boy said. "You've been serving Mama and me for years. Now it's my turn to service you."

Bomber cringed.

"Kind gesture, but not necessary," Marty said, clearly uncomfortable with the developing situation.

"Won't take 'no' for an answer," Ron-Boy said. He stepped up, toe-to-fuzzy-toe with Bruce. "And as for you, you communist turd, you better pack up your furry little costume and your group of sissies and get the hell outta here. We ain't gonna stand by and watch you harass Mr. Marty."

To Bruce's credit, he didn't back down, but Bomber couldn't tell if it was bravery or paralysis brought on by fear. Bomber put up his hands to de-escalate the situation.

"Whoa, whoa, whoa," he said. "Nobody's harassing anyone. The workers have formed a union and they have every right to—"

He was interrupted by Ron-Boy's bratwurst-like finger in his face.

"I ain't forgot about our little disagreement," Ron-Boy said. "I don't like you, but I never figured you for a socialist sympathizer."

He spat on the ground at Bomber's feet.

"Who the hell's a socialist?" Bruce said, coming out of his paralysis. "Aren't you and Big Mama on, like, every form of welfare assistance? If anybody's a socialist, it's you. Fat socialists are the worst socialists."

The teen protesters seemed to find a second wind in this mantra and began chanting. "Fat socialists are the worst socialists!"

"Don't chant that," Bomber yelled. He wanted to grab Bruce and shake him, but Ron-Boy beat him to it. Putting both hands on Foxy's shoulders, he rattled the boy inside the mascot.

"I ain't no Commie," Ron-Boy yelled. "You are!"

"Help!" Bruce shrieked. "Hate crime!"

Bomber leaped forward to break up the altercation. This startled Ron-Boy who pushed Bruce, sending him sprawling backward onto the pavement. Then, as more of an impulse, he swung his arm around, catching Bomber with a stiff backhand. Blood spurted from Bomber's nose and he pinched it tight while he sank to his knees.

"You fat clod," Bomber shouted, peppering blood droplets across the pavement.

Ron-Boy looked remorseful for half a second, then tightened his stance.

"Now we're even," he said. He turned to Marty again. "I hear the rest of your employees went limp inside the store or something."

Marty chewed his lip.

"Yes," he said. "They're calling it non-violent resistance."

"Want us to make it *violent* resistance?" Ron-Boy puffed his chest. He began waving the rest of the Apple Knockers forward toward the door. Marty began to protest, but then gave up and gulped the rest of his whiskey.

"Let's round up some Commies," Ron-Boy whooped, leading his cohorts through the market doors.

Bomber was already trying to call Sheriff Connie. When she didn't answer, he sent a text. He got to his feet and wiped his hand on his shirt, which was already ruined with nose blood. Bruce watched him from the bed of his truck, where he'd resumed his position and incited a new chant of "Apple Knockers are off their rockers."

Bomber was torn between chastising Bruce and following Ron-Boy's pretend army to ensure they didn't hurt anyone inside. He didn't think they would, but then again, he'd just been punched in the nose. Before he could decide, the automatic doors hissed open. Customers, employees, and Apple Knockers alike began sprinting out of the store, all of them wearing looks of shock and horror.

Bomber stopped a stock boy as he ran past. "What's going on in there?"

"Someone lit the store on fire," the stock boy cried.

Marty clapped his hands gleefully, as Bomber stepped back to survey the store. Sure enough, black smoke billowed from the back of the roof.

3:30 p.m.

The parking lot outside of Fox Hollow Middle School was jam-packed with vehicles already spilling into the soccer fields. After wasting her time in the orchard with McConnell, Sheriff Connie decided to spot-check her officers setting up for the mayoral debate, which was set to kick off in thirty minutes. She'd expected a good turnout but hadn't imagined it would fill the parking lot.

The American flag waved high outside the front entrance and Connie listened to the hoist rope clang against the pole as she walked by. The clatter drew memories of a particular eighth-grade morning when Sly Fox had bullied a sixth-grader named Jimmy Fletcher into removing his pants and hoisting them up that same flag pole. He then forced Jimmy, sobbing in yellowed whitey-tighties, to solicit salutes for his own lofted trousers from the throngs of arriving students. The concept of the prank had been derived from a children's television show popular at the time. The school faculty had put a quick end to the abuse, of course, but Jimmy's adolescent life was permanently marred. To this day, less-sensitive members of the community still salute Dr. Fletcher in passing.

Sheriff Connie clenched her fist at the memory. There were too many people in Fox Hollow with stories like Dr. Fletcher's. Too many memories of harassment by the likes of Sly Fox. And Bomber Merridan for that matter.

The school halls were packed with people milling about, but most whispered in isolated groups, hugging rows of battered lockers. Connie weaved through the clusters, catching bits of conversations. She heard mentions of Pastor Mast, Ms. Carol Meyers, and of course the former mayor, their names intermingled with those of wild animals. Bears. Cougars. Dogmen. One man spoke loudly about a documentary he'd watched on the black-market tiger trade. Other discussions were about the candidates. Accusations and rumors rippled in whispers through the crowd and clusters of one loyalty glared at clusters of the other. Allegiances were easily identified, with the school colors split and bastardized by each camp: bright white shirts for the Gloria supporters and orange trucker caps for the Longstreeters.

Most groups went silent when Sheriff Connie passed. They eyed her suspiciously and she eyed them suspiciously right back. From behind her, someone snorted like a pig.

The gym itself was still mostly empty and the janitorial staff was placing metal folding chairs in front of fully-extended bleachers. The smell of lacquered floors and old sweat dredged up memories of demeaning dodgeball bombardments.

On the other side of the gymnasium, she saw Sergeant Householder giving instructions to two other officers who were placed as security near the doors leading outside. The whole concept of "heightened security" in Fox Hollow seemed absurd to her, but in light of recent events, she felt the need to keep people's minds at ease.

Sergeant Householder noticed Connie and walked over as people spilled through the door behind her, taking seats in the bleachers and rows of chairs.

"How are things going here?" Connie asked. "I see the town's finest have come out this evening. Maybe our boys should have brought their riot gear just in case."

She laughed. Householder laughed. Neither was sure if she was serious.

"We're all good here, ma'am," Householder said. "We're probably going to have half the crowd exit out those side doors at the end. Send the other half the way they came. Might help keep them from razing this place to the ground."

Sheriff Connie nodded approvingly. She checked her watch. Twenty minutes until showtime.

"Where are the candidates?" She asked.

Householder shrugged.

"Busy politicians," he said. "They'll probably slide in with a minute to spare. How'd the trip out to the orchard treat you? Are you a Gloria convert now?"

Sheriff Connie guffawed. "Gloria wasn't even there. She'd already left. Took all of McConnell's pickers with her."

"With her? With her where?"

Connie shrugged. Her phone dinged, derailing her thought.

She snatched it from her pocket, hoping it was finally something from Bruce. She hadn't seen him in over two days.

She looked at her phone and scowled when she saw Bomber's name. His text read: "Apple Knockers at the market. Send help."

"What the hell does that mean?" she grumbled and then showed Householder. "What's an 'apple knocker'?"

Householder's phone dinged, too. His message was from Bruce, stinging Connie with a flash of jealousy before her phone dinged again with the same message: "FIRE AT MARTY'S MARKET."

5:05 p.m.

When the Fox Hollow Fire Department arrived on the scene, the inferno had spread through most of the store, only slowing slightly when it hit the freezer and cooler aisles. By the time Sheriff Connie and Sergeant Householder arrived, it was clear there wouldn't be much to salvage from the old store. Sheriff Connie left the police work to Householder and immediately sought out Bruce, but he'd evidently hopped in his truck and slipped away during all the commotion. Half the town was already gathered at the back of the parking lot watching the chaos, while the other half was working its way over from the debate, which had been canceled in light of the circumstances.

Bomber had led the effort to get all customers, employees, protesters, and Apple Knockers safely away from the building. With no other means of accounting for all customers, he began matching members of their gathered group with the cars currently in the parking lot, which had now been blocked from leaving by fire trucks. They successfully identified and located all vehicle owners except for one: a 1996 Buick LeSabre, which was well known to belong to Ms. Doris Grayson. The fire department was notified and redoubled their efforts, but Bomber couldn't shake the awful feeling in the pit of his stomach. The back corner of his mind still hung onto hope she'd, in her confusion, stumbled into some untouched corner of the store, locked herself in the dairy cooler, or simply ambled out the dock doors in search of the restroom. The crowd collectively held its breath until half an hour later when her charred body was found in what remained of the pet food aisle. Her body had been identified by the orthopedic shoes melted to her feet and a blackened hand-basket full of canned food for the cat she didn't own.

For an hour or so there was unity in the town once again, as people mourned the loss of yet another community staple. They hugged one another and uttered reassuring lies in order to soften the blow of the loss:

"She probably fell asleep from the smoke and died peacefully."

"She didn't know where she was anyhow. She's not suffering anymore."

"She was old as hell. Probably only had a few months left."
And:
"She'd always talked about being cremated."
This last uttered by Tommy Coughlin, who waited eagerly with his two brute sons to take possession of Doris's blackened corpse.

"Sad as it is, maybe this will be the catalyst to get everyone in this town to pull their heads out of their asses," Sheriff Connie told Bomber.

Though crass, it was a nice sentiment from Sheriff Connie and a rare display of optimism, which unfortunately ended up being misguided. The communal mourning of Doris Grayson *was* a nice reprieve from the past week of partisan bickering but unraveled quicker than the spools of fire hose being used to drown the market fire. It was impossible to tell which side laid claim to Doris's memory first. Fond recollections of her two distinct personalities—the flitting liberal youth and the staunch old conservative—bubbled up, at first in cooing whispers, which then gave way to venomous hisses as disagreements erupted over which personality was Doris Grayson's true self. Each side was desperate for a martyr. Each side was angry, looking for a fight, and the sweet catharsis of theatrical outrage.

"She loved everyone equally," Tammy Schmidt screamed, pointing an angry finger at a cluster of Apple Knockers. Tammy was the hot yoga instructor at Wild Goose Yoga just down from the ash-heap that was now Marty's.

"She was the angriest woman I ever met. But she's the only reason I knows how to read," Ron-Boy howled, his eyes brimming with tears. He stepped forward, toe-to-toe with Tammy.

Tammy struck first and there was a scuffle. A flurry of poorly-strapped imitation body armor and Lululemon leggings. Each side pulled back their gladiator before Sheriff Connie or Sergeant Householder could intervene. Connie issued warning after warning, but her words were drowned out by more threats.

Threats gave way to accusations, with each side blaming the other for starting the fire that killed sweet, angry Doris Grayson and leveled the town's only grocery store. The Longstreet camp concocted the theory that the fire was lit intentionally by one of the disgruntled stock boys protesting within the store. They even made up unfounded details about where the fire was started, the means of ignition, and a store-stocked cleaning agent used as an accelerant. Each made-up detail lent undue credibility to a fabricated story and each retelling within the group cemented the lies as truths in their rage-addled minds.

Gloria's side was no better and they pinned the arson on a particularly hapless member of the Apple Knockers, claiming the doughy freedom-fighter had set off a flash-bang grenade in an attempt to scare the dozing protesters inside. Instead, the grenade had ignited a nearby cereal box and the rest was history. No one seemed to recognize the accused Apple Knocker, which fueled rumors of Carl Longstreet recruiting soldiers of fortune—or in this case, *mis*fortune—to bolster the ranks of a private militia. It wouldn't be until the following day that the true origin of the fire would be discovered. Though a flash-bang had been used, the inept thrower had failed to pull the pin and it never discharged. The fire, instead, came from several blackened apple pies, which had been left in the oven by accident when the store's team of bakery workers had executed their walkout. In a way, Bomber found it ironic that such a nostalgic symbol of Americana was ultimately to blame for such destruction. Of course, once the truth came to light, each side was so sold on their own telling, they simply dismissed the provable facts as lies made up by an establishment attempting to pacify them.

None of that mattered at the moment though because reason had taken a back seat to blame and both sides continued to shout at one another. As the evening light faded, Sheriff Connie called in several more officers to assist her and Householder, as they tried to keep the seething, growing masses apart. Bomber watched as people he'd known since childhood, people he'd gone to church with, spit at one another across some imaginary divide. People shook fists and raised middle fingers. Bomber was sick. He turned away and watched the flames still licking the southwest corner of the gutted building. Across the parking lot, Marty stood alone, staring off into the void.

"I bet you're on cloud nine right now," Bomber said, coming up behind him. He slapped a hand across Marty's back. "You know. Aside from Doris and all."

Marty looked over just as the parking lot lights kicked on. The light caught a thin tear sliding down his cheek.

"I'm sorry," Bomber said. "I thought you hated this place."

"I did," Marty said. Bomber couldn't tell if Marty's eyes were misty with emotion or glazed with bourbon. "But all I am is *this* place. I don't know anything else. I've always hated it, but you live with the anger long enough, you don't know what to do when it's gone. You forget how to be any other way. I never recognized my potential. Playing the victim of some unchangeable past was just an easier route, you know? Blame is an easy thing to twist, but ultimately it's all on ourselves. I could've been so many other things. But you can't fail if you don't try, right?"

His rhetorical question was a punch to Bomber's gut.

Marty forced a weak smile and lifted the bottle of whiskey in his right hand, his knuckles white around the neck. Then suddenly his grip eased and the bottle hung slack. He pushed it toward Bomber.

"I'm sorry," he said.

"What are *you* sorry about?" Bomber asked. He took the bottle, interpreting the gesture as more of a surrender than an offered drink.

"I'm going to have to let you go," Marty said quietly. He blew out a sigh like he was trying to blow out the flames and then walked away without another word.

Bomber stared down at the half-empty fifth in his hands. Marty had splurged on himself and gone for the top-shelf liquor. The bottle of WhistlePig bourbon stared back at him. He looked over his shoulder at the savages shouting and shoving. Then back at the flames, blackening the bones of a comfortable, riskless life. He pulled the stopper from the bottle-top and took a long swig.

Unbeknownst to the fire department, or anyone for that matter, the southwest corner of Marty's Market—the corner that was still in flames—was the location of the store's propane cage, where employees could one-for-one exchange a customer's empty from its abundant supply of full tanks. So it caught everyone by surprise when the bastards blew, sending successive fireballs into the night sky. Most surprised was Tammy Schmidt, who finally shut her big mouth long enough to watch metal shards of propane tanks, hunks of cinder blocks, and flaming milk cartons smash through the front window of Wild Goose Yoga studio, setting it completely ablaze. The Longstreeters and Apple Knockers whooped and cheered. They rushed forward toward the flames and danced like heathens in its flickering light. Someone in the group recited an obscure fire-and-brimstone piece of scripture, while the firemen tried desperately to work through the chaos.

"Joke's on you, I'm fully insured, you white-trash hillbillies," Tammy screamed. She picked up a loose piece of asphalt and launched it at Ron-Boy's van. It skipped off the hood and lodged in the windshield, spider webbing the glass. Ron-Boy howled. He ran to the van and dropped to his knees, which were protected by tactical knee pads made of old potholders covered in strips of duct tape. He stroked the rusted front bumper tenderly.

"You'll pay for this, you flexible bitch," he yelled.

From there the evening unfolded into a series of progressive retaliations lobbed like artillery shells at the opposing sides. By 8 p.m. the town had descended into madness. At first, the acts of aggression were small potatoes. Opposing sides broke down into smaller factions and wandered neighborhood side streets kicking in campaign signs, spray-painting bumper stickers, and occasionally putting a rock through a house window.

Sheriff Connie was in a whirlwind as she dispatched officers to all corners of the town while simultaneously calling for reinforcements in riot gear. Things really slipped out of control around 9:30 p.m. when The Coalition of A.S.S.E.S departed the vacant lot beside Harold's Hamburger Shack and, using the existing chaos, executed an incursion into the heart of Old Town.

Their target? Robinson's Family Pet Shop. While Sheriff Connie and her officers were dispersing small bands of aggravators, the A.S.S.E.S. were smashing in the store's front window and setting loose the animals inside. Cats, dogs, rabbits, hamsters, gerbils, mice, spiders, lizards, and snakes meandered down Main Street's sidewalks, unsure of where to go or what to do, while the A.S.S.E.S shooed them along, enthusiastically encouraging them to be free. Most disturbing was the release of Alice the American Alligator, who sauntered her six foot frame out the front door dragging bits of broken glass under her belly, while Ms. Chitters, the comedian's macaw, swooped overhead, screeching insults at passing vandals.

When news of the raid on Robinson's Family Pet Shop circulated around the Fox Hollow Community Facebook page, the Longstreeters took it as an attack on their personal liberties, their pursuit of happiness, and the infallible capitalistic system of which they were mostly ignorant. They promptly retaliated in kind. Unsurprisingly, it was Krystal's Crystals that bore the initial brunt of their anger, being a beacon of everything liberal and everything Team Gloria had come to represent. Ron-Boy and his Apple Knockers were there, but due to their aversion toward exercise had opted to watch from the far side of the street, periodically waving their rifles in the air and yelling things like "Freedom isn't free" and "Somebody swipe me a Himalayan salt lamp," while ordinary citizens, fueled by the fury of mob mentality, shattered windows, smashed dream-catchers, trampled tapestries, looted oils and incense, and defecated in no fewer than three tie-dyed bean bag chairs.

The escalations continued in a tit-for-tat style along Old Town's main drag. The Glass Jaws smashed in Peterson Sporting Goods because of their pro-Second Amendment and pro-hunting stance, Sully's Hardware Store because fixing things allegedly perpetuates the patriarchy and promotes toxic masculinity, and Fairhaven's Financial Advisory Service because personal financial responsibility is abhorrent and is a representation of capitalism, which they too were mostly ignorant of. Likewise, the Longstreeters pillaged Rita's Vegan Bakery for obvious reasons, Terry's Appleseed Diner because Ron-Boy was still sore at Terry, and Ming Dynasty Chinese Buffet, partly because of a pro-Gloria sign in their window, but mostly because the Longstreeters were getting hungry—for this, they were dubbed racists by the opposition, though none of them had anything against the Chen Family on a personal level. The only establishment left untouched by the mobs was The Tree of Knowledge Bar, probably because it was common knowledge that Snake, the bartender, kept a loaded double-barreled sawed-off shotgun tucked behind the bar.

Bomber had stayed at Marty's Market, watching the fire department put out the last of the flames, their hoses saturating the blackened remains of his former life. Even after they'd moved on to quell the inferno ironically burning the hot yoga studio, Bomber remained, moving ever closer to the ash heap until he could finally feel the remaining heat and steam across his face. Part of the store's front remained intact, its large windows had melted, bowed and warped, but still displayed the partly burned ads for this week's specials:

"White Bread - $0.99 per loaf"
"Reduced Sodium Thick Cut Bacon - $2.99 per package"
"Fox Applesauce's Bloo Goo - $3.99 per box"

He couldn't stop thinking about Doris Grayson and he wondered, at the end, who she'd been when she died, the lighthearted, young Doris or the beleaguered, old Ms. Grayson. He supposed it didn't matter. Young and optimistic or old and realistic, when the world burns around you, everyone feels the flames the same way.

On the ground at his feet, wet with the ash-water trickling from the store, was an undamaged pouch of Bloo Goo Applesauce. Bomber put down the whiskey bottle and picked up the pouch, wiping away the grit. A fitting souvenir, he slipped it absentmindedly into his pocket.

He left the store and the whiskey behind him, tripping down Main Street in a daze and heading in the direction of Old Town. The rain clouds had regrouped and a cold mist filtered down, occasionally giving way to large fat droplets lasting in only seconds-long fits, as if the clouds themselves were confused. The flashing lights of firetrucks faded while police squad cars zipped back and forth, responding to calls down seemingly every side street in town. Bomber barely saw them. He just trudged forward, semi cognizant that he didn't know where he was heading. The town he'd lived in for thirty-three years looked completely foreign. He marveled at how lost he could feel in a place so familiar.

By now Old Town was boiling. Groups of protesters and rioters clashed with each other in earnest, with Sheriff Connie's limited supply of police officers, in full riot gear, intervening where they could. Longstreeters brandished their guns, but to their credit never pulled the triggers. Instead, they threw punches and took prideful poses while a photographer from *The Fox Howler* snapped pictures. The Glass Jaws pulled their shirts over their faces, hiding their hateful snarls, but doing little to protect from the clouds of tear gas now creeping down the street. Cars parked along the curb were smashed with bats or tagged with spray-painted campaign slogans. Bomber trudged on, weaving loosely between the hordes of people he knew who ran from smashed windows with hidden faces and arms full of stolen treasures.

Up the street, old Earl stood outside his barbershop. His shoulders were slumped and he stared through the broken front window. His old barber chair lay on its side amid a glass-covered sidewalk. Inside, the assortment of mismatched chairs was smashed to splinters, his flags shredded. The candy-striped barber pole, ripped from its holder, now leaned dented and dirty across the kicked-in door. Earl didn't move as Bomber approached. He was dressed only in a stained undershirt and slacks, held up by fraying red suspenders. He shivered against the cold and didn't react at all when Bomber draped his coat over the old man's shoulders.

"Is it bad?" Earl asked, squinting through cataracts and mist-covered glasses.

"Yeah, Earl," Bomber said. "It's bad."

Earl nodded. His lip trembled, but then stiffened and a single tear slid from his eye before mixing with the rain. A photographer from *The Fox Hollow Post* kneeled quietly in front of them and snapped pictures, the shudder clicking relentlessly.

"Those are gonna be real tear-jerkers," he said, smiling like a goon. Bomber swiped at his camera, but the photographer bounced away, giggling.

Bomber looked back to Earl and the two stood quietly for several minutes.

"We always tried to do the best we knew how," Earl said.

"I know you did," Bomber said.

"Hopefully people will remember what used to make them happy," he said.

Bomber wasn't sure they would.

"Help me move that thing," Earl said, pointing a knobby finger at the barber pole blocking the entrance.

Bomber lifted the pole and leaned it in the other direction as Earl shuffled in. The old man picked up his broom and set to doing the only thing he could think to do, sweeping his little shop while the world crumbled around it. Bomber collected a few broken chairs into one corner and then left the old man to his business, receiving a curt nod as he went.

7:45 p.m.

Fox Hollow was burning and Patrick McConnell was furious. He wasn't really angry about mass looting or the wanton destruction of property. Nor was he upset about the roving bands of radical nutjobs that kept sweeping through his neighborhood and kicking over his trash cans. What irked him was the call he'd just received. Apparently, a group of Gloria supporters was now occupying the parking lot of the Fox Applesauce Company's production plant and blocking the second-shift workers from entering the building. They claimed to be protesting "unfair labor practices" or some such nonsense and he would have to go and set things right.

McConnell felt the weight of the brass knuckles in his pocket as he locked his front door. Despite the anger and irritation of having to return to work, he felt almost giddy with anticipation at the thought of bashing a few liberal punks.

He made his way down the sidewalk to where his massive diesel truck was parked along the city curb. At least the mobs had had the good sense not to disturb his truck. His street was quiet now, but sirens could be heard coming from the direction of Old Town.

As he rounded the truck, he noticed movement up near his garage. A child dressed in a werewolf costume was standing near the small gated fence that connected his house to his garage, separating the front yard from the back.

"Hey there," McConnell yelled over the hood of his truck. He stuck his hand up in an attempt to get the child's attention. No response.

"Hey there," he yelled again. "You're two days early for Halloween."

The child turned, facing the gate to the backyard. The tail on the werewolf costume was swishing back and forth.

Spoiled kids and their expensive costumes, McConnell thought. He missed the days of toilet paper mummies and bedsheet ghosts.

He started back up the walkway. At the same time, the child lifted the latch on the gate and pushed through to the path between the house and garage.

"Hey!" McConnell yelled, starting to jog now. "You can't go back there. That's private property."

He felt stupid saying it. Of course this kid knew it was private property and he was going back there anyway. McConnell shoved his hand into his pocket, then pulled it out, the polished metal of brass knuckles now shining on his fist. He didn't love the thought of threatening a child with violence, but at that moment, he didn't hate it either.

By the time he reached the walkway, the child was already standing in the back yard near the corner of the house, still facing away. The werewolf costume appeared to be a fitted bodysuit with no seams or gaps. A larger version of one of those baby costumes new parents shove their toddlers into for Instagram photos, so they can prove later that they were cool and attentive parents.

"The jig is up, kid," McConnell said. "It's time to come out of there."

The child didn't move.

"You can either leave or I can make you leave," McConnell said. He punched the brass knuckles into his opposite hand for added effect.

The child lifted his head slightly at the sound and then walked casually around the back of the house and out of sight.

"You gotta be kidding me," McConnell said. "Alright kid, have it your way. But don't say I didn't warn you."

He jogged down the walkway and around the corner of the house.

8:18 p.m.

Bomber was in a foreign land. Some Third World country, rocked by the unrest of a toppled dictator. A tornado inside a power vacuum. Everyone around him shouted in tongues. No one he'd ever met was who they claimed to be. The street had a pulse.

Hooligans from both sides smashed the bulbs in streetlamps and the new darkness made it hard to tell who was who or where anyone's allegiances lay. Chaos owned the night and the dueling mobs merged into one fevered entity. On the west end of Old Town, a line of riot police advanced up the road clattering batons against plexiglass shields, which they used to deflect rocks, bricks, and beer cans thrown by the mob as it backpedaled toward City Hall. Three tear-gas canisters landed between Bomber and the compressing crowd. White smoke billowed from the canisters and crept toward him. He was rocked from his daze when the first molecules seared the membranes of his eyes. He blinked desperately. Turning on his heels, he ran west, rubbing his eyes and dodging masked marauders, who ran toward the confusion, hands clutching wine bottles with rags stuffed in the top.

He hurtled along, stumbling over debris and past cars whose alarms whooped, honked, and screeched on an endless loop. Everything was a blur of movement and flashing lights and distant fires until suddenly it wasn't. Bomber found himself at the base of the Sly Fox statue. The bronze soldier looked like he was leading a charge toward the Battle of Old Town. Bomber gulped air and spit a foul-tasting wad onto the sidewalk.

He looked up at the statue and spit another on the soldier's boot.

"You'd have absolutely loved all this," he said. "You prick."

The motion lights were on in the front lobby of City Hall. From the darkened windows of the mayor's office, a flash caught his eye. Inside, a flashlight beam cut across the half-drawn blinds. Before Bomber could register what was happening, the window was flooded with light and a gunshot rang out. There was shouting muffled by the windowpanes and Bomber raced for the front door.

Inside, Edith stood in the doorway of the Mayor's office,

facing in.

"Edith," Bomber said, "what is going on here?"

She glanced over her shoulder and Bomber could see the small Derringer pistol gripped in her shaking, withered hands.

"I caught him red-handed this time—rifling through Cecil's desk," Edith said. "Call the Sheriff. I'll keep him right where he's at."

Beyond her, Buck was sitting at the desk, his face white, his hands raised above his head.

"Buck?"

"Now hold on," Buck said. The "World's Greatest Mayor" mug had exploded across the desk, leaving shards of porcelain, pencils, and pens scattered in front of him. "Hold on just a damn minute."

"Shut your burglarizing mouth," Edith shouted. "You won't get another warning shot."

"I can explain everything—" Buck started.

"I was actually aiming for his head," Edith whispered over her shoulder to Bomber. "Now be a dear and pull your head out of your ass. Call the Sheriff. My arms are getting tired."

Bomber stepped forward, with both hands reaching out.

"He's a friend, Edith. I asked him to come here tonight. I didn't think there'd be anyone else here," Bomber lied. "Please put down the gun."

Edith looked back and forth between Buck and Bomber, before dropping the gun to her side. She sighed and stooped to pick up her enormous purse.

"I don't believe you," she said. "But I also don't care. I just came in to get my gun before those no-good looters make it down this far and ransack the place. The whole town's going to hell in a handbasket."

She trudged past Bomber, shaking her head.

"Please take the back way out," Bomber said. "It's getting ugly out front. I don't want you getting mixed up in it."

She waved the pistol over her head. "I've got five shots left. I'd love an excuse to use 'em." She shuffled to the front door, muttering more things Bomber couldn't make out. He turned back to Buck, who'd regained his color.

"She nearly killed me."

"I don't blame her," Bomber said.

"You don't, huh?"

"I don't," Bomber said, stepping into the office. "It's been a taxing day, so you'll forgive me for being blunt, but things haven't really been adding up."

"How so?" Buck asked. He leaned back and the old chair wheezed.

"Well, for a number of reasons, actually," Bomber said. "Most of which I overlooked initially because I was so excited to work with you. I wanted to believe you too badly."

Buck motioned for him to elaborate.

"First, the timing of everything. You showed up on the exact day Cecil was murdered and you've been conveniently unaccounted for whenever anything bad has happened since. That doesn't mean I think you're killing folks, but more drama makes better ratings, right? So you can see why I'd be suspicious. Second, your gear, which could outfit a small militia. Let's not pretend you bought it at an army surplus store. You either bought it from some bad people, stole it, or you're a—"

"Fed," Buck said.

"What?"

"Fed," Buck repeated. "That's what you were going to say, right?"

"Actually, I was going to say 'mercenary,'" Bomber said.

Buck threw his wallet across the desk, spinning it like helicopter blades. The wallet landed open. A stoic, mustacheless photo of him in a starched white shirt and black tie stared up next to big navy-blue block letters reading: FBI. On the other side was a sharp, gold shield with an eagle perched on top.

"So you're impersonating federal agents now?" Bomber asked. "Does that help you gain access to places you shouldn't be?"

"It's not a counterfeit badge," Buck said. "I *am* FBI. Special Agent Raymond Ross."

Bomber looked down at the badge again.

"Is that supposed to be some kind of superhero alter ego name? Like Peter Parker or Bruce Banner or Mickey Mouse?

"Did you think 'Buck Wildes' *wasn't* a made-up name?" Buck asked.

"Are you working with him?" Bomber asked.

"Working with who?"

"Drop the act," Bomber said, surprised by the force in his own voice. "Are you working with whatever that thing was? In the orchard. Was it Mr. Fox?"

"No to both," Buck said. He looked at his watch and then out the window. There were flashes from down the street, followed by sharp cracks. Angry shouts were getting closer. "I don't have time for this, I need to find your uncle's secret files."

"Secret files?"

"Incriminating files," Buck said. "He told me he had dirt on the Fox family, but he wouldn't send me documents. He thought they'd get intercepted, like the KGB was hiding in the damn mailbox or something. Paranoid old coot. He tried to fax them, but he couldn't figure out the fax machine. I kept getting blank pages. And of course, navigating email was out of the question."

"So he told you he had secret files when you were pretending to be an FBI agent?"

"I *am* an FBI agent," Buck repeated. "I'm undercover. *Deep* undercover. That's all I do is undercover. That's what 'Buck Wildes' is, a way to gain access to places most agents can't. And I'm currently working a case that'll bring the Fox family down."

"They've already been brought down."

Buck laughed. "Smoke and mirrors," he said. "You people only know what the rich want you to know."

"Prove it."

"I would, if I could find the files."

"And what if I just call up the FBI and ask them to verify your employment?" Bomber said, pulling his phone from his pocket.

"I don't think they have a hotline for that sort of thing," Buck said. "Nor do they just pony up information on deep-cover agents." He paused. "And I'm not sure anyone would be able to confirm my story anyway."

"Not sure—because you're a liar?"

"Because there are only a handful of people that know I'm

still an agent."

"That's convenient," Bomber said.

"It's true," Buck said. "I'm with the Department of Cryptozoology."

"Bullshit. The FBI doesn't have a Department of Cryptozoology."

"The FBI *did* have a Department of Cryptozoology," Buck explained, "though its existence wasn't general knowledge, even by those within the bureau. A sub-department of the FBI's Science and Technical Services Division, The Department of Cryptozoology was established in the early 1970's as a response to a wave of Bigfoot sightings and inquiries coming out of the Pacific Northwest." Buck grinned. "They called it Sasquatch Fever. It eventually died out, but the department was kept active due to its unique ability to infiltrate and assimilate into rural communities rife with counterfeiters, dope smugglers, moonshiners, and meth labs. As it turns out the Venn diagram of Bigfoot enthusiasts and meth-heads has a rather large overlap. Throughout the 1980s and 90s, the department was on continuous loan to various DEA, ATF, and FDA task forces, making them the secret spies of the War on Drugs. By the early 2000s, the drug war had ebbed, along with the crypto-hunting communities. The department was deemed obsolete and earmarked for dissolution, but we were ultimately saved due to several fortuitous clerical errors within the bureaucracy. Still, our budget was all but severed, leaving funding for only one remaining agent." Buck jabbed his thumb at his chest and gave Bomber a meaningful look.

"What agency are you on loan to now?" Bomber pressed. He was interested to see how intricate the lie really was.

"Environmental Protection Agency," Buck said.

"Okay, so you're telling me, the FBI loaned a deep-cover cryptozoologist field agent to the Environmental Protection Agency, to come to Fox Hollow to look into the conspiratorial rants of its elderly, dementia-addled mayor?"

"You should write headlines for *The Fox Howler*," Buck said.

Bomber lifted his phone. "I'm calling Sheriff Connie."

"March 9, 2007," Buck said.

Bomber stopped. "What?"

"March 9, 2007," Buck repeated. "Buckley, Washington, outside of Tacoma." He sucked his teeth. "Dr. Oslo Hornsby, Chief Chemical Engineer and head of Research and Development at Earth Mother Chemical Company was brutally murdered in his laboratory. The lab was ransacked so thoroughly that it took a full week to confirm the only thing missing was Dr. Hornsby's personal laptop. Cause of death was ruled an animal attack."

He took a breath and continued.

"July 15, 2009. Parking lot of Green Grow Labs LLC, Flushing, Indiana. Senior Chemist Dr. Walter Whitmore was found disemboweled in the back seat of his Audi Roadster. His left arm was severed at the elbow. The appendage and the briefcase previously chained to it were never recovered. The arm had been chewed off."

Bomber lowered the phone. Buck relaxed a little.

"May 12, last year. Central Valley, California, ChemX Corporation's R&D test fields. Three-time Chemy Award winner and renowned fertilizer expert Doctor Ellie 'E.E.' Ellis was brutally attacked between rows of Northern Highbush Blueberries on her way to conducting field experiments with a chemically-enhanced fertilizer—a fertilizer that would revolutionize agriculture by accelerating growth rates in organic material. Dr. Ellis' throat was not the only thing missing. Her duffle bag, containing the experimental compound, was never found."

Bomber searched Buck's face.

"Those are only three of a dozen such attacks, murders, and abductions," Buck said, "but the Dr. Ellis attack has a particularly interesting caveat."

Bomber took a seat opposite the desk.

"When the authorities arrived on the scene, officers found nine migrant workers huddled in a nearby shed. Most were in shock. Too terrified to speak. One of the older men finally spoke up. He swore Dr. Ellis had been attacked by a Chupacabra."

"No shit," Bomber whispered.

"No shit, indeed," Buck said. "The Tex-Mex Dogman."

"So what is the EPA's interest in all of this?" Bomber asked. He hated himself a little for getting sucked into the story.

"Neither the chemicals nor the research in question were ever approved by the U.S. government and could have serious environmental implications in the wrong hands. And that's where Great Uncle Cecil comes into the picture. As you may or may not know, your great uncle liked to take lustful walks in the orchard with an old lady friend—Doris, I believe."

"Yes," Bomber said. "I'm unfortunately aware."

"Well, apparently they stumbled across some—abnormalities."

"Abnormalities?"

"Abnormalities," Buck stated again. "Apples as big as a man's head and an odd shade of blue, as he reported them."

Bomber felt the Blue Goo packet still in his pants pocket.

"So he finds a few freak apples and that prompts him to call the EPA?"

"That coupled with numerous concerned letters from a town busybody alarmed about the rising rate of dementia cases at The Golden Years Assisted Living Facility. Would you like to guess who the busybody was?"

"Ms. Carol Meyers," Bomber whispered.

"Bingo."

Bomber felt deflated. He'd been delighted at the notion that his great-uncle had held a secret passion for the mystery of the Dogman and that his political life had prevented him from letting his freak flag fly. Now, come to find out, Cecil had only been concerned about the potential poisoning of the town.

"But you said the EPA got the call," Bomber said. "I still don't see how you got involved."

"I'd done some work for the EPA in the past and an old handler of mine filled me in on a small town in Michigan with some anomalies—"

"Abnormalities," Bomber corrected.

"Yes, Abnormalities," Buck said. "He'd cross-referenced the town name with bureau files and found another case referencing Fox Hollow. One of my cases."

"A case about what?"

"One of the first cases I ever worked was a strip-club massacre in Kentucky, just outside of Fort Knox. Fine Fillies was the name of the joint, I think. Everything down there is horse-themed. It's weird. Not unlike the overdone apple theme here. Seven people dead, including two soldiers. One soldier MIA. A Private Sylvester Fox of Fox Hollow, Michigan."

Bomber's mouth hung open.

"Coroner ruled the deaths as an animal attack. They figured a freak incident with a cougar, given the geography. At first, everyone assumed Private Fox was dead. Carried off by the mountain lion. Though that'd have to be one big-ass lion."

"At first?"

"Yes," Buck continued. "There were two survivors. One soldier. One stripper. The soldier had been lucky enough to be in the bathroom during the attack. They had all just graduated Basic Training, you see, and had snuck off base to get crazy and make up for the previous nine weeks of misery. The soldier claimed Sly Fox never even made it to the strip club and had split from the group beforehand. Allegedly, he'd had intentions of going AWOL, which is why he ended up dishonorably discharged and I'm assuming why his father lied to the town about his death. The massacre was clearly an animal attack, so he was never suspected of the deaths. The Army doesn't really follow up aggressively with Basic Trainees who bolt, so he just kinda fell off the radar."

"But if they thought it was a cougar, why'd they call in the *monster* hunter?"

"The stripper was a local girl who, coincidentally, went by the stage name of Foxy Roxy," Buck said. "She swore up and down that it was some sort of miniature wolfman that tore everybody up. And she believed it. She was completely distraught. I mean, really freaking out. Turns out she was high on meth, which is why they ultimately called me in. Figured if I could connect with her on the wolfman deal, I might be able to get a bead on the local meth labs."

"And?"

"Never found the meth labs," Buck sighed.

"Not that, you idiot," Bomber said. "The attack. You said the creature was miniature?"

"I didn't. Roxy did. I wasn't there to validate her claim though, so that all just got ignored. It wasn't until I heard the name Fox Hollow again that I started piecing things together."

The chaos outside was growing louder, but the blinds were closed, giving the noise the effect of a movie playing from another room.

Bomber stood, intending to look out the window, but his eyes caught something in the shattered "World's Best Mayor" mug. In the middle of pens and porcelain was a small brass skeleton key. Buck's eyes followed his and they jumped for it simultaneously, with Bomber barely beating him out. Bomber came around the desk and with a twist of the key, the drawers that had been a mystery to him were unlocked. Buck opened the bottom drawer, finding it empty and letting out a tired groan. Bomber opened the top drawer and this time both of them groaned. The only thing inside was a yellowed old newspaper. Buck leaned back in the leather chair and rubbed his eyes.

"Another dead end."

Bomber plucked the newspaper from the drawer and unfolded it. The paper was an issue of the long-dead *Fox Hollow Gazette* dated Thursday, October 16, 1947. The headlines were all of national news: a piece about Chuck Yeager's historic supersonic flight, flown two days earlier a fear-mongering column about communists in Hollywood; and an opinion piece about Harry S. Truman's recent televised public address—the first of its kind— and how it was a trend unlikely to continue. Bomber thumbed through the paper finding nothing of note. Glass clinked behind the pages and Bomber lowered the paper to find Buck had removed the highball glasses and the whiskey bottle from Cecil's other drawer.

"You got any better ideas?" Buck asked. Bomber looked toward the window where more shouts came from the street.

"No. I really don't."

Bomber folded the paper closed and took a quick glance at the back page. He was about to throw it onto the desk when he stopped. At the bottom of the page was a small article, tucked in the lower corner.

"Listen to this headline," Bomber said. "*WILD BEAST STALKS LOCAL ORCHARD*"

Buck stopped pouring and Bomber continued reading: "'Yesterday, two Fox Hollow residents claim to have witnessed something earth-shattering. While walking the rows of Orchard #42, the couple claims to have spotted the form of a wild beast near the drainage pond which the town youth have dubbed The Kissing Pond. The individuals, who wish to remain anonymous, claim the monster appeared to be a species of canine, having a 'wolf-like body, but ambulating bipedally.' They claim it stood roughly four feet tall and was an orange hue. The witnesses state the wolfman was preoccupied, feeding on the carcass of a dead animal, which allowed them to avoid detection. Though this reporter is skeptical, it's worth noting that black bears, coyotes, and red foxes do frequent the Fox Hollow area. It should also be noted that the eyewitnesses smelled distinctly of apple brandy at the time of the interview. Finally, as a reminder, the Orchard 42 Drainage Pond is private property owned by Fox Applesauce Corp. and trespassing, regardless of your innocent (or not so innocent) intentions, is illegal.'"

Bomber set the paper down and the two men stared at each other.

"I don't see how it changes anything," Buck said. "Other than that it confirms you're not the only crazy person in town."

"See what I mean about having alcohol on your breath," Bomber said.

Buck shrugged and knocked back his glass of whiskey. There was a flash outside and a large boom. Bomber jumped.

"Flash-bang grenade," Buck said. "Sheriff Connie's getting serious."

Bomber could hear the front door rattling and he was glad he'd locked it behind him. Buck edged the other glass of whiskey toward Bomber.

"You might as well drink it," Buck said. "It's the end of an era. Ain't nobody going to trust anybody about anything anymore anyway."

Bomber pulled the glass toward him. He didn't have the heart to tell Buck he'd folded hours earlier and taken a pull from Marty's bottle.

"It's a shame," Buck said. "Fox Hollow seemed like a pleasant place. At least from the outside." He pointed to the wall of photos, the pictorial history of Bomber's entire world. "All that's not going to mean shit after today. Even when people look back at it, trying to reminisce about happier times, it'll all be tainted. It's funny what we sometimes choose to ignore. Something has been bubbling in this town for a long time. There's something insidious behind each of those pictures."

Behind those pictures, Bomber thought. He jumped to his feet and with the newspaper in hand, ran to the wall of photos.

"What are you doing now?"

"This paper was from October 16, 1947," Bomber said. "The article said the sighting was the day before."

"So?"

Bomber scanned the pictures which hung in chronological order, starting with Cecil's inauguration. His eyes stopped on the third picture in, dated October 15, 1947. While the rest of the photographs were significant markers in the town's history, this picture was of a young Cecil and a pretty young woman, both dressed in bathing suits, near a small pond surrounded by apple trees. A brass placard under the picture read:

October 15, 1947
- Kissing Pond -

"Is that Doris Grayson?" Bomber wondered out loud.

Bomber reached up and lifted the picture from its nail. Buck let out a soft whistle as he walked over. Behind the photograph was a perfectly hidden wall safe.

"Well, I'll be damned," Buck said. "How do you suppose we open it?"

There was more commotion from outside and a single gunshot sounded. Bomber hoped Edith hadn't murdered anyone.

"Probably with this," Bomber said. On the back of the picture was a sticky note. He flipped it over to reveal a lock combination.

Buck raised an eyebrow.

"Doesn't seem like a real secure method."

"He was ninety-three years old," Bomber said, "with rapidly progressing dementia."

"Still," Buck said. "Can you imagine thinking that someone

might find a secret key, to open a locked drawer, to decipher an old newspaper, to find a hidden wall safe, but decide not to flip over a sticky note to reveal the combination?"

Bomber was already twisting the dial and the last number gave a satisfying click. The two men looked at each other and the small handle *ka-chunk*ed as Bomber pulled it down. The door swung open and they both gagged. The smell was a punch to the nose. Inside, the safe was divided into two shelves. The bottom shelf was stuffed with trash, rotten apple cores, banana peels, empty Bloo Goo pouches, and what appeared to be a pair of soiled, whitey-tighty underwear.

"What the hell?" Buck said through the shirt pulled over his nose.

"I told you. Rapidly progressing dementia."

"There. On the top shelf," Buck pointed.

Bomber pulled out a manila folder and opened it.

The first document in the stack was a vehicle title for the '67 Cadillac in Cecil's garage.

"That's curious," Bomber muttered. The title was still in the name of its previous owner, Gloria's deceased husband, Edgar Scott Glass. Half of the title transfer section had been completed by Gloria, only three weeks prior.

While Bomber was pondering the implications of the vehicle title, Buck had pulled the remaining documents and was grinning like an idiot.

"It's all here," Buck said. "Everything. Soil sample results. Medical reports, which he apparently linked to the soil samples. Bunch of photos of some weird-ass looking apples."

He was thumbing through a stack of photos when he suddenly stopped.

"What?"

Buck handed Bomber a photo. It was a grainy image, but showed a wolf-like creature, standing on two legs over a blurry mound on the ground. Buck handed him a second photo.

"Oh god," Bomber said. "A little warning would've been nice."

The photo was of a mutilated corpse. The man in the picture appeared to be of Hispanic descent. His eyes were wide, frozen in horror. His bottom jaw had been ripped away, along with most of his throat, giving the appearance of an elongated scream. Several long claw marks opened a forest green polo shirt, darkened with blood. A fox-head emblem was sewn over the right breast. Bomber recognized the shirt. It was the same style worn by the landscape crew at Fox Mansion. The man's intestines lay in a heap next to him.

There was a loud thud and Bomber looked up. Buck was lying on the ground. Papers and photos were scattered across the floor.

"Buck!" he yelled. "What the—"

He stopped when he saw it: a dart sprung from Buck's neck, its feathered blue end still quivering.

8:42 p.m.

Connie shifted her weight forward and dug her knee deep between Ron-Boy's shoulder blades. He was face down on the ground screaming for Big Mama, his thick neck wrenched upward. He choked on cries as he tried to keep his fat cheeks off the concrete. A spent tear gas canister lay only feet away and while the wind had carried off its contents, Connie could still feel a sting behind the visor of her riot gear.

"Police brutality," Ron-Boy screamed. "Mama! Help, Mama! I'm being brutalized!"

"You have the right to remain—"

"Mama, help!"

Connie read him his rights, albeit robotically. He wasn't listening anyway and her attention was focused on the scattering mob. She figured Bruce was out there somewhere. She'd spent the last several hours pulled in every direction, responding to a never-ending barrage of emergency calls reporting vandalism, destruction of property, noise violations, aggravated assaults, domestic disturbances, and even two separate instances of indecent exposure.

Citizens who two weeks ago would've waved cheerful greetings were now hurling rocks and insults and the occasional Molotov cocktail. They fought with the police and they fought with each other. They no longer had any intention of coercing one another into a new line of thinking or swaying anyone's vote. They wanted only the complete destruction of the opposing side. They screamed political mantras with the fervor of religious radicals, their bodies quaked with the rush of casual conflict. At the center of it was Gloria Glass and Carl Longstreet, but there was something more, something else loomed in the background. Something she couldn't quite put her finger on.

And through it all, Connie could only think of Bruce. She couldn't bring herself to believe that he'd played a conscious role in inciting the night's violence. She'd raised him better, hadn't she? Or maybe she hadn't raised him enough. She scanned the crowds, as she groped for Ron-Boy's wrists.

"You're on my spine," Ron-Boy whimpered. "I've got the

scoliosis."

"Consider me your chiropractor for the evening," Connie said. She had Ron-Boy's rifle slung across her back and she struggled to recall if she'd placed the weapon on safe. Something Ron-Boy should have done to begin with, before a careless trigger-finger caused him to fire an accidental round. The round had ricocheted off the Sly Fox statue and seemed to have caused no further damage, but it was enough excuse, and distraction, for Sheriff Connie to take one of the riot ringleaders out of the mix. Especially since reinforcements hadn't arrived yet.

Connie had reluctantly called the Cedar Mills Police Department, but their Sheriff was less than gracious and refused to send more than three officers due to the anti-Cedar Mills rhetoric that had been spilling from Fox Hollow on the lips of the Longstreet disciples. It turns out, when you preach isolationism, sometimes you get what you ask for, or at least that's what the Cedar Mills Sheriff told Connie before he'd hung up on her. A few other departments around the county had reluctantly agreed to send officers, but between spin up and travel time, it was hard to tell when they'd actually arrive.

Ron-Boy yelled something about his scoliosis again and Connie missed a transmission crackling over her radio.

"Shut the hell up," Connie snapped, finally cinching handcuffs around his biscuit-wrists.

She eased off her knee and he sighed, letting his face sink to the concrete.

"Say again, over," Connie said into the radio.

"Roger," said the static voice of Sergeant Householder. "Just got word from Fire Chief Douglas. They're responding to another fire."

One hell of a night, Connie thought.

"Did it spread from Wild Goose Yoga?" She asked.

"Negative," Householder said. "An isolated incident. Private residence."

"Who?"

There was a pause from the other end.

"Patrick McConnell's house."

8:44 p.m.

The fox sat in the mayor's chair with its feet propped on the desk, Buck's stolen tranquilizer gun in its right hand. Or was it a paw? It appeared to Bomber to be a combination of the two, but his mind was more concerned with the prospect of being shot. The gun barrel was leveled at Bomber's chest and the fox had the casual manner of an Old West gunslinger dominating a dirty saloon.

There was a tense moment before the fox's shoulders slumped and the gun's barrel drifted toward the ceiling. Bomber breathed easier. The fox was larger than before, at least a foot taller, or longer, or however you'd classify it. Its torso and arms were puffed with new, sinewy muscles that bordered on comical, considering the creature's height. If nothing else, the black fanny pack was the same. The fox wiggled his clawed toes and stretched his chiseled arms behind his head, grasping his own elbows, while the tranq-gun rested across furry thighs.

The fox opened his mouth into a terrible, toothy smile and the office's fluorescent lights glittered off a single gold tooth.

The right canine.

"Goddammit," Bomber said. "I knew it."

"You didn't know anything." Sly laughed. "Sit."

He motioned to the chairs opposite the desk. Bomber looked at them warily.

"If I wanted you dead, I could've done it a thousand times by now," Sly said. "Sit."

Bomber walked over and sat.

"Good boy." Sly smiled, which appeared to be an unnatural state for his fox face and his jowls quivered in an involuntary snarl. "I'm disappointed in you, Bomber. All you had to do was stay out of it."

Sly lifted the whiskey bottle off the desk and added more to Bomber's untouched glass, until it was nearly overflowing. Bomber picked it up, not knowing what else to do.

"I'm ten years sober," Bomber said. He used his finger to drag a fox-hair out of the brown liquid, before setting his glass back on the desk.

Sly put his hands behind his head again. "You had a drink earlier tonight. I can smell it." His nose twitched and he nodded at the glass. "The alternative is I rip out your throat." A real snarl rippled through his lip.

Bomber tipped his glass and drained the whiskey. It burned his throat and he coughed. "What happened to you, man?" he asked, setting the glass back on the table.

"I could ask you the same thing," Sly said, adding another healthy pour to Bomber's glass. His bushy tail poked from the back of the chair and swished lazily behind him. "Drink."

Bomber slugged back another glass full. It still burned, but no cough. He knew the liquor would be kicking in soon, so he started firing off questions.

"How long have you—?"

"Since I was nine."

"But when did you first—?"

"When I was nineteen. At Basic Training."

"But what triggered—?"

"Beats me. Bloodlust?"

"What happened to your mom?"

"Dad ate her."

"Ate her?"

"Yup. When I was nine. But only her liver. It's the most nutrient rich organ in the body."

Bomber didn't try to hide his look of disgust.

"It's what predators do," Sly added, pouring more whiskey.

"What happened to your dad?"

"Story for another time, I'm afraid. Drink."

Bomber drank. His thoughts were beginning to dance.

"How often are you like *this*?" he asked, motioning to Sly's body.

"All. The. Time," Sly said. "Long story. Science is great and all, but you can't break a curse with chemistry. At least, not yet."

Bomber noticed a small tube containing a vibrant orange liquid protruding from the fanny pack and disappearing under the fur at the top of Sly's hip. Sly noticed him noticing it and shifted his posture to hide the tube.

"You look bigger than you did the udder night." Bomber

heard his words begin to slip.

Sly smile-snarled, but remained silent as he slid the whiskey bottle across the desk.

"Why are you doing all this?" Bomber asked.

Sly's laugh was a hollow, hissing thing.

"Listen," he said. "I didn't come here to have a heart-to-heart with you or catch up on old times. I came here to tie up loose ends--" he pointed to Buck and the mess of documents on the floor "--and to offer you a fair warning. Stop looking for me. Stop the Dogman nonsense. Forget about 'Buck Wildes' and go back to being your normal mediocre, self-absorbed self."

Bomber tried to wrap his fairly drunk brain around the cursed half-man-half-fox sitting in front of him, chastising him about "Dogman nonsense." Blue and red police flashers bled through the window blinds and Sly drummed his claws against the chair as Bomber fought to clear the fog thickening his thoughts.

"Did you kill Uncle Cecil?" Bomber asked.

"Obviously," Sly said. "Do you have any idea how frustrating it is trying to bribe someone with dementia?"

"I liked it better when you died in Iraq," Bomber said. He hadn't meant to say it out loud, but bourbon is a vocal lubricant. He raised the bottle and sloshed the brown liquor.

"Finish it," Sly said. He leaned back and put his feet on the desk again.

Bomber snickered at the sight of the red tufts of hair between Sly's toes. He raised the bottle, drained it, and grimaced out of habit, no longer feeling the burn.

"So, what?" Bomber said. "I get-ta walk away? Free to spill yer story to anyone and anyone who'll liszen?"

Sly laughed.

"You go right ahead," he said. "An alcoholic falls off the wagon and makes outrageous claims about the magical creature he only sees while drunk? And this time, it's a cursed incarnation of his estranged best friend from high school, who by the way died a war hero? I'm sure everyone will be fascinated by your new, robust story."

Bomber smiled through numb lips. "Imma be honest," he said. "I'm feelin' a pretty bit tipsy. I only caught about half-a what you juz got done blabbering about. But people will look for Buck when he don't turn up."

"You're quite right," Sly said. "In fact, I won't be surprised if there's a nationwide manhunt for the disgraced grocery store manager accused of killing him and all the good people around Fox Hollow."

"I feel like yer imply'm yer gonna make it look like I did all thad stuff," Bomber said. "Too mag my dogman talk look real."

"Correct."

"Ats smart," Bomber nodded. His head was swimming. "I don't suppose I could convince you nadda do thad part?"

"Depends on how much noise you make," Sly said.

"Oh!" Bomber said, excited by a new thought. "What abou Paztor Mast? Why'd he deserve ta die?"

"Nobody said he was dead," Sly said.

"Good puppy," Bomber said. He half stood and tried to pat Sly's head.

Sly snapped at him.

"Bad dog!" Bomber scolded.

"Alright, I think we're done here," Sly called.

The office door creaked open. Carl Junior stood in the doorway.

"Holy shid!" Bomber explained. "Hey Junior! What're you doin her? Juz guess'n, but your name isn't really Carl Junior, is it?"

"Of course it's not Carl Junior, you ass," Junior said.

"'Of course it's not Carl Junior,'" Bomber sassed in a mocking voice. "I'm gettin' real frickin' sick of you, Carl—"

He interrupted himself with a burp.

"Classy," Sly said.

"Can ya at leasz tell me who Junior is?" Bomber asked. "You guys are a cute couple. Is it serious?"

Sly picked at his nails impatiently.

"He is a survivor of the Fine Fillies Massacre," Sly said. "And a devout Pagan. He thinks I'm the reincarnation of some ancient Celtic Wolf Goddess. The Morgan, he calls it."

"The Morrighan," Junior corrected.

"Right. What did I say?" Sly said. "Anyway, he worships me as some sort of war god. He also handles most of my day-to-day, front-office business. Face-to-face meetings, intel gathering, weapons purchasing, all that jazz. It's been a beneficial friendship."

Sly looked over at Bomber, who appeared miles away. There was a glaze over his eyes and his breathing was slow and shallow.

"Ats adorable," Bomber finally slurred. "Good fer you two."

"No use in fighting it," Sly said, checking his watch.

Bomber's face flushed. "Fighting what?" He stood up, suddenly belligerent, but still swaying. He glanced down at the empty bottle in his hand and then lofted it casually behind him where it shattered on the floor in front of the bookshelf. "I ain't drunk, if that's what yer sayin'."

"Sit down or you'll hurt yourself," Sly said.

"*You* sid down," Bomber said to Sly who was still sitting. "I'n tired of yer shid. I'm outta here. I don't think you've got da stones to stop me. You or dat wuss, Carl Juner."

Bomber turned to find Junior now directly in front of him.

"Outta my way, lacky," he said, putting his hand to Junior's chest.

There was a prick in his shoulder and he turned his head to see the blue fuzz of a tranq dart flowering from his shirt. The glint off Patrick McConnell's brass knuckles, now bridging the fingers of Junior's fist, brought his attention back around front, right before they connected with his nose.

October 30, 2017

6:30 a.m.

Sergeant Householder sat at his desk stirring a bowl of instant oatmeal. He closed his eyes, but all he could see was the mangled corpse of Patrick McConnell, still spread like a meat blanket on the grass beside the smoldering ruins of his home. He opened his eyes again. Steam danced from a cup next to him and he breathed in coffee vapors, trying to force the tension from his shoulders, neck, and face. In his ten years on the force, he'd never seen anything like the past two weeks, let alone the chaos of last night. He longed for mundane traffic stops, cat rescues, and maybe even a nasty egg salad sandwich.

He closed his eyes again. Pink entrail-tentacles crawled from McConnell's open chest cavity. They'd been chewed.

"Quite the night."

Householder opened his eyes to find Sheriff Connie standing beside his desk.

"You could say that," Householder said.

Connie sank into the empty chair of a neighboring desk. The office had finally calmed: all the rioters who needed to be processed were processed, those who needed to be jailed were jailed, and the rest, who could be released with warnings, were lectured and let go. All but Ron-Boy Carson, who sat in the rear holding cell taking up the majority of the six-foot bench. Sheriff Connie was still determining his fate and doing her best to ignore Big Mama who was making angry loops around the waiting area in a shiny new electric scooter. Between each lap, she'd stop to condemn the Fox Hollow P.D. for the injustice being brought upon her household and spouted ill-advised legal counsel to her caged son—mostly recommendations of nonviolent resistance in the way of "self-defecation."

"Shit yer britches, boy, and they'll have'ta send ya home," she kept yelling.

Connie looked over at the stack of files, born from the riots, that threatened to bury her desk completely.

"What are we going to do?" Householder asked.

"About what?"

"What do you mean, 'about what'? About the whole town imploding. About another dead body, which, by the way, is looking like straight-up murder now."

"Not really much we can do," she sighed. "About the town, that is. Except enforce the law where needed and hope things fizzle out after one of those two sociopaths gets elected."

Householder nodded.

"As for McConnell, we'll treat it as a homicide," she said.

"Suspects?"

"After last night?" Connie sighed. "Everyone. But honestly, I'd like to have a nice, long chat with Bomber's new friend, 'Buck Naked.'"

"Buck Wildes," Householder corrected.

Connie leaned forward in her chair. The smell of Householder's oatmeal was making her stomach churn. She couldn't remember the last time she'd eaten.

"Do you think we'll ever find McConnell's head?" Householder asked.

Connie shrugged.

They sat in silence for a long minute, smelling Householder's breakfast and listening to the violent quakes of Connie's empty gut.

"Which sociopath are you voting for?" Householder asked,

giving in to curiosity.

"I'm not," Connie said. "I don't like the idea of voting for my own boss."

"But what if, by not voting, you let the bad candidate win?"

Connie raised an eyebrow.

"Sorry, you let the *worst* candidate win," he corrected.

"That's the problem," Connie said. "I can't tell who the 'worst candidate' is."

As if on cue, the front door burst open and Carl Longstreet strolled in, clicking his cane on the tile floor. The dull drone of chanting voices swept in with him, bouncing off the plexiglass divider that separated the waiting area from the workspace.

The sun wasn't yet up, but a gaggle of Apple Knockers had formed under the streetlights, hoisting poster boards reading "Free Ron-Boy" and "Fox Hollow Gestapo" and "Sic Semper Tyrannis," which had a small picture of a Tyrannosaurus Rex underneath it, leading Connie to believe they weren't entirely understanding the Latin phrase.

Connie looked at Carl with tired eyes. His mere presence sapped what little energy she had left. He made eye contact with her and then Householder before spitefully tapping the silver bell at the service counter. The muscles in Connie's neck and shoulders tightened.

"What do you want?" Connie asked, her jaw clenched.

"I'm here to post bail for a Fox Hollow patriot," Carl said, puffing his chest. He clicked his cane on the floor for emphasis.

"Who?" Connie asked.

Carl deflated.

"Ronald 'Ron-Boy' Carson, of course," he said.

Big Mama gasped.

"My hero," she gurgled in what must've been her attempt at a flirtatious voice. Carl looked alarmed.

"What reason do you have to post bail for Ron-Boy Carson?" Connie asked.

"My lady—" Carl started.

"You'll address me as Sheriff," Connie interjected.

Carl hemmed and hawed. "My apologies," he said, doffing his tiny top hat. "My *Sheriff*, I am just a concerned citizen trying to right a simple wrong. An injustice, if you will. I believe that poor Ron-Boy was a victim of unfortunate circumstances. Circumstances created by Gloria Glass's left-wing, socialist agitators. You can hardly expect a person with Ron-Boy's civic passion and limited mental capacity to be able to maintain his composure. The poor boy was probably scared for his life. The whole deal is clearly self-defense."

"Ain't nothing wrong with my mental capacities," Ron-Boy shouted from the cell.

"Shush yer mouth," Big Mama yelled at him.

Connie was too tired to explain to Carl how Ron-Boy had been a key instigator of the entire fiasco.

"So you're saying he's not cognitively fit to possess a firearm?" Connie asked.

"Waz that mean?" Ron-Boy shouted.

"Means yer too dumb for guns," Big Mama shouted.

"Everyone has the right to bear arms," Carl said. "It's in the Declaration of Independence."

"It's in the Constitution," Householder corrected.

"See," Carl said. "At least someone here has some sense."

"So which is it, Carl?" Connie asked, stepping closer. "Is he smart enough to know better or too dumb to tote a gun?"

Carl straightened his bowtie and gathered his thoughts.

"I don't believe you can bar me from posting bail for a fellow citizen," he said. "How much has it been set at?"

"Ten thousand."

"Ten thousand?" Carl gasped. "Based on what charges?"

"Well," Connie said. "Disturbing the peace. Accidental discharge of a firearm. Resisting arrest. Assault. Public urination. They add up pretty quickly."

"Live free or die hard," Ron-Boy yelled from the cell.

"Isn't that a Bruce Willis movie?" Householder asked.

"I think he means, 'give me liberty or give me death,'" Connie said.

"Yeah, that one," Ron-Boy nodded.

Carl huffed as he pulled a checkbook from his breast pocket and began writing. Connie motioned to Householder who walked over and let Ron-Boy out of the cell. Ron-Boy glared at Sheriff

Connie as he waddled toward the exit.

"Where's my rifle?" he spat.

Connie scoffed.

"I'll be holding onto your rifle for now," she said. She watched as Ron-Boy and Big Mama's scooter nearly collided when both tried to move through the exit simultaneously.

"Where's yer manners boy?" Big Mama snapped. "Ladies first."

"I'm surrounded by fascists," Ron-Boy grumbled.

Even Carl looked bewildered as the two Carsons bickered their way out. He doffed his cap one more time to Connie and Householder before reluctantly following them out of the station. A muffled cheer rose from the Apple Knockers as their hero emerged onto the front sidewalk and Connie shook her head.

"What the hell is going on around here?" she asked.

"The whole town's mentally ill," Householder said.

7:58 AM

A shiver brought Bomber back. His cheek was pressed against rough, cold concrete and he could smell dirt and grass and autumn leaves. His tongue was sandpaper, scraping the dry walls of his cheeks. He opened his mouth, spilling a cloud of stale whiskey and vomit vapors. Memories crept in like burglars. He remembered the mayor's office and Buck and—Sly Fox. He flicked an eye open, but then shut it again. The movement ignited a pounding on each lobe of his dehydrated brain. He focused every ounce of his being on remaining perfectly still.

He opened his eye again, this time forcing it to stay open. In front of him was the first step to his front door. Overgrown grass and weeds choked the concrete walkway between, making him feel like he was lost in a jungle. With heavy arms, he rolled onto his back. The few stars still clinging to the western sky were losing ground to the first signs of dawn. The thought of daylight made his eye burn more. He tried to touch his other eye but stopped when pain slammed through his head again. It was swollen shut.

"Buck," he whisper-groaned.

He held his breath, partly in suspense and partly to quell the taste of bile. Mustering his will, he pushed himself to a sitting position. His stomach roiled and his guts bubbled. The yard was empty and Bomber, his mind fully rebooted, was filled with grief and fear. He had no idea how he'd gotten home, but was thankful he hadn't triggered any of the Dogman-booby-traps littering the yard.

There was a mound on his lap and he lifted his shirt to find a black fanny-pack strapped around his waist. His fingers fumbled with the zipper. Inside was a note written on stationery from the mayoral desk:

Bomber,

You disappoint me, but then again you disappoint everyone. I thought you, of all people, would understand me. After all, I am clearly the victim in all of this. My abundant wealth will probably prevent any sympathy from you and your judgmental, closed-minded kind, but you have no idea what it's like to be forced to live in luxuriant isolation. An abomination of nature, doomed to damnation for sins committed a century before my birth.

But I believe in second chances among friends. Something you didn't afford me. Enclosed in the fanny-pack (which I think you'll find quite practical) is $100,000. In addition to being payment for your discretionary silence and atonement for the whole "Gloria" business, I must insist you use this money to start your life anew somewhere other than Fox Hollow. If you stay, I will be back for my money.

Don't make me come back for my money, Bill.

Your friend (whether you like it or not),

S.F.

Bomber unzipped the fanny-pack further. The inside was packed with banded stacks of one-hundred-dollar bills. It was more money than Bomber had ever seen. He sat for several minutes, stroking the stack of bills like a long-lost pet and weighing the option of skipping town. Buck was probably dead already and he was out of a job with the grocery store gone.

He stood up slowly, steadying himself under the weight of his throbbing swollen head. Before he could move for his door, there was a clatter from the shed at the end of the driveway. A pail rolled a half circle on the asphalt, triggering one of the many motion sensors. Floodlights kicked on, bathing the side yard in intense white. Bomber looked out over the knee-high grass and weeds. A patch near the shed waved in the breeze.

Except there was no breeze.

Bomber backed up and the grass went still. He allowed himself to breathe and to feel a little foolish. He would've laughed right then, had a tripwire not triggered, sending a leftover Fourth of July firework booming into the early dawn. The explosion rattled his teeth and sparked wild barking from the tall grass where he'd seen the movement. The frenzy was accompanied by several seconds of thrashing and then silence once again.

"Probably a big raccoon," Bomber whispered. He stood on his toes again trying to get a peek. Smoke still wafted from the spent mortar tube and he imagined Gloria in her raccoon costume, Army-crawling through his yard. He picked up a chunk of concrete broken from the path and lofted it into the weeds where he imagined the animal had settled.

A yelp. Followed by a savage snarl and more barking. Bomber retreated toward the house. The ruckus subsided into low hissing and spitting and the patch of waving grass crept forward. Bomber took slow steps backward. As he moved, so did the grass. Whatever it was, it was now stalking him.

"Stay back," he shouted, as if wild animals obey verbal commands. He was answered by loud snuffs and snorts. Bomber's heel hit the first step behind him and he nearly toppled backward. He tried to fish the keys from his pants pocket, but the waistband of the fanny-pack interfered.

At the end of the walkway, the grass parted and a beast emerged, as though birthed from the jungle lawn. Bomber stumbled back again, this time losing his footing. The keys he'd finally snagged slipped from his fingers and slithered into the gap between the stairs.

The creature could have been a raccoon at one time, or perhaps the distant relative of one. It slinked across the walkway, studying Bomber. Its face was etched in a permanent snarl, lips arching over purple gums, and gleaming yellow fangs reflecting floodlights. Its fur was scattered in matted clumps across a sea of dead gray skin. Thick veins were visible everywhere. They pulsed and bulged, marring the smooth sinew that glided like mud over stone muscle. There was no symmetry to the creature, save its eyes which sat deep inside a band of black fur. Two cool gray orbs cracked with glowing channels of orange lightning. Like fire pits left to smolder.

The creature snarled at Bomber, then paused and shook its head erratically. It hacked like a hell-cat with a hell-hairball, and blood spurted from its nose, dribbling down to its chin. It shivered. Then regained itself. It took in a mighty breath and seemed to inflate, its throbbing veins expanding. The blood frothed in its mouth and it arched its back, then stepped into the weeds on the other side and out of sight.

Bomber's eyes followed the parting grass, as he groped for his keys beneath the steps. The creature was making an arc through the lawn, seeking the best angle of attack. The keys jingled against an errant knuckle and the movement in the grass stopped. With a swipe, Bomber had them and was on his feet.

Thrashing came from behind him. He lunged for the door and looked over his shoulder. With the elevation of the steps he could see the beast rushing toward him, its eyes now two orange flames. He thrust his key at the knob, but in his haste he'd produced the wrong one. He nearly dropped them again as he looked back. A wild bark. The beast lunged forward, its claws sending grass up in its wake. The next key fit but the knob stuck. He slammed his shoulder into the door and sank down, holding out his hands in futile self-defense.

SNAP

The teeth of Bomber's rusty bear trap slammed closed around the creature and it exploded like a ketchup-filled balloon, sending forward a spray of crimson.

Bomber sat in shock, dripping in a thick red gore. Around him, the blast had created a circle of carnage. Bits of tissue and fur decorated the siding of his house. Entrails draped across the branches of his untrimmed boxwoods. He watched in dazed wonder, as these larger pieces of flesh seemed to melt, dripping to the ground, their color morphing from red, to purple, to a deep neon blue. He wiped his face, finding smears of blue across his fingers, and the smell of decaying flesh brought the taste of bile back to his mouth.

An hour later, when Bomber stepped from the shower the rancid smell still lingered in his nostrils. He checked himself in the mirror. The blood had stained his skin like tattoo ink and even after vigorous scrubbing, dull blue speckles remained, blending nicely with the purple swelling around his eye. He stood there, wallowing in self-loathing, and staring at the mess in the mirror of his childhood bathroom. He was suddenly very aware of his surroundings and the comfort of his parent's home now felt bleak and artificial. The house had become a monument to his mediocrity.

He shuffled out to the open expanse of his basement-bedroom-command-center, still wrapped in his bath towel. A figure in the corner of his eye made him jump and he dropped the towel. Rex, the hodgepodge-Dogman statue, made of black market taxidermy, watched him from the base of the stairs.

"Dammit, Rex," he said. Without thinking, his fist snapped out, catching the Frankenstein-Dogman in the chin. The head tilted back and rocked forward again. It felt good.

Bomber took another swing.

This time stitches ripped from where it was connected to the stuffed fur torso.

Fake-ass Dogman, he thought. He didn't bother to pick up his towel and he turned to his command center table. The television monitors still picked up live feeds from around the yard. The camera at the front door showed a discolored circle around the old bear trap. The black-and-white cameras made the spot look like a scorched crater, as though a meteor had plunged from the heavens, narrowly missing the house. That story would be less weird and unbelievable than the truth. But he didn't dwell on it. Instead, he grabbed the table's edge and flipped it with all his might. The monitors crashed to the floor and flickered out. He picked one up and spiked it on the ground for good measure.

"Fake-ass Dogman," he yelled.

He reached up and tore the town map from the wall. Pushpins tinkled to the floor in every direction. He found more things to destroy. At his trap pile, he sent several smaller steel-jaw traps sailing across the basement, embedding one in the Buck Wildes poster above his bed.

"Fake-ass Buck," he yelled.

He was breathing heavily and blood pulsed painfully through his puffy eye. He looked down at his wrists. The veins in his forearms bulged, the muscles contracted and he bellowed, feeling nothing by white-hot rage.

Rex stood, his head cocked inquisitively to the side. Ten years of wasted time and self-sabotage. Bomber lunged forward, grabbing Rex by the waist. He hoisted it up, moving his grip to the ankles, and with one solid, overhead swing, smashed the statue over the stair banister.

"Fake-ass Bomber," he yelled.

He stumbled across the room and fell flat on the mattress of his pullout sofa. Swaths of sheet and comforter balled up in his white-knuckled fists. He pressed his face into the bed and yelled until his lungs threatened to crack his ribs.

The tension released from his back. His fists eased and his fingers creaked open. He lifted himself onto his elbows and looked down at his wrists. The bulging veins had retracted. The pulse slowed in his eye. He rolled onto his back and stared at the ceiling, regaining control of his lungs and heart, as sweat trickled across his brow.

He tilted his head back. Buck Wildes stared down at him from the poster behind his bed. Bomber slid a pillow over his manhood for good measure. He thought about the fanny-pack full of money, now buried in a heap of tainted clothes on the bathroom floor, and how easy it would be to disappear. Then he thought about all the times he'd taken the easy way out. The myriad missed opportunities to do the right thing. To make his town a better place. Flawed as it was, Fox Hollow didn't deserve to rot from within, and, fake or not fake, Buck Wildes didn't deserve to go out at the hands of Sly Fox.

12:15 p.m.

Connie rubbed the bridge of her nose.

"You told him *what?*" she asked again, though she'd already heard.

Her grandfather, Chief Hayes, sat across the desk. He was nursing an extra-large soda from Harold's Hamburger Shack. Every time the straw sputtered, he'd twirl the Styrofoam cup like a lowball.

"I told him about the curse," he said matter-of-factly. "He came asking about it."

Connie made no attempt to hide her irritation. "You can't tell people like *him* about things like *that.*"

"Why not?"

"Because he's going to believe you. And not just believe you, *obsessively* believe you."

"Why shouldn't he believe me?" Chief Hayes asked.

"Because it's a myth, Paw Paw."

"Myths have to come from somewhere," Chief Hayes said. A smile blipped at the side of his mouth.

Connie had grown up hearing the stories about the Fox family and the origin of the town. Certainly a great many injustices had been brought against her people—up to and including mass murder—and she had no doubt her people had sought retribution, but she always figured the legend of the curse was the godfather of all other town gossip. The first edition, issue one.

"So what *did* you come here for?" she asked.

Chief Hayes twirled his cup. "I'm worried about Bruce," he said.

"We're all worried about Bruce," Connie said. "Always."

Chief Hayes shook his head.

"No, this is different," he said. "Yesterday, I saw him outside of Marty's. Before the fire. He was in his silly fox get-up again, yelling at the store with a megaphone. Much of what he said was not repeatable. That is not normal behavior for a boy his age."

"I'll talk with him," Connie sighed.

"I would like him to come hunting with me," Chief Hayes said. "I think killing something would be good for him."

"I'll talk with him," Connie repeated. "If I can ever find him."

3:03 p.m.

Bomber crept down a row of gnarled, unkempt trees in Orchard 42, hating every minute of it. His righteous ambition to save Buck had petered quickly when he realized he had no idea where Buck was or if he was even still alive. He was fairly certain, given their conversation, that Sly was still living at his parent's mansion. This revelation had given Bomber momentary pleasure. With all his riches, Sly was also living in his parents' house—though he probably wasn't residing in the basement surrounded by taxidermied animal parts. Even if Sly was operating from the mansion, there was no way to be certain it's where he'd taken Buck. Fox Applesauce owned facilities and properties all over town and Bomber didn't know what kind of sway Sly still held with the company or if the company itself was now an evil entity, entirely aware of the sinister misgivings of its phantom president.

After much deliberation and a microwave burrito, Bomber had decided the mansion was the best place to start. Returning to his bed, he'd stared at the ceiling, contemplating any realistic means of accessing the mansion without being gunned down immediately by the mansion's armed guards. He could think of none, but he knew that every minute he spent lying there, the chances of recovering Buck alive got smaller and smaller.

Not going to make any progress lying here on my back, he thought.

That single thought had triggered a domino effect in the back of his brain and soon he was thinking of Doris Grayson and what she'd said to him:

I don't make a living on my back.

She'd said this in reference to the prostitutes smuggled in and out of the old brothel-turned-mansion via the storm drain that fed the Old Kissing Pond. He'd sat bolt upright, recalling her addled retelling of the Dogman legend and how it was rumored to live in the same tunnel. A plan had snapped into place like the teeth of his rusty bear trap.

As he drew closer to The Kissing Pond, he began to notice a change around him. The deeper he ventured into Orchard 42, the larger the apples became and by the time he reached the last rise before the pond, the apples were the size of melons, their skin a magnificent purple hue. Inversely, the trees had become especially pitiful, their trunks shriveled and brittle, limbs sagging under the weight of freak fruit. Some branches had snapped leaving splintered white wood jabbing at the sky like fractured bone.

Bomber got low as he neared the crest of the hill overlooking the Kissing Pond, finally getting down and crawling to peek over the top. He was dressed in his apple-drape camo, which didn't afford pockets, so he'd begrudgingly strapped Sly's fanny pack around his waist and now had to admit to finding it surprisingly functional, though he had to swing it aside to keep it from dragging in the dirt. In it, he'd placed a pocketknife, a pair of small binoculars, a length of paracord, and two expired protein bars in case the rescue mission took him past dinnertime. His cell phone was missing from the inventory, as he hadn't seen it since his encounter with Sly the night prior.

A skin of blue-green sludge bubbled across the surface of The Kissing Pond, swallowing the sunlight. He could smell the rot of algae spiked with bitter, pesticide runoff. Behind the pond was a concrete spillway, leading up to the storm drain which was large enough for a person to stand upright in. An iron gate had been fitted over the drain's entrance and, with his binoculars, he could see there was a lock securing it.

He rolled onto his back to brainstorm how he'd open the lock. Looking up, he found one of the engorged apples dangling a foot above his head. Curiosity got the best of him and he reached for it. The moment his finger touched the soft skin, the apple began to shake violently. Bomber scrambled, retreating as the apple swelled further.

POP!

The dancing apple was gone in a spray of neon blue. A thick sauce splattered across leaves, branches, and grass, and a familiar fruity scent overpowered the Kissing Pond's bog water. The small explosion disturbed nearby apples, which repeated the process until the tree was completely spent of apples and soaking in a puddle of Blue Goo. The chemical laden mixture seeped into the soil leaving a thick, black muck.

The sweet smell of the sauce filled the air and Bomber had the sudden urge to eat some. The desire was small and quiet at first but stacked exponentially until he felt a painful pressure in his chest. His heartbeat hammered in his ears and he looked down at his forearms to find his veins purple and bulging again. He squeezed his fists and they emerged like a tangle of snakes. Stumbling over the hill, he ran toward the pond, and as the smell of rotting algae overpowered the apples, his heart settled and his veins retreated.

What the hell was that? he wondered.

He approached the storm drain from the side, scanning the area for any signs of surveillance cameras or sensors. Seeing none, he approached, keeping a wary eye on the pond itself, which occasionally sprung to life with fits of bubbles trickling up from its murky depths. As he neared the edge, a noise from deep within the black tunnel caught his ear, a faint chirping. Bomber tried to imagine what type of bird would build its nest in such a dark, dank tunnel, but as he listened, the chirping maintained a ceaseless rhythm. A steady, cyclical, metallic squeak, like a flimsy wheel on a Marty's Market shopping cart. The noise grew louder and soon Bomber could hear hushed voices, as if the tunnel was speaking. The amplified whispers slipped out in guttural mutterings of "dude" and "sucks" and "stinks."

Bomber retreated into a cluster of arrowwood shrubs near the mouth of the tunnel and hid. The gate began to rattle. Two thick, white arms emerged through the rusty crossbars, one holding a large skeleton key. The hands were clumsy, but the key eventually found its mark, and the lock was removed. The gate swung open, a scream escaping from its rusty hinges, and a shock of red hair emerged from the dark.

"What the hell?" Bomber whispered.

One of the Coughlin twins stepped out of the storm drain, into the light. His face contorted in the sun and he held a freckled white arm above his eyes.

"Stupid sun," he grumbled.

"Hurry up and help me," came another voice from inside the tunnel. "It stinks in here."

"Stinks out here, too."

The first twin turned and grabbed a flat metal surface that emerged from the door. He grunted as he lifted it and stepped backward, careful not to step into the pond. The metal surface became a rolling gurney, with large deep-tread wheels. A black body bag lay on it and threatened to slide forward from the incline.

Bomber felt sick. He was sure it was Buck in the bag.

The second twin followed behind the gurney, stepping down into the concrete spillway.

"My eyes," he shouted, crushing his eyes shut.

"Stop shoutin'," Twin One snapped. "You want somebody to hear?"

Twin Two was too busy trying to hide his eyes in his armpit to respond.

"I wish we didn't have to do this in broad daylight," Twin One continued. "Third time this week." He grunted again as he started pulling the gurney up the embankment to a service road above.

"What do you think they got going on in there?" Twin Two asked, barely pushing on the back end.

"Dad said not to ask questions," Twin One grunted.

"I know," Twin Two said. "I'm just sayin', all these Mexicans ain't dyin' from work accidents." He patted the body bag.

Bomber was relieved to hear it wasn't Buck in the bag but quickly felt guilt for his relief.

The twins crested the embankment and brought the gurney to rest on the road. Twin One doubled over gasping, his hands on his knees. Twin Two was barely breathing and leaned over the edge, peering back down at the storm drain.

"You forgot to lock the gate," he said.

Twin One looked up and wiped the hair from his eyes.

"Me?" he snarled. "You were bringing up the rear. That's your job."

"You were movin' too fast," Twin Two said. "You didn't stop so I could do it. Besides, I went back last time. It's your turn."

Twin One looked nervously at the pond, then began shuffling down the hill, cursing. As he neared the bottom, a large cluster of bubbles formed on the other end of the pond. Twin Two pointed at them, but Twin One had already seen and began moving at twice the speed. He secured the lock, removed the skeleton key, and looked over his shoulder. The bubbles had morphed into a low wave, cresting the back of whatever lurked beneath.

"Shiiiiit," he sang. He tucked the key behind a nearby rock and scrambled up the hill.

Bingo, Bomber thought.

The wave came within ten feet of the pond's edge and then dissipated into nothingness.

"I don't know what that is," said Twin Two, "but I think it'd be worth mentioning to Mr. Junior next time."

The two brothers bumped off down the service road and Bomber listened until the sound of the squeaky gurney disappeared completely. Keeping a wary eye on the pond, Bomber retrieved the key. The tunnel was cold, dark, and musty, which is exactly what you'd expect of a century-old storm drain and had he not witnessed the sons of the town's funeral home director exiting the tunnel with a corpse, he would've assumed he was following a false hunch. But now he walked headlong into the black void, questioning the sanity of his mission. He left the gate unlocked with the key still protruding from the faceplate. He didn't know if he'd come back this way again, but if he did, there was a good chance he'd be coming fast.

3:48 p.m.

Sheriff Connie sat in her patrol car fighting back tears. Her cheeks, nose, eyes, and forehead spasmed, as she struggled to keep composure. She had to stay professional.

But why?

Farther down the wood-lined road, her officers were conducting a thorough search of Bruce's truck, which was jackknifed into the ditch. Two out-of-town monster hunters had been wandering the woods when they'd discovered the truck an hour earlier. They were now giving statements to Sergeant Householder, telling him the vehicle was unoccupied when they found it. The poor hunters had no idea why the police had responded so quickly to a simple, abandoned vehicle call, but that was before they'd found blood in the cab and Patrick McConnell's signature brass knuckles wedged between the driver's seat and center console.

There's going to be nothing simple about any of this, Connie thought. *Bruce, what have you done?*

She blamed herself, of course, for allowing the violent video games, the horror movies, the rap music, the nightly news. If only she'd put her foot down over some of the rotten things he'd been consuming.

Consuming.

Another problem. What kind of stable mind could maintain itself on a diet of processed cakes, soda, and neon applesauce? She felt as if she'd failed her son in every conceivable way.

"Sherriff?"

Connie lifted her head to find Sergeant Householder, standing over her. She made her face of stone. "What is it, Sergeant?"

He held a small evidence bag. Inside was a shred of fabric.

"We found this caught in the driver's door," he said. "Fabric look familiar?"

The way he asked let Connie know he'd already placed it, too. The fabric was a thick red flannel, identical to the trademark cutoff shirt of Buck Wildes.

Relief flowed over Connie, followed by another wave of anxiety. If Bruce wasn't responsible for McConnell's death, he was surely involved and definitely in danger. With a faint sniffle, she wiped the back of her hand across her nose. She hated showing so much emotion.

"You okay, boss?" Householder asked, eyes wide.

"Fine," Sheriff Connie said. "Put out an APB on Buck Wildes and his pedophile van." She paused for a moment. "Better add Bomber Merridan, too."

5:12 p.m.

Bomber walked the dark tunnel, guided by a single row of dim orange rectangles, not unlike the lights used to line the aisles of commercial airliners. The small bulbs were mounted to the center of the ceiling and extended forward, disappearing into the darkness. He didn't dare use his flashlight, for fear of triggering sensors or drawing otherwise unnecessary attention. Behind him, the light from the gate shrunk until it was nothing more than a pinprick in the distance.

The overhead lights were too faint to provide any real illumination and he walked on for what felt like an hour, half-stepping through the unknown. The darkness was so complete it began to play tricks on his eyes and he imagined the lights to be incandescent ants marching single file through the cold endlessness of space. Drones to some distant, uncaring queen.

The lights ended abruptly, bringing Bomber out of his trance. Beyond the last light was nothingness. He reached out, held his breath, and took several steps forward before finding his hand against a cold, smooth surface. The area felt metallic, unlike the rough concrete of the tunnel walls. He moved his hands in wide arching strokes, starting from the top, eventually finding first a hinge and then a handle on the opposing side.

He expected the door would be locked, considering it was the secret entrance to the underground lair of a mutant supervillain bent on municipal domination.

Kur-chunk.

The handle turned and the door creaked open. For a fleeting moment, he felt unbearable disappointment. A locked door would've been an acceptable criterion to turn back and to do so with the semi-clear conscience of a reasonable effort. He wanted nothing more than a roadblock. A reason to be a chicken-shit and take the safe route. But destiny prodded him forward through each disheartening success.

The door spilled into a dimly-lit corridor with stone floors and walls. The ceiling was railroaded with ancient timbers that disappeared into the rock on either side. Before letting the door close, he felt the interior handle. It was locked, which meant Sly was more concerned with keeping people in than keeping them out. From the fanny pack, he removed one of the energy bars and placed it between the door latch and the frame.

Across the hall, an ancient wood placard read: "Sex Dungeon," carved in a scrawling, sophisticated font. An arrow pointed forward to where the hall turned sharply. Bomber paused briefly to listen for sounds of impending doom and then, satisfied doom was still farther ahead, crept down the hall until he reached the corner.

Lining the new corridor's left side were two long tinted windows. Behind the windows was a large expanse of sterile white and brushed silver. It took Bomber's eyes a moment to adjust to the fluorescent lights of the laboratory in front of him. Men and women in white lab coats stood at desks, peering down through microscopes or mixing vibrantly colored liquids with tiny eye droppers. Some milled from desk to desk with clipboards, taking notes on the work of their colleagues. Others huddled in small groups, appearing to have hushed conversations while discreetly pointing at clearly unpopular holders-of-clipboards. All wore thick collars around their necks, with small black boxes placed directly over their spines.

Directly in front of Bomber, one scientist had turned and was now staring directly at him. Neither man moved. Bomber was about to make a run for it, when the scientist leaned forward and picked at something in his teeth. He pulled his gums back and furrowed his brow, then dug into his teeth again with a long, neglected fingernail. The scientist was suddenly startled by a clipboard-wielding colleague who had approached him from behind. The two men turned to his desk and he began speaking, using the same long fingernail to point emphatically at his work.

A one-way mirror, Bomber thought. *And soundproof.*

He stood slowly, getting no reaction from anyone inside the laboratory. He breathed easier. A stone staircase was at the far end of the hall and he moved toward it while keeping an eye on what was happening in the lab.

In the back of the lab, against the far wall, Bomber could see four cavernous openings, each covered with wrought-iron gates, similar to the one covering the storm-drain entrance. Bomber figured these were the remnants of the brothel's old "Sex Dungeon."

"Rich people are disgusting," he whispered.

He strained his eyes, thinking maybe Buck was being kept in one of the cells. At first, he saw nothing, but then his eyes picked up dark shadows moving in the dungeon's depths. Hulking black forms paced in and out of view. From one gate a pair of orange eyes appeared only for a second before evaporating into imagination.

Not far from the iron gates, a group of scientists had gathered around a metal table. An overweight man with a bad mustache was arguing with a birdlike woman. She was clearly annoyed, as he waved one hand wildly in the air. His other hand held a plump white rabbit by the scruff of its neck, keeping it pinned against the table. The mustache man picked up a syringe and waved it about. The woman scientist pointed to a glass enclosure that was spattered with blue smears, marked "Test Area 1". The man only shrugged. With one quick motion, he plunged the needle into the rabbit's bottom and pushed in a light blue liquid. Everyone froze. Mustache man pointed both hands toward the rabbit and nodded. Suddenly, the rabbit, who'd barely reacted to the needle, began to shake violently. This was all the warning needed. Scientists scattered with great urgency. Bomber watched their faces twist in unheard shouts as they flipped tables to use as shields. They'd been through this before. The rabbit wrenched back. Its eyes were fire. The plump, white body inflated like a parade float, thinning the fur and exposing pink hide. It opened its mouth in what looked like a scream, but Bomber couldn't tell if a sound was produced before it exploded. In an instant the rabbit was gone, replaced with a smear of blue sludge.

Bomber gagged.

There was chaos in the lab. The scientist with clipboards ran in frantic circles, shouting at everyone without clipboards. Several others were already in the far corner donning HAZMAT suites and an isolated sprinkler-head activated over the area. Mustache man was on the ground in the fetal position, while two clipboard scientists kicked him repeatedly from behind.

What the hell is happening here? Bomber thought.

There was nowhere to go but up. The staircase was uneven, but the stone steps were polished smooth in the center, worn from a century of traffic. The wall to his left was marked in intervals by enclaves that housed life-sized bronze statues. At the bottom, the first statue had been of a grotesque demon, but as Bomber climbed, the statues slowly morphed until, at the very top, he was greeted by a divine angel. Only the eyes of each statue had remained the same.

Bomber tried the door, finding it locked.

Keeping people in, he thought.

From below, he could see a flashing red light. Someone had tripped an alarm after the rabbit explosion. On the other side of the door, there was a rush of feet. Bomber ducked quickly into the angel enclave and pressed himself against the stone wall. The door opened and two uniformed guards rushed past him. He made his move, slipping through the door before it could swing shut behind the guards.

He stood alone in a hallway of Fox Mansion. The vibrant red carpet and aggressive apple decor were a shock to his senses after the dark tunnel and dungeon basement. The hall was identical to those he'd navigated with Carl Junior a week earlier. The whole mansion seemed to be designed to disorient.

He chose a direction and began cautiously down the hallway. Realizing Buck could be behind any of the identical doors, he began stopping at each, listening for signs of life. As he moved farther, his bravery mounted and he began testing doorknobs, finding each locked. He recalled the giant ring of keys, carried by Carl Junior. He peeked carefully around a corner and was relieved to see the main foyer at the far end of the hallway.

Before he could move, he heard voices behind him—the security guards were returning from the basement. He moved quickly down the hall, scanning for a place to hide.

Just before the foyer, Bomber found a door left ajar. He slipped inside and latched the door behind him. The room was larger than he'd expected and dimly lit by three wall lamps, each muted by lush red scarves that hung like rivers of blood, ending just before the floor. Candles burned on a vanity in the far corner, making shadows shudder on the walls.

On the far side of the room, a four-poster bed stood like a Gothic castle, sprung from a landscape of silk pillows. Sheer curtains were drawn along all sides, but Bomber could see the silhouette of a person lying propped against the headboard, knees raised and open. One arm was outstretched, reaching toward the corner post.

"Is that you, Puppy?" came a sultry voice. Bomber recognized it immediately. "I could only get one handcuff by myself. I'll need your help with the other."

Bomber sidestepped to where he could see through a gap in the curtains. Gloria lay on the bed, the light skin of her bare thighs in stark contrast to the deep purple duvet. A black sleep mask covered her eyes. The rest of what she wore—which wasn't much—could best be described as "raccoon lingerie." A ringed black tail stretched out across the bed from between her legs. On top of her head, holding back waves of golden hair, was a headband adorned with pointed black ears.

Rich people are soooo weird, Bomber thought again.

"Puppy? Is that you?" Gloria called, sitting up. "If you can just do this other handcuff— Sorry, I hope it doesn't kill the mood for my big bad wolf."

Bomber moved to the side of the bed. Grasping the clasp of the cuff, he raised Gloria's other arm and secured it to the bedpost.

"Big bad *fox*," he whispered.

Gloria's face washed white under the black mask and, up close, Bomber noticed she had painted a black dot on her nose, with thin whiskers on each cheek.

"You two psychos are into some kinky stuff, huh?" Bomber said. "We would've never worked out."

Gloria screamed. "Get out of here! Help!"

"Shush," Bomber hissed, slapping a hand over Gloria's mouth. "You're going to tell me where Buck is or I'm going to—to cut you or something."

He quickly pulled the pocket knife from the fanny pack with his free hand and waved it well away from Gloria even though she couldn't see it through the mask. He slowly released the pressure on her mouth.

"You don't have the balls, you loser," she spat. "And your hillbilly friend is probably dead by now. Hell if I know. I don't concern myself with the prey."

"The prey?"

Gloria launched into a full-on tantrum. She thrashed her legs in Bomber's direction, arched her back, and began to shriek.

Bomber tried to hush her as he backed toward the door. He reached for the knob, but it was gone. In its place was Sly Fox. He no longer stood a meager four feet tall but was now eye to eye with Bomber's six-foot frame. Muscles rippled under thinned fur, rolling across his chest like cable cords. His enormous shoulders occupied the entire doorway.

"My, what big paws you have," Bomber said.

"That's so unoriginal," Sly growled.

Sly drew back his massive fist and Bomber's world went dark —again.

* * *

8:27 p.m.

Bomber woke. His eye, and now his nose, pulsed painfully, as he pushed himself up and spat grit and blood from his mouth. The side of his face was coated with sand and he wiped it away with his wrist, sending clumps of congealed blood to the ground beneath him. He looked around. It was dark, but he could see that the white sand stretched out in all directions and then ended abruptly, colliding with walls the color of bleached bone. The walls reached high, maybe fifteen feet or more, and then angled out and away from him, as if retreating into the night sky. In the stars above, he traced the familiar straight line of Orion's Belt, reminding him of orange lights he'd once followed through a storm drain.

A storm drain? He thought to himself.

He rubbed his sore head.

Only then did he remember the events of the day.

He scrambled to his feet, senses suddenly heightened. Everything was still. Something pinched his neck and he reached up, finding a thick collar around his neck. He remembered the scientists as he traced his hand around to where a small box sat below the base of his skull.

"Sly!" he yelled.

Blinding lights kicked on above him, forcing him to look down and shield his eyes. The lights reminded him of his football days. He was in some sort of stadium—or arena.

A small handle stuck out of the sand on the ground at his feet, his pocketknife. Behind him, there were two sets of tracks leading toward the wall and he could see the outline of a door. Between the two sets of tracks were two continuous grooves, where his toes had been dragged through the sand.

Bomber heard the distinct sound of latches uncoupling on the other side of the arena. He turned slowly, squinting against the lights. A panel opened in the wall. The space behind it devoured the light. A low rumble, more vibration than noise, escaped the pitch-black hole and Bomber felt his chest contract; goosepimples prickled his limbs. He could feel the veins in his arms swell.

A pair of orange eyes opened in the dark, floating and

growing. Bomber had seen the same orange before: in the eyes of the deformed raccoon and the ill-fated lab rabbit.

Now, around the eyes, black fur and blue-gray flesh materialized out of the abyss. A head took form, massive and misshapen, with ripped, rounded ears. The shoulders that followed were broad and muscular, the body enormous. It carried itself in the manner of a bear, though it was bigger than any grizzly Bomber had ever seen. It paused outside the door and sniffed the air. Its fire-orange eyes locked on Bomber, its lips quivered, and the air rumbled once more.

Bomber held up the pocketknife, as the bear paced along the circular wall. It lumbered slowly and Bomber turned with it, as its circle became tighter and tighter. The closer it came, the more Bomber could make out of its grotesque form. Its fur, like the raccoon's, was stretched thin so that rigid muscles and tendons could be seen beneath its hide. Its mouth was drawn in a permanent sneer and purple blood dripped from its nose and gums. It breathed in turbulent fits that escaped like the mad laughter of a hyena.

The circling lasted several long minutes. The monster's muscles, which at first had rippled in concert with its movements, now took on a life of their own, roiling beneath the surface like small ocean waves. It turned toward its prey and let loose a savage roar that sent shockwaves through its flesh and shook the sand around it. Bomber barely heard it. His heart thundered in his ears with the hollow cadence of jungle drums, summoning a primal feeling that coursed through every engorged capillary. Purple blood oozed from a cut on the bridge of his nose. He felt focused and strong. He felt free and confident for the first time in years. He felt—bigger. Planting his feet, he sucked the air from the arena and roared back.

The bear gave pause and for the first time closed its mouth. It cocked its head and then shook violently, like a dog leaving water. It turned back to Bomber and pawed at the ground. Bomber crouched with the small pocketknife raised and ready. The bear lunged forward, picking up speed. The arena floor shook.

"Aaaaaaahhhhh." Bomber let loose another wild scream.

POP

Still fifteen feet away, the bear exploded in a rain of guts and blue mist. Bomber leapt backward, avoiding the toxic spray by mere inches and then sank to his knees.

"Dammit!" came Sly's voice from above. "I thought we had the timing down on the bears."

Bomber squinted, searching for Sly. The lights dimmed and Bomber could now see the empty amphitheater seating around the arena. Above the open gate where the bear had emerged, and above the wall and rows of seats, was a raised platform with gold guardrails. Behind the bars was a regal granite throne with a fierce fox head carved above the backrest. Sly sat beneath the stone head, sharpening his claws against the armrests.

"Bring him to me," Sly commanded.

The hidden door behind Bomber opened and three men entered. Two were dressed in identical gray-and-green pressed uniforms and toted submachine guns. The last man to enter had to turn sideways to fit his wide shoulders through the narrow door. His uniform was similar to the first two, but with elaborate piping and arm-patches denoting some type of rank. Bomber recognized this mountain of a man immediately.

"Ex-Sheriff Barnstorm," Bomber said, spitting the name to really drive home his disgust.

Barnstorm sneered. The arena lights reflected off his bald head and several highly polished stars along his uniform's shoulder boards. Barnstorm had a particular disdain for Bomber. It was rumored that he'd lost a small fortune in a not-so-legal high school football gambling ring when Bomber threw the big game.

"You know," Barnstorm said. "They call you 'Bomber' because you choked in the championship."

Bomber didn't miss a beat.

"You know, they don't call you anything," he said. "Because they're happy you're gone."

Bomber had barely finished his sentence when Barnstorm's fist connected with his gut, leaving him doubled over and gasping. His pulse quickened. He clenched his fists. The veins in his arms became more pronounced but did not bulge like before.

"Eh, eh, eh," Barnstorm clucked. "Let's not do anything stupid." He lifted Bomber's chin to show him the small device in his other hand. It looked like the remote for a dog's training collar. "There's just enough C4 in that box on your neck to take your head clean off."

Bomber took several deep breaths to steady his heart.

"Let's go!" Sly called from above.

Barnstorm gave Sly a submissive wave.

"Walk," he hissed at Bomber.

The two guards prodded Bomber forward and they all followed Barnstorm. The door led to a long, narrow room with smooth cement floors and cinder-block walls painted blood red. Wooden benches lined both walls and the distinct vinegar smell of a locker room stung Bomber's nose. On the wall, was an ancient-looking wooden sign, carved with the phrase, "*Whores Gotta Eat.*"

"It *does* exist," Bomber whispered.

"What?" Barnstorm asked.

Bomber pointed. "That inspiring sign."

Barnstorm grunted.

They continued through another doorway and then up several flights of stairs before emerging at ground level behind the arena, which Bomber could now see was dug into the earth with the back of the great Fox Mansion looming over it. Following a series of ramps, they emerged onto the platform where Sly was still perched on his ridiculous throne. Beneath them, a teal tarp was being mechanically drawn across the open pit of the arena. From above, it would look like nothing more than a large swimming pool.

Sly didn't bother getting up. He lounged across the throne with his furry legs dangling over the armrest closest to Bomber. He pointed his big, clawed toe at a lesser chair next to his.

"Sit," he said.

Bomber sat.

"Leave us," Sly said with a wave of his paw-hand.

"But, sir—" Barnstorm began.

"Leave. Us."

Barnstorm's big chest deflated and he shot Bomber a sour look before leaving the platform.

Sly thumbed at the zipper of his fanny pack, no longer trying to hide the tube tethered to his hip. Bomber wondered if the orange liquid inside had anything to do with Sly's increase in size. Even through his fur, Sly's muscle definition was obvious.

"Been working out?" Bomber asked.

Sly smiled. He'd always liked a compliment.

"I have to say," he said, "you impressed me out there." He jerked a nubby thumb sideways to indicate the arena and the bear fight. "What got into you?"

He sat up straighter and peered down at Bomber's forearms and then squinted to study Bomber's eyes.

"It would appear you've had some performance enhancement," he smiled. His one gold fang sparkled. "Did you eat the forbidden fruit while you were trespassing?"

"Raccoon exploded on me," Bomber said. "In my front yard."

Sly laughed.

"Damn," he said. "That'll happen though. They eat the apples or get hit by the sprayers and they start swelling. Once they're huge, they're pretty hard to contain."

"What have you done with Buck?"

"Special Agent Ross is fine. For now."

"And what about Pastor Mast?"

Sly grimaced.

"Last I checked, he wasn't dead," he said, sucking his sharp teeth. "But I have to say, I don't like his holier-than-thou attitude."

"Well, he *is* a pastor," Bomber said. "So he is. Holier. Than thou."

"And I don't like that he held so much sway over people's thoughts and moods. No one should have that power, unless it's me. Especially if he's going around peddling happiness and hope. I can't have that. When people have hope, they walk with their heads high. They see more clearly. I need people to be focused down, on a consecutive chain of problems." He chopped one hand into the other a few times for emphasis. "And those problems need to stay positioned directly in front of their faces. Even if I have to create those problems myself."

"But why?" Bomber asked. "All so you and your uppity friends can sit up here, drink champagne, and make bets on which of your animal-abominations will win?"

"None of them are my friends," Sly said.

"You're like the Jay Gatsby of freaks," Bomber said. "So, how do you hide what you are from your guests?" He motioned to Sly's entire body.

"I don't," Sly scoffed. "If you're rich enough, nobody cares what you look like. Besides, as soon as they set foot on this property, I own them. I have lists of people who'll do anything I ask, whenever I ask, all because I have proof of the sordid things they did here. Pictures, signatures, compromising videos—hell, even DNA. Mostly DNA, actually."

"Gross."

"Leverage makes lasting friendships."

"See, you have friends after all," Bomber said snidely.

"I don't need friends," Sly said. "I had a *friend* once and he betrayed me."

"I sure hope you're not talking about me," Bomber said, feeling his blood pressure rise. "You stole *my* girlfriend, remember? Not the other way around."

"Oh, please," Sly said. "You were going to break up with Gloria anyway. Or have you conveniently forgotten? You told me the day before. I remember it clearly because we'd just been kicked out of the Robinson's pet store for the hundredth time, for harassing that stupid parrot. What was its name? Mr. Chipper?"

"Ms. Chitters," Bomber said.

"That's right," Sly laughed. "Then you got all sulky and told me Gloria had gotten into MSU and you knew the Spartan football scouts were going to be at the next game, but you weren't sure you wanted to go there. And 'boo hoo hoo,' you said you weren't sure you even wanted to keep playing ball at all." Sly sighed. "You didn't bomb that pass because you were pissed at me. You bombed it because you're a coward.

"In a way, all this," he raised his furry arms, "is your doing. If you want my honest opinion, I think the day I started to change was the day you tossed our friendship away. You had always held the worst of me at bay. But when you bailed—well, the floodgates opened."

Bomber stared at the ground. "I couldn't be friends with you anymore," he whispered, so quietly he himself almost couldn't hear it.

"Why?" Sly snarled. Nothing got past his pointy ears. "And don't say it's because I was 'mean to people.' Let's not forget, Bomber, you were right there with me, every time. You and I are the same. I just had the guts to embrace it."

Bomber sat quietly, his heart thumping in his ears again. He looked down at his forearms, but the veins stayed hidden.

"It wears off after some time," Sly said, seeing him analyze his wrists.

"What *is* it?"

"It's none of your business, is what it is," Sly said.

Bomber saw him exhale deeply. The arena lights began to click off one by one around the great circle. The lights from the mansion intertwined with the beams of moonlight, giving Sly's silhouette an air of menace.

"This all started with my old man trying to get a leg up on the competition," Sly said. "Corporate espionage is quite a thing. He'd send me all over the globe to 'collect free samples' from chemical fertilizer specialists. I can be very persuasive." He flashed his teeth. "But dad's ambitions were small potatoes, though, and he bulked at the idea of using the research, any research, to manipulate my form. With him out of the way, a whole world of opportunities has opened up.

"The applications of what we're creating in that lab go far beyond use in an apple orchard. I'm a living testament to that. We're talking about cellular regeneration. New, improved growth."

"So, like a cure for cancer?"

Sly considered this.

"I was thinking more about military applications. Defense contracts and whatnot," he said. "But yes, I suppose we could make a ton of money off sick people, too. Desperation is a great driver of wealth. Not as good as war profiteering, but what can you do? I tell you, getting rid of the late-stage eruptions was a huge tick in the right direction."

Bomber recalled the exploding rabbit in the lab and wondered if the kinks had really been worked out like Sly thought. Then he thought about the splatter he'd taken from the raccoon in his own front yard.

"You shouldn't have anything to worry about," Sly said, seeing his concerned look. "Secondary exposure in such a low dose shouldn't last long. You'll be fine in twenty-four to forty-eight hours. Unless you get hit with a second dose. Then you'll be nothing but a blue stain."

He said this last bit with a wicked smile.

"BAAA!" He screamed, lunging toward Bomber with teeth and claws on full display.

Bomber scrambled back, toppling off his chair.

Sly wheezed with laughter.

"You're too easy," he gasped. He wiped a tear from his eye with the back of his paw-hand before he turned toward the ramp and shouted: "Guards."

Ex-Sheriff Barnstorm ran up the ramp, where he'd clearly been eavesdropping.

"I sent the men back to their quarters, sir," he said. "I can handle this pansy."

Sly nodded and Bomber got to his feet.

"Oh, and Bomber," Sly said, "you were wrong about one thing earlier. When you said me and my 'uppity friends' place bets on chemically-enhanced animals."

"Oh?"

"It's not just animals fighting."

Sly looked at Ex-Sheriff Barnstorm again.

"Have him processed and throw him in with the rest of the gladiators," he said. "And Barnstorm, don't rough him up too much. Tomorrow's a big day. I need every contender prime to fight."

The White Whale wasn't hard to find. Within an hour of putting out the APB, one of Sheriff Connie's patrolmen had radioed in that Buck's van was parked in the lot behind City Hall. While finding the van proved easy, accessing the back was another story. The cab had been no challenge, as the driver's door was open when the patrolman discovered it, prompting him to approach the vehicle with his weapon drawn, only to find the front seats ransacked. The upholstery had been shredded and the glove box hung empty from one hinge, papers, and coins littering the floor. The stereo had been stripped and the center console emptied of its contents. Making things weirder, several fecal specimens were left on the front seat, which Sergeant Householder noted were similar to those found at Pastor Mast's home.

Another jackpot of excrement, Connie thought, recalling Bomber's terminology.

The cab of the truck had been sealed off from the rear by thick steel plating and the back doors were secured with metal bars three inches in diameter, though it appeared someone had attempted to pry the doors open, probably with a crowbar. Even when the fire department brought in a jaws-of-life tool it took several hours to gain access. Abandoning attempts to enter through the reinforced walls, Connie had ordered her troopers to cut away the roof, peeling it back like the lid of a tuna can. Once inside, they were blown away—figuratively—by an arsenal larger than that of their own station.

"Where does a small-time, reality show star get access to all this gear?" Connie wondered out loud from her seat on a black case labeled "CLAYMORE."

Sergeant Householder was crouched low and scooting around the van, cutting locks off containers and weapons racks with a large bolt cutter. He was currently working on a particularly thick lock securing a small firebox toward the back.

"All of this stuff looks government-issued," Connie said.

"Probably because it is," Householder said. Connie looked up to find him holding a file folder he'd plucked from the now-open firebox. "Looks like copies of requisition forms. And look where they're from."

"Federal Bureau of Investigation," Connie read off the letterhead. "And the signee is a Special Agent Raymond Ross."

"What would the Feds be doing in Fox Hollow?" Householder asked. He'd resumed flipping through papers in the firebox.

"And how does it involve Bruce?" Connie added. "Anything else in there?"

Householder handed her a thick file folder. Inside was a jumble of documents, article clippings, and photos. Connie thumbed through, finding a newspaper article from *The Fox Howler* breaking the news of Carl Longstreet's lottery win, several grainy photos of either a fox or coyote, more articles about kidnapped or murdered scientists spanning several years, and overhead imagery of the Fox Family Mansion dated from three weeks prior.

Connie studied the imagery and handed it back to Householder.

"Can you believe the size of that damn place," she said. "The pool out back is the size of a small lake. I never even knew there *was* a pool." She sighed.

"Rich people and their damn pools," Householder said.

"Now this is interesting," Connie said. She pulled a final packet of paper from the folder. The top sheet was a Form DD214, which she recognized from her own service as military discharge paperwork. This particular DD214 was made out for: Fox, Sylvester V., VI. The "Character of Service" section had been listed as "Entry Level Separation" and in the remarks box, the administrator had noted: "Missing / Presumed Dead."

"'Entry-Level Separation' is usually only reserved for soldiers who can't hack it in their first 180 days of training," Connie said. "If this is true, the whole town's been fed a load of bullshit about Sly Fox being a war hero."

The rest of the packet was a sanitized incident report that was more redacted than not. Connie was able to glean small parts of a story about soldiers going AWOL, strippers, and some sort of wild animal attack. The final page was a picture of a lifeless cougar, splayed across the back of a pickup tailgate. Blood stained the cougar's white underbelly, while two potbelly policemen flanked the cat on either side, looking very serious in aviator sunglasses, Stetsons, and hunting rifles.

"This keeps getting weirder and weirder," Householder said.

"Ma'am," came a voice from above them.

They both looked up to find the officer who'd found the van, poking his head over the hole in the roof.

"We found something up front you may want to see," he said.

At the front of the vehicle, the officer pointed out that they'd opened the driver's side sun visor, which had the standard covered mirror inside. Connie was unimpressed by her officer's discovery of the van's baseline features, but then the officer flipped up the mirror cover revealing a sticky note stuck inside. On the note were two names, Cecil and Chuck, each with a phone number below them.

"Thought you might want to call and see where they lead," the officer said.

Connie nodded.

"You guys finish up here," she said to Householder. "Make sure everything inside gets removed and properly cataloged. I don't need any Bureau Boys bitching me out if this turns out to be legit. I'm going to go make some calls and have a look around inside."

In the mayor's office, it was clear something had gone down. A bourbon bottle had been shattered on the floor in front of the bookshelf. Connie felt a faint pang of pity for Bomber, assuming he'd fallen off the wagon after the burning of Marty's. On the mayoral desk, a porcelain coffee mug appeared to have exploded, leaving white dust, mug-shards, and a bouquet of pens and pencils scattered across the surface. Along the far wall, a picture had been removed from the historical timeline and a small wall-safe hung open, nothing inside but soiled pair of men's underwear and an assortment of trash.

She pulled out her cell phone and dialed Bomber, but it went straight to voicemail. She took the sticky note from her pocket and, on a hunch, dialed the number under "Cecil." The phone on the desk began to ring. She'd figured as much. She then dialed the number under the name "Chuck." The phone rang several times before going to voicemail:

"Hello. You've reached the desk of Director Charles Rostad, Department of Kinetic Operations, Office of the Environmental Protection Agency. Our regular office hours are..."

"Kinetic Operations?" Connie leaned back in the chair, trying to process all the new bits of disconnected information. She swiveled around in the chair and that's when she saw the bullet hole in the wall behind the desk.

11:47 p.m.

Bomber scratched his shaved head and leaned against the dungeon door. The scientists, who'd scuttled around the laboratory earlier, were gone, herded off by guards to some unknown corner of the mansion. They'd forced Bomber to strip down, making him stand on a pedestal in the center of the lab where they poked and prodded him for far longer than seemed necessary. The scientist who appeared to be in charge had walked around Bomber, scrutinizing his body and slapping at various muscle groups as if he were a side of beef, even going so far as to stand on a chair to check his mouth for sores or rotten teeth. He'd at least had the courtesy to do this before the hernia and hemorrhoid checks. After this, they drew blood samples and administered a series of shots they vaguely referred to as "inoculations." When Bomber asked what he was being inoculated against, the scientists would pretend not to understand English, even though he'd heard them speaking it moments earlier. He was then put through a rather humiliating delousing process, which involved the shaving of his head, before being placed in a cell for the night in case any of the shots caused him to explode, which Bomber was sure was not a side effect of any normal inoculation. To top it off, his clothes had been replaced with a strange buckskin costume, complimented by a raccoon-skin hat.

"The boss likes his battles—theatrical," Barnstorm had said with a hint of disdain.

The hide was stiff and unwelcoming, and the hand-stitched seams showed no signs of previous wear. The shirt had leather-strip tassels dangling from the arms.

"You look like Daniel Boone—you know, if Daniel Boone had been a middle-aged loser," Barnstorm had laughed.

The dungeon cell extended off into blackness and the smell of feces drifted in from the back. Bomber wondered if these cages might be connected, somewhere in the darkness, to the underground arena where he'd met the mutant bear. This thought stoked the fear that something else might be lurking in the dark, so he sat with his back to the cage door, staring into the void and thinking about all the ways he'd botched the rescue mission.

He could hear breathing from the next cell over, slow and raspy, but the position of the doors prevented him from seeing anything. Dark thoughts crowded his mind, as he wondered what new terrifying beast he'd face in the arena tomorrow. His heart raced and he began to wonder if he were reacting to the "inoculations". He imagined the scientist finding his cell empty in the morning, a blue puddle of sludge on the floor. He wiped the sweat from his palms onto the buckskins covering his knees and took several deep breaths.

Bomber lifted the coonskin cap from the floor in front of him and as it moved past his eyes he noticed a small "B.H." had been written in black marker along the inside band.

Bruce?

The overhead lights in the lab flickered on. Bomber turned to see a familiar top hat appear over the tabletops, followed quickly by the bobbing head of Carl Longstreet. The old man leaned heavily on his apple-knobbed cane as he came down the row between tables. A tattered bathrobe leeched at his gaunt frame, a robe which was much too short and revealed far too much of his veiny white thighs. Bare feet sported nails so long they click-clacked on the tile floor as he dragged his tired toes. His eyes were bloodshot, but alert, darting every which way. He ran his free hand casually across the top of a table, littered with vials and other sciencey stuff, and for the briefest of moments, Bomber saw him finger a small object before it disappeared into his palm.

"Oh, look. A two-faced weasel," Bomber said. "To what do I owe the pleasure?"

Carl mustered a weak smile. His eyes shifted over his shoulder toward a camera mounted on the wall. Its red light was no longer on.

"How did you manage that?" Bomber asked, noticing the camera.

"One doesn't spend a lifetime skirting security systems without learning a thing or two about deactivating them," he said proudly. "You'll have to excuse my appearance. Mr. Fox does not allow me to wear my 'going-out clothes' unless I am, indeed, stepping out."

"To *what* do I owe the pleasure?" Bomber repeated, louder

this time.

"I want to be clear up front," Carl said. "I'm very grateful for everything Mr. Fox has done for me. He lifted me out of squalor, like a glorious garbage phoenix. He's allowed me to live in his wonderful home—though I wish he'd provide me a proper bed. I sleep on a pile of hay, you know?"

Bomber could see bits of hay clinging to the wooly fabric of the robe.

"But that's neither here nor there," Carl went on. "The point is, he has completely changed my station in life. Risen me up to a position of influence. A position where I can feel dignified among those who used to mock me. A position of power, where I can crush my enemies—with his approval." He paused.

"But?" Bomber asked.

"But lately, I've grown—concerned."

"About?"

"Well, as you may have noticed," Carl fished for words, "Mr. Fox lacks a basic moral compass."

"You don't say."

"It's true," Carl nodded. "In fact, he seems to have been born without a soul at all. Look what he did with Pastor Mast." Carl's eyes shifted briefly to the neighboring cage. "I can't say I ever really liked the guy, but he was a man of God. You've gotta be a devious bastard to do *that* to a foot soldier of the Lord."

"What did he do to Pastor Mast?" Bomber asked.

Carl didn't register his question. "I just feel like, when Sly is done with all of this—with me—he may discard me."

"Oh, he'll definitely discard you," Bomber said. "Now what happened to Pastor Mast?"

"But he needs me," Carl reasoned, ignoring the question again. "He needs me. He needs a face for his fortune. The face of Fox Applesauce."

"*Millionaire Recluse Not Seen Since Lost Election*," Bomber said, pretending to read a newspaper headline.

"He wouldn't," Carl said, eyes wide.

"My guess is you'll end up in the arena like the rest of us. Or maybe he'll pump you full of The Sauce and lock you in the ol' Exploding Chamber."

He pointed over to the blue blood-stained, glass enclosure.

"So, if I can ask one more time," Bomber continued. "What happened to Pastor Mast?"

Carl was staring at the glass enclosure.

"Who else have you told?" he whispered.

"What?"

"You knew about Mr. Fox's—condition—before you came here," Carl said. "Please tell me you notified someone. It seems unlikely that Special Agent Ross's colleagues will be following up anytime soon."

"How did you know—"

"When you're poor, you get good at going unnoticed," Carl said. "I hear lots of things in this old mansion, Mr. Merridan. Did you tell anyone else about Mr. Fox? Did you tell Sheriff Connie?"

"Who would believe any of this?" Bomber spat, waving his arms around. "Who's going to believe a millionaire werewolf, who's supposed to be dead, is secretly rigging town politics, producing chemical weapons, and hosting gladiator deathmatches for the world's elites? Are you out of your damn mind?"

Carl threw his hands over his face and shook his head.

"The debate tomorrow is going to be an absolute bloodbath," he mumbled.

"What?"

With surprising speed, Carl reached through the gate and snatched Bomber's wrist. Clasping Bomber's hand with his own, he pressed something cold against his palm.

"There's only one chance now," Carl said. "Only a couple of drops will do it. I think. For the town's sake."

Bomber looked down to find a small glass vial of blue liquid in his hand.

"And Bomber," Carl said. "If we make it out of this alive, please tell Mr. Wildes how I tried to help."

Bomber made a fist around the vial, as Carl turned and walked away, his butt cheeks sagging beneath the bottom of the robe.

"Wait, Carl," Bomber shouted, shielding his eyes from the butt cleavage. "What did you mean about the debate?"

"An absolute bloodbath," was all Carl said as the door slid

shut behind him.

"What do you know, Carl?!" Bomber shouted.

He was answered by a low growl from the next cage over.

October 31, 2017

5:59 a.m.

Sheriff Connie opened her eyes and, for a moment, struggled to place where she was. She'd fallen asleep on Bruce's bed, still in uniform, her hands folded across her stomach. Spiderwebs crisscrossed the ceiling fan above and an unpleasant odor wafted up from the comforter below. Her nose wrinkled at the stink. She'd long ago entrusted Bruce to clean and care for his own space, which he'd neglected almost entirely. She used to nag him, of course, especially when food scraps began to rot and stink or when his accumulation of cosplay costume material reached fire-hazard status, but her increase in responsibilities at the precinct pushed domestic tidiness farther down her priority list.

She shifted on the bed and her holster dug at her thigh. The last couple of nights she'd broken her own rule and hadn't put her gun in its lockbox. Instead, she'd left it on her nightstand, a full magazine in the well. No round chambered. Safety first.

There was a knock at the front door.

Connie checked her watch. 6 a.m.

"Crap," she grumbled.

It'd been midnight when she walked in the door the night before. She'd laid down on Bruce's bed for a moment of reflection. Now, six hours later, it was time for work. At least she was already dressed.

Another knock. This time hard and aggressive, rattling the door.

Who the hell comes to the door at 6 a.m.?

She pushed herself up and navigated the minefield of dirty underwear and lonely socks.

Another knock. Hard. Violent.

The apartment was dark and Connie slipped quietly down the hall, unbuttoning the holster of her 9mm Beretta as she went. She reached the door as it rattled again. When it settled, she pressed her eye to the peephole. Nothing. Well, almost nothing. A few strands of gray-blue hair danced at the bottom of the peephole.

Connie sighed and buttoned her holster.

"Good morning, Edith," Connie said as she opened the door and flicked on the lights. Edith had been their downstairs neighbor since her kids had determined she was too old to live in a multistory house on her own. She had disagreed and not gone quietly.

"Good morning, dear," Edith said, looking up at her. She wore her normal frown and held, between two large oven mitts, a tin containing a loaf of bread. "I baked you something. It's banana walnut."

Connie smiled. She was allergic to walnuts, but she reached for the bread anyway.

"Thank you, Edith," she said. "I—"

"Ah ah ah," Edith chided, pulling the bread back. "Child, don't you see these mitts? This bread is fresh out of the oven. It'll burn the shit out of your hands."

She tottered past Connie into the apartment.

"Come right on in," Connie muttered. "Isn't it early for baking bread?"

"Nonsense," Edith said. "I've been up for two hours already."

She sat the tin on the coil of a stove burner.

"It's gluten-free banana bread," Edith said. "I know how all of you kids these days have sensitive bowels. First time baking gluten-free, so forgive me if it's crap."

She shuffled back toward the door.

"Your son seems like the type who'd have sensitive bowels," she said. "I heard that he's been missing. Rumor mill and all. I just wanted to let you know I don't believe what they're saying he did. He's a good boy. A little strange, but a good boy."

"Thank you, Edith," Connie said.

Edith stopped in front of the open door.

"And he's got a good mother," Edith said. There was kindness in her eyes and she picked up Connie's hand in her oven mitt, still warm from the bread. She gave the hand a meaningful squeeze and let it drop. "A good mother doesn't have to be a traditional mother."

She gave Connie a wink that could've been her face spasming or a mini-stroke.

"Thank you, Edith."

The old woman tottered back out the door and then turned around as sharply as an 82-year-old can.

"Oh," she said, holding a mitt in the air. "I almost forgot. A favor?"

Connie nodded.

"The school administrators weren't too keen on allowing tonight's debate in any of the school buildings after what happened in Old Town the other night, so it's been moved to the football field where people can do less damage."

Connie had forgotten about the debate entirely.

"I was hoping you could be up on stage with me?" Edith asked. "Bomber was supposed to be the moderator, but since he seems to have skipped town, or been involved in multiple homicides, the task has fallen to me. I'd just like a little firepower on stage," she pointed to the gun on Connie's hip, "in case the crowd gets rowdy."

"I will be there, but it looks like you're already prepared for any trouble," Connie said, cocking an eyebrow. She pointed to the handle of the holstered Derringer sticking out of Edith's apron.

Edith patted the handle.

"Never can be too careful," Edith said.

"Would the caliber of that gun match the bullet hole I found in the mayor's office wall?"

Edith smiled.

"Get a warrant, Sheriff."
With that, she turned and tottered off down the hall.

7:32 a.m.

The scientists returned to the lab early in the morning looking oppressed and bleary-eyed. Several seemed genuinely surprised to find Bomber unexploded and equally relieved at not having to clean him off the walls and floor. Bomber tried fruitlessly to inquire about their work and appeal to their humanity, but they bowed their ragged heads and busied themselves around the lab. The little red light on the surveillance camera blinked obnoxiously on the wall behind them.

The lab door slid open and Barnstorm entered. The scientist kept their heads down and continued to scurry about looking very busy.

"What now?" Bomber groaned.

"Congratulations," Barnstorm laughed. "You've cleared medical—which is a fancy way of saying you didn't die—you get to join your fellow fighters for the day."

They exited the mansion the way they'd come and the labyrinth of identical hallways spit them back onto the "poolside" patio. Mansion servants scurried about, opening sun-umbrellas over rows of beach chairs and unfolding bright red tablecloths over glass tables, completing the pool illusion. The servants were dressed in similar crisp red uniforms with forest-green piping, and resembled employees of a fancy hotel. The men sported crisp suit pants cut evenly with highly polished black shoes, while the woman wore pencil skirts, high heels, and very low-cut blouses. All sported flesh-colored collars with black boxes at the base of the neck. Not a single worker turned to acknowledge Barnstorm and Bomber as they passed.

Bomber looked behind him as they walked. On each side of the patio, elegant staircases wrapped to a second-floor deck, which was also lined with chairs and tables. Behind the seating area was a wall of windows and glass doors leading into the mansion's large ballroom. The ballroom was still lit and house servants could be seen vacuuming and setting tables, no doubt in preparation for the day's "big event."

"Are these people all kidnapped migrant workers?" Bomber asked, already knowing the answers.

"They're volunteers," Barnstorm said. "Kidnapped volunteers."

The eastern sky was turning a mix of oranges and purples as Barnstorm stiff-armed Bomber down a cobblestone walkway that led around the far side of the arena before opening up to the large expanse that was the back of the Fox Estate. Far off to the right were tennis courts and a two-story driving range, with yard markers emerging in the distance. On the left, the southeast corner of the estate had been walled, creating a compound within a compound. The walls matched the height of the exterior perimeter and two small guard towers sat on opposing sides. Bomber could see a guard on the eastern-most tower, his rifle silhouetted by the orange dawn. The compound walls had been painted completely with strange murals of woodland creatures fornicating in a lush orchard. Deer, squirrels, skunks, and raccoons copulated in various settings, some panting with eyes rolled back in their erotic pleasure.

"What in the hell?" Bomber whispered.

"Rich people are real perverts," Barnstorm said disdainfully.

They stopped in front of a large steel door. Beside it, two possums were entangled in an unnatural, Kama Sutra position.

Bomber looked at the possums and then at Barnstorm, whose eyes flicked over the painting and then closed. Bomber caught a sense of embarrassment, as though he couldn't believe he'd been reduced to working for such people.

Bomber coughed deliberately and Barnstorm opened his eyes again.

"I hate these goddamn—possums," Barnstorm said.

"Possums are the worst," Bomber nodded.

Barnstorm grunted a sound that sounded suspiciously like agreement, as he flashed his badge across an electronic pad. Somewhere inside the great door, a latch flipped. Hydraulics kicked in and the door slid slowly open.

Beyond the door was a ten-foot buffer of open space surfaced with a sea of broken glass applesauce jars. This no-man's-land of shards was split by a narrow walking path leading to an inner chain link fence. Like the perimeter walls of the compound, the fence was lined with coils of razor wire that buzzed with electric current. Somewhere down the line, an unfortunate moth touched the wire and a sharp thwap of electricity snapped and sizzled. Beyond the chain link, and along the exterior walls of the compound, were eight ramshackle houses, four on each wall. Some of the roofs were sagging into wide holes and the walls were gray, weathered wood, with faded patches of colored paint here and there.

The shacks looked out with paneless windows onto an expanse of dirt and brown grass, littered with iron dumbbells, weight benches, and medicine balls like a prison courtyard in a Hollywood movie. At the center of the courtyard was a circle of barefoot men, their attention turned inward. They hooted and shouted between crisp clacks of wood against wood. Some were shirtless against the morning cold, their bulging backs and arms covered in dark tattoos. In the gaps between, Bomber could see the movement of quick bodies, and the ends of long wooden dowels would occasionally rise above the gathered heads before disappearing again with loud, violent cracks.

Barnstorm unlocked the gate and shoved Bomber inside the fence.

"Fresh meat!" he called, immediately closing the gate.

Bomber looked up to find the attention of the circle was now on him. The cheers and clattering sticks, replaced with the thunderous beating of his own heart. The men in the circle lowered their heads but kept their eyes on him. Lions sizing up a meal.

"Wait," Bomber sputtered, but Barnstorm was locking the gate. The men moved toward him in a human wall of muscle. Their eyes were fire and they bore their teeth. "What are they going to do to me?"

"Looks like they're gonna beat you to death," Barnstorm said. He was already strolling back across the path to the metal door. "Establish dominance. You'll be fine." He shrugged. "Maybe."

Bomber looked back. The horde was closing in. They wore hard expressions above their black collars and their fists were balled into mallets.

Establish dominance, Bomber heard Barnstorm's words again.

He held out his hand, flat toward the advance, and wished the violent aggression of The Sauce hadn't worn off.

"Stop right there!" Bomber shouted, his voice giving way to an unfortunate crack.

The men were nearly on him now. Their dark eyebrows curled down in anger forming deep folds in the tan skin of their weather-beaten faces.

For no reason at all, Bomber's mind went to the fornicating possums near the outer gate.

Play possum, he thought. He dropped to the ground in a heap, as though all his bones had been plucked from his body.

The giant men parted around him. They continued past and crashed against the fence like a wave against ocean rocks. They kicked the chain links and rattled them with their large hands, shouting in Spanish and spitting as the exterior door slid shut over the last glimpse of Ex-Sheriff Barnstorm. The men were red with rage and continued shouting even after the door was closed.

"What're you doing down there?"

Bomber looked up. Buck stood over him, his bare stomach and recently shaved head glowing equally white. He carried a long wooden mop handle, which rested across his shoulder and over the black box on his neck. One of the huge men had doubled back from the fence and scooped Bomber up under his arm, lifting him back to his feet.

"Sorry, amigo," he said in a thick Spanish accent. A big smile spread across his face. "Got to keep Barnstorm on his toes, you know? Keeps him from lingering."

"Th-thank you," Bomber said. The rest of the men were returning from the fence. Some patted him on the back and offered greetings in Spanish and English.

"Bienvenido."

Bomber made awkward half waves before turning back to Buck, who was smiling with deep purple bags under his eyes.

"I thought you were dead," Bomber said.

"But you came to find me anyway," Buck said.

"I'm still mad at you for lying to me."

"I did it for your own safety."

Bomber looked around.

"It didn't work."

"So when is Sheriff Connie and her team raiding this place?" Buck asked.

"What?"

"Or did you find the information in the van?" Buck asked eagerly. "Did you talk to Chuck Rostad? He's a good dude, but sometimes it takes the EPA a while to spin up their team since direct-action operations aren't their primary function."

Overhearing Buck, the other men gathered around, listening expectantly.

"I-I didn't—" Bomber started. "I didn't do any of those things."

Buck blinked at him.

"Okay," he said, drawing it out. "So what's the plan then?"

Bomber looked around at all the sculpted and scarred faces, looking back at him with a dim glimmer of hope.

"I didn't think anyone would believe me, so—so I just came on my own. No one knows I'm here."

The faces sagged. Shoulders slumped.

"We're all gonna die," Buck said.

The muscle-bound man with the big smile stepped forward and placed a hand on each of their shoulders.

"Cheer up, amigos," he said. "Only half of us will die."

His smile was suddenly replaced with grave sincerity.

"But you two will definitely be in the half who dies."

4:47 p.m.

The bleachers were packed to capacity and people stood along the football field fence. Closer still, people congregated on the stretch of running track that separated the fence and the field, where Edith stood on a portable stage. On either side were empty podiums and behind her, Sheriff Connie sat with the remaining aldermen in a row of metal folding chairs. One chair had been left empty, supposedly in a symbolic gesture of mourning for the late Patrick McConnell, but really it was just a miscount by the janitorial staff.

Sheriff Connie surveyed the throngs of people as they filed into the bleachers and onto the field, instinctively dividing themselves by tribal alliance. Carl Longstreet's adoring fans were decked out in orange attire and sported orange trucker hats with the slogan "Take The Longstreet To Victory." Those who couldn't afford Carl's campaign-approved merchandise simply sported orange hunting vests and hats they'd pulled out for the upcoming deer season. Connie had spotted several Apple Knockers milling around the crowd, still dressed in their trademark DIY body armor. She was keeping a special eye out for Ron-Boy, but so far there was no sign of him or Big Mama.

On Connie's left, Gloria's horde continued to grow, dressed in their campaign color, pure white, no doubt to emphasize the purity of their self-righteousness. Signs reading "LOVE EVERYONE," "END POVERTY" and "LIVE AND LET LIVE" were intermixed with "DEATH TO THE PATRIACHY," "ONCE A BUM, ALWAYS A BUM" and "ABORTIONS FOR ALL." Connie watched as a man with a giant posterboard peace symbol spat at a Longstreet supporter heading for his own side. The man turned, revealing the slogan "Gloria Glass Can Kiss My Ass" on his orange sweatshirt. The Longstreeter was clearly loving the attention and he waggled his hips suggestively at Gloria's crowd, pointing to his sweatshirt.

The two groups were growing rapidly and the shrinking no-man's-land between them was a hotbed of tension. Neighbors shouted at one another across self-made battlelines. Connie was on edge, her nerves only tamed by the knowledge of an armored truck of riot police she'd had Householder stage in the parking lot.

"Good evening," Edith said, her voice crackling over the loudspeaker.

The noise of the crowd continued at a dull roar.

"Please quiet down now," Edith said politely.

No change.

Before Connie could stop her, Edith pulled her Derringer from her coat pocket and fired a shot in the air. There was silence around the football stadium.

"Jesus, Edith!" Connie hissed.

"Gunfire seems to be the only way to get anyone's attention these days," Edith said. "As I was saying, 'good evening.' I was going to thank you all for attending tonight's Mayoral Debate, but I'll forgo the pleasantries. I *would* like to say that Mayor Merridan would be rolling in his grave right now. Bomber was right about there being monsters in this town. It's all of you."

People in the crowd studied their feet.

"You all should be ashamed," Edith added, shuffling some index cards.

The silence was interrupted by a venomous "boo" from Gloria's side. Then another from Longstreet's people. Within seconds the whole crowd was booing and cackling together.

"Finally, some unity among morons," Edith huffed. "Here are your stupid candidates."

At the far end of the football field, two of Connie's officers swung open the fence gates. Two figures stood, backlit by the late afternoon sun, one in a slick, fitted white pantsuit and the other furry, with two pointed orange ears.

"Bruce," Connie whispered.

Relief swept over her. She wanted to run to him, as he and Gloria marched across the field. In fact, she almost did, but when she tried to stand, she felt a soft, wrinkled hand on her shoulder.

"Don't rush it," Edith said. "Sometimes children need to reach conclusions on their own."

"He may have been involved in a murder, Edith," Connie said.

"Last week, I saw him outside releasing a spider he'd caught in your apartment. He's too big of a pansy to murder anyone," Edith said. "And besides, this place is a powder keg already."

Connie didn't like it, but Edith was right. The crowd was aching for conflict and like it or not Connie was an authoritarian presence. Intercepting a candidate's righthand-man could be perceived as an act of aggression or favoritism to the opposing side.

Connie sighed and sat back in her seat. She waved to Bruce but received no response. Instead, Foxy ran clumsily along the front of Gloria's crowd, hyping them up as he went. People screamed and whooped. When he reached the edge of no-man's-land, he stopped and raised two plush middle fingers toward the Longstreet supports who booed and cursed and threw anything they could find.

Connie covered her eyes in embarrassment.

The ruckus of the crowd was suddenly drowned out by music blaring from the loudspeakers: "Who Let the Dogs Out" by Baha Men.

"What now?" Connie moaned. She looked to the gates as a motorized scooter, souped-up with a V8, revved its engine. Carl Longstreet stood on the back and waved to the crowd. Big Mama was poured into the driver's seat. She revved the engine again and smoke billowed from four curved exhaust pipes. Carl coughed but continued to wave.

"Who let the dogs out? Who? Who? Who? Who? Who?" The Longstreet crowd chanted. "Who let the dogs out?"

Connie pinched the bridge of her nose and tried to recall the things she used to love about Fox Hollow.

"I do love this song," Edith said, bouncing lightly.

The scooter clipped along the field, leaving muddy ruts and kicking up chunks of turf before power sliding up to the stage stairs. Carl climbed up to his podium, waving his top hat to great fanfare from his side. The two candidates glared at one another in a prolonged pose as their respective paparazzi snapped photos. Edith took her spot at the center podium as the speaker system emitted a high-pitched screech, causing everyone to cover their ears.

Edith jiggled the connection at the base of her microphone.

An alarming amount of duct tape had been used to mend the cracks and frays in the cords coming from all three podiums.

"Before we launch into our topics," Edith said, "each candidate will introduce themselves, with a brief overview of where they stand on key issues that are important to you, the voters of Fox Hollow."

"Woo! Fox Hollow!" someone cheered.

"Please save your shouting for the end," Edith said. "As is customary, we'll have ladies go first. Gloria, please begin."

Gloria leaned into her podium.

"It's *Ms. Glass*," she said, "and I don't need any head-start charity from you. Please put your faux chivalry and outdated patriarchal tendencies aside for the debate, Edith."

"You gotta be shitting me," Edith mumbled and the audience gasped. She turned to Carl. "Carl—er, Mr. Longstreet, would you please start us out?"

Carl cocked his top hat like he was about to charge into battle.

"Thank you, Moderator Edith. And if I could ask you, please refrain from using obscenities. We have good, clean, Christian ears in attendance. " Carl said. He was inexplicably popular with the evangelicals in town. Probably from his days of being their outreach poster-child.

Edith balled her fists at her side.

"My name is Carl Lenard Longstreet Senior and I'm running for Mayor of Fox Hollow. Many of you know me as a prominent businessman—"

Gloria scoffed.

"—and man about town. Most of you know my rags to riches story, a mixture of resilience, good fortune, and guile. Just twelve years ago, I was a vagrant. A hobo. A beggar, living off the goodwill of this fine town. But fate has smiled on me and now it can smile on you, too. If you elect me mayor of Fox Hollow, I will champion new legislation promoting the aggressive expansion of Fox Applesauce leading to a dramatic increase in jobs and household income. Together we'll wipe out homelessness in Fox Hollow."

There actually wasn't a homelessness problem in Fox Hollow,

but people liked the sound of increased household income, so his side of the crowd cheered all the same. The cheers emboldened Carl.

"If you elect me Mayor, I will tighten the borders between Fox Hollow and Cedar Mills, so good people like Pastor Mast will no longer fall victim to senseless acts of violence."

"Amen!" The Longstreet crowd was whooping and hollering now.

"It's time we stop letting towns like Cedar Mills push us around," Carl shouted. "It's time we stop taking a back seat and start fighting back. It's time we place—Fox First!"

His crowd roared with a chant of: "Fox First!"

"Everyone calm down," Edith yelled. "Quiet down now. This is a political debate, not one of your cockamamie campaign rallies."

Connie looked over to find Foxy standing next to the stage with his arms crossed. He shook his big furry head in overdramatic turns.

"Bruce," Connie shout-whispered as the crowds settled down. There was no acknowledgment from her son.

Edith turned back to Gloria.

"Your turn," she snapped.

"Well, you certainly are a feisty one," Gloria said like she was talking to a child.

Edith growled and the smile fell from Gloria's face.

"All kidding aside," Gloria continued. "My name is Gloria Glass and I am running for Mayor of Fox Hollow. Unlike my adversary, I can't brag about rising from poverty on sheer luck and laziness or about having the luxury of watching our small-town decay from the expanse of a decadent mansion. No. My life has been rife with struggles and personal tragedy like many of yours. From the heartbreaking, but heroic, death of our beloved soldier Sylvester Fox on the glorious field of battle, to the untimely death of my late husband," she paused and it seemed to Connie she was trying to remember his name, "but in all of these things, the community of Fox Hollow has been my rock and my anchor. My love for you all has never wavered. I have held a seat on the Board of Aldermen for the last five years, where I've continuously fought for those outside the protective umbrella of certain large corporations who shall go unnamed."

There were boos directed at Carl.

"We love you, Gloria," someone shouted.

"And I love you back, Fox Hollow," Gloria yelled, as her crowd cheered. "With me as Mayor, we will work to get the town's minimum wage increased and narrow the disgusting income gap between the hard-working citizens like yourselves and the privileged aristocrats who hoard their wealth in fancy mansions."

She pointed at Carl, who was absentmindedly polishing the golden apple on his cane.

"Together, we will open our community," Gloria continued, "and generate new wealth through free commerce with Cedar Mills and welcome their youth as friends, not enemies."

This actually garnered some boos from the Longstreet side.

Edith waited impatiently for the crowd's fervor to subside and then began lobbing questions at the candidates. Connie did her best to stay present as Carl and Gloria traded trifling criticisms over each other's past positions on everything from zoning ordinances to mandatory minimum wages, union rights, and crackdowns on the area's burgeoning methamphetamine production. All the while, neither offered any real solutions of their own.

Connie's attention continued to wander to the mystery of Bomber's absence and his association with a federal agent, both of whom were now suspected in the murder of Patrick McConnell and possibly more. She wondered if the town could ever return to the way it'd been—and if it could, whether that would be a good thing or not. Whatever all of this was, with all the riots, the angst and the anger, it was clear it didn't blossom from nothing. This was a climax. A bloodletting, after years of simmering frustrations.

Another round of boos and heckles jolted Connie out of her daydream. Edith shuffled index cards at her podium, squinting at each as if it were in a foreign language. Carl and Gloria looked smug, as their rabid fans rocked tensely on their heels and in their bleacher seats. The whole place was primed to ignite.

"And lastly," Carl said, continuing whatever point he'd been making. "Under my plan to reduce city taxes, public school funding would be reallocated away from the unnecessary spending I mentioned before: teacher's wages, staff pensions, overpriced text books, and generic rectangular sheet pizzas."

Gloria's side of the bleachers erupted with anger. They were barely looking at the candidates now, instead, they were staring across no-man's-land at enemy soldiers. Carl's people cheered wildly and made lewd gestures to the infidels.

"School's fer dummies!" someone shouted.

"Now might be a good time to mention," Carl went on, "my son, Carl Jr., will be opening Fox Pup Primary School for next fall's enrollment. Sign up fast, for a top-of-the-line education in a state-of-the-art facility. In all honesty, it won't be cheap, but I hear public school funding is about to take a major cut around here." He winked at his side of the crowd.

There were nervous, confused laughs on Carl's side and some folks wrung their hands.

"Okay, Mr. Longstreet," Edith chastised. "You've been warned before. Please refrain from promoting private business ventures during the debate."

Carl smiled politely and doffed his hat toward Edith.

"Next question," Edith said. "Many community members have voiced concerns over the Fox Applesauce orchards encroachment on residential areas, a problem so prevalent it has been dubbed Agrarian Sprawl. They feel it has a negative effect on the aesthetics of local neighborhoods—as pertaining to property value. But most importantly, it poses significant environmental and health concerns due to the regular spraying of pesticides. What are your plans to address these concerns?" Edith looked up. "Carl, we'll begin with you."

"How come he always gets to go first?" Gloria snapped. "This is sexist."

Edith's face twisted into an angry mass of wrinkles.

"Listen, you uppity bit—"

"I'd be happy to go first," Carl cut in. "Let's keep this civil, ladies." He masked his mouth from them with one hand and jerked a thumb toward them with the other hand. "Women. Am I right?"

He laughed and winked at the crowd, but was met with silence.

"Anyway," he said, "I think one thing we can agree on is that we'd like to see this town, not just prosper, but *thrive*. Am I right?"

Cheers from his side.

"This town was built on and by Fox Applesauce. It's the lifeblood of our economy. In order to continue to grow, to continue to thrive, we need to not only continue to *produce*, but *expand*. And I think any true Fox Hollowinian would understand that in order to do so, sacrifices must be made. And anyone who's unwilling to sacrifice for the good of the town, for the good of their neighbor, is our direct enemy and should be shipped right on outta here!"

He zipped his thumb over his shoulder for emphasis. His side of the crowd went nuts. Chants of *"Fox First"* were intermingled with *"Ship Them Out."*

Connie looked around the crowd. Faces were contorted into ugly jeers or awash with the vacant bliss of mob mentality.

"And what about the accusations that the pesticides are environmentally dangerous?" Edith pushed on with her next question. "Some claim they are responsible for the uptick in Alzheimer's cases in Fox Hollow in recent years. What are your thoughts?"

Carl's face went blank and he tossed up his arms, raising and lowering them in a bad zombie impression.

"Where am I? *Who* am I? I think I just pooped my pants," he said, laughing a little too long at his own joke. The boos from Gloria's side drowned out the laughter from Carl's.

"But seriously folks, we use only industry-standard pesticides. The town's safety is our number-one concern and there's no secret conspiracy to make you all a little forgetful."

Carl suddenly looked ill at ease.

"You're just appalling, Mr. Longstreet," Gloria said. "The Agrarian Sprawl happening around this town is a real and present threat to our citizen's livelihood. Not only that, but you openly mock concerns of those who simply want reasonable distance between their homes and the noxious gasses you spray that ravage our bodies."

"I wouldn't ravage your body if you paid me to," Carl snapped.

"Mr. Longstreet!" Edith shouted. "That is quite enough."

"The only thing you've ravaged is a dumpster," Gloria shouted.

Laughs erupted from the crowd. Carl's face reddened.

Gloria continued unphased.

"When I'm Mayor, we will be rezoning all agricultural areas—including Fox Applesauce orchards—to be kept a minimum distance from residential areas."

Cheers from her fans.

"Further, I will be pushing legislature making it illegal for the town's residents to participate in neo-western lawn mutilation. Even the simple, unnecessary act of mowing one's lawn destroys potential habits for wildlife and pumps carbon exhaust fumes into the atmosphere."

The cheers dwindled.

When the crowd settled, Edith continued: "Our next topic will be—"

"What about the attacks?" someone yelled. "Where is Pastor Mast?"

Edith hushed the crowd.

"We have limited time here, folks," Carl said. "And a prescribed list of questions—"

"I want to hear your answer," Edith interrupted, then turned to Gloria. "And yours."

Gloria flashed a smirk, quick as a wink, but Connie caught it. There were shouts of approval from the crowd.

"Well," Carl started. "It appears these attacks are being caused by a beast of some sort."

"You said it was Cedar Mill's teens," someone from Gloria's side shouted.

Carl laughed. "Well, they're beasts in their own right," he said. "But after consulting with Conservation Officers, I've come to believe it to be an animal."

Whispers rippled through the crowd.

"Bomber was right!" someone shouted.

"Under my administration," Carl went on, "we'll be taking preventative measures in case something like this ever happens again. Several miles of chain-link fence, topped with coils of razor wire, will be erected around Fox Hollow's borders. Checkpoints will be set at all major entry points to town, which will allow traffic in and out, but no more beasts."

"Sounds like you want to trap us in with the creature," Gloria laughed. "Like you want to turn Fox Hollow into a prison camp for its own residents."

Angry agreement rose from her side.

"The opposite, in fact, young lady," Carl said. "It's my intent to make sure that each citizen of Fox Hollow is in possession of at least one, preferably two, assault rifles to protect themselves and their families."

"New guns!" someone yelled from Carl's side and everyone cheered.

Carl threw up his hands in celebratory solidarity.

"Typical man," Gloria scoffed. "And once you've caged us in with this 'beast,' what then? Watch as it devours us one by one? You'd probably like that. Then you could bulldoze our vacant homes for more orchard property like you did with poor, dear Ms. Carol Meyers and old Cecil Merridan himself."

"I've actually—"

Gloria steamrolled ahead: "Perhaps instead of barricading the town, we could try a less authoritarian approach. Perhaps we must remember the beast was here first and it is we who are trespassing. Perhaps Fox Applesauce's Agrarian Sprawl has finally enveloped the beast's last remaining refuge and it is lashing back out of fear. Perhaps *we've* been the beasts the whole time."

The whole crowd was silent.

"Fuck that thing!" somebody shouted, followed by confirmations on both sides.

Gloria motioned for calm.

"I'm simply saying, perhaps we could take back some of the ill-gotten lands from the corporate greed machine and repurpose it into a wildlife sanctuary, where the beast can be isolated and free."

There were claps from Gloria's side, but nothing overly

ambitious.

"And then, perhaps, leave animal sacrifices to the beast, giving thanks to it for ending its bloody reign of terror."

The applause stopped. People looked at each other in bewilderment.

"And who is going to pay for this wildlife preserve and these animals you wish to sacrifice to your beast-god?" Carl asked. "No doubt you'd ask the citizens to foot the bill."

Gloria smiled. "I was thinking we'd raise the income tax on the super-wealthy."

Cheers erupted once again from her side. A few folks on Carl's side clapped briefly.

"The safety of Fox Hollow is my number-one concern," Gloria called, to more cheers. To their credit, Carl's side opted out of booing a call for community safety.

"Oh, I agree," said Carl. "That's why I've already been in contact with a group of security contractors who agreed to hunt the creature at a discounted rate. These guys are top of the line, I can tell you. They've been hunting humans in Iraq, Afghanistan, and Syria for the last fifteen years, so they really know their stuff. They seemed real anxious to get their fingers back on the trigger."

Cautious applause from Carl's side.

"In fact, this whole conversation is a non-issue," he went on. "They've already come and gone and I paid for them out of my own pocket, because I love this town."

"And they killed it?" someone yelled.

"Even better," Carl smiled.

Carl pointed to the press box and Guns N' Rose's "Welcome To The Jungle" started blasting over the loudspeaker. An engine revved from outside the fence. Connie looked over as Ron-Boy, dressed again in his homemade armor, rounded the corner onto the track hunched over the handles of an ATV. With his assault rifle still confiscated by the Fox Hollow PD, he now wore a rocket-propelled grenade launcher, or RPG, strapped across his back. The 4-wheeler was towing a large trailer covered in an orange sheet with "Longstreet 2017" printed on the side. The sheet billowed, as Ron-Boy pulled to a stop beside the stage.

"What is this, Carl?" Connie asked warily, as Ron-Boy

dismounted the ATV and stood next to the mystery trailer.

"Ladies and gentlemen," Carl called like a carnival barker. "We've captured—the beast!"

Ron-Boy took his cue and jerked the sheet off the trailer revealing a circus cage. Behind the bars, a giant creature paced. It had the long body of a timber wolf but carried the weight of a bear. Its thick muscles wrapped like vines around its legs, visible beneath sparse hair. It was easily twice the size of any wolf Connie had ever seen and its eyes shined a brilliant orange.

Someone in the crowd screamed.

"What is this, Carl?" Connie said, getting to her feet.

"What is it?" someone echoed from the crowd.

"Does it matter?!" Carl yelled. "It's a monster. What more proof do you need that this creature has been the source of your fear? The source of your pain. We've allowed the beast to plague our town for too long. Even our own police department has failed to quell the bloodletting. But I'm not here to discuss the bumblings of Sheriff Connie Hayes."

Connie clenched her jaw.

"You've all suffered long enough," Carl said. "I say we kill it. Right here and right now."

Cheers rose from each side. People shouted at the beast in the cage, agitating it further. It shook its head violently and then lunged against the door causing it to rattle on its hinges. Those closest shrieked and tried to back up into the wall of people behind them.

"It's got parasites," someone yelled from the front row. Bubbles formed on the creature, moving slowly along under its taut skin. Purple blood oozed from its mouth.

"Goddammit, Carl," Connie said. "You shouldn't have brought that—*thing* in here."

She leaned into her hand-mic.

"Send in the cavalry," she said over the radio. Her signal to send in the riot police.

"Who wants the honor of killing it?!" Carl yelled. A hundred hands shot into the air.

"You can't kill it!" Gloria screamed. "This creature has as much right to be here as you or I. I demand this creature be released immediately."

"Maybe *immediately* isn't the best idea," Edith said.

"Immediately," Gloria screamed. She was staring straight at Foxy, who nodded his huge furry head.

At that precise moment, three things happened in such rapid succession, they all blurred into one. First, Foxy began running toward the cage, barely staying upright as he tripped over giant furry feet. Second, Ron-Boy, still having a bone-to-pick with Bruce, zeroed in on Foxy and began groping for the RPG strapped across his fat back. Finally, Connie, who'd intended to arrest Ron-Boy after the debate, began running across the stage to intervene before someone got themself blown up.

The resulting actions were perceived by everyone in dramatic slow motion.

Aided by the momentum of the heavy suit, Foxy hit the cage bars with tremendous force and, having discarded his fuzzy gloves, popped the latch. With one solid heave, he yanked the door open and sandwiched himself against the trailer. The creature, who was now in a rightful frenzy, leaped from the cage, as the audience pushed desperately away. It shook its head, spraying purple blood in all directions, before zeroing in on the largest and closest threat, the massive frame of Ron-Boy Carlson, who was still entangled in the strap of the rocket launcher.

The creature sprang forward, yellow teeth flashing.

Ron-Boy screamed.

Connie drew her pistol on the run and fired three shots, but one was enough. The first bullet hit the beast, center-mass, as it sailed toward Ron-Boy. The sound produced was that of a balloon bursting, and a slosh of blue jelly rained around Ron-Boy's leather combat boots. Connie skidded to a halt at the top of the stairs.

Beyond the steaming pile of blue goo, still gripping the steel bars of the cage door, Foxy dropped his head to his chest. Two patches, wet and red, blossomed like roses against the pristine white of his "Gloria Be To God" campaign shirt. He let go of the door and it squeaked shut as he dropped to his knees and then to his side, his big, hollow, furry head bouncing on the turf.

Twenty-eight gladiators sat on the wooden benches in the staging room leading to the arena. Bomber shivered. His buckskin costume was clammy with sweat. They'd spent the day training for what was feeling more and more like a human sacrifice, rather than a fight with any real chance of survival. Several of the migrant laborers were already veterans of Sly's arena of terror and they did their best to prepare the new recruits. None were true experts in combat, so most advice came in the form of ways to avoid immediate death. They noted that the chemically enhanced beasts always targeted the largest threat on the arena floor first, whether it be the biggest man or biggest weapon. Armed with this intel, the motley crew of damned fighters had strung together several loose battle plans for baiting and attacking their would-be killers.

Bomber looked down the row of men sitting shoulder to shoulder, grateful for the kindness they'd shown in the face of true horror. Knees bounced nervously. Some folded hands and bowed their heads. Half were dressed in buckskins and furs, like he and Buck, and half were dressed in stereotypical Native American attire, complete with war paint, claw necklaces, headbands, and a few elaborate feathered headdresses. They were all characters in some sick play and in the back of their minds, each knew, when the beasts were dead, they'd undoubtedly have to fight each other.

Bomber read the words on the old wooden sign.

"Whores Gotta Eat"

The sign read differently to him now and he wondered if the senior VanGovern hadn't crafted it as a crude joke but as a sad resignation. An acknowledgment that his profession was not the fulfillment of a lifelong goal, but an inglorious means of survival in a world dominated by immoral men. Dirty hands in a dirtier world.

Bomber mulled this over as he tried not to imagine any scenarios where he'd be forced to fight the men sitting beside him. In their training, there'd been whispers of a mutiny or an uprising of sorts, but their half-baked schemes—usually concocted by

Buck—were quickly crushed by the veteran fighters who'd already seen plenty of good men lose their heads.

If it weren't for these collars, we'd have a fair chance, Bomber thought, as he thumbed the thick, inflexible collar.

"Woven Kevlar," Buck said.

"What?"

"The collars," Buck said. "They're made of woven Kevlar. Or something similar. That's why they're impossible to cut." He sighed. "What I wouldn't give for a weapon."

Bomber removed his coon-skin hat and turned it over, exposing the inner band where "B.H." was written on it.

"I've got a weapon—of sorts," he whispered.

Buck looked at him questioningly.

Bomber slid the vial of blue liquid through a gap in the stitching.

"Is that—?" Buck started.

"It is," Bomber said. "A last resort."

"How?"

"Carl," Bomber said. "He knows you're FBI and he's interested in self-preservation."

"So he probably wanted you to give that to me," Buck said.

He reached over, just as Ex-Sheriff Barnstorm rounded the corner with his entourage of submachine-gun-toting guards. Bomber slipped the vial back behind the band of the hat.

"On your feet!" Barnstorm shouted. His voice was muffled by a mask covering half of his face. The mask was screen-printed with the mouth and nose of a cat and two ears stuck out from the top of a black baseball cap. His guards were in similar attire, with full rubber dog snouts strapped around their heads and long droopy ears hanging from gray patrol caps.

"I said, On! Your! Feet!" Barnstorm shouted.

Everyone jumped from their bench.

"Forward," Barnstorm barked. "Move!"

At the end of the hall, a narrow door slid open and one by one they entered the arena, each shielding their eyes against the stadium lighting. Cheers filled the air as the gladiators stepped into the loose sand. Bomber was confused by a feeling of exhilaration. He felt at home in the arena, under the brilliant lights.

More armed guards stood inside dressed in half-assed animal costumes. As Bomber's eyes adjusted, the reason became clear. The stadium seats were packed—with animals.

They were not real animals, of course, but elaborate masks meant to hide the identities of those who'd come to satisfy their curiosity, sadism, and blood lust. Most of the men, to compensate their cowardice, wore the fearsome face-coverings of great predators, decorated to complement fine suits and tuxes. The women, with their elegant hair, donned posh cat masks and fur coats over tight, sequined cocktail dresses. Some—the more dedicated of the bunch—wore full-body costumes with oversized plush heads. Several individuals were surrounded by serious men in identical black suits, no doubt Secret Service or some other hired security.

"It's a 'furry party,'" Buck whispered over his shoulder.

"A *what* party?" Bomber called back.

"A furry party. It's when a bunch of weirdos dress up as animals and do weird stuff."

"Why?"

"The masks keep them anonymous and they can shift any shame or guilt onto their animal alter ego or something."

"You know a lot about this," Bomber said.

"I've dealt with furries before," Buck said. "Don't let the costumes fool you. These people are dangerous. They don't want their secrets getting out. There's nothing more dangerous than a cornered furry."

The gladiators were herded into a long cage set along the arena wall, like the team bench of a prison hockey rink. Some of the new gladiators were instructed by the guards to sit closest to the cage door. They would be the first to fight. A warm-up for the furry crowd.

The intercom crackled with a low buzz. "Welcome, ladies and gentlemen."

Bomber looked to the platform where he and Sly sat the day before. Deep crimson drapes were tied back to four ornate posts framing the platform, giving it the feel of a Roman emperor's box. True to the fantasy, Sly stood before the crowd in a white toga, a half-wreath of golden laurel leaves rested on his head above the ears. He wore no mask. He hid nothing.

"Do we have an evening in store for all of you!" he shouted.

The crowd cheered.

Sly was massive. His chest was a billboard and lines of sinew were visible through his fur, which somehow seemed thicker and more lustrous. When he stood straight, his head nearly touched the canopy stretched overhead. He raised the microphone to his mouth with both paws and Bomber thought his biceps might rip right through the skin of his arms. A sneer curled his lip, as he looked down on the expendable men in the cage.

"Let's all give a big round of applause for our brave volunteers," he said, holding a paw-hand out toward his captives. The arena was filled with the muffled clapping of gloved hands. A few of the veteran gladiators waved. "I'd like to thank each and every one of you for being here tonight on All Hallow's Eve. I hope you're enjoying your stay at the Foxy Howl Inn and that our staff is treating you like kings and queens. If they're not, we'll have them put to death."

There was a beat of uncomfortable silence and then Sly barked a laugh and the whole arena joined in.

"Seriously though," he said. "If there's anything we can do to make your stay here more…*memorable*, feel free to abuse the staff until you get it. Anyway, I know most of you are here purely for the sport and that's fantastic, but I know some of our esteemed guests out there are interested in an investment opportunity. Namely, the purchase of our Strategic Performance Enhancement drugs which will be on full display tonight. If you're on the fence or you're just hearing about our products, feel free to flag down one of our concession workers and they'll provide you with a brochure outlining the three varieties we're offering."

Three? Bomber thought. He only knew about two. The Sauce and whatever it was Sly was juicing on from his fanny pack.

"We have a lot of interesting fights on the docket tonight," Sly went on, "and maybe even a few surprises along the way. But before we get started, there's somebody I'd like to recognize." He turned around and waved someone forward. "Get up here, dummy," Sly said.

Slowly, sadly, a furry brown hat became visible.

"I'd like you all to welcome my good friend, Bruce," Sly said, now staring directly at Bomber. Bruce stood next to Sly, dwarfed by his enormous size. He was dressed from head to toe in an elaborate beaver costume, equipped with fake front teeth and a comically large, flat black tail. "Bruce here is an expert at costume design and a bunch of other really useless nerd junk. He's been hard at work over the last few days, sewing the costumes for our gladiators and some of the pieces you've seen our staff wearing around the mansion. Let's all give Bruce the round of applause he deserves."

Again, the arena was filled with the sound of pillowed hands.

"Sit your ass back down," Sly said to Bruce, barely off-mic. Bruce shuffled over and sat awkwardly in the low seat next to Sly's throne, where he shifted uncomfortably around his tail.

"Well," Sly said to the audience. "That's just about enough out of me. I mean, we're all here to see some carnage, are we not?"

The crowd roared.

* * *

6:25 p.m.

For the first time in her life, Sheriff Connie lost positive control of her sidearm, as her pistol slipped from her fingertips and clattered to the stage floor. A woman in the crowd screamed. It didn't matter from which side. A horrified paralysis tried to take her, but Connie slipped free, forcing her training to own the moment.

Render first aid, she thought.

She leapt from the stage. Rushing to Foxy's side, she rolled the costumed body over and applied pressure to the bullet holes in his chest.

"Someone call 911," she yelled. "I need a medkit, now."

One of the officers wrangling Ron-Boy jumped up and darted off toward a patrol car.

"Stay with me, Bruce," Connie said. She could no longer contain it and tears slid down her cheeks. "I'm so sorry, Bruce. I'm sorry for everything." She repeated this over and over, as bright blood continued to spill through her fingers.

"Stay with me, baby, stay with me."

The padding of the costume was too thick to apply adequate pressure.

"We gotta get this stupid thing off him," she shouted, as Householder slid up beside her.

Householder grabbed the mascot's head and stumbled back as it slipped off. The crowd murmured and the pale head of Carl Junior bounced like a ripe melon off the ground.

He spat blood and wheezed.

"Oh, good God," Connie said.

She found the zipper at the back of the costume's neck and then wrenched down the front, quickly applying pressure once again to the wounds.

"Where is my boy?" she hissed, but Carl Junior wasn't long for the world. He stared past her, his eyes glassy and distant. He lifted a trembling hand toward the man on stage, for whom he'd pretended to be a son.

"Father," he coughed.

"Oh, for goodness sake," Carl said. "Can we quit this

already?"

"Father," Carl Junior coughed again. "Tell Mr. Fox—tell Mr. Fox I died well. Tell him I was his servant 'til the end."

"No," Carl said. "I won't do it."

"Mr. Fox?" Connie asked. "What are you talking about?"

She watched the last life slip from Junior's eyes.

"Where is my son?!" she yelled, shaking the bloody, lifeless body, before letting it drop to the ground.

She was interrupted by the distinct sound of a pistol hammer locking back. Householder raised his hands above his head. Connie turned to find Carl Senior had recovered her pistol and was now pointing it directly at them. The Aldermen behind him had their hands above their heads and Edith stood clutching her handbag as if she were being mugged. Gloria had disappeared entirely.

"I only did what I was forced to do," Carl said, his voice trembling.

"Take it easy, Carl," Connie steadied her voice and put both hands out in front of her. "Nobody else has to die tonight, Carl. Why don't you put down the gun and fill us in on what's going on?"

She spoke in a soothing tone, but in her head, she was calculating the distance from where she was crouched to where Carl stood on the stage. Six steps. Maybe seven. Four stairs, but she could clear that in one jump.

"Mr. Fox said everything would be fine," Carl said. "He said everything would smooth out after the election. After he was in charge."

Carl's cocky, affluent facade had crumbled away.

"I didn't know Mr. Fox was going to kill anyone," Carl sputtered. "I swear it."

"Mr. Fox has been gone a long time, Carl," Connie said. "He skipped town right after he sold *you* Fox Applesauce. Remember?"

Carl shook his head so hard he nearly lost his top hat. "Not *that* Mr. Fox," he said. "The kid. Sly Fox, the sociopath."

Connie stood slowly. "Carl, do you believe Sylvester Fox—the Sylvester Fox whose memorial statue is out front of City Hall—is alive and influencing the election?"

Carl pushed the gun forward. "Saying it like that makes me sound crazy," he snapped. "You're trying to discredit me."

"Carl, it was all over the news," Connie said. "We've all read the story."

People in the crowd nodded cautiously.

"What news?" Carl asked. "*The Fox Howler?* Well, guess what, *The Fox Howler* is owned by Gloria Glass." He turned to point at her with his cane, finding her podium empty. Connie took the opportunity to take a step forward.

"Of *course*, she's gone," Carl said with a rueful laugh. "She's been in on it from the beginning. Ever since she had him kill her husband. They're secret lovers, you know? How many articles about Sly Fox did you read that weren't from the *Fox Howler?* Huh? How many of you have checked government records about your so-called war hero?"

Everyone was silent.

Connie took another cautious step forward.

"Stay back," Carl warned. He looked out to the crowd. "He's been feeding you all lies. I'm not a rich guy. I'm just a pawn. You know the new *Fox Hollow Times?* Well, he owns that one, too. He's been playing you all from both sides. Divide and conquer."

"Carl," Connie said again. "Just put the gun down."

"I'd have thought you'd be madder than anyone, Sheriff," Carl said.

"Why's that, Carl?"

"Because he's got your precious Bruce," Carl said. "He's got him locked up in that disgusting mansion right now, sewing costumes for his freak-show friends and their sick parties. Parties I never got invited to, even though I lived there. Why wasn't I allowed to party with the rich people, Sheriff? I love to party."

"I'm sure you do, Carl," Connie said. She took another step.

"Get back!" Carl shouted.

Bang!

Carl dropped the gun and shrieked.

Connie looked down at her chest. No holes.

Carl dropped to the stage floor, clutching his butt and howling. Edith stood behind him, smoke rising from the barrel of her tiny Derringer pistol. In an instant, Connie and Householder were on stage, zip-tying Carl's wrists and securing Connie's pistol.

"Thank you, Edith," Connie said.

"I'm *not* missing my Wheel Of Fortune," Edith said. She checked her watch and slipped the tiny gun back into her purse.

"You know I'm going to have to confiscate that pistol, Edith," Connie said.

"Blow it out your ass, Sheriff," Edith said with a polite smile.

Connie looked out over the crowd, who all stood silent and slack jawed. She stepped toward Carl's empty podium, unsure what to say.

"Let him go," someone yelled from Carl's side.

"What?" Connie blinked incredulously.

"Yeah, let Carl go," someone else yelled. "He's one of us. We have to fight back against the rich elite and he just admitted he ain't rich."

"He's trying to pin everything on Gloria," one of her supporters shouted. "Lock him up."

"The liberal media lied to us," cried someone.

"It's their fault," someone else yelled, pointing at Gloria's crowd.

"The conservative media lied to *us*," cried someone on Gloria's side. "It's all *their* fault."

"Maybe it's *all* of your faults for not thinking for yourselves," Edith said into her mic.

Both sides erupted in boos. From somewhere in the middle of Carl's crowd, a full water bottle sailed into the air and crashed into the face of Janice Cartwright, who was wearing a "Team Gloria Tiger Mom" T-shirt, made with black and orange puff paint. She let out a fierce roar and all hell broke loose. Both sides charged, closing the gap in no-man's-land in a fraction of a second, sandwiching a row of riot-gear-clad officers. Punches were thrown, landed, and dodged. In the bleachers, people were pushed over bench seats and down the stairs. In the center of the fray, several members of the Apple Knockers had been yanked to the ground by their own homemade body armor and were being stomped mercilessly by wine-buzzed soccer moms in Lulu Lemon yoga pants.

Three gunshots sounded in rapid succession. Everyone

stopped, looking toward the stage. Connie stood at Edith's podium with her pistol over her head.

"Look at yourselves," she yelled in the microphone. "Look at what you've become. This used to be a community of good people who cared for one another. People who were able to put their differences aside and be neighborly. A community of tolerance."

She pointed at Carl and at Gloria's empty podium.

"These two jackals have torn us apart. They used fear to fuel anger. This is what they want. It's how they grab for power. Don't let them do it. You're all better than this. I've seen it."

Connie looked around at the downcast eyes of the crowd.

She cleared her throat. "There's an old story I'm reminded of," she said, feeling more confident. "It's a story about a fight. A fight inside us all. A terrible fight between two wolves. The first wolf is wickedness. She is anger, hate, arrogance, resentment, and ego."

There was silence over the crowd and Connie felt a twinge of hope.

"The second wolf is goodness. She is love, hope, kindness, empathy, and truth."

Some people in the crowd were nodding.

"This fight is going on in each of you," Connie said, pointing out over the crowd. "It's going on inside of me. Our souls are at stake."

Connie paused for effect.

"And do you know which wolf wins the fight?" Connie asked. "The wolf who wins is the one you feed."

The crowd was silent for a long moment, shame etched in every face.

"Sometimes it's the most chemically-enhanced wolf who wins," Carl said from the floor.

"You stole that," someone yelled from Team Carl. "That's an old Indian proverb."

"*Native American*, please," someone from Gloria's side chastised.

"*Indigenous person's* proverb," corrected someone else.

"The point is, you jackasses are feeding the wrong wolf,"

Connie said.

"That's a Cherokee proverb," someone yelled from Gloria's side.

"So?"

"So you're an Ottawa. That's 'inter-cultural misappropriation'."

Shouts of affirmation came from Gloria's side.

"Trust me, they're not going to care," Connie said.

"I'm one-sixteenth Cherokee Indian," someone yelled. "And I'm offended as hell."

Shouting and jostling began again.

"What would Mayor Meridian think of this behavior," Connie yelled. To her surprise, the crowd settled down again. "The man was mayor for forty-eight years with hardly an incident and you people can't make it two weeks without destroying what he built."

"What do you mean, 'you people'?" someone shouted.

"It's Mayor Merridan's fault we're in this mess," cried Tammy Schmidt. "This town's been stagnant for forty-eight years. Some geezer's romantic notion of the past shouldn't be a reason to impede progress. We finally have a chance to grow, to break free of his outdated thinking."

"I'm not sure you all understand how limited the mayor's power is," Connie said.

"Cecil could've at least left us with someone competent in charge," Tammy shouted. "Instead he left us with his alcoholic, monster-chasing, failure of a nephew—who, by the way, couldn't be bothered to show up today."

"Yeah, where is he?" shouted someone else.

"He's also at the mansion," Carl interjected. "Really, all your answers are at that mansion. I'm not sure what you're all still doing here."

"Listen," Connie told the crowd. "It sounds like we've all been duped. By Carl. By Gloria. And by the Fox family. I don't have answers for you, but I plan to get them. And if that mansion is where my son is, then that's where I'm heading. You can either stay here and kill each other over corrupt politicians or you can come with me and get to the bottom of this, once and for all. Frankly, I don't really care what you do. I'm going to get my son back."

With that, Connie jumped from the stage and jogged off the field.

* * *

315

6:36 p.m.

The arena floor was dotted with puddles of vibrant blues and dark, oily reds. The rusty smell of blood rolled into the stands, filling the nostrils of masked tycoons, movie magnates, divas, fat cats, barons, CEOs, fund managers, fixers, and other big shots, feeding their primitive lust. The crowd pulsed. Their shouts and screams were no longer words. They hooted, grunted, and whooped like chimpanzees, their language indecipherable to the men in the arena. The calls for blood rolled down in tidal waves, crashing against them.

Two by two, the gladiators were pulled from the cage, their collars removed and dull swords or wooden clubs placed in their hands in the sullied name of "good sport." Each round began the same. The gladiators were ordered to the middle of the arena, where they stood stoically while the crowd spit and pelted them with old apples, passed out by concession agents. Then the far door would raise and it was always a gamble as to what would emerge. The beasts started small. The first round featured seven beefed-up raccoons, not unlike the one Bomber had faced at home. Their numbers were too much for the inexperienced gladiators and the fight was over in seconds. The raccoons, still building toward their explosive finale, turned their attentions to the cage where they swiped and scratched their humanlike hands through the metal bars until they finally melted into bright blue puddles.

The fifth battle had been the strangest. A giant whitetail deer had galloped from the door, blood already dripping from its black nose. The Sauce hadn't affected the size of the buck's antlers, but that didn't stop it from impaling one gladiator against the wall. The poor man's body hung lifeless from the buck's rack as it trotted in circles, blinded by blood and dangling arms. The impeded vision had allowed the remaining gladiator to zig and zag until the stag burst behind him. The crowd had booed, denied their blood sacrifice, only stopping after a disapproving look from Sly, who gave the gladiator a thumbs-up.

This went on for ten rounds, culminating with a massive cougar who killed its victims so fast, Sly had to remote detonate its collar before it could jump the wall and mangle his guests. The cat's head had rolled to a stop just inches from where Bomber sat in the cage. He watched in horror as it lost its form. Fur, teeth, whiskers, and all, melting into the dirt.

Bomber ached to help the men he'd watched die and those who remained in the cage. He looked around to find that he and Buck were the only fighters left dressed in the fur-trapper costumes.

"Got a plan yet?" Buck asked.

"What?"

"A plan," he repeated. "For getting out of this mess? I've been racking my brain, but it all comes back to me losing my head." He tapped the collar.

"They're removing the collars before the fights," Bomber said. "I think that's our window. Once they're off, we should have enough time to hoist one or two of us over the wall before they can react. They won't shoot into the crowd. I don't think so, anyway. Seems like our only shot."

The rest of the men had been listening. They all nodded in agreement.

"Okay," Buck said, "but give me The Sauce. Maybe I can give you guys enough of a distraction to make something happen."

Bomber shook his head.

"No," he said. "It's got to be me. I helped create the monster. I need to take it down."

The lights dimmed and a spotlight settled on Sly standing in front of his throne.

"What a show so far, right folks?" Sly said into a headset microphone. "Let's give a big round of applause for all our dead gladiators tonight."

The crowd clapped obediently.

"For our last—structured—event this evening, we have a special treat in store," Sly said. "Our remaining fighters will be putting on a piece of 'performance art,' if you will. An homage to the origins of this very town and to its honorable and most patriotic founder, my great-great-great-grandfather Silas Morgan Fox. As you can see, some of our remaining gladiators are dressed as humble fur trappers," he pointed to Bomber and Buck, "who entered the forests of Michigan with nothing more than the hopes of a peaceful existence, living close to the land. The others," Sly's voice took an ominous tone, "are dressed as the merciless savages who tried to cut them down."

The crowd booed.

The buzz from the cage-door latch sent vibrations down the benches. The door creaked open on its own.

"On your feet," the guards yelled. "Get to the center of the arena. Then divide up into your teams."

The men exchanged glances, as they rose solemnly from the bench.

"Good luck," Bomber whispered.

One by one they stepped out onto the sand, their legs tensed, ready to run. But the collars never fell away. Each man instinctively raised his hand to check his neck.

Sly smiled from his place on the platform.

"We'll be keeping the collars on for this event," he said. "Just to spice things up a bit."

* * *

6:38 p.m.

Sheriff Connie buzzed the intercom at the mansion's front gate. In the distance, the great building was haloed with an unnatural glow and the low roar of a distant crowd spilled around its edges. The lawn had been turned into a makeshift parking lot, packed with long black limousines and audacious sports cars. Another signature Longstreet party, but this time Carl wasn't inside. Perhaps there was truth in the old loon's ramblings.

"Longstreet Manor," came the voice over the intercom. "State your business."

"This is Sheriff Hayes," she said. "I need to ask a few questions. Please buzz me in."

There was a moment of silence.

"No can do," the intercom said. "Mr. Longstreet isn't home. Neither of them."

"I'm aware," Connie said.

Silence.

"I'm afraid there's no one here who is authorized to answer your questions."

"I'm looking for my son," Connie said.

"Haven't seen him."

"I have reason to believe he is here."

"Nope. But maybe he just needs some space," the intercom offered.

"I'd like to get a look around the grounds," Connie said. "Just to be certain."

"Come back with a warrant," the intercom said.

Headlights illuminated the gate and a Fox Hollow P.D. patrol car crunched to a stop behind her. She shielded her eyes as Sergeant Householder emerged.

"You didn't have to come," Connie said.

"I know."

"I'm getting in that mansion," Connie said. "And it's probably not going to be legal."

Householder nodded.

Connie grabbed the wrought-iron posts and gave them a good shake.

"The question is," she said, "how to get through to these rich bastards?"

Householder shook his head.

"Maybe they can help?" He jerked his thumb over his shoulder as "Mollie's Revenge," the department's light-armored vehicle, pulled up. Behind it came the Carson's rickety van, with Ron-Boy in the front seat grinning apologetically. Next was Tammy Schmidt's white Prius, still sporting the smeared remnants of "Team Gloria" written in window chalk. Connie stepped out to the road and looked down at an endless row of headlights.

"But wait, there's more," Sly said. "When the final showdown between settlers and savages took place on these very grounds, the Indian braves were led by an evil witch doctor who called upon their demon gods to transform them into vicious, wild beasts—as if they needed help with that."

Sly winked and the crowd jeered behind their masks.

"But this was no ordinary witch doctor. So I couldn't just let her part be played by any old gladiator. No, it takes a religious kook to play a religious kook."

The beast-gate slid open and the gladiators took up defensive stances. From the door, an old man, dressed only in a loincloth stumbled from the shadows and dropped to his knees. Armed guards followed behind and hoisted him up by his elbows. Every square inch of the man's body was covered in a patchwork of fresh tattoos depicting religious and satanic symbols of every origin, the skin beneath still crimson and bloodied.

"Ladies and gentlemen, former Pastor William J. Mast Senior of the Third Christian Reformed Church will be playing the role of the crazy witch doctor: Poca-Haunts-Us!"

The crowd went wild and began chanting, "Poca-Haunts-Us," as the old man was led to the far side of the arena.

"Pastor Mast," Bomber yelled, as he rushed forward. Pastor Mast turned his head just in time to see Bomber dropped by a jolt of electricity coursing through his collar.

"Uh, uh, uh," Sly clucked. He waved the remote control in his paw-hand. "Those collars have more than one setting, you know. We can't have you fraternizing with the enemy."

He motioned to the armed guards on the ground.

"Take your places, everyone."

The men dressed as Native Americans were herded to the far side, where they immediately dropped their clubs and swords to lend support to Pastor Mast, an act of kindness that drew more boos from the crowd. Only Bomber and Buck, in their fringed leather jumpsuits and coonskin hats, remained on Sly's end of the arena.

Bomber, recovering from his jolt, watched Sly while the men took their places. Ex-Sheriff Barnstorm had appeared, a look of concern on his face. He lifted to his toes and whispered in Sly's ear. Through the din of the crowd, Sly's responses were faint over the microphone.

"I don't care if the whole goddamn town is out there... They are?... Well, security is your job, isn't it? Take care of it or I'll take care of you."

Barnstorm turned to leave, but Sly grabbed his shoulder.

"Take this little shit with you," Sly said. "As leverage."

Barnstorm yanked the sullen beaver-Bruce from his seat and pushed him forward by his neck until they were out of view.

Sly turned back to the arena, replacing his long, dog-faced scowl with a sadistic grin.

"Seven savages against two red-blooded Americans?!" he yelled. "Seems unfair, right?"

The crowd shouted affirmation.

"Perhaps I should level the playing field," he said.

The crowd cheered as he pulled the toga over his head. His chest muscles contracted and he made a show of flexing his huge hairy biceps. The crowd whistled and cat-called. His black fanny pack hung down from his hips, doing little to cover his small, furry genitals, which Bomber found weirdly inoffensive in the way he might view an unneutered dog.

Sly leapt from the platform and plunged into the arena, doing his best superhero landing into the sand only a few feet from Bomber and Buck. He towered over them.

"My," Buck said, "what big teeth you have."

Sly rolled his eyes, as he pushed between Bomber and Buck.

At the center of the arena, he turned back to address the crowd but paused when something caught his attention above. Bomber looked up, past the crowd, to see a group of armed guards running in the direction of the mansion.

Two days ago, half of Fox Hollow had been rioting against the other while Connie tried to put down both sides. Now, the whole town was ready, once again, to destroy private property—but this time, together.

Connie pressed the button to the intercom again.

"Listen," she said. "I don't know what's going on in there, but this is your last chance. The entire town is out here and we want answers. I won't be able to stop them from tearing down this gate. And I'm not sure I'd want to if I could."

"Trespassers will be shot on sight," came a voice from the other end. This voice was different, but familiar. Unnerving. At that moment, several flares rose into the sky from behind the mansion, burning high overhead.

"You were warned," Connie said.

"So what do we do now, boss?" Householder asked. "Ram the gate with ol' Mollie?"

Connie thought for a moment and then pushed into the crowd until she came to Ron-Boy's van. He was leaning against the hood and trying to maintain a safe distance from Connie and her officers, who'd manage to lose track of him in the mayhem following the football-field-stand-off. As Connie approached, he stood and straightened his homemade armor.

"How can I be of service, Sheriff?" Ron-Boy asked, his chins held high.

Connie sighed. She couldn't believe she was asking.

"You still have that RPG handy?"

Sly spent several moments rallying the crowd like the headliner in a Pro-Wrestling match. Ted Nugget's "Cat Scratch Fever" played ironically in the background and several sets of pyrotechnics were shot overhead, garnering oohs and ahs from the crowd. Finally, he signaled for the music to stop and stood at the center of the arena, his chest rising and falling like a barrel bobbing in the sea. He adjusted his earpiece and microphone, which had been jostled out of place during his ridiculous preening.

"Alright, alright," Sly said, chuckling to himself the way cocky assholes often do. "That's enough of that nonsense."

"We love you, Sly!" someone shouted.

Sly took a deep bow and the white tip of his orange tail pointed skyward.

"As I mentioned earlier in the evening, we have multiple performance-enhancers on display for you tonight. The animals you've seen so far have been dosed with a short-term, but highly effective compound we call, The Sauce. Extremely effective if you'd like to see your enemies rip each other apart for no reason. The Sauce is actually best dispersed as an aerosol in low doses for prolonged effects, unless you can trick your target into ingesting it. Fun colored applesauce has proven to be an effective vehicle. In high doses, though, there *are* negative side effects, including nausea, diarrhea, and spontaneous full-body eruption."

The crowd laughed.

"I thought we'd pit the final two enhancers against each other, to best highlight their difference. For the rowdy bunch of savages over there," Sly pointed to the group huddled around Pastor Mast, "each of their collars contain a small dose of a compound we call Brute. This lovely cocktail brags all the characteristics you love about of The Sauce, such as increased strength and unrelenting aggression, without the nasty side effect of exploding into blue gloop. Brute is an excellent choice for increasing performance in your favorite fighting dogs, giving an edge to Third-World military coup d'états, or simply upping the challenge level in the people you hunt."

A disgusting number of people clapped at the "people hunting" comment.

"Finally, we have our third compound," Sly said, patting his fanny pack. "Our premium product, Warrior Poet. Those of you who've been here before can tell what it's done for *me* in just a short time. Warrior Poet will increase physical performance, while allowing the subject to maintain critical cognitive functions. The enhancer has been fortified with high levels of Omega-3s and fish oils and all kinds of crazy shit too, not only maintain mental cognition, but enhance the mind's performance as well. The Warrior Poet can be used for purely cosmetic purposes," Sly flexed his huge arms, "or to enhance performance in black ops soldiers, paramilitary intelligence spooks, and run-of-the-mill mercenaries. Hell, even your day-to-day security teams would benefit from the Warrior Poet. And, folks, once this stuff hits the streets, you don't want to be the only one without it."

The crowd began to clap, just as an explosion echoed through the arena.

Sly looked toward the mansion, his eyes narrowed to slits. Several more guards ran toward the mansion.

"What the hell was that?" Members of the audience stood, looking toward the source of the explosion, their masks hiding their concern.

"It's nothing to worry about. Please take your seats," Sly reassured. "It's nothing my staff can't handle. Let's get on to the main event."

Connie and her officers had pulled everyone back from the main gate, shielding them behind a perimeter of squad cars, with Mollie's Revenge in the middle. Connie had planned to fire the RPG herself, but Ron-Boy refused to give up his prized possession, citing the astronomical amount he'd paid for the damn thing. The price turned out to be an outright lie, later coming to light that Ron-Boy had actually attained the weapon from the recently deceased Carl Junior, who'd supplied it with the intent of furthering the chaos of the debates.

Ron-Boy positioned himself behind the squad car nearest the gate, before going through a series of tedious preparations, the last of which was to recruit a fellow Apple Knocker to snap several dramatically, heroic photos for Ron-Boy's social media accounts.

"For god's sake," Connie yelled. "Shoot the damn thing."

The Apple Knocker withdrew and Ron-Boy heaved a deep breath.

"Backblast area, all clear," he yelled, a procedure he'd learned from military-themed video he'd Googled minutes earlier.

He jerked the trigger.

The rocket rushed forward, leaving a winding tail of smoke. It ricocheted off the gate's central post and careened up the driveway, where it slammed into the hood of a limousine, immediately igniting the luxury vehicle.

"Wicked," Ron-Boy said, unable to hide his smile.

"Damn you, Ron-Boy," Sheriff Connie said.

Ron-Boy frowned and stood with the empty RPG tube on his shoulder looking like somebody had just killed his puppy.

"Plan B," Connie said to Householder. "We're going to use Mollie to ram the gate."

Householder nodded.

"In retrospect," she said, watching the burning limo, "that should've been Plan A."

Householder nodded again.

Far down the road, a horn began blasting erratically and two headlights snaked toward the gate through the mess of vehicles parked along each shoulder. Marty VanGovern's jacked-up diesel truck pulled up next to Connie and Householder, its monstrous tires grinding on the gravel road. The window dropped and Marty pushed his head out, strands of gray fly-aways sticking out from his crown of hair. Connie could smell the bourbon before he even spoke.

"I hear yer have'n some trouble up here," he slurred. "Lemme help out."

"I appreciate the offer," Connie said, "but we have the situation under control."

The burning limo reflected in Marty's watery eyes.

"Do you?" he asked. "Lemme help. I ain't done one adventurous thing in my life. Been stuck in that damn store and now that it's gone, I can't figure out what it was all for. I ain't got one damn story to tell anyone."

He wiped a tear with the back of his hand, which still clutched an open bourbon bottle.

"Let me make a story fer myself, Sheriff," he said.

"I think you should get out of the truck," Connie said. "You're flashing a half-empty liquor bottle to a police officer for god's sake."

"Not half-empty, Sheriff," Marty said, forcing a quivering smile, "half-full."

"What?"

"Whores gotta eat," he said quietly.

"I don't see what that has to do with anyth—"

"WHORES GOTTA LIVE," Marty yelled. He slammed his foot on the gas pedal and the back tires sprayed gravel, sending everyone diving for cover.

The truck fishtailed forward and slammed into the iron gates, which bowed only slightly at first. The truck's engine revved. Connie hollered. Gravel sprayed into the air, arching like a rooster tail. There were several loud pops and the gate toppled down with a heavy clatter. The truck lurched forward over the mangled metal and came to a stop twenty feet inside the wall.

For a moment, no one moved. The mansion was still and all was quiet except the chugging of Marty's diesel engine. Finally, the door swung open and Marty jumped to the ground. He raised his hands in celebration, like an ace pilot returning from another successful dogfight. The town went wild.

The cheering was so loud that the distant report of a rifle may have been missed had Connie not seen the muzzle flash on the mansion roof. A spray of blood and flesh erupted from Marty's abdomen. He dropped to his knees and then to his face, his arms still raised victoriously above his bald head.

Everyone heard the gunshot. The entire arena looked to the mansion as one. From the arena floor, Bomber could barely make out the mansion's castle-like roof, but through the bright lights, he swore he could see men moving along the parapet. People began to point and a steady murmur rippled through the crowd.

"Everyone sit down and shut up," Sly snarled. "We're doing this, dammit."

The people obeyed, but hesitantly.

"They're coming for you," Bomber said. "The whole town is coming. They'll have your ugly dog-head on a platter."

Sly reached his paw-hand into the fanny pack and produced

the collar remote.

"If I lose my head," he said, "you'll lose yours."

Sly turned to face the faux Indian warriors and their painted medicine man.

"What do you think, old man?" Sly yelled. "You've been wasting your life, trying to save souls on cursed ground. This is the town that sin built. Will you fight me for its ugly soul?"

"The only ugly souls here are yours," Pastor Mast said. He swept his hand across the crowd. The crowd hissed. "The Lord teaches us to reject violence and to love our fellow man unconditionally." He bent down and retrieved a club, dropped by one of the gladiators. He pointed it at Sly. "But you're no man and we all fall short of the glory of the Lord."

Sly smiled, pulling loose jowls back into a snarl. "That's the spirit," he growled.

The lights reflected off his gold fang and the sound of not-so-distant gunfire became nothing more than background noise to the enraptured crowd.

Connie leaned around the stone wall and tried to get a look at Marty, who was moaning on the ground beside his truck. Her face was barely past the wall's edge when a bullet cracked into the stone, sending chips of rock into her cheek.

She'd tried to reach Marty after the first shot, but a volley of fire had erupted from the mansion's roof, raking the truck and kicking up gravel around her feet. She dove for the cover of the wall like everyone else, and now Sergeant Householder sat next to her, clutching his pistol.

"What do we do now, Sheriff?" he asked.

Connie shut her eyes and tried to block out everything as the guns on the roof barked in alternating spurts. She breathed deep and forced her nerves to calm. Her mind took her back to the night before Bruce's first game as Foxy the mascot. She'd sat with him on the edge of his bed, as he battled an anxiety attack. She could still feel her hand rubbing his back over that stupid costume, reassuring him that, fox or no fox, he'd be okay. He'd needed her then and he needed her now.

She stood up against the wall.

"Sheriff?" Householder asked, looking up.

"Gimme the keys to Mollie," she said.

"Sheriff, what are you planning to do?"

"Gimme the keys."

Householder stood and pulled the keys from his belt. "Okay, but I'm coming with you."

"Like hell you are," she said. "You're in charge here. Keep these people back and don't let anybody try to be a hero. Especially Ron-Boy."

Before Householder could protest, Connie was dashing for the light-armored vehicle.

Inside, the cab smelled like a rancid mix of sweat and chew juice. She cranked the engine, killed the headlights, and lurched Mollie forward, creeping through a sea of squad cars and people running for better cover. She moved the vehicle through the gate, veering hard left to avoid crushing Marty's prone figure. She made it a full ten feet before a large caliber bullet ripped through the engine block, leaving a two-inch hole in the hood. Mollie coughed to a halt.

Connie slammed her fists into the steering wheel just as the windshield burst into a web of shattered glass. She doubled over in the seat, getting her head below the dash as a second volley peppered the very un-bulletproof windshield, sending white seat-stuffing up like confetti at a parade. She cursed Barnstorm for cutting corners, even while wasting the tax payers' dollars. The air around her was pulverized by the overpressure produced by the large caliber rounds. She could feel the concussion in her chest and it felt like her heart had shifted rhythm. Suddenly the pressure stopped, but the steady beat continued. She spilled from the vehicle's cab and looked up as a shadow glided overhead, like the silhouette of a shark beneath black waves. A spotlight kicked on from the helicopter hanging above and shone onto the roof ridge from where the gunfire came.

BRRRRRRRRRRRTTTTTTTTTTT

The aircraft let loose a long belch, accompanied by the tinkling of spent brass casings as they fell to the asphalt driveway. The mansion's parapet disintegrated before Connie's eyes.

Miniature figures of men were vaporized or plummeted from the roof in the dramatic fashion of dying cowboys in a spaghetti western.

Thirty-millimeter chaingun, Connie thought.

The helicopter hung in the air in front of her and then a faint whistle announced a trail of smoke that rushed toward the mansion.

Hellfire missile, Connie thought.

An explosion rocked the rooftop and a large radio antenna wavered and then toppled to the ground below. A second helicopter came buzzing low behind the first and Connie caught a glimpse of the large white lettering on the side.

"EPA"

What little of the crowd's attention Sly still held vanished when the roof of the Foxy Howl Inn erupted in a great fireball. The crowd watched as a radio antenna crumbled out of sight and men engulfed in flames leaped from the rooftop. The smile melted from Sly's face as screams echoed through the arena. His guests scattered. Masked cowards in tuxedos and slinky evening gowns clawed and pushed their way out of the pit of depravity.

A helicopter buzzed overhead, spilling a floodlight over them before lurching on. Bomber looked up and read the lettering on the side.

"You were telling the truth," Bomber said to Buck.

"You have trust issues," Buck said.

"You did this!" Sly shouted. He stalked forward. His feet sank into tacky, blood-saturated sand. "I'm going to have to start over completely now."

"It's over, Sly," Bomber said as he and Buck back-pedaled.

Sly's hand slipped into the fanny pack and he twisted a dial. His neck spasmed and his shoulders wretched forward. His biceps bulged with a spiderweb of veins. He grew in front of their eyes, inflating like a marshmallow in the microwave.

Buck stopped and stood his ground.

"Run," he said. "I'll buy you some time."

Bomber pulled the coonskin hat from his head and thumbed

the vial in the band. He wasn't going to take an easy out. Not this time. Heart thumping, he stepped up and stood even with Buck. He slid the vial out and gripped it discreetly in his hand.

"We'll do it together."

Sly was nearly on top of them now and Bomber could smell awful dog breath as it stabbed out against the cold in rolling, gray clouds.

"I should've killed you both at City Hall," Sly snarled. He lifted a massive hand equipped with claws, ready to slash.

There was a dull thud and Sly yelped like a kicked mutt. He turned, rubbing the back of his head as a wooden club settled in the sand. The entire band of migrant-workers-turned-gladiators were on a dead sprint across the arena, leather skins flapping and feathers trailing from Bruce's elaborately decorated headdresses. Behind them, Pastor Mast struggled to keep up.

Bomber felt a twinge of hope, but it would not last. At the sight of the charging gladiators, Sly held high the collar remote, and Bomber's stomach dropped.

"Enough," Sly barked. The gladiators kept coming. Bomber could see horror register in each of their faces and then wash away in grim resignation. Still, they came.

Sly's big thumb hovered over a red button.

Bomber dove at Sly's arm, but it was too late. The button was down.

He closed his eyes and waited, wondering if his brain would continue to fire neurons long enough for him to watch his head fall away from his own shoulders.

Nothing happened.

Bomber opened his eyes. Sly pushed the red button over and over, not seeming to notice the two-hundred-pound adult male hanging from his hairy arm.

"What the goddamn hell?" He grumbled, slapping the remote with his other paw-hand.

There was a simultaneous moment of clarity and they both looked to where the collapsed radio antenna had stood on the roof.

The gladiators were still charging, rejuvenated by the high one experiences when one's head doesn't explode as expected.

Sly crushed the remote in his hand, dropped it, and with the upward flick of his elbow, lofted Bomber into the air, catching him by the buckskin leather shirt. Bomber dangled there, the fringes of his costume swaying behind him.

"Two Merridans in two weeks," Sly bellowed. "Maybe I'll track down your parents and make it four."

From behind them, there was a loud crack. Sly howled and dropped to one knee. Buck stood behind him, wooden club in hand. He made to raise it again, but Sly was too fast. Five razor claws swept Buck's chest, sending him sprawling into the sand.

Sly hurled Bomber like a ragdoll at the approaching gladiators. Fortunately for them—and less fortunate for him—Bomber's flailing body missed them completely. Somewhere in the rolling and sliding and cursing, Bomber lost the vial.

He looked up as the lean, muscled men, who, just days ago had made their living peacefully picking fruit, descended on the massive Dogman. But they were nothing to him now. Fleas on a dog. They clubbed, punched, stabbed, and yanked. They kicked, bit, grappled, and clenched, but Sly would sweep his arms and clear them all in large swoops.

Bomber scoured the sand for the vial. Only another beast could kill the beast. He knew there'd be no coming back, but it was the only option he could see. The only chance they had.

He spotted the vial, ten feet away and he crawled toward it. When he looked up again, the vial was there, between two bare feet. The feet were coated with bloody sand, barely covering blue tattoo ink. A peace symbol on one. A pentagram on the other. Bomber followed a maze of tribal designs up the tattooed legs of Pastor Mast. The old reverend gave him a weary smile as he bent to retrieve the vial.

"There is no greater love than this," he said, as he popped the rubber stopper from the end. The word "Don't!" had barely escaped Bomber's lips, before the good Pastor gulped down the blue liquid inside.

No sooner had the helicopters arrived than two blacked-out SUVs swerved up and skidded to a halt, creating an even bigger jumble of vehicles and confusion, as throngs of townsfolk began to venture out from where they'd taken cover. Connie had rushed to Marty and found him still breathing, though his lungs were making strange wheezing noises and a good portion of his upper intestinal tract was showing. Connie did her best to stop the bleeding until two of her officers showed up with a fancy medkit and took over first aid.

A man in black body armor stepped from the lead SUV with a tricked-out AR-15 strapped across his armored chest and began barking orders at other dark figures emerging from other SUVs. He was a short man, thick in build, with a dense beard and the strong, sturdy index finger of a man who's spent his life directing people where to go.

"Who are they?" Householder whispered.

"E.P.A. spooks, I think," Connie said.

"The Environmental Protection Agency has spooks?"

The man spotted them and walked over, removing one of his tactical gloves to shake Connie's hand.

"Special Agent Chuck Rostad, E.P.A. Department of Kinetic Operations," the man said, shaking Connie's hand for much longer than is socially acceptable. "But everyone calls me Chuck Roast. You must be Sheriff Hayes?"

"I—"

"I got your message, Sheriff Hayes, and I appreciate the heads up. When our boy didn't provide his scheduled Situation Report, we started to suspect something was up."

"How'd you know to come here to the mansion?"

"We've had our eyes on this place for some time now," he said. "It was one of Agent Ross'—Mr. Wildes' areas of interest. If he was going to go missing, there was a good chance he'd be going missing here."

"Well, we appreciate you coming, Chuck," Connie said. "Are your men going to assault the mansion?" Connie asked. "My son is in there. I don't want anyone rushing in there, guns blazing."

"Assault the mansion?" Chuck patted the thick armor plate carrier on his chest below a novelty Velcro name tape reading "CHUCK ROAST" and a Punisher-skull patch. "Negative. Our birds have identified our target behind the mansion. I'll be taking my team around back. Our top priority is neutralizing the beast and extracting our agent."

"The beast?"

"Besides," Chuck said. "It looks like your motley militia here is already assaulting the mansion just fine."

He pointed a beefy finger toward the gate where Ron-Boy and his band of merry Apple Knockers were leading a mob of townsfolk past Marty's truck toward the mansion.

Pastor Mast was on his knees, his arms wrapped around his stomach in an effort to contain the bone-cracking spasms. He didn't scream or moan. He barely made a sound until his neck elongated and even then, he only grunted through a locked jaw. Tough old codger. Muscles in his back jerked and swelled. Connective tissue rolled and bulged and pulsed. He began to look less like a man and more like a shaved mountain gorilla or one of those bonobo monkeys if you pumped it full of steroids and then exposed it to radiation. The fresh tattoos trembled at first and then bubbled above traveling sinew. They stretched and expanded every which way, their origins lost as they transformed to fit a new form. Blood seeped from open wounds, turning from crimson to deep purple, until it appeared the religious symbols were melting, blurring into a slick mass of anger and confusion.

Everyone—even Sly—had stopped to watch. Pastor Mast, or the creature who used to be Pastor Mast, was now the size of Sly. There was no trace of humanity left in its eyes, which had gone dark like windows to a lightless house, and then cracked with streaks of orange fire.

Bomber was still lying prone at the feet of this new beast, not daring to move for fear of stirring the Pastor's aggression. He remembered what the other fighters had taught him about the dosed-up predators focusing on the largest threat first, which was most certainly Sly.

Pastor Mast lumbered forward, his enormous feet leaving craters in the sand. Sly braced for impact but the momentum was too great. He toppled backward, nearly crushing Buck who was struggling to his feet, looking pale with five bloody gashes across his chest. The other gladiators scattered, knowing, if Sly were bested, Pastor Mast would be after them next.

Sly sprang up, but Pastor Mast was at him again, swinging wild haymakers with blind fury and connecting more often than not. Sly battled back, landing blows of his own, each one sending tidal waves of flesh across Pastor Mast's face and chest. Each one threatened to rupture the clergyman and reduce him to a blue puddle. But Sly couldn't compensate for the Pastor's raw, savage rage and he raised his arms to protect his head from a rain of thrashing arms beating tirelessly against him.

Bomber ran to Buck and supported him under the arm as they both ran for the door. Bomber turned his head just in time to see it happen.

One of the Pastor's wild swipes went low and made purchase on the waistband of Sly's fanny pack. It ripped free like it was nothing. Sly made a grab for the bag but was too late. The Pastor yanked back, pulling the long IV tube free from the flesh of Sly's hip. Orange liquid squirted into the dirt and the Pastor tossed the whole ordeal to the side like trash.

Sly lunged for it, but the Pastor snatched his tail and pulled him back. The change was nearly instantaneous. The vivid light of Sly's eyes dulled and his chest deflated like a balloon releasing air.

Bomber pushed himself out from under Buck's arm. They were nearly at the door, where the remaining gladiators were prying the edge with a discarded sword, trying to make an exit. He dashed back across the arena floor, too close for comfort to the raging beasts. The Pastor was on top of Sly, choking him. Veins bulged in his tattooed arms, like jungle vines wrapped around two totem poles.

Bomber grabbed the fanny pack and turned to run, but something had his foot. From his supine position, Sly had managed a desperate grab and was now clutching Bomber's ankle in a shrinking paw-hand.

Sly's eyes were dark and cold, and he choked for air as Pastor Mast pushed into him. Blue blood streamed from the Pastor's chin and dripped into a puddle beside Sly's head. The skin of his face bubbled. A tooth fell from Mast's mouth, followed by another. His eyes were red-hot coals.

Still grasping Bomber's ankle, Sly wriggled his feet with his fox-flexibility and planted both on the Pastor's heaving chest. He thrust and sent the old man flying backward, arching toward the ground in slow motion. For Bomber, time stopped and the Pastor's body floated flat above the ground. In that split second, Pastor Mast reappeared. Perhaps even a younger version of the old reverend, the lines and wrinkles of his face smoothed away as his tissue melted and his cells released their natural bonds. His arms, rippling in slow motion, were extended at his sides and his face was placid and pale beneath the blotted ink-blue symbols of the past.

It's hard to say whether he exploded before the impact or *due* to the impact. If you ask Bomber, he'd tell you the Pastor was still six inches from the ground when he ruptured, sending a wave of goo sloshing across the sand.

Sly scrambled back, releasing Bomber, in an effort to avoid contact with the Pastor's contaminated blood and brains and intestines and whatever-the-hell-else was liquefied and heading their way.

They were both on their feet and Bomber turned to find Sly had shrunk to eye level. Sly snarled, his eyes searching the ground for his synthetic advantage. Buck stood ten feet away, the fanny pack in one hand and a clear plastic IV bag in the other. The bag was torn wide and the last orange drops of Warrior Poet splashed to the ground.

Sly tipped his head back and let loose a mournful howl, as if whatever remained of his soul was escaping. It would've been most impressive, and eerie too, had it not been cut short when Bomber socked the whining Dogman straight in his furry jaw.

Sly stumbled back, sucking in the battered jowl before spitting his gold canine into the dirt.

"What the hell?" he yelped.

"What?"

"You sucker-punched me," Sly said, rubbing at his face. He had to look up to meet Bomber's angry gaze.

Bomber puffed his chest.

"You wanna do gladiator shit?" he said, putting up his fists. "Let's do gladiator shit."

Sly lifted his paw-fists, as if to fight, and then darted off across the arena. The other gladiators were now gone and the door they'd wrenched open hung wide from one rail. Sly's diminished size lent to greater speed and he was through it in a flash.

The front lawn of the Fox Family Mansion was a warzone. A melee of epic proportions. The EPA's helicopters continued doing gun runs, silencing occasional rifle reports coming in tandem with muzzle-flashes from various mansion windows and inadvertently providing cover fire for the advancing hordes of Fox Hollow residents. Ron-Boy and the Apple Knockers led the charge across the expanse that separated the front gate and the rows of fancy cars, though it was more of a "clamber" than a full-on "charge." They were followed by hordes of regular citizens, armed with gardening tools, bricks, bats, rocks, and whatever else they could scrounge up to be used as weaponry. Even the dullest mind can be creative when put to the task of destruction. Yoga instructor Tammy Schmidt advanced through the crowd gripping the necks of two empty wine bottles, wielding them like fat-ended billy clubs.

The mob filtered through the labyrinth of parked sports cars and tricked-out SUVs. They slashed tires, keyed doors, stomped hoods, and smashed windshields along the way. Car alarms sounded and echoed off the perimeter walls. As they reached the Original Sin Fountain, the front doors of the mansion burst open like floodgates and a wave of rich, entitled ass-bags spilled out. They were still in their creepy party masks, dressed to the nines in tuxedos, tailored suits, fancy evening gowns, and cocktail dresses. Some appeared to have dressed hastily, coming from the dens of debauchery inside, their collars and hemlines askew, shoes missing or in-hand, hair still frazzled from whatever depravity had been cut short. Some were without shirts, others without pants. All without pride. The first wave made mad dashes toward their cars. Men tripped on untied laces as their fancy dates clattered along behind them, snapping ankles in toothpick stilettos and calling for them to be chivalrous for once in their worthless lives. They were met by the mob's unflinching resolve. Fists and feet flew freely.

From where Connie stood in the gate entrance, she could hear the sharp sound of meat on meat and the yelps and groans of people not accustomed to life's discomforts, let alone physical pain. Masks flew off, revealing a CEO here, a movie star there, a supermodel, a sitting U.S. Senator.

Sheriff Connie had an inclination to put a stop to the violence and destruction. But something gave her pause. Gnawed at her gut. She knew that every last one of these people had it coming and she'd be lying if she didn't admit a deep satisfaction in seeing them pummeled. She continued to scan the crowd for any sign of Bruce. She knew she needed to stop the mayhem. Her duty was to keep the peace, regardless of personal feelings. She was about to do just that when she looked toward the mansion doors and out spilled a dozen naked bodies—the apparent remnants of an orgy. In the center of the group, a fat man still grabbed mirthfully at the breasts and butts of several, much younger, women and men in his party. All at once, he seemed to realize the mayhem around him and he snapped upright, his hairy gut bouncing. It was at that precise moment of disgusting clarity that Connie had a moment of clarity all her own. She was not going to help these monsters. Not one bit. Not even when Yoga Tammy charged forward up the mansion stairs like a lunging lioness and walloped the fat man across the temple with an empty bottle of merlot, crumpling him to the stone steps and sending his band of perverts scattering into the ruckus.

"Are we going to stop this?" Sergeant Householder asked.

Connie realized, somewhat sheepishly, she'd been smiling.

"Do what you need to do to keep anyone from getting killed, I guess," Connie said, heading back toward her patrol car.

"What are you going to do?" Householder called after her.

Connie opened the back door. Carl lay in the fetal position on the backseat, his hands still cuffed behind his back.

"Get up, Carl," Connie said. "You're gonna give me a tour of the mansion."

Pursuing Sly was easy. All Bomber and Buck had to do was follow the trail of carnage. The breadcrumb trail of bodies started with three of the mansion's staff members' eviscerated amongst the tables of the fake poolside patio, which led to their decision to enter the mansion through the same door Bomber had taken with Ex-Sheriff Barnstorm instead of venturing around the mansion's outside. Had they rounded the outside of mansion's east lawn they would've been surprised to find a heavily armed team of EPA Operators trying fruitlessly to subdue several frantic migrant workers oddly dressed in Native American garb and ranting about "perro del demonio."

The labyrinth of identical halls inside the mansion was now clearly marked, littered with dead or dying mansion slaves and masked elitists alike. No one was safe from Sly's wrath.

The trail of blood led them to the door to the dungeon laboratory, which had been hastily left ajar.

"He's heading for the tunnel," Bomber yelled, but when there was no response he looked back. Buck was several yards back, doubled over with one hand braced against the wall and one hand across the gashes on his chest. When he looked up, his face was pale and glistening under a slick of sweat.

"Maybe you'd better take a seat," Bomber said.

"I'll be okay," Buck grunted, but took a seat anyway. "I think this is where I leave you. Or rather, you leave me."

Bomber started back toward him, but Buck put up a hand.

"No," he said. "You have to finish this. I only need to catch my breath. You can't let him slip away or all this," he swung his hand around to indicate the depraved former brothel, "or all of this will happen again, somewhere else."

Bomber pointed down the hall.

"The front entrance is that way," he said. "Find Sherriff Connie."

Buck nodded and then pointed to the open door.

"Go!"

Sheriff Connie had a heck of a time getting Carl through the warzone that was the mansion's lawn. Despite her firm grasp on his tuxedo collar, townsfolk accosted Carl all along the way. A kick here. A jab there. A thrown rock. A yank of his greasy hair.

Whether or not he was being mistaken for one of the rich sickos was up for debate, but Connie suspected the pissed-off people of Fox Hollow knew exactly what they were doing.

By the time they reached the mansion steps, Carl had been punched in the face no less than five times, kneed in the gut thrice, his jacket was ripped, his shins bloodied, and he'd received one solid drive-by bash to the testicles from Big Mama Carson, who'd ripped by in her electric scooter.

"This is police brutality," Carl shouted.

"I haven't done a thing to you," Connie said.

In fact, Connie had stopped Yoga Tammy from clocking Carl with her twin wine bottle clubs, fearing another blow to Carl's head might render the old vagabond unconscious—and therefore, useless.

The mob's mood was shifting. They grew tired of simple assault and began looting what they could from the mansion. People spilled in and out like worker bees around the entrance of a hive. Connie and Carl entered the front door to find two looters had dislodged the mural of "The Fox Hollow Massacre" from the far wall.

"Put it down," Connie called. She raised her pistol and stepped to the side for a clear shot around the bronze fox statue. She would not have the glorified slaughter of her ancestors decorating some random idiot's living room.

The looters leaned the frame gently against the staircase banister.

"Get out of here," Connie said, beckoning with her pistol. "Go find other shit to steal."

They rushed off down the east hall, but Connie was too distracted to care. Behind where the painting had hung on the far wall was an ancient wooden door, held together by ornate ironwork. It was secured shut with three thick iron drop bars.

Carl opened his mouth to say something misguided, but never got a chance, as Sheriff Connie turned and pistol-whipped him across the cheek. He squealed like a stuck pig.

"Now *that* is police brutality," she said. "Is that where they're keeping Bruce?"

"I don't know," Carl said, blood dribbling down his chin. "I've never seen that door before."

Connie crossed to the door and heaved back the heavy drop bars. The door's hinges cried out a warning as it swung out. The inside of the door was marred with long desperate scratches, dug deep into the old wood.

Connie peered into the darkness, but could only see the top of a stone staircase descending into abysmal darkness. She rushed back to Carl and hit him again, this time dragging him forward toward the door.

"Is he down there, Carl?" she yelled. "Is he?"

"Tsk, tsk, tsk, Sheriff," came a familiar voice from the platform above. "Beating up on the elderly homeless now? Looks like the Fox Hollow P.D. has really gone downhill."

Connie had to backpedal a few steps to see the giant man at the top of the staircase.

"Barnstorm." Connie frowned.

"And I brought a friend," Barnstorm said with a smile.

He pulled Bruce forward, placing him in front. Barnstorm's huge arm was wedged under Bruce's chin and the barrel of a Remington Rand 1911 pistol was pressed tight to his temple.

At the basement floor, Bomber stared in horror at the wall of one-way windows, now coated with spattered blood. Through gaps in the gore, he could see white lab coats stained red, lying motionless on the tile floor.

The lab door was open, pushed off its sliding track and clicking relentlessly as it tried to right itself. Bomber stepped tentatively into the lab because that's how one enters a room of recently deceased bodies. The lab was in shambles. Mixed among the bodies were overturned desks and smashed lab equipment. The floor was covered in the shards of broken test tubes and puddles of bright colored liquids. Bomber dared not enter further.

Suddenly, something grabbed his ankle and he nearly fell backward out the door.

He looked down to find the bird-like scientist who had objected to injecting the rabbit when he'd first arrived. She coughed and wheezed. Her eyes already bore a glassy sheen of death. Blood soaked her white lab coat. She was trying to say something, but the words were faint.

"He has the samples," she whispered. "He has the reser-research."

Her eyes went wide.

"Oh, God. He has everything."

As if uttering this phrase completed her mission, she closed her eyes and exhaled her last.

"Bruce," Connie shouted. "Are you okay?"

"I've been better," Bruce said. "They cut my hair off."

"It looks good, honey," Connie said.

"Shut up!" Barnstorm barked.

Connie swung her pistol off to the side and removed her finger from the trigger.

"There's no getting out of this, Barnstorm," Connie said. "Let him go."

"I will," Barnstorm said. "Just like you're going to let *me* go. You see this here?"

He flashed the hand he'd been using to hold Bruce. In it, was a small remote.

"The collar around little Brucey's neck is equipped with enough C4 to separate his head from his spine. This remote is what triggers the charge. I'm going to let your boy go and I'm going to walk out of here with no trouble from you or anyone else. One wrong move and 'pop goes the Bruce.'" He grinned at Connie. "Do we have an agreement?"

"We have an agreement," she said without hesitation.

"Good," Barnstorm said. His forehead glistened with sweat. "I'm releasing him now."

He slowly eased his arm off Bruce's chest and held up the remote in his left hand, in case anyone forgot it was there. He pointed his pistol in Connie's general direction. She remained motionless. A statue next to a statue.

Connie caught movement in her peripheral vision and turned her head to find a man dressed in a bloody frontiersman costume stumbling into the foyer.

"You!" she exclaimed.

Carl spun around, his eyes the size of dinner plates over a bloody nose and bleeding cheek.

"You!" Buck shouted and popped Carl in the eye. Carl dropped like an overripe apple.

Behind Carl, Buck could see Sheriff Connie, splitting her attention between him and something on the upper floor. Buck stepped further into the foyer where he could see Ex-Sheriff Barnstorm and the teenage beaver-kid from the arena.

"Holy shit!" the kid exclaimed. "It's Buck Wildes!"

Buck flashed a woozy smile.

"Stay back," Barnstorm shouted, his pistol now alternating between Connie and Buck, remote still held up in the air.

"Stay back," Connie repeated, holding her hand up toward Buck. "We're letting Mr. Barnstorm go, so he doesn't blow my Bruce's head off."

"He won't," Buck said, matter-of-factly. "He can't."

"What do you mean, 'he can't'?" Connie asked.

"Like hell, I can't," Barnstorm said.

"He can't," Buck said. "The collars don't work anymore. Helicopter blew up the repeater tower." He thumbed his own collar casually. "He's bluffing."

"Like hell, I am," Barnstorm said. He held the remote higher and mashed the red button.

"No!" Connie yelled.

Nothing happened.

Barnstorm pressed it again. And again. He pulled the remote down to look at it.

"What the fu—"

A shot rang out and everyone jumped. Everyone except Sheriff Connie and Barnstorm. Connie didn't jump because she'd pulled the trigger. Her pistol breathed a wisp of smoke. Barnstorm didn't jump because the majority of his brain was spattered on the staircase wall behind him, blending perfectly with the apple themed wallpaper. The bullet caused Barnstorm's head to jerk back, while his body pitched forward. He somersaulted over the staircase railing and fell, landing squarely on the razor-sharp tail of the bronze fox statue, impaling him like bait on a fishhook.

Bomber sprinted headlong through the blackness of the tunnel, the dim lights overhead zipping by in a never-ending line. He knew the end must be near. His legs burned and his swollen nose throbbed, but he had one thought: catch Sly Fox. That is, if Sly didn't catch *him* first. Sly's canine eyes would give him the upper hand in the dark. His mind raced to formulate a feasible plan to overpower the dangerous Dogman and he weighed the pros and cons of drowning his one-time best friend in the toxic stew of the Kissing Pond.

He ran on, his heavy breathing echoing off the tunnel walls.

"So much for stealth," he thought. He was cursing himself for leaving the tunnel gate unlocked, though he was sure Sly would have a key. But at least a locked gate would slow him temporarily.

In the distance, Bomber heard the squeak of metal hinges. His heart leaped into his throat, while his stomach plummeted to his knees.

Bruce nearly toppled down the stairs as he ran to Connie who wrapped her giant child up like a mama bear embracing her cub.

"I'm so sorry, Bruce," she said, squeezing him tight. She never wanted to let go. "I'm so sorry for everything."

"Sorry for what, mom?" Bruce asked.

Connie snuffled back the emotion.

"I'm sorry for putting work first so much," she said. "I know it hasn't been easy."

"Are you kidding, mom?" Bruce said. "My life is always easy. I'm sorry I don't try harder. I'll try harder to try harder."

Connie chuckle and then cried.

"With your hair gone, you look like Lex Luthor," she said.

"Thanks, mom."

"Can we get the hell out of here now," Carl yelled. He was up off the floor and staring at the swaying legs of Barnstorm.

Sheriff Connie turned her attention back to Buck.

"Mr. Wildes," she said. "Or should I say Special Agent Ross?

—You appear to be losing a lot of blood."

She pointed at his chest.

"I should probably—" Buck started, but he was cut short when a doleful howl escaped the ancient door at back of the foyer.

Sly stood in the open gate, silhouetted by the moonlight. He was no bigger than a standard fox now. His once human-like hands had all but retracted into padded paws and the satchel dangling from his shoulder scrapped the ground.

"I'd honestly hoped you'd just let this alone," Sly said. "Why couldn't you have just done what you always do and given up?"

"I'm not that guy anymore," Bomber said.

"You'll always be that guy," Sly said. "Fox Hollow's favorite failure."

He looked at his watch.

"So what?" Bomber said. "You're going to have to kill me now?"

Sly turned back and looked into the sky outside the gate.

"You know me, Bill," Sly said. "I could never kill you. Have someone else do it? Yes. But not me."

Bomber stepped closer.

"I'm serious Sly," Bomber said. "It's over. Turn yourself in and they might even help you get back to—normal—before they send you to jail. You're rich; you'll probably get some cushy low security cell anyway."

Sly seemed to consider this. "There's never been any normal for me," he said, "and nothing's over."

Bomber raised his fists and stepped forward, as Sly turned to face him. His snout was low and his jowls wrinkled into that familiar sneer or snarl. Bomber could never quite tell.

"I'll wager my razor claws and teeth against your soft hide any day."

Bomber stopped his advance. Beyond Sly, he could hear the distant *thump, thump* of an approaching helicopter.

Another slow howl filtered up the stairs and into Sheriff Connie's spine.

"What the hell was that?" she asked.

From outside, the sounds of the melee could still be heard, intermixed with the rhythmic chopping of the EPA helicopters still circling the mansion. Down the inkwell of the stone passage came slow, heavy footfalls and the scraping of nails.

Sheriff Connie drew her pistol.

From the abyss stepped a small, withered creature. Not quite a dog, it walked on all fours. Its long snout was drawn, with paper-thin jowls, and ribs protruded from its emaciated frame. The fur of its legs was rubbed away, the skin red and raw, as though it had been bound in clasps. Its nails were worn to bloody nubs. The fur on its head was black, with two lightning streaks of gray hair above pointed ears. It stepped forward slowly, timidly. At the base of the statue, under the stiffening legs of Ex-Sheriff Barnstorm, it reached its front paws forward and pulled itself up to stand. Connie stared in disbelief. The creature stumbled forward until it reached the banister, where it seemed to consider the painting a moment before propping itself up and panting with a long, pale tongue. Connie could hear gasps from the front door behind her.

Bomber took a step closer.

Sly flashed his razor fang, still formidable despite the missing gold tooth.

"Don't be a hero," he said. "It's not your style."

Behind him, the moon reflected off the scummy surface of the Kissing Pond into an elongated orb. Bomber watched as the outline of the moon bubbled and broke and sloshed. Something was moving through the water. Sly, with his back to the pond, didn't notice, and Bomber, still weighing his options, felt no urgency to tell him.

Sly pulled a small medical kit from the satchel. "Sooner or later," he said, "the truth of tonight will come out, if only in rumors. Some may even call you a hero for a spell. But when Fox Applesauce goes under, when people's lives start to erode and their kids go to bed hungry, they'll come to blame you for upsetting the applecart. They'll hate you for it. And you've seen what monsters they can be."

The trail of bubbles and swirling scum moved slowly toward the tunnel's spillway. Sly inserted a syringe into a vial filled with bright orange liquid and pulled back the plunger.

Bomber stepped again. "My whole life, I've taken the path of least resistance," he said. "And it started with you. I was complacent to your abuse, to your bullying. I was complacent because it was easy."

Sly paused to laugh. Bomber watched as the bubbles reached the water's edge, where the bottom lip of the spillway disappeared into the sludge. In the distance, the rhythmic thumping of the helicopter rotors drew nearer still.

"So you're blaming me for your crummy existence? *Boo-hoo, life's unfair and nothing's my fault,*" Sly pouted. "How original. The battle cry of the downtrodden."

"No," Bomber said, shaking his head. He had to shout now, to be heard over the din of the helicopter. If he could keep Sly talking, he might be able to signal the EPA agents somehow. "No. I made my choices. I accept responsibility. Just like I'll accept responsibility for killing Fox Hollow, if it comes to that. But I'll never choose the easy-wrong over the hard-right again."

"You're a goddamn after-school special, you know that?!" Sly shouted.

"That's an outdated reference," Bomber yelled back.

A small crowd of Fox Hollow residents had gathered outside of the mansion's front door and they stood wordlessly watching a small fox-man ambulate bipedally across the foyer floor.

"Mr. Fox?" Connie whispered.

The small animal's ears perked and there was recognition in its yellow eyes.

"It's me, Mr. Fox, Sheriff Connie Hayes."

Connie holstered her pistol and raised her hands to show the old dog they were empty. She took a step forward and Mr. Fox shrunk, cowering like a beaten dog.

"No one's gonna hurt you," Connie said.

"Kill it!" Ron-Boy yelled. Big Mama Carson rose from her scooter and slapped her boy across the back of the head.

Connie edged forward, holding her hand out. The old Dogman growled insincerely and then crumbled to his knees. Connie looked to Buck, who, all things considered, should be the expert in the situation. Buck only shrugged because, after all, he had no experience with *real* monsters.

Connie removed her jacket and swung it over Mr. Fox's shivering back.

Perhaps triggered by the warmth of her jacket, but more likely by the undeserved kindness, Mr. Fox's form began to change. The fur on his body receded. His limbs elongated and became human in shape. His long snout retracted into a scraggly, gray beard. A long sigh escaped his lips, a sound that Connie would later describe as "the burden of a hundred and forty years slipping away."

She helped the old man to his feet and walked him toward the door.

The townsfolk parted for her, offering murmurs of support as she passed. She felt a new comradery with them, right then and there. For the first time, probably ever, she felt like part of her own town—she felt like she belonged.

The wind was ripping outside the tunnel and Bomber knew the helicopter must be overhead. The bubbles in the pond had stopped, or maybe they hadn't, but the water and scum and muck were being churned by the blades whipping above. Sly looked remarkably calm. A searchlight kicked on, illuminating the orchard on the far side of the pond for an instant. In a far-off tree, Bomber caught a bright flash of color before the spotlight moved.

The light traced the edge of the pond and then stopped at the entrance of the tunnel.

"I told you it was over," Bomber said. "Run for it and the EPA will gun you down."

Sly placed the vial back in his satchel and stood. Syringe in hand, he stepped out onto the spillway, his red-orange mane ablaze in the spotlight. The rotor wash kicked his fur so that it looked like licks of flame.

"I'm sure they would!" he yelled. "If they were anywhere nearby."

Behind him, the coiled end of a rope ladder dropped from the sky and clattered against the concrete. Sly placed the full syringe in the side of his mouth like a hypodermic cigar and jumped onto the ladder. He had difficulty grabbing the rungs, as his hands were now mostly paws, but he was able to steady himself with the crook of his elbow.

"I could have made Fox Hollow great again!" Sly yelled through a clenched jaw.

"You were the one who ruined it in the first place!" Bomber yelled back.

Sly tried to give Bomber the finger, but it was barely visible beneath his fur.

Bomber watched the water, hoping whatever was down there would make a move. He imagined a giant snapping turtle dragging Sly to the depths, but the spotlight clicked off and Sly began to climb.

Bomber ran to the edge of the tunnel and looked up at the helicopter, hovering thirty feet overhead. By the moonlight, he could read the words printed on the helicopter's tail:

Fox Howler: Eye in the Sky

At the top of the ladder, in the open side door, Gloria stood in her tight, white pantsuit. She gripped a handle overhead while her golden hair whipped dramatically behind her. She was shouting something at Sly but the words were lost in the torrent.

Bomber grabbed the ladder, suddenly wishing he hadn't made that lofty speech about choosing the hard-right over the easy-wrong. He started to climb, chanting four-letter words as he went. When he was ten feet up, the helicopter slipped sideways, causing the end of the ladder to splash along the surface of the pond. There was an eruption from the depths.

The pulsating head of Alice the alligator burst from the water like a missile. The body that followed was impossibly large and ghostly gray. Alice's eyes glowed like the pits of hell.

On pure instinct, Bomber curled his legs and the gator's open maw snapped on a rung, inches below his heels. The helicopter pitched from the added weight until the rung snapped, sending the gator crashing back to the water. Bomber looked up, to find Sly and Gloria both staring at him in amazement and terror.

"Just die already!" Gloria yelled.

Bomber pulled himself to a higher rung. The pilot tried to gain altitude, but before he could, the gator lunged again. This time its teeth became ensnared in the nylon rope and when the full weight of the old dinosaur hit the end of its slack, the helicopter wrenched violently. Bomber was looking up when Gloria fell. Not right away, of course. Her firm grip on the overhead handle left her legs dangling into thin air. The futile kicking lasted for only a moment before her fingers slipped loose and she plunged, screaming, into the murky water below. A bed of lily pads swallowed her luminescent white ensemble, and Alice, choosing the easy-right over the hard-right, released the rope ladder and submerged to find her snack.

Bomber looked up.

Sly still had him by about ten rungs and was looking down at the dark water. He'd just witnessed the love of his life fall into gator-infested waters, but he managed to maintain a look of utter indifference. He plodded on, up the ladder, no doubt intending to cut it loose when he reached the top, sending Bomber to the same fate.

Bomber climbed with everything he had. Sly's narrow paws forced him to climb slower and Bomber closed the distance quickly. The helicopter lurched sideways over the apple trees, leaving Alice and Gloria behind. Sly was level with the helicopter skids when Bomber caught him. Or rather, caught his tail as it swished past.

Bomber yanked and Sly yipped. The syringe, which was still gripped between Sly's teeth, slipped free and fell, nearly grazing Bomber's shoulder on the way down.

Sly growled a dramatic "No!" and reached for it, but the syringe was gone. Bomber used the moment to push up two more rungs and grab at Sly's satchel, landing his arm through the strap just as Sly's foot connected with his jaw. The blow stunned him and he lost purchase on the ladder completely. His full weight came to rest on the arm he'd hooked over the canvas bag, which was strung around the neck of a three-foot-tall fox-man, who was, himself, dangling from a local news helicopter. The absurdity was not lost on him.

"Let go," Sly strained.

"I can't," Bomber yelled. "I have unresolved issues."

"What do you want from me?!" Sly yelled. He knew what Bomber wanted, but the moment was intense and this seemed like a normal thing to yell given the situation.

"Polly want a cracker!" Bomber yelled.

"What?" Sly's fox-eyebrows arched in confusion.

"Polly want a cracker!" Bomber yelled as loud as he could.

The helicopter pitched again and the satchel strap snapped. Bomber was weightless. He fell in slow motion, staring up at Sly, who was now undoubtedly sneering. But his smug grin was short-lived and his face sank into horror. Or was it surprise? Maybe shock?

Fox emotions are so hard to read, Bomber thought in one of those queer moments of clarity you sometimes get in moments of crisis.

An explosion of color burst past Bomber's head. Red followed by yellow, followed by a flurry of blue. The wind blew upward. The whole thing of it—the color, the sound, the sensation— awakened Bomber's senses and he grabbed for the ladder, snagging a rung near the bottom.

Above him, Sly yelped hysterically as a pterodactyl-sized macaw beat its wings around the suspended fox-man.

Ms. Chitters.

Bomber had known instantly what the flash of color in the tree had been once Alice emerged from the pond. As always, the two animals were inseparable and Bomber was grateful that at least one friendship in Fox Hollow had stood the test of time.

Enraged by Bomber's recitation of Sly's age-old taunt, the mutant bird nipped at Sly with her razor-sharp beak. Sly's chickens—or rather, his macaw—had come home to roost.

The bird made several swoops before finally finding its mark. On its last pass, it clamped its beak around Sly's leg, mid-shin. There was a sickening crunch and the bird flew on, as though nothing had happened, Sly's lower leg still grasped in its beak. The action was so quick and clean that Sly hadn't even lost the ladder. He looked at his stump in shock, then down at Bomber. He did not scream. He simply turned upward and redoubled his efforts to make the top.

Sly's paw had just reached the side door when Bomber saw it.

Ms. Chitters had come full circle, this time high above the helicopter. She banked sharp and dove like a peregrine falcon after her prey. Bomber suspected that the poor old macaw couldn't see the nearly invisible blades of the helicopter. The massive bird tucked its wings and, in an impressive show of aerodynamics, approached the helicopter like a ballistic missile.

She hit the blades with impressive force, showering the orchard with bits of blue-blood-soaked plumage. The splatter coated the windshield in a thick goo, leaving the pilot flying blind, which didn't matter anyway considering the impact had knocked the rotors off-kilter and they clipped irregularly in a desperate bid for lift.

The helicopter pitched and circled violently. Sly dangled from the doomed aircraft's skid, his remaining leg kicking in the wind behind his orange and white tail. The tops of the trees were roughly thirty feet below him, but Bomber was out of options.

His heart stopped as he let go of the ladder. He fell backward into the night, watching the helicopter, and Sly, spin away.

* * *

9:25 p.m.

The double doors of a federal SUV hung open, giving Bomber a commanding view of the entire mansion estate. Across the lawn, agents in navy-blue nylon jackets with F.B.I. printed in bold yellow on the breast and back, hurried about. After a short search, a team of federal agents had found Bomber still cradled in the branches of a Golden Delicious tree five feet off the ground in Orchard 42. They'd carried him back through the tunnel, to the mansion where the FBI was keeping everyone corralled to, as they stated, "contain potential contamination issues."

An FBI medic had hurriedly attended to Bomber's assortment of cuts and bruises, giving him an informal once-over for any broken bones or hidden head trauma before scooting off to help the long line of wounded elitists—most of whom appeared to be faking injuries with the hopes of future lawsuits—leaving Bomber sitting on a stretcher in the back of the SUV. The dynamics of the scene had taken an interesting shape in just a short time. The federal agents, who'd arrived on-scene well after the melee, had corralled everyone inside the compound walls into three distinct groups. To the far east of the compound, the remaining mansion security personnel had been rounded up, zip-tied, and placed up against the stone wall, where several armed agents stood watch. In the center of the lawn, lounging around the Original Sin Fountain, were all the patrons of the Foxy Howl Inn who'd just come off the beating of a lifetime. Federal agents wandered the group, providing medical aid and passing out emergency mylar blankets, starting with those elitists who still had no clothes. The headlights from the SUVs shined off the silver-foil blankets, making the whole scene look like some weird alien refugee camp, while still more federal agents served them hot food from green mermite containers.

On the west end of the lawn, the townsfolk of Fox Hollow and the mansion's involuntary staff had been gathered and left largely to fend for themselves. And fend for themselves they did. Bomber watched with a touch of pride and hope as members of his community, who'd been at each other's throats hours earlier, smiled and slapped each other's backs with newfound comradery.

Sergeant Householder led a group of Fox Hollow officers as they administered first aid to those in need, both citizens and involuntary mansion-staff alike, and Bomber couldn't help but chuckle as he watched Ron-Boy mime a punch in front of a group of onlookers, no doubt regaling them with a war story from his charge across Fox Field. He ended the big show with a fist bump to none other than Tammy Schmidt. They were all bruised and battered, but they were bruised and battered together.

A few from the group caught him watching and gave him a smile and a wave, which he happily returned.

"Everyone's talking about how the great Bomber Merridan slew a vicious Dogman."

Bomber looked over to find Sheriff Connie smiling next to the SUV, with Buck at her side.

"Actually," he said. "I just pestered the guy until his own creations got him."

"Either way," Connie said. "There are a lot of folks in town who owe you an apology for calling you a lunatic all these years."

"Is that your way of apologizing?" Bomber asked.

Connie shrugged.

"That's the best you're going to get," she said.

"Does anyone know what happened to Mr. Fox?" Buck asked. "I've been looking all over—"

"He's gone," Connie said. "The feds took custody of him. They shoved a black bag over his head, stuffed him in a truck, and were gone before you even made it to the aid station."

Buck shook his head. A large white bandage was taped across his bare chest.

"Figures," he said. "Finally something worthy of the Department of Cryptozoology and I get shut out." Buck sighed. "Not that it matters anyway. Agent 'Chuck Roast' informed me this whole ordeal drew the attention of the Director of the FBI who was quite interested to learn that the Department of Cryptozoology was still in operation. '*Was*' being the operative word there. The Department has effectively been shut down and I was to be folded into another department. '*Was*' being the operative word there, too, because I quit."

They stood silent for a moment, watching one of the elitist

hotel guests have a heated exchange with a federal agent, apparently over the quality of the food they were being served. The agent appeared to be apologizing profusely.

"What will the world do without the great Buck Wildes?" Bomber finally asked.

"I never said I was done with 'Buck Wildes,'" Buck said. "Hell, I make way more money as Buck Wildes than I ever did as Special Agent Raymond Ross. Lot more fun, too. But I *was* thinking the show could use a co-star?"

He patted Bomber on the shoulder.

Bomber looked again to the gathering of his town's people. It was they, not a corporation or some pompous wealthy politician, who were the hope of Fox Hollow. They would find their salvation was there all along, in themselves, in their community, in their friendships, and in their love for one another. They would carry on here, mending the burned buildings, the smashed windows, and the broken hearts, together. And they would be tested again, many times, for there is no shortage of monsters in this world. Their shared experience would bind them, strengthen them, like scar tissue hardened over an old wound. Bomber wished he could stay to watch the town grow back, blossom, and bear fruit. To watch it return to the town he thought he knew from his youth. But he couldn't. And he wouldn't. He was done pushing forward toward the past. He had more monsters to hunt.

SUBJECT: Aftermath

DESCRIPTION: The sections below outline key events following The Incident and are meant to provide closure and catharsis for those readers who would not be able to sleep otherwise.

SECTION ONE: KEY LOCATIONS

<u>CITY HALL</u>: Immediately following the events of October 31, 2017, the people of Fox Hollow descended on City Hall and destroyed the statue/false war memorial dedicated to PFC Sylvester "Sly" Fox, III.

On the one-year anniversary of The Incident (October 31, 2018), a new statue was dedicated in memory of the late Pastor William Mast, Sr., though federal nondisclosure documents prevented the town from affixing a placard to explain the mysterious and heroic circumstances of the pastor's death and why he has been immortalized riding on the back of a great alligator with a parrot perched upon his shoulder. It has served as an excellent conversation piece for visiting tourists.

<u>ORCHARD 42</u>: At the time of this writing, Orchard 42 is still off-limits to the general public. Preliminary tests of the orchard soil by agents of the Environmental Protection Agency yielded high levels of harmful chemicals, though their exact composition has not been shared for "national security reasons."

Several chunks of Gloria Glass were dredged from the blue-tinted waters of the Kissing Pond after it was confirmed empty of large carnivorous reptiles.

A thorough search of the *Fox Howler: Eye In The Sky* helicopter wreckage turned up only the remains of one person, identified as the newspaper's contracted pilot.

During their search of the area, the FBI recovered a canvas satchel. The bag, stained blue, was filled with broken vials. It was recovered in an area infested with grotesquely-sized ants.

The full syringe of orange serum dubbed "Warrior Poet," initially reported by Bomber Merridan, was never recovered.

<u>FOX FAMILY MANSION (A.K.A. THE FOXY HOWL INN)</u>: The hidden passage behind the Fox Hollow Massacre painting yielded more than just access to a rank dungeon cell. In the depths of the cavernous dungeon was an old wooden box containing the original land grant issued to, and from, Silas Morgan Fox in the eleventh month of 1877. The land grant was unanimously voted invalid and unlawful by the Town's Board of Aldermen and the entire property was turned over to the local Ottawa tribe, led by Chief Herman Hayes. Taking a cue from several other local tribes, Chief Hayes had the mansion renovated and converted into Mishiimin County's first full-service casino. The establishment of the Swinging Timber Casino has resulted in a fifty percent increase in employment in Fox Hollow, with total employment numbers surpassing that of Fox Applesauce and simultaneously increasing tourist revenue by over three hundred percent.

<u>SECTION TWO: KEY INDIVIDUALS & ENTITIES</u>

<u>FOX APPLESAUCE COMPANY</u>: The company didn't tank as Sly predicted. In fact, the overall operation of the company didn't so much as waver, save for a brief set of strikes by Local Apple Pickers Union #43, who demanded better work conditions and fewer gladiatorial deathmatches. Carl Longstreet, though incarcerated, retained controlling interest in the company until a board of counsel could be established and take over operations.

* * *

CARL LONGSTREET: In return for his forced cooperation with authorities, Carl's sentence was reduced and he was placed in the Mishiimin County Correctional Facility, a local minimum security prison, where he enjoys three square meals a day and a bed with sheets. He was allowed to keep his top hat, but not his apple-knobbed cane.

RON-BOY: Following the glorious "Charge of Fox Field," Ron-Boy and his fellow Apple Knockers created a Limited Liability Corporation of the same name, hiring themselves out as private security contractors. They dreamed of large government contracts in the vein of Blackwater and Triple-Canopy, but most members simply provide floor security for Swinging Timber Casino.

BIG MAMA CARSON: Through the Mishiimin County "Write A Convict" program, Big Mama Carson began a long-distance romance with the recently incarcerated Carl Longstreet. They were married in a state-funded wedding in the Spring of 2019.

TAMMY SCHMIDT: Tammy spends her weeknights drinking hard seltzers at the Tree of Knowledge Bar, regaling patrons with war stories from the "Charge of Fox Field," where she was responsible for the bludgeoning of two prominent State Senators. Her bravado does little to hide the ghosts behind her eyes. She is haunted by wine bottles.

TOMMY COUGHLIN & SONS: When the federal agents arrived at Coughlin Funeral Home, they found nothing but several cheap coffins and an overworked crematorium. U.S. Marshals caught up with Tommy and his sons at the Port Huron border crossing, as they attempted to enter Canada. All three are currently serving 30-year sentences in the Ionia Correctional Facility, a maximum-security prison, where they are forced to manage the inmate-operated morgue.

* * *

<u>MARTY VANGOVERN</u>: Beating all the odds, Marty survived his gunshot wound. According to doctors, the excessive scar tissue on his liver slowed the bullet, reducing the overall damage to surrounding organs. When he slumped forward, the liver's excessive size blocked the exit wound preventing further blood loss. A normal person with a normal-sized liver would have surely perished. Marty recovered and was recently elected Chief Operating Officer of Fox Applesauce, replacing the late Patrick McConnell.

<u>MR. FOX</u>: Sparse reports appeared in the regional media about Mr. Fox's reappearance and subsequent arrest for his involvement in a major scandal of "human cock-fighting," prostitution, kidnapping, murder, conspiracy to commit murder, tax evasion, extortion, and the intent to break international chemical warfare treaties. He was seen on television only once, as the media prepped for his trial, where it was rumored, he'd be "naming names" from his family's list of high-profile clientele. He was found dead in his jail cell the following morning from multiple stab wounds to the back. His death was ruled a suicide.

The "outrageous claims" by townsfolk that Mr. Fox was a werewolf or Dogman were explained away as a collective hallucination caused by weaponized hallucinogens created in the dungeon laboratory, and secretly dispersed during the melee.

<u>EDITH (ADMINISTRATIVE ASSISTANT TO THE MAYOR)</u>: In an apparent "Upon My Death" order, set in place by Carl Junior, a kill team of foreign mercenaries was dispatched to Fox Hollow to eliminate anyone with incriminating information against the Fox family—starting with the sitting mayor. The scene inside the mayoral office on the following morning was an absolute bloodbath. The bodies of four military-aged males were found with gunshot wounds from a small-caliber pistol. At the center of the room was the bullet-riddled body of Edith, still clutching her tiny Derringer, a permanent smile etched on her wrinkled face.

* * *

<u>SERGEANT HOUSEHOLDER</u>: Following the events of The Incident, Sergeant Householder, for his steadfast loyalty and dedication, was promoted to the position of Deputy Sheriff and delegated a good percentage of Sheriff Connie's workload. As his first major project, Deputy Sheriff Householder led an initiative focusing on the "de-orchardization" of properties within the Fox Hollow city limits, an effort to combat Agrarian Sprawl. He still hates egg salad sandwiches.

<u>BRUCE HAYES</u>: With Marty's Market gone, Bruce floundered at home for several months before picking up a part-time gig sweeping floors and learning to cut hair at Earl's Barber Shop. He insists all customers refer to him as an Associate Cosmetologist, which is a fancy way of saying "barber's apprentice."

He still makes cosplay costumes on the side and has begun selling them online, though he does not report his income to the IRS—nor to his mother.

<u>SPECIAL AGENT RAYMOND "BUCK WILDES" ROSS</u>: The day following The Incident, Special Agent Ross submitted his formal resignation to the Federal Bureau of Investigation, whose HR Department spent the better part of three months simply trying to find any record of his employment. He has permanently adopted the moniker "Buck Wildes" and continues to roam the country in search of the nation's mythical fauna. As the ratings on YouTube would suggest, the addition of a costar to his already popular videos has dramatically increased the quality and entertainment value of his productions.

<u>SHERIFF CONNIE HAYES</u>: With a newly minted Deputy Sheriff and most of the town's rabble-rousers nursing a fledgling gambling addiction, Connie's workload decreased dramatically. She has since been able to spend more time with her "adult" son and elderly grandfather. All three recently took a hunting trip to

Michigan's upper peninsula where Connie harvested an impressive eight-point buck and Bruce cried for several hours. In return, Connie was forced to accompany Bruce to the annual Cedar Mills Comic-Con, where they dressed as Supergirl and Lex Luthor. Several photographs of the event have surfaced, but no one in town has the guts to post them to social media.

<u>WILLIAM "BOMBER" MERRIDAN</u>: Since his departure from Fox Hollow in the winter of 2018, Bomber has made a name for himself in the niche world of online monster hunting videos, co-starring alongside his friend in the wildly popular, bi-weekly *Buck Wildes Monster Hour.* Rumor has it, they have been in talks with a major streaming service, who has shown interest in acquiring the rights to the show.

In a recent phone interview, Bomber did not rule out the possibility of returning to his hometown of Fox Hollow, though he did not anticipate it would be anytime soon. When asked if he'd ever consider running for mayor, he laughed, saying he thought "a reality T.V. star would make a terrible politician."

* * *

*** ADDENDUM #4 ***

(Added Post-Publication on November 13, 2021)

SUBJECT: Encounters

DESCRIPTION: "The Great Halloween Fox Hunt" has become a favorite annual tradition in Fox Hollow, taking the place of the old "Harvest Festival." Members of the community and surrounding towns gather in the parking lot of the new Darling Doris Grocery Store for what has evolved into a combination carnival and tailgate party before heading out for an afternoon of insincere fox hunting. Because of the hunt's high level of merriment—and intoxication—no foxes have ever actually been harvested.

This year, however, a small party of hunters reported the event's first-ever sighting, claiming to have glimpsed a mangy three-legged fox before it disappeared into the underbrush. A cigarette butt was found on the scene.

<u>ACKNOWLEDGMENTS</u>

The story of Sly Fox Hollow has shifted and morphed through many drafts over the last several years and I owe a lot to all the people who have been willing to read my unpolished work over it's many forms and have offered their constructive criticisms or have flat-out told me to rein in my crazy. Thank you to my beta readers: Paul Wright, Grant Velie, Joey Shier, Adam Hillary, Travis Klempan, Brian Wilk, and Travis Russell. Thank you for your feedback, your edits, and your encouragement. Without you all, this may have ended up a normal novel.

Many thanks to Matt Gallagher and the Spring 2021 Words After War class for the valuable feedback on the first dozen pages of the novel.

Thank you to the incredible David Abrams for his editing expertise, his pacing recommendations, his insights, and his invaluable words of encouragement.

Both of my book covers have been created by the insanely talented Lucas Stump of Handsome Dog Creative Studio. Lucas is the best type of collaborator in that he takes a concept you think you want and gives you something much, much better. Thank you, Lucas, for another masterpiece!

The world of self publishing can be full of stumble-stones, so thank you to Ryan Young for answering my countless questions regarding independent publishing and for creating the coolest book trailer I've ever seen.

Thank you to my coworkers, Harlee Alexander and Jacob Tighe, for putting up with my divided attention in the office and my often manic shifts in mood.

And finally, thank you to my hometown of Fremont, Michigan for providing the structural bones of Fox Hollow. Go Packers!

ABOUT THE AUTHOR

Brett Allen is a humor writer and Michigander. He grew up on the mean streets of Fremont, Michigan, (the town whose structural layout served this novel) where he spent his teenage years working for the local grocery store as a Food Supply Systems Engineer. Brett is a graduate of Michigan State University's Supply Chain Management program which, oddly enough, provides little to no help when writing novels. He now resides in Ada, Michigan with his wife, two kids, and two dogs, Gatsby & Fitzgerald. Brett is also the author of *Kilroy Was Here*, a dark comedy inspired by the events of his 2009 deployment to Afghanistan as a Cavalry Officer with the U.S. Army. Recently, Brett's short story, *Project Valhalla*, was awarded the 2022 Colonel Darron L. Wright Award by *Line of Advance Literary Journal* and his writing has appeared in *O-Dark-Thirty*, *Walloon Writers Review*, *Task & Purpose Magazine*, and *Real Clear Defense*.

READ MORE!!!

Brett maintains a Substack (http://brettallen.substack.com) where he frequently posts new short stories, book reviews, and more. Subscribe today, so you don't miss updates on upcoming books!

Or... you can visit his website at: http://hogwashwriting.com

OTHER WORKS

Kilroy Was Here – Published 2022 by A15 Publishing
Available on Amazon.com / Barnes & Noble.com / or order at most book stores

Post – Published 2018 by Hogwash Publishing (Short Story)
Ebook available on Amazon.com

The Kherwar – Publish 2017 by Hogwash Publishing (Short Story)
Ebook available on Amazon.com